MW00627069

LIKE A COMET:
THE INDESTRUCTIBLES BOOK 4

by
Matthew Phillion

Like A Comet: The Indestructibles Book 4

Lost Continuity Press
P.O. Box 1044
Salem, MA 01970

First Printing: PPF Publishing, May 2016
Second Printing: Lost Continuity Press, November 2018
Printed in the United States of America

ISBN-13:978-0-9979165-8-4
(also available in eBook format)

Front cover design:
Sterling Arts & Design

Praise for *the Indestructibles* series

It's refreshing to have the book's one truly indestructible hero be female... But there's plenty that you haven't seen before... Phillion ramps up the action often enough to keep things moving... in the end, it's the heroes' well-drawn personalities that make *The Indestructibles* fly... And [he] doesn't give the villains short shrift either... It's the rare young superhero fan who won't find him—or herself plowing through *The Indestructibles* in as few sittings as possible—and the rare older fan who won't want to scoop it up as soon as junior finishes."

—Peter Chianca *Gatehouse Media*

* * *

"Three cheers for Solar, Dancer, Fury, Straylight, and Entropy: the five brightest stars in the sky . . .a young woman with Supergirl-like strength and abilities; Kate Miller, who wasn't really a superhero at all; a teenage werewolf; a kid with an alien super symbiote living in his brain; and a girl who could control gravity . . .In other words, the superteam was filled with a disparate mix of monsters and freaks. Or, we suppose, they could simply be called Dr. Strange and the Furious Five . . .[an] indefatigably entertaining novel."

—Eric Searleman - Superheronovels.com

* * *

"Like the first installment, [in *Breakout*] superhero fans of all ages are likely to appreciate the plot's action-packed twists and turns, the pop culture references, the revolving door of special guest heroes and villains and above all the humor, which comes both from well-placed one-liners and the characters' well-drawn personalities... Phillion juggles the multi-pronged plotlines well, even managing to fit in a burgeoning subplot involving the resurgence of the generation of heroes that preceded the current crop. And the action is impeccably choreographed, no small achievement when you don't have panels full of artwork to fall back on . . .But the novel's strength is no doubt its characters: the superheroes of *Breakout* are people first, Spandex-clad adventurers second. Add in the particular depth of Phillion's female characters—heroes and villains both—and you've got a superhero saga that really does deserve to break out"

—Peter Chianca, *Gatehouse Media*

* * *

"Superheroes are famous for being perfectionists. Bruce Wayne, Big Barda, Natasha Romanova, Matt Murdock—they all trained diligently to reach their utmost physical and mental potential. And so it is with Kate Miller too ("The Soloist"). In two excellent novels Miller fought evildoers as a member of a superhero team called the Indestructibles. But she was the only member of her crew who wasn't bit by a spider, hit by lightning, or cursed by Galactus. She had to work hard to be a badass. They called her Dancer because she moved like a ballerina and hit like a mixed martial artists fighter. Now, in a prequel to the first *Indestructibles* novel, we get an insight into Miller's motivation. As it turns out, being a ballerina is excellent training for being a crime-fighting vigilante. You never know when a perfectly executed grande jeté will come in handy. Coda: the author recommends listening to Samuel Barber's "Adagio for Strings" while reading his story.

—Eric Searleman - Superheronovels.com

Acknowledgments

For the record, this isn't the last of the Indestructibles.

It feels a bit like an ending, though, because this story—Indestructibles... in... space!—is the last of a series of stories I already had plotted out and waiting to be told when I first started writing about Jane, Kate, Billy, Titus, and Entropy Emily, and to know that that original quartet of stories has actually seen print is amazing to me.

And it only happened because of you.

Yeah, you.

And I want to acknowledge you first. The readers. Because without all of you, we never get to meet Plague and visit the Labyrinth, we never travel into a dystopian future, and we most certainly never get to see Indestructibles... in... space! (Sorry, it's just so much fun to type. Blame the Muppets.)

So this book is for you. Everyone who read the series. Every time you told a friend, or picked up an extra copy to share. Some of you dropped off postcards at your local comic book shops. (I got chills seeing the cards on a counter next to the latest releases, you know.) Some of you cosplayed Kate or Emily or Doc Silence or Straylight or even Agent Black, and I want to let you in on a secret—there's a saying among writers that you really haven't made it until someone cosplays your character. That's when Pinocchio turns into a real boy.

Thank you for your sketches of the heroes, or naming your video game avatars after the Lady, for stopping by at conventions just to say hello and talk about the next book. Thank you for inviting me to your wedding (congratulations, Ben and Megan!). Thanks for all of it. Because writing the Indestructibles has been the best thing I've ever been a part of, and I don't get to keep doing it without you.

But before the books ever hit the shelves, there's a lot of people who do a whole lot of saving me from myself during the writing and editing process, and I should thank you as well.

Stephanie Buck has the great misfortune of hearing me talk to myself as I'm channeling Entropy Emily, when I get ridiculously excited about researching Saturn or time travel theories, and for those months when nothing goes on in my head except these characters. Thanks for letting me test my jokes on you. I'm sorry for the ones that bomb.

Peter Sarno, publisher with PFP Publishing, who originally published the series: thanks for taking a chance on a first-time author writing a prose comic book about super-powered kids. We wouldn't have come this far this fast without you.

Colin Carlton, Christian Sterling Hegg, and Jen Howland—my Geek Sounding Board. Thank you for letting me ping ideas off you all day while I'm writing to make sure I'm staying true to this genre we love. And for on more than one occasion inspiring some of the one-liners inside. Double thank-you to Christian, who heads up Sterling Arts & Design, for another great cover.

Rebecca Gianotti, thank you for being one of my first readers through the whole series. You make me a better writer with your questions.

Christine Geiger and Jay Kumar, you've both worked incredibly hard during the series to be the last sets of eyes on the books. Your editorial expertise has always been appreciated. (And I owe you both beer.)

And of course my family—you were supportive through every crazy endeavor getting here, and you've been more than supportive as the series continued and the world of superheroes and nerdiness took over my adult life the past few years. Thanks for letting me be your artsy, geeky son and brother (and nephew and cousin too). And for giving me the chance to be the uncle who shows up with the superhero swag whenever he can. I don't plan on stopping, by the way. Ever.

For my family, both the one I was born into and the one I found.
I could never do this without you.

And especially for Adelyn. Welcome to the world, little star.

PROLOGUE: BIG SKY

Billy Case landed in a field outside the City, an old playground gone to seed where his parents used to bring him on those rare days when they both could get away from work. Rusted swings creaked softly in the light breeze, the entire field cast in a dark pink light as the sun set, turning the City's skyline into shadowy spires.

Billy, the superhero known to the world as Straylight, looked up at the sky, deep blue darkened to indigo and black, stars so faint as to be almost invisible. A city sky, the sort where the ambient light devours the glimmer of stars and turns the night into a neon-bathed eternal day.

"I didn't really notice stars 'til that time Jane took us to her parents' farm," Billy said, as if to no one. But he wasn't alone. Billy Case was never alone, not with the symbiotic alien sharing his body acting as his constant companion, his conscience, his Jiminy Cricket.

This is something you Earthlings do far too infrequently, the alien Billy had dubbed Dude, much to the creature's annoyance, said. *I've been on your planet a long time, and I've never understood why you look up so rarely.*

"We get busy," Billy said. "Distracted. And then, I guess… then, before you know it, it's too late. The stars pass us by."

They had only recently returned from a trek into an alternate future, Billy and Dude and the rest of the Indestructibles team. None of them had come back the same. Billy, in particular, felt more pensive, more inclined to melancholy. But then again, he'd suffered a unique trauma there, sharing memories with his future self,

1

witnessing his own death in that timeline. Things just seemed a little less funny now, though he did his best to keep those worries to himself when he was with the others.

And—just a few days ago—after returning to their home timeline, an alien had crash-landed on Earth, one sharing Billy's powers, with a symbiote just like Dude living inside him. The alien traveler had been more than half-dead, desperate to find his counterpart here, to warn him. An invasion was coming. Another species, and not the friendly and charming kind like Dude. Headed for Earth-fall. Dude called them the Nemesis fleet.

Billy spent a lot of time during the past few days looking up at the sky.

Now he saw the others approaching, Jane flying through the evening air like a ball of fire, Entropy Emily far less gracefully drifting behind her in one of her "bubbles of float." Billy knew they were looking for him. They needed to figure out what to do. How to stop this invasion. If they *could* stop this invasion. He sat down on a rusted swing, hoping it would hold his weight, and let himself rock back and forth, taking unexpected comfort in the soft squeaking of the chains as he moved. Jane landed nearby, then Emily. Together the girls approached him. Jane stopped in front of him and folded her arms across her chest, her hair moving and dancing like open flame. Emily plopped down on the swing next to him and began to swing for real, legs kicking to stay in motion.

"You know I'm going to have to go up there and scout things out," Billy said to Jane.

Her mouth formed a tight line of worry across her face.

"I can go with you," Jane said. "You shouldn't travel into space alone."

"Can you believe we're having a conversation about this?" Emily said. "Heading into space? I mean, seriously. Eighteen months ago I was getting in trouble for jaywalking and now we're talking about interstellar travel. Space. The final frontier."

Emily began whistling the theme song to *Doctor Who* softly. When Billy gave her a dirty look, she immediately switched gears to "Binary Sunset" from *Star Wars*.

"What?" Emily said. "Tell me that's not apropos."

Billy smiled then turned back to Jane.

"No, I have to go alone," Billy said. "You're the big gun. Everyone will need you here if I don't come back."

"I think we're both the big guns on this team, Billy," Jane said. "Especially after what happened to you in that other timeline."

She had a point. They had always been the two most powerful members of the Indestructibles, and Jane seemed to get stronger every day as her solar-powered abilities built up over time. But Billy had absorbed some of the strength of his future self while they were in that other timeline, and it seemed to be permanent. He could do things he hadn't been able to before. It had changed him physically, too; his eyes glowed blue-white all the time now, the way their mentor Doc Silence's glowed violet. They both, Billy and Doc, had scars from trying to take on too much power now. Billy wondered if he should get some signature sunglasses like the ones Doc wore.

"I'll be fine on my own, Jane," Billy said. "I won't engage them. I'm just going to put some eyeballs on whatever is headed our way and then come right back."

"Maybe the alien will wake up and give us that answer," Jane said, referring to the Straylight-like creature who had come to warn them of the pending invasion. The other being remained unconscious at the Tower. Dude told Billy his counterpart inhabiting the traveler would try to heal its host, but for now, both were in stasis, and thus unable to tell them anything else about what was headed in their direction.

Billy said nothing, listened intently to the creaking of Emily's swing, and rocked his own to create a call and answer between the two. *Creak swing, creak swing, creak swing.*

"The two of you," Jane said, smirking. "You can't even stop yourself from doing stuff like that when you're together."

"We're a team, yo," Emily said.

Billy leaned back and gazed into the night sky again. It felt so overwhelming. Like it went on forever.

It makes me feel insignificant, Dude, Billy thought.

It makes us all feel insignificant, Billy Case, Dude said. *And it should. If*

3

outer space doesn't make you feel small, I would be worried about your ego.

You already worry about my ego, Billy thought.

True enough, Dude said.

"It's amazing how big it is, isn't it?" Billy said.

"What," Emily said.

"The sky."

"That's kind of what it is. 'Big' is its defining characteristic," Emily said.

"I know what you mean," Jane said. "On my parents' farm I used to lay on my back, look up and be amazed at how it felt so endless. Only stars and blackness."

"I was born in the City," Billy said. "I grew up there. The sky was just that sliver of blue you saw between buildings on those rare occasions you looked up. We didn't have stars. Didn't have big sky."

"This is known," Emily said. "Seriously, the first time I went somewhere without ambient urban light I thought I was struck blind."

"If you want, I can scout and you can stay here," Jane said. From anyone else it would have felt like a taunt. From Jane it was simply an honest offer to take away some of a friend's pain and fear.

"No," Billy said. "This one's my job."

"Okay," Jane said.

Billy and Emily continued their rhythmic swinging while the sun crept closer to the horizon.

"You're not leaving right now, are you?" Emily said.

"No," he said. "Got a few things I should do first."

"Like write a will?" Emily said.

"Emily!" Jane said.

Billy laughed.

"As if I have anything to leave behind," he said.

"You do," Emily said. "I, William Byron Case, bequeath to Entropy Emily *sole custody* of our dog Watson in the event I die tragically in a battle in outer space."

"It's all about the dog with you, isn't it, Em?" Billy said.

"Don't get me wrong. I'd rather you come home," she said. "But you better make sure the dog stays with me if you don't."

4

CHAPTER 1:
THE TOWER

Long ago, a young Doc Silence and his friends found a space ship in the desert.

No one could tell how long it had been there buried in the sand. Years, decades, centuries, it didn't matter. It was a ghost ship, a derelict craft long forgotten, buried deep in a lifeless place.

Doc and his friends excavated it. They opened the ship up. And when they made their way inside, they found a living, breathing craft, a great and mighty machine, waiting to fly once again. But the world wasn't ready for alien starships then, not yet, and so they built a skyscraper, a tall and vapid structure, and one night, under the cover of darkness, they landed their found ship on the roof, like the world's ugliest cake topper. It became part of the building, part of this "Tower," and for many years it stayed there, home base of operations for more than one team of superheroes, a hidden starship in the City's downtown.

While living within its walls, they came to realize something: this ship was not a weapon of war, but rather a mobile hospital, a refugee ship, a rescue vessel. Someone on another world, in another time, built it to house the sick, to save the imperiled, to keep safe those who needed it. Part life raft, part floating medical facility.

They never learned how the ghost ship came to be buried there, devoid of life. Not even the corpses of its former passengers could tell its tale. After a time, it simply became "home."

Doc Silence sat in a room in the Tower's medical bay, looking at the unconscious alien laying in stasis, watching the creature's scaled skin rise and fall in shallow breaths.

The alien had crash-landed on Earth a few days before, apparently inhabited by a Luminae, the same species of symbiotic pure-energy being as Billy's companion Dude. Another Luminae, another hero from a different world, come here to warn them that an invasion was imminent. Jane, Billy, and Emily had found him there, half-dead, rasping out his final words of warning.

Doc had known Dude, through multiple hosts, for a long time. He'd worked with Billy's predecessor, and he'd known Straylight's partner, another Luminae-human pairing named Horizon. Horizon quit Earth entirely when Dude's former partner was killed. The aliens and their human hosts never explained why there were two of them here, though they'd hinted that having a pair of Luminae on Earth was an unusual precedent, that there were many inhabited worlds out there among the stars with only one to watch over them.

To watch over them. That was a very specific term, Doc thought. To watch over the world, just in case something terrible came from the stars. Well, here we are. Something terrible is coming from the stars.

"Neal?" Doc said out loud, invoking the attention of the disembodied Artificial Intelligence who controlled the Tower. Neal was with the ship when they'd found it, but he had been clearly a newer modification, something Earth-born. Neal was a late addition to the ship's arsenal, and he'd never revealed how he got there either. Maybe he came from the future. That was Annie's theory, that Neal had been created further along the time stream and installed like a software improvement.

And we still don't know anything about who did that, Doc thought.

"Yes, Designation: Doc Silence," Neal's gentle voice said. Neal wasn't the ship itself, so to speak, but the AI was everywhere, living within the walls and computers and electrical currents. The ship was his body in many ways.

"Neal, do we know what species this alien is? We know he's a host to a Luminae, but I'm wondering about the host-body itself,"

Doc said.

There was a pause as Neal searched his extensive library of knowledge.

"Records show he is most likely an Ank-tar," Neal said. "A species from a planet approximately 23 light years away. Relatively nearby."

"Relatively nearby," Doc said, laughing a little. It was strange, confronting the cosmic like this. Doc had spent his entire life amid the arcane and magical, seeing things impossible and mind-bending, but when it came to science, it was as foreign to him as it might be explaining elemental magic to an engineer. "What do we know about his species?"

"We have moderate biological knowledge based upon old data from previous patients, Designation: Doc Silence," Neal said.

Doc nodded.

"See what we can do to help him. I don't want this guy dying on us, Neal."

"I will do what I can."

"You always do," Doc said.

Doc left the med bay and headed toward the command center, meeting the returning trio of Jane, Billy, and Emily on the way.

"What have you three been up to?" Doc asked.

"Watching *Firefly*," Emily said.

"Trying to figure out our next move," Jane said, leading the way toward the control center. The door hissed open, allowing everyone to enter.

"I'll head out soon," Billy said. "Scout things out."

Doc put a hand on Billy's shoulder as the younger man headed for his designated seat at the table.

"You're going to be careful up there," Doc said.

"Oh you don't have to tell me twice," Billy said. "Momma Case didn't raise no daredevil."

Jane sat down wearily in her own seat and looked up at the bank of computer monitors behind her.

"Has anyone recalled Kate and Titus yet?" Jane said.

"I didn't," Billy said. "I figured we don't really know what we're doing yet, so why disturb them before we have to. I mean, 'hey, your vacation's over, world is ending.'"

Emily hopped into her chair and sat on the back, feet where her bum should be, balancing precariously.

"No offense to either one of them, but why do we need them to come back yet?" Emily said. "I mean, they're good at what they do but who brings a werewolf to a spaceship fight?"

Doc rested his arms on the back of his chair and leaned forward tiredly.

"Because while Billy is scouting out the incoming invasion, we're going to try to figure out what we can do to get ourselves ready here," Doc said. "There's a good chance if these... invaders, whatever they are, have picked out Earth to attack, they already have people here spying on us. We should try to find out what they know."

"And we need Assassin Barbie and Cujo for that?" Emily said.

"You're being obtuse, Em," Billy said.

"I'm trying to buy the love birds a few more days' vacation," Em said. "I know why you're bringing them back. They are our detectives."

Doc shot a wide, bright smile at Emily.

"Exactly. And we have some detective work to do," Doc said. "That includes you, by the way. I have some research for that big old science brain of yours to dig into that I don't understand."

"Did you just stay I'm smarter than you?" Emily said.

"In this case, you might know more than I do about certain things," Doc said.

Emily held out her hand for a high five from Billy.

He just stared at her.

"Come on, Billy Case. Give a girl a victory high five," Emily said.

"What else can we do," Jane said. "We can't start building warships. Whatever's coming at us is... what's the word I'm looking for? More advanced than Earth? We're not ready for this."

"But we can be," Doc said, rubbing his eyes behind his red-lensed glasses.

"All right," Jane said. "So we just have to figure out how to stop an alien invasion. I mean, we've time traveled. This should be easy by comparison."

"If I throw up in space, does it float?" Billy said, as if he'd tuned out of the conversation completely.

"In space, nobody can hear you puke," Emily said. She put her hand to her mouth and made a motion like the inner jaws of the xenomorph from the Sigourney Weaver *Alien* movies at Billy. "Hiss. Rawr."

"Jane," Doc said, "Get Titus and Kate on the line. Fill them in. And then we have one more thing I think we need to do before we start moving."

"Last meal?" Billy said.

"Ask George R. R. Martin if we can get a peek at the end of *Game of Thrones* in case the world gets invaded before he finishes?" Emily said.

"No," Doc said, turning to Billy. "I think Straylight should tell us a story."

"'There are those who believe… that life here began out there, far across the universe…'" said Emily.

"Not the opening narration to *Battlestar Galactica*, Em," Doc said. "I think Dude is going to tell us about where he came from."

Everyone looked at Billy. His eyes went slightly blank, the way they did when he listened most intently to Dude's voice inside his head.

"Yeah," Billy said. "Dude says we should tell you the whole story. But just once. Let's get Titus and the scariest vigilante on the planet on the monitor so they can hear. He says the explanation is overdue. And he's sorry."

CHAPTER 2:
BREAKFAST OF CHAMPIONS

Kate would like to say she wasn't sure how she ended up with a man pinned to the counter of a diner bending his arm almost to the breaking point, but she'd be lying. She knew exactly how she got here.

The real question was whether or not Kate, better known to the world as the vigilante Dancer, was going to break his arm.

The night had started off innocently enough. She and her teammate and sort-of-but-nobody-said-it boyfriend, the werewolf Titus Whispering, had been training with some of his mentors at a camp near the Canadian border. The two older werewolves, laconic Gabriel and chatty Finnigan, had been excellent teachers, showing both Kate and Titus new techniques for hand to hand combat they'd never used before, and the werewolf couple had proven to be enjoyable company as well, full of stories about their heritage and their travels.

But the camp proved isolated and lonely, and Kate had never really lived outside a city before. The quiet had begun to affect her. That and the lack of action. She'd been fighting crime on her own before she was old enough to drive. Training out in the woods was all well and good, but this was the longest she'd gone without hitting someone in years.

So she and Titus drove into the nearby town, little more than a single main street, with Gabriel and Finnigan in tow, and the quartet hit up the local diner for breakfast-as-dinner.

In retrospect, perhaps they should have re-acclimated Kate to being around regular people a little more slowly. She remained anti-social even on her best days.

They ordered their meals, and while Finnigan attempted to convince the waitress into adding white and black pudding on the menu in the future and Titus devoured a stack of silver-dollar pancakes, Kate went to the restroom. Kate disliked public bathrooms. They made her uncomfortable. Forcing her to become vulnerable in an unfamiliar environment, she found them disconcerting as well as unsanitary.

When she returned she discovered that Titus had left their table, though Gabriel and Finnigan, their backs to her, still sat munching away. Kate wondered where Titus had gone and, at the same time, pondered why you can never really get your hands completely dry using a public bathroom. At that moment, she felt a hand paw at her unexpectedly.

A regular person might have become instantly surprised, or frightened, or simply confused. But instead, as someone who'd been in a state of battle-readiness for years, she relied on her instincts. Blindingly quick, Kate battered the hand away, grabbed the person's wrist and bent it back, dragging the offender—a twenty-something man in a red baseball hat and a poor excuse for a beard—to the counter.

"What the hell!" the man yelled, his surprised shot cut off when his face bounced off the countertop.

"Who sent you?" Kate growled in the man's ear.

"What?" he whined.

"Where'd you come from?"

"Lady, he didn't mean anything," another man, bigger, maybe a year or two older, said, hands up and palms out. "Just let him go. Nobody has to get hurt."

"You're crazy!" the man on the countertop said.

Kate twisted his wrist a millimeter more.

"Call me crazy one more time," she said. "And you'll never have full use of this arm again."

"What?" the man said, his face turning bright red.

11

The diner door opened and closed again, and Titus' familiar voice cut through the air.

"I was only gone for three minutes!" Titus said. Faster than should have been possible, he stood by her side, carefully positioning himself between Kate and the pinned man's friend.

"Tell your lunatic girlfriend to let him go," the friend said.

Kate glanced back at their table to see where the older werewolves were. Finnigan sat there, nibbling a piece of bacon with one hand, watching the altercation with glee, while his other rested on Gabriel's shoulder to keep his partner from intervening.

The friend reached for Kate's arm, but Titus grabbed his wrist. In his human form, Titus was a solid sixty pounds lighter than the other man, but his grip stopped him dead in his tracks. Kate watched as the friend tried to pull his arm free, but Titus held him perfectly still.

"I like to think of myself as a pacifist," Titus said, "but if you try to lay a hand on either one of us again my lesser angels will take over and you won't like that at all."

"Crazy tourists," the friend said, shaking his head.

"You have no idea," Titus said and then turned to Kate, "We good?"

"He grabbed me," she said, applying just a little more pressure on her captive's fingers.

"You did?" Titus said. "Man, you're lucky to have any teeth left right now. Very lucky."

"Look, I'm sorry! I wouldn't have touched you if I knew you were a ninja!" the first man said.

"Would you have accosted me if you knew I wasn't dangerous?" Kate said.

"Can I just apologize?" the man said.

Titus exchanged a long look with Kate before shrugging his shoulders at her.

"I want to break a finger," Kate said.

"Maybe not," Titus said.

"Just the pinky then," Kate said.

"If you must," Titus said.

12

On the other side of the restaurant, Finnigan guffawed.

Kate released the man and pushed him away.

He began to flex and rub his arm, then glared at her.

The waitress behind the counter stared at Kate with wide eyes.

"I should have taken that outside. I'm sorry," Kate said.

"That's okay. I've wanted to do that to him for at least six months," the waitress said.

* * *

Outside, as the quartet walked away, Finnigan couldn't contain himself. "I just want to break one finger!" he said. "Titus, lad, I just love this girl."

"I actually just loved your response—not apologizing for almost breaking the guy's arm. You apologized for not dragging him *outside* to break his arm," Titus said.

Gabriel shook his head.

"Where did you go, anyway?" Kate said.

Titus rubbed his eyes in a very Doc-like manner, then gnawed on a fingernail anxiously.

"Tower called. They need us back," he said. He looked to Gabriel and Finnigan. "Sorry, guys."

"Off to save the world again?" Finnigan said.

"I don't actually know," Titus said. "Jane wouldn't give me any specifics. Said it was too much to explain over the phone and that we should both be there to get the whole story."

"Back to the City for ye then," Finnigan said.

"Let us know if you need any help," Gabriel said.

"Thanks to you both," Titus said. "We'll head back to camp, get our stuff and hit the road. You okay with this, Kate?"

Anticipation bubbling up inside her, Kate—somewhere between anxiety and joy—grabbed Titus by both shoulders. "I hope they've found us somebody to punch. I can't wait to get home."

She let go of him and walked away, leading the walk back to the campsite, a lightness that might almost be mistaken for happiness evident in her step.

CHAPTER 3:
PARENTS AND CHILDREN

Emily sat in the living room in Billy's parents' home, knitting her replacement replica Fourth Doctor's scarf. She found the process a bit Zen, with the repetitive motions, the way it consumed time, but she was also out of practice and she kept screwing up, dropping a stitch here and there and having to undo a lot of her work. She'd given her original scarf to Anachronism Annie when the notorious time traveler went back into the dark, alternate future the Indestuctibles had tried to save a few weeks before, and she'd felt good about that—Emily didn't, by nature, give gifts very often—but had she realized she was going to have to make herself a new one, she might have just as easily given Annie a gift certificate to Apollo's Coffee or something.

Speaking of not sharing well, Emily also found herself shooting daggers at notorious dog-hogger Billy Case, who had Watson curled up on his lap as he talked with his parents. Ma and Pa Case, or as Emily called them, Al and Lori, looked worried. They tended to appear this way whenever Billy came to visit, because Billy—lacking a certain amount of skill lying to his own parents—came around to visit more often when he thought he might get killed on a mission for the team. It was, in Emily's opinion, the worst, most upsetting, and yet strangely hilarious "tell" she'd ever seen in another human being.

"So you really can't give us a hint about anything that's going on?" Billy's mother said.

"Is it classified or something?" his father said.

"No," Billy said, scratching Watson behind the ear. Emily also noticed that Billy employed the dog as a small child would while

14

hugging a teddy bear, a source of tactile comfort when he worried.

I can read you like a book, Billy Case, Emily thought, before catching yet another dropped stitch in her scarf and backtracking to undo the mistake.

"So once again, you've come by with the goal of making us worry like crazy people about you," Lori said.

"I... pretty much. Yeah, that's accurate," Billy said. "And I have a favor to ask."

"Whatever you're doing, you can't borrow the car," Al said. Lori shot him a look of motherly worry that was so annoyed Emily had to bite her lip to not laugh at it. "What? It's either crack a joke or start pacing, Lor. I went with the joke to save the finish on the floors."

"What do you need us to do?" Lori said, turning her full attention to her son.

"If anything happens, I was hoping we could leave Watson here with you," Billy said.

"Hey!" Emily said, chiming in. "If you... do a thing... like... and can't keep Watson, I get full custody."

"And you might be doing some other thing that makes taking care of him really difficult, because you're also a superhero," Billy said.

"Can't argue with that," Emily said, returning to her knitting.

"You really think something's going to happen where you won't be able to take care of him?" Lori said.

"Can I make a joke about how we always knew if we got a dog I'd be the one who had to walk him?" Al said.

Lori repeated her look of intense exasperation. "You realize this is where he gets the smart mouth thing," Lori said.

"The ability to offer jokes in the face of adversity and terror is a sign of intelligence, darlin'," Al said. He turned his attention back to his son. "We'll keep an eye on your dog if you need us to, of course."

"We talked about getting a dog instead of having you when we first got married," Lori said.

"And you've regretted it ever since," Billy said.

"Well, you *were* harder to potty-train," Lori said.

"And he gets those smart mouth traits from me?" Al said.

15

Billy rummaged around in his pockets, pulled out a card, and handed it to his mom.

"And if things get really bad out there, I want you to call that number," Billy said. "That's Sam Barren's direct line at the Department of What."

"The Department of What," his father said, incredulous.

"It's a long story," Billy said. "If you need help, he'll send people to come get you. Promise me you'll call if anything happens."

"Well I'm past the point of fighting off anxiety with humor," Al said. "What's really going on, Billy?"

Billy threw his hands up in the air. "Hopefully nothing. I'm just being careful because I might not be close enough to come get you myself," he said.

"And by close enough, you mean…" Lori said.

"I may, in fact, be in outer space," Billy said.

"Way to keep a lid on your top secret mission, Billy Case," Emily said.

"You texted your mom ten minutes after we found out about this, don't judge me," Billy said.

Lori turned her attention to Emily.

"Your mom have a card for this Sam Barren, Department of When, Where, and Why too?" Lori said.

"My mom can fly. She's got things covered," Emily said.

"Melinda can fly?" Lori said.

"Just blew your mother's secret identity, Em," Billy said.

"Are you kidding?" Emily said. "I already told her to check on your folks if things get bad! They were going to find out anyway."

"Melinda… can fly?" Lori repeated.

"I had pretty much the exact same reaction when I found out, Mrs. Case," Emily said. Her phone chirped. She set aside her knitting to answer and said, "Talk to me."

"Billy with you?" Jane said.

"Is he ever not?" Emily said.

"Fine. Come back to the base. We'll patch Titus and Kate in from the road and get them caught up."

"Roger-Roger. On our way. Over and out," Emily said. "Hey

16

Billy, time to make your PowerPoint presentation."

"I don't really want to," Billy said.

"Well, I don't really want to knit a ten-foot long scarf by hand a second time, but we all have things we'd rather not do," Emily said.

"Does my son really have to prepare a PowerPoint presentation?" Lori said.

"Nah," Emily said. "I'm just being metaphorical."

"I was going to say, I don't think he knows how to work PowerPoint," Lori said.

"Thanks for the votes of confidence, everyone," Billy said. "We have to go now, Em?"

"Her majesty says chop-chop," Emily said.

Billy stood up, letting Watson jump to the floor. He looked at Emily.

"I'll bring him back if we need to," Emily said. "Right?"

"Right," Al said. "We'll be waiting. The Department of Who info will be taped on the fridge."

Billy pointed at his father, his face almost comically serious.

"You call them."

"We will," his dad said.

"You promise."

"Promise," Al said. "What's got you so worked up? What's happening, an alien invasion or something?"

Billy and Emily shot each other identical horrified expressions.

"We're going to be late!" Emily said, grabbing Billy by the arm and dragging him and the dog out the front door. "It was good to see you Mr. and Mrs. Case! We'll be back again soon!"

Emily bubble-of-floated all of them into the air before Billy had a chance to answer. Dragged off the ground, he waved to his parents and scooped up Watson—who had become bizarrely comfortable when floating with Emily—into the crook of his arm.

"Well, now they know we're being invaded by aliens," Billy said.

"I think it's time to admit neither one of us can lie," Emily said.

"There are worse things," Billy said, watching his family home grow tiny on the ground below.

CHAPTER 4:
THE MISSION IS GO

A well-dressed woman sat alone at a table at an outdoor café in Seville. Large sunglasses covered her face, a floral scarf hid her close-cropped, dark hair. She sipped a short glass of beer, golden in the warm sunlight, and drank in the smell of orange blossoms. Sometimes, she thought, it almost became possible to forget how many people wanted her dead, how many enemies she had, and all the many ways her life and career had gone wrong.

Her legs crossed, her elevated foot rocking rhythmically, she watched families walking by pushing strollers, small children in button-up shirts eating little cups of ice cream with tiny spoons, school girls dressed in classic uniforms scurrying home from class. She wouldn't stay here long. She never did. Movement remained the key to her survival, she knew. But this place, the orange blossoms, the crowds, the old buildings blending Christian and Muslim and Jewish architectures in elegant displays… this place could be home, if she gave it half a chance.

But people like her never get to go home. It's the choices we make, she thought, and the actions we perform.

Her phone rang, a soft classical tune. She looked at it, wondering who might have the number. It was a burner phone, a temporary device to be discarded once it outlived its usefulness. But then again, the people who knew her, both allies and enemies, had ways of finding a temporary cell phone number if they needed her.

She answered.

"*Hola*," she said. "*Quien es?*"

"No need to pretend, agent," the voice on the other end of the phone said. "Don't worry. You're among friends."

"I have no friends," the woman said in American-accented English.

"With skills such as yours, you'll always have friends," the voice said. "We remember the good work you did for us."

"So you're a client," she said.

"Your very best client," the voice said. "We told you we would need you again someday."

The woman sighed, sipped her beer again, and gazed at the humanity passing around her. This had been nice for a little while, she thought, allowing herself a few more moments to muse on the illusion of a different life. I wish I'd had more time.

"What do you need?" the woman said, her tone becoming more formal and business-like. If you're going to take my peace away from me, she thought, it had best be for a good reason.

"We told you when you worked for us before that your job was to stockpile the best human weapons you could find," the voice said.

"Well, that didn't end well," she said.

"To the contrary, madam, your work invigorated the right people. It moved a new generation of super humans to action. You played the foil perfectly. And you got them prepared."

"It would have been nice to know that was the plan from the beginning," she said. "I might have played the game differently."

"We apologize. But we had our reasons for keeping it close to the vest."

The woman stood up, leaving twice the cost of her beer in cash on the tabletop, and drained her glass before placing it on top of the Euros. She scanned the crowd for anyone who might be watching her. Seeing no one, she moved away. Though unarmed, she was far from defenseless. She possessed powers herself and knew how to use them to deadly effect.

"So what's your game now?" she asked, slinging her bag tightly across her chest in the event she had to start running.

"Our worst fears have been realized," the voice said. "The most terrible thing that has ever happened to our world is on its way."

"Why are you telling me this? I'm a little short on miracles here."

The voice on the other end of the line laughed.

"Oh, but my dear, you know where all the miracles are buried. That's what we paid you to do all those years, wasn't it?"

The woman stopped, the phone still pressed to her ear, and stared at an expensive black car that hadn't been there moments before. She waited for enforcers to step out and grab her, but they never did.

"That car is empty. The keys are in the ignition. You'll find travel papers in the glove box," the voice said.

"I'm perfectly capable of getting my own papers, thank you," the woman said.

"Just trying to save you time. You do have a lot of work to do."

"And what type of work is that, exactly?" she asked, taking off her sunglasses and opening the car door.

"Welcome to the side of the angels, my dear," the voice said.

"My fee structure hasn't changed. I don't care if I'm working for Heaven itself," she said.

"And we'd not have it any other way," the voice said.

The woman slammed the car door and drove away, heading for the nearest airport.

CHAPTER 5:
THE ORIGIN OF DUDE (OR: ALL THE FLYING ELEPHANTS ARE GONE)

illy toyed nervously with a remote control, the device which it controlled a complete mystery to him, as Emily and Jane tinkered with the futuristic videophone in the Tower's command center. They were trying to patch Titus and Kate in from the road, and for some reason neither of them wanted to ask Neal to do it.

Billy looked at Doc, who watched the small argument between the two women with weary confusion.

"Why don't they ask Neal to patch them in?" Billy whispered to Doc.

"I…" he said, before making a vague, confused gesture with his hands.

Working on the assumption it controlled the television in Emily's room, Billy pointed the remote control at the videophone anyway, pressed a few buttons, and suddenly Titus' face lit up on the room's main monitor.

"Oh, there you are," Titus said.

"I told you I could figure it out," Emily said.

Billy and Doc exchanged looks, then both shook their heads "no," but didn't correct her.

"Where are you?" Jane asked the giant Titus-face on the screen.

"We're on the highway. Kate's driving." The werewolf angled his phone so that everyone could see Kate in the driver's seat. She looked through the camera from the corner of her eye and then turned her attention back to the road.

"Kate can drive?" Emily asked.

"One of us should know how," Titus said. "Do you?"

"I don't drive, I float," Emily said.

"So what's going on?" Titus said.

Jane gave him the thirty-thousand-foot overview—alien crash landing on earth with the same powers as Straylight, possible invasion imminent, Billy's plan to go scouting while the rest of them prepared. The worry on Titus' face was comically apparent projected on a screen so large, and even Kate, steadfastly trying to remain her usual stoic self, kept looking over at the camera as if to verify Jane was telling the truth.

"So this is a nightmare," Titus said.

"I wish," Emily said.

"What do we know?" Kate asked, eyes remaining on the road.

"We believe this is an invasion force that Straylight's species has faced before," Doc said.

"Which is helpful," Titus said, his voice dripping in sarcasm, "given that we know almost nothing about Straylight's species in the first place. So what's the deal, Billy? Does Dude have some good intel for us?"

"That's the other reason we've patched you in," Doc said. "Billy is going to translate for us so Dude can fill us in on the big picture."

"I don't know if translate is the right word," Billy said. "I'm mostly just going to repeat what he says inside my head—does this sound as crazy to everyone else as it sounds to me? It seems nuts to me."

"Not gonna lie, Starbuck, it *is* pretty messed up," Emily said.

What about you? Are you ready for this? Billy thought.

Honestly, I should have told you all this a long time ago, Dude said.

Why didn't you? Billy thought.

Because at first I needed to make sure you'd be a worthy partner. And then we were too busy saving the world a few times, Dude said. *I did have every intention to share this information with you.*

Anything I'm about to translate for the rest of these guys that's going to make me super uncomfortable? Billy asked.

Truthfully? Probably all of it, Dude said.

Well that's reassuring, Billy thought. Where are we going to start?

At the very beginning, Dude said. *You should know where you come from.*

Last time I had this conversation, it was a very awkward afternoon with my dad, Billy said. Let's get this over with.

"Hey Billy, you've got that slack-jawed look going on," Emily said. "You talking with Dude?"

"Yeah," he said.

"Whenever you're ready, Billy," Doc said. "No rush."

How do I begin? Billy thought.

Like you would any story, Dude said. *You start, and I'll tell you what to say.*

* * *

And Straylight said:

Once upon a time.

"A long time ago, in a galaxy far, far away?" said Emily.

"Quiet, Emily," said Jane. "Let him talk."

She's not wrong, Straylight said. *It was a long time ago in a galaxy far, far away. My people, the beings you call the Luminae, had a home world. It was a planet made of light.*

"Humans call you the Luminae," Jane said. "But that's not your real name, right? What should we really call you?"

"Oh sure, you get to interrupt him and I can't," said Emily.

"Hush, Em," said Jane.

No, it's okay, said Straylight. *My real name, our real name, is made up of light, a certain tone and glow. It can't be translated for human language. Your people called us the Luminae, and that is a fine name. A strong name. We accepted it gladly.*

"You said once upon a time you had a home world," Titus said. "It's gone?"

We had a home world made of light, Straylight said. *It was the most beautiful thing you would ever have seen. And we swam along its surface like fish,*

23

glittering in the daylight. It was paradise.

But it had a flaw. All worlds have a flaw, you know. All worlds, great and small, have some crack, some imperfection, and because of that imperfection every world is one bad day away from becoming nothing. This is the way of the universe. Nothing is perfect, and nothing is forever.

"Does our world have a flaw?" said Jane.

Of course, Straylight said. *More than one. As did ours. And when our world died, we fled. We ran to the stars. We rode the cosmic byways like dolphins along the prow of a ship. A school of shooting stars.*

"Is your world gone?" Emily asked.

Gone like a dream the moment you wake. A haunting memory in the corner of your mind, something you can't quite recall, a thing you love but can never touch. There was nothing like it in the universe. We know this for sure, because in our search, we looked for a new home, a place like ours, with seas of light and mountains made of moonbeams.

"Well this is off to quite a depressing start," Billy said, deviating from the script. He felt Dude admonish him silently. "Sorry. I was editorializing. I'll continue."

As I was saying. We went to the stars, in search of a new home. And we found one, on a large planet not unlike your own. Temperate, filled with life. Its dominant species welcomed us, but we couldn't survive there. We needed to live as they lived, to breathe as they breathed. We needed their ability to survive to survive ourselves.

This was how we learned to share bodies with hosts. One of the eldest among us, and the bravest, tried first, bonding her energies with one of these beings. And in bonding, she gained the being's abilities, and the being gained hers. The two, together, were more than the whole.

"So, if Billy had powers, you would have absorbed them?" Jane said. "If you and I bonded would you have my powers?"

Not necessarily, Straylight said. *We absorb survival instincts and genetic necessities. We absorb the ability to survive as the host does. I suppose it might happen, that one of us could mimic the powers of someone such as yourself, but I've never seen it. Our ability is to grant strength to those who need it, not to steal from those who have it. The opposite, in fact, of our enemy, but I'll talk about that later. We are symbiotic in nature. The sum of the parts is better than the pieces.*

We stayed on this host world for centuries. We became part of their culture. We grew to love each other, as brothers in peace. It was the second time we found a home. It did not replace in our hearts our luminous birthplace, but here, among these kind and noble beings, we found a sense of belonging.

"Were they like us?" Emily asked.

No one is like you, Straylight said.

"No, I mean were they like us physically. Two arms, two legs…?"

The closest Earth species I am aware of that these beings resembled, said Straylight, *is your elephants.*

"Wait," Billy interrupted again. "Your first host species were… flying elephants?"

Please just tell the story and stop interjecting with your own comments Billy Case, Straylight said. *And no, they weren't elephants. I just said that the closest physical approximation to them here on earth were elephants. May I continue?*

"Please," Jane said.

We stayed so long that this new world became our home. Entire generations came and went. Our host bodies became heroes and leaders. We began to travel the stars together. We learned of other civilizations just beyond our reach and dreamed of ways to communicate with them. To build a bigger universe. To touch the hands of gods.

And then the Nemesis came to our doorstep, and nothing was ever the same.

"The Nemesis?" Kate said. "What is this?"

I have called my species symbiotic many times. We share with our hosts. We give them benefits they cannot achieve on their own. They give us a home. A way to survive. The Nemesis is a species much like ourselves. They require hosts. They require bodies. But they do not do what we do.

The Nemesis are parasites. The words symbiotic and parasitic are not so dissimilar, in some ways, but know this: one leeches off the host, takes and takes and takes until there is nothing left. And the Nemesis is truly a parasite. They seek out worlds, and they devour them. They take just enough to continue their never-ending search to quench their hunger, stealing bodies, stealing technology, but they leave each world they touch a dead husk, a graveyard of dust and ruin.

"They destroyed your second home," Jane said.

We would later learn that others had encountered them as well. Many species know of them, and each have their own name for these creatures. The Devourers. The Locusts. One of your writers here on Earth learned of them and called them

Outer Gods. But to us, they were the Nemesis, our dark shadow, a vulgar and brutal reversal of the shared life we tried to create.

We were not ready. Their armada struck hard and fast, terraforming the beautiful world of our hosts. Friends and allies died fighting them. Some might call it a war, but it was not. It was a slaughtering field. It was genocide.

But our noble hosts, these great and brave beings, knew they could not save their own world. They knew they couldn't protect it. They knew they couldn't escape. But they knew we could.

"The Luminae," Titus said.

They told us to flee. To run back to the stars from whence we came. Our surviving hosts came with us, brave souls, rising into the darkness of space as their world crumbled to dirt and ash behind them. But this time, we did not swim as school of shooting stars. We fled in pairs or in trios, or sometimes alone. We flew in every direction. We aimed ourselves at every star. We went looking for life.

We knew the Nemesis would not stop at the world of our hosts. We knew they would wipe the blood from their lips and hunt again, looking for another meal, for another world to rend limb from limb. For the Nemesis is always hungry. They never stop moving. They never stop eating.

We went to the stars to find worlds bountiful enough, beautiful enough, alive enough to attract the monstrous attention of our Nemesis. We found these worlds, and we waited. We became the watchers on the wall. We found new homes and turned our eyes forever skyward. Waiting for the day the monsters found us.

"What about the hosts you left with?" Titus asked.

Many didn't make it. We were young then, and unsure of how to survive in space. For many, the host worlds we found were uninhabitable. Still others died at the hands of natives, afraid of outlanders invading their pre-spaceflight worlds.

"Are there any left of those original hosts?" Jane asked.

They are all gone now. I have not seen one in millennia. Such great and noble warriors.

"All the flying elephants are dead," Billy interjected. "That's horrible."

Please stop editorializing, Billy, Straylight said.

"Sorry. Keep going."

In our escape we learned much of ourselves. Of our ability to turn ordinary beings into heroes. Our ability to travel at the speed of light. We discovered in ourselves a talent for war. Of this we are not proud. But we have saved worlds.

26

We've lost worlds as well. More than we've won. And we have learned much about our Nemesis, their tactics, their hunger. We have learned that they send advanced scouts to new planets, and we have rooted them out and destroyed them.

"Here?" Kate said.

Not in your lifetimes, Straylight said. *But long ago. My partner and I destroyed agents of our enemies on Earth more than once.*

"Where is your partner?" Kate asked. "We've heard the name more than once. Horizon. Where did he go?"

Straylight was silent a long time.

Billy felt the eyes of his friends on him, waiting, and the worry and sadness in his symbiotic companion as well.

"Where did he go, Dude?" Billy said.

My partner went looking for another world to save, Straylight said. *We were here together a very long time. We watched the rise of mankind. We watched and we waited. And we saw what Earthlings could be like.*

"He gave up on us," Titus said.

Again, Dude was silent. But this time, Billy waited patiently for his partner to be ready to speak.

Horizon believed perhaps there was a world worthier of saving, Straylight said.

No one spoke.

Emily rubbed imaginary smudges from her fingernails; Jane studied her shoes. Doc looked away, his face pained with memory. Billy knew, through Dude's shared memories, that Doc had been friends with Horizon. He wondered what they witnessed together that made the other Luminae so determined to give up on all of them.

"What about you?" Billy said. "What did you think? Why did you stay?"

Because, Straylight said, *I love your world so very much. And I do think it's worth saving.*

"Well then," Jane said, and as always, her voice set the tone. She filled the room with hope. "We're in agreement about that. Let's figure out what we need to do to save our world."

* * *

Billy looked back and forth between all his friends and allies, drained by the story; he felt an inexplicable sadness, a sense of loss and melancholy he could not put into words.

I'm sorry for everything you've been through, Dude, he thought.

But if I hadn't been through all of this, Dude said. *I would never have known you, Billy Case.*

Now you're just buttering me up because you're about to ask me to go on a suicide mission with you, Billy thought.

Then he experienced that surreal sensation in the back of his mind that he knew meant Dude was laughing.

"So what's our next move?" Titus asked through the monitor.

"I'm going to go play tag with an alien parasite armada," Billy said. "I have no idea what you guys are going to do."

"First of all, we're going to make sure they don't have any sleeper agents that are already here on Earth," Doc said. "I know Straylight and Horizon have been vigilant about finding their scouts, but we also realize they've been here before. They may have some allies on Earth relaying information to them."

"We could start by figuring out who has the capability to send a signal deep off-world," Emily said.

"How do you even do that?" Billy said.

"I have some ideas," Emily said.

"Okay," Doc said. "You and Titus will work on pulling together a list."

"Me?" Titus said.

"Like it or not, you two are our science brains, " Doc said. "Pull together some leads and we'll split up to investigate."

"What are the rest of us going to be doing?" Jane said.

"We're dramatically short on defenses," Doc said. "I'll pay a visit to the Department of What and see if they've got anything in the vaults we can use. Maybe Henry's been tinkering on something new."

"I'll come with you," Jane said.

"No," Doc said. "Right now, we've got two, maybe three of us who are capable of doing some real damage in outer space. I'm not counting myself, either, because magic isn't nearly as effective off world as it is on Earth."

"You want me to start recruiting?" Jane said.

"Kate and you both know some people who might come in handy if the Nemesis fleet reaches Earth," Doc said. "There's a fair chance we can't stop them before they get here. We need to be prepared to fight."

"What about the press?" Jane said.

"You think you can keep your pet reporter on a leash?" Kate said through the telephone. "Because if we can't stop them in time, having someone who can help us get the word out to the civilian world in a trustworthy way might save some lives."

"I can prep Broadstreet," Jane said. "He'll listen if I tell him we shouldn't start a panic."

"Then we have our assignments," Doc said. "Neal?"

"I will alert all of you if I detect any anomalous signals from off-world, Designation: Doc Silence," the AI said.

"Be careful out there, everyone," Jane said.

She looked at Billy last. "And you. Don't leave without saying goodbye."

CHAPTER 6:
BUILDING A BETTER EMILY

Doc Silence materialized outside the front door of the Labyrinth, the superhuman prison that had been used to hold some of the Indestructibles last year, which had since become the de facto central office for the Department of What. The Department—the international task force in charge of monitoring and working alongside superhumans—had cleaned up its act since that time, in no small part through the leadership of Doc's friends and allies. Formerly retired agent Sam Barren had returned to limited service as an advisor, and Doc's old teammate, Henry "Coldwall" Winter, had been named director in charge of getting the agency back on its feet.

Why they'd chosen the Labyrinth to be their home office, Doc didn't quite understand, except, perhaps, because it was close to the City. Or maybe because it was familiar—Henry had been locked up here against his will for years by a rogue element of the Department and presumed dead by everyone he knew. Perhaps it felt more like home than anywhere else to the former hero.

Doc approached the front doors, the massive gateway opened with a mechanical hum, and Sam Barren waited for him just inside, whip-thin and still sporting the best silver moustache Doc had ever seen.

"I hope you're here to talk about whatever crash-landed the other night," Sam said. "We know you took it into your possession immediately."

"And you knew we'd call on you as soon as it was safe," Doc said.

"Safe's a relative word. You going to fill us in?"

"And ask for your help," Doc said.

"Now I'm really worried," Sam said. "Come on inside."

* * *

Sam led Doc to a small conference room, where Henry Winter, looking older than he should be but still dapper in a tailored suit, waited for him. Henry stood up to greet his old friend, leaning heavily on a cane.

"You ever going to tell me what happened on that little excursion you and the kids went on?" Henry said, referring to their recent time travel adventure. None of them had really spoken about the specifics upon returning. It had been an ugly future and one they'd hoped to avoid repeating.

"Maybe someday," Doc said out loud. Probably never, he thought. Nobody needs to know all the details about how their world could die. "Different problem this time. We've got ourselves an alien invasion on the way."

"You realize I have to say the word 'again,' right?" Henry said.

"This is the big one," Doc said. "You know that thing Straylight and Horizon always warned us about? The one they were sent here to watch for?"

Henry's face wrinkled into a deep frown. Their former teammates had never given them a full account of what their enemies were capable of, but they all knew whatever it was, it was worse than anything they'd faced before.

"And we're short one Luminae," Henry said. "Screw Horizon for bailing on us. Judgmental son of a…"

"We're short staffed in a lot of ways," Doc said. "Only Billy and Jane are really capable of fighting in outer space. We're going to need help. Got anything kicking around we should be looking at?"

"… " Henry said, pressing a button on the intercom docket on the center of the table. "Send Doctor Bohr in please."

"So our little preemptive recruitment idea is bearing some fruit," Doc said.

"You were right. He's a genius," Henry said, sitting down. "Some of his ideas are wonky, but with the right guidance and motivation, he's a real outside the box thinker. We're getting good work from him. He has something to show you, actually."

Sam sat down as well, grunting like the old man he was as he settled in.

"We have some old gear in storage," Sam said. "Space suits. Ray guns. Stuff we've confiscated over the years."

"Did you just really say ray guns?" Henry said.

"What, that's what they are. Buck Rogers junk."

Henry laughed, shaking his head.

"We really don't have a lot for deep space. We didn't have the brain power, and we never stole the right stuff to reverse engineer," he said.

Doc joined the other men sitting down and rubbed his eyes beneath his glasses.

"I'm thinking about talking with his highness about coming out of retirement to help if we can't stop them," Doc said.

The smile left Henry's face.

"Not that jerk," he said. "Not to mention there's no way he'll help."

Doc held his hands up in a vague gesture of frustration.

"I don't have much choice, Henry," he said. "And also… you know the one thing he couldn't resist is a challenge. This would be right up his alley."

"No it wouldn't," Henry said. "He might just tell you to sink or swim without him."

"There's no harm in asking," Doc said.

"There's harm. You actually have to talk to that—" Henry said.

"Are we talking about the big guy?" Sam said.

"Yeah," Doc said.

"Y'know," Sam said, leaning back. "He was always nice to me."

"Then you talk to him," Henry said. "I'm not."

"Yes you are," Doc said. "We're both going."

"Why," Henry said.

"Because I'll need you there to corroborate a few facts."

"He'll believe you if you say there's an alien invasion coming," Henry said. "Whether that properly motivates him to come out of his little monastery of selfishness or not is debatable."

"I might need you there to verify some familial information for me," Doc said.

Henry stared at him for a long, hard second, caught off guard and clearly curious. Before he could speak, the conference room door opened and in walked Keaton Bohr.

The scientist looked healthier than the last time Doc had seen him—in an alternate future the scientist had unintentionally helped to destroy. Without telling Henry and Sam the specifics, Doc and the Indestructibles had told the agents to recruit him. The other option was to kill him, but despite Doc's fury towards the man for the choices he made in another timeline, he was, in fact, still innocent here. And he was as brilliant as they said he was. Giving him a job with the Department was a better alternative than locking him up or murdering him in cold blood.

Bohr had a box in his hands when he walked in, looking around nervously.

"You're Doc Silence," he said. Doc forgot that they'd never actually met in this timeline, but Doc was a public figure, and an easily recognizable one at that.

"I am. How are you settling in, Doctor Bohr?" Doc said.

"You know I spent my whole life trying to invent things to make the world a better place and nobody would let me," he said. "I figured, I'm offered a job in the Department of What and I'll be, I don't know, making weapons of war and the like. And instead they've got me working on alternate energy sources. It's like I've found the dream job I never knew I wanted."

"Glad to hear that," Doc said.

"What's in the box?" Sam said.

Bohr set the box down on the conference room table nervously. He looked at Henry, who gestured for him to speak.

"I know we were under orders to not look too deeply at how the

Indestructibles powers work," Bohr said.

Doc looked at Henry angrily. Henry held up one finger, gesturing for him to wait.

"I don't like where this is going," Doc said.

"Give it a second," Henry said.

Bohr pulled a glove out of the box, a mechanical gauntlet in bronze and black.

"But we were discussing how Entropy Emily doesn't have a way to defend herself during a fight," Bohr sad.

"I am really unhappy with how this is progressing," Doc said.

"Give it a chance, Doc," Henry said.

Bohr's eyes flitted nervously between Henry and Doc. Henry gestured for him to continue.

"All we've done is—do you remember Emily learning how to… what did she call it, Henry?"

"Her 'Wall of Slam,'" Henry said. "Do you remember *that* unfortunate incident?"

Doc almost laughed despite his anger. He'd specifically told them not to tinker with Emily's powers to avoid Bohr repeating the actions he took in the alternate timeline. Somehow, he had reversed the gravitational powers Emily possessed, turning her into a bomb capable of tearing the whole world apart. Everyone—with the possible exception of Emily herself—knew that she had more power than any of her teammates if she ever learned how to use her abilities, but she was still young, and still very unpredictable, and Doc wanted her to learn how to use those powers on her own, not through scientific interference.

"She actually used them against suits the Department designed based on an item acquired during the Indestructibles' first public battle—the Distribution suit," Bohr said. "Kinetic energy stored, redistributed, and used as a weapon. So we got some crazy readings."

"What does this glove do," Doc said. "Simple words. Pretend I'm not smart."

"All these gloves do is let Emily aim her 'Wall of Slam' into a single place. A… punch," Bohr said.

"Does this drain her powers at all? Tap into her power source?"

"It just points the wall, Doc," Henry said. "It's just an idea."

Doc picked up the glove, turned it over in his hand, then placed it back on the table, frowning. He looked back and forth between Henry and Bohr. They were lying to him. He could feel it. Not about the gloves—which, he hated to admit, might be helpful if things got bad—but something else. He decided not to call them on it. Not here and now. For the moment, they had bigger worries.

"We can talk about this later," Doc said. "For now, she doesn't use these. You and I both know she'll be a better hero if she doesn't have rely on technology to cheat, Henry."

"I agree," Henry said.

Doc turned to Sam.

"Will you make a list of toys you might have to help us? Not just in space. There's a good chance these creatures make Earth fall. If they do…"

"We'll have all hands on deck," Sam said.

"I have a few more stops to make," Doc said. He looked at Henry one more time. "And you're coming with me to talk with the big guy later."

"If I must," Henry said.

"I don't like him any more than you do," Doc said. "But at the end of the world, you can't be as picky about your friends."

CHAPTER 7:
LITTLE GODS

The sky above the City filled with clouds, rain threatening to fall, like a glass of water resting on the edge of a table. A cool wind blew in from the East, the sort of wind that has purpose, a personality, a reason to be. The air itself had a tense, busy sensation to it, that electrical hum before a thunderstorm. And because of all these signs, Jane knew her friend had come to town.

Jane didn't fly to the park, choosing instead to walk on foot, dressed in civilian clothes, one of Emily's knit hats hiding her flame-like hair. She stuffed her hands in the pockets of her jacket and watched the ordinary people stride by. Ordinary people. The humanity Jane needed to protect. They had no idea the threats that came their way every single day, the ones the Indestructibles, or the Department, or someone else diverted or defended them against or were sometimes sidestepped by simple, unadulterated luck. Like meteors hurtling by in space, we dodge terrible events all the time, Jane thought, and turned her eyes skyward.

We're not escaping the next one, are we? I just hope we're ready.

And speaking of ready: sitting on a nearby park bench, Valerie Snow looked nearly human.

Valerie, the girl the Children of the Elder Star had merged with a sentient hurricane and called "Project Valkyrie," had met with Jane and the others sporadically the past few months as she learned to control her powers. She talked with Billy a bit at first, thinking that perhaps his relationship with Dude would be a good starting point for building a connection with the living, breathing storm that now shared Val's body. But they soon found that not to be the case. The storm was a feral thing, acting and reacting on a wild, emotional level, the polar opposite of Dude's cool, detached demeanor. The Straylight entity acted as a calming, rational force on Billy's human fallibility; Valerie, instead, had to be that calming factor for the wild creature she now shared a life with.

It was not a battle she always won, but today, sitting on a park bench in a dress Jane gave her a few weeks before, a large summer hat covering her sky-blue hair, Valerie looked under control. Today, she was winning.

Jane sat down next to her and smiled. "How are you?" she said.

"Feeling almost human today," Val said. Her skin pure white, but uneven, changed colors like clouds, with wisps of silver and gray mottling through. Her appearance shifted with her mood. When they first met, she'd been dark gray like a thundercloud, lightning dancing across her skin in violet ripples. The air around her always indicated her mood, too, be it fury or fear, sadness or peace. Jane wondered what overcast and breezy meant.

"Have you done that thing we talked about?" Jane asked.

"I can't," Val said. "I've flown over my parents' house a few times, I've creeped through their windows, but I'm… I'm not ready for them to see me like this."

Jane put her hand on the back of Valerie's, trying to reassure her.

"I want to tell you that someday this will all be normal, but…" Jane said.

"I know. I'm beginning to be okay with that. With not being normal," Val said.

"Where are you staying?"

"There's a lighthouse. An abandoned lighthouse. I stay there sometimes," Val said. "I don't sleep much anymore, so I have trouble staying still. I think that's the thing that feels the strangest. Not flying, not controlling the weather, but… not being able to sit still anymore."

"I wish we knew more about what they did to you, so we could help," Jane said.

Val shook her head softly.

"It's okay. I'm figuring things out on my own," Val said.

"Well, you know you'll always have a home with us," Jane said.

Val tinkered nervously with her oversized hat.

"I don't think I'm ready to live like a normal person just yet," Val said.

"Trust me, none of us are normal," Jane said.

"That's not exactly it," Val said. "I mean... I don't feel right indoors anymore. It makes me feel cut off. I feel trapped."

"That makes sense, you know," Jane said.

Val nodded, almost to herself.

"I suppose it does," she said.

A light rain began to fall. Jane turned up her collar. Val looked at her apologetically.

"Sorry," she said.

"It's okay," Jane said. "So I have something to ask you."

"Of course," Val said. "Anything."

"Something bad is coming our way. We're hoping we can stop it before it becomes a problem, but if it does.... We could use your help again."

"You know, when you freed me, I thought I was destined to be the villain forever," Valerie said. "I thought they'd made me into something evil. That they'd made me into a weapon."

"And we've asked you to be a weapon already once," Jane said. "I'm sorry for that."

"No," Val said, raising her face to the air, letting rain splash against her skin, which had deepened to a pale gray. "When Kate asked me to help free you from the prison, she gave me a chance to be a hero instead of a villain. To be better."

"I think you've always had it in you to be a hero," Jane said.

Val vigorously shook her head no.

"I never would've been a hero if this hadn't happened to me. At best I would have been ordinary. At worst I would've been a statistic. In some weird way, everything I went through at the hands of those people made me better than I ever could have been."

"You don't have to help us if you're afraid," Jane said.

Valerie stood up, spinning on one foot, playing in the rain she'd made fall from the sky. It gleamed on her bare shoulders.

"This is what we were all made for, Jane," she said. "We're like little gods. The weather elemental, the goddess of the sun. And we're here to keep our tiny world safe from harm. This is what those terrible people gave me, and this is what you and your friends have taught me."

Jane watched her dancing, barefoot in the park grass, her lonely friend, this elemental being with no home. She remembered how they almost had to kill her, to put her down to save thousands of lives. And here she was, a being with the power of a hurricane, dancing in the rain and prepared to go to war beside them.

"How will I know when you need me?" Val asked.

Again, Jane looked to the sky. She could feel the rain soaking her knit cap.

"We won't have to tell you," Jane said. "Everyone will know when it happens."

CHAPTER 8:
UP, UP, AND AWAY

Billy stood on the landing platform of the section the Indestructibles thought of as the "docking bay" and entrance for the Tower, an open area littered with hoverbikes, technology and hardware none of them really understood, and the clutter where Kate spent time tinkering and personalizing her own equipment. He was alone, except, of course, for Dude, and stared up into the growing darkness of the evening sky.

"I have absolutely no concept how big space is," Billy said.

No one really does, Dude said.

"Have you ever been to the edge of it? Does it end somewhere?"

Rumor has it there's an end point somewhere, but I don't know anyone who's laid eyes on it, Dude said. *And I've known beings who have ranged very far.*

"Not like we're going that far, are we?" Billy said.

I fear we're not even leaving your solar system.

"What do you mean, fear?"

If we don't leave your solar system, it means the Nemesis is very, very close, Dude said.

"Great."

Billy walked up to the very outskirts of the landing platform, looked down at the City below, something that used to give him vertigo. Sure, just when I get used to flying, we go into space. New vertigo. Vertigo 2.0.

"So let's break down the ground rules here. You give me the ability to breathe in space."

Not exactly.

"Not exactly?" Billy said, his voice cracking.

Not exactly. I remove the need for you to breathe in space. The shielding I generate also provides you with enough of the necessary airborne elements you need to maintain respiratory function.

"I have no idea what you just said," Billy said.

I give you the ability to breathe in space, Dude said, resigned.

"And all the other stuff that happens in movies. My head won't blow up? I won't freeze to death in three seconds?"

Dude sighed in Billy's head, which always meant he was at his wit's end.

Imagine that, being connected to me, you have as part of your actual body the best spacesuit ever invented. Personalized to your biological needs. This is what I do for my host. I grant the same ability to live in the vacuum of space I myself have.

"Great. Next question: What happens if someone hits us with a null gun and we separate?"

You probably die, Dude said.

"Dude!"

Would you rather I lie to you?

"Yes," Billy said. "Yes, in fact, I would prefer you lie to me about stuff like that."

In that case, don't worry about anything if we get hit with a null gun. You'll be dead before the surprise reaches your brain.

"I hate you sometimes," Billy said.

"I love when you talk out loud to Dude and you think nobody's listening," Emily said, emerging from the interior of the Tower. Frustrated by the progress of her replacement Fourth Doctor scarf, she'd begun testing out different signature items, and tonight she wore one of her hand-made Jayne Cobb wool hats over her neon-blue hair.

"Hey, Em," Billy said.

"You're leaving right now, aren't you?" Emily. "You sneaky git."

"Well, I was going to, but clearly you're going to rat me out," Billy said.

Emily walked up to the edge of the platform as well, dangling one foot over, fearless.

"I want to come with you," she said.

"You can't," Billy said.

"One: we don't know that for sure, and Two: yeah, I know. I'm kind of jealous, y'know," Emily said.

"Of scouting out an invading army of aliens."

"No, man, you get to do what I've wanted to do since I was three years old," Emily said. "I want to just…"

She waved her hand vaguely at the empty sky above them.

"Go where no man has gone before. Up, up and away. Into a galaxy far, far away. Take me out to the black, tell 'em I ain't coming back," Emily said, the last part sing-songy.

"Now you're singing theme songs," Billy said.

"I'm serious, though," Emily said. "This world is such a drag, man. Why do you think I do the things I do? I'm bored. I want to be out there."

"Maybe you'll get your chance."

"Y'think?" Emily said. "Maybe someday, right? We save this stupid, mean, boring world, we make sure it's okay, and then you and me and Dude and Watson, we can find ourselves a Corellian stock light freighter and go travel the star lanes?"

Billy stared at Em for a moment, watching as she playfully stepped off the platform and floated herself back onto it repeatedly.

"I can't tell if you're being serious or not," Billy said.

Emily looked up at him, a huge, almost feral grin on her face.

"C'mon, Billy Case, you know you want to go explore the universe. Meet yourself an alien princess from a faraway world. I'll learn how to duel with a laser sword. It'll be awesome."

"You're a space cadet, Entropy Emily."

"I prefer the term 'starship captain,'" she said. "Look, just come home safe, okay?"

"I will."

"Tell Dude I told him he needs to take care of you."

I heard her, Dude said.

"He heard you," Billy said.

"Good." Emily took her hat off and stuffed it on Billy's head instead. "It's dangerous to go alone. Take this."

"You said the same thing to Annie when she left," Billy said.

"Well, the same logic applies," Emily said. "Now you're a meme."

"How do I look?" Billy said. "I know the answer to this ques—"

"Man walks down the street in that hat, people understand he's afraid of nothing."

"I knew you were going to say that," Billy said.

"It's a cunning hat."

"Be safe when I'm gone, Em."

"Don't die, Billy Case."

"I won't," Billy said.

"Watson will be so mad at you if you don't come home."

"I'll keep that in mind."

Billy looked once more into the sky, held his hands loosely at his sides.

"Up, up, and away, huh, Dude?"

'To infinity, and beyond,' the alien said.

"Did you just make a *Toy Story* joke, Dude?"

I did. Why are you so surprised?

Billy laughed, his first real laughter in as long as he could remember.

"No reason," He said. "Okay. Here we go. 'To infinity, and beyond.'"

Billy Case rose into the air, fast as a rocket, swifter than a shooting star, a streak of white and blue light darting heavenward. The world grew tiny below him, his friends, his family, the Earth itself, a tiny marble adrift in eternity. He watched his world shrink into a bauble, something blue and beautiful he could put in his pocket, the galaxy expanding around him in infinite blackness. A blanket of stars enveloped him, the sun bright and hopeful in the distance. The moon was a nickel spinning in shadows. He looked out into the blackness of space, into the void, and the silence of it, the vacancy, made his heart beat faster and faster.

I've never known what it feels like to be truly alone until now, Billy thought.

But you're not, my friend, Dude said. *I'll be right here with you.*

And together, boy and alien, heroes and partners, flew like an arrow into the darkness, in search of an armada.

CHAPTER 9:
E.T. PHONE HOME, LONG DISTANCE

When Titus and Kate returned to the Tower they found it eerily quiet. They wandered the halls wearily, backpacks slung over their shoulders, wondering where everyone went.

"You're the werewolf," Kate said, raising an eyebrow at Titus. "Sniff them out."

Titus shook his head.

"Neal keeps this place too clean. The whole place smells like intergalactic disinfectant," Titus said. "Speaking of..."

"Entropy Emily is looking for you in the library, Designation: Whispering," Neal said unexpectedly.

"Not the first choice I had in mind, but fine," Titus said. Kate held out a hand to take his backpack, and he handed it to her gratefully. "Thanks."

"I'm going to shower. Good luck with Baby Einstein," Kate said.

Titus sighed and headed for the library, a circular bay on one of the lower levels. Both he and Emily had found it on their own and discovered the library to be surprisingly full of print books dating back hundreds of years. The center of the room held an electronic research hub, which Titus used to dig into werewolf history and past exploits of the residents of the Tower. Emily mostly used it like the galaxy's best Wikipedia, pulling at threads of subjects she knew nothing about until she fell asleep sitting at the terminal. More than once Titus had found the blue-haired girl passed out while sitting up, random subjects displayed in front of her, like evolutionary theory,

45

the schematic plans for the Eiffel Tower, or a dissertation on the history of fennel.

As soon as he walked into the room, Emily latched onto him.

"I need your brain," she said. "I broke something."

"Great," Titus said, pulling up a chair next to her. A holographic projection of planet Earth spun in front of them.

"Watch this," Emily said. "Library: Display all outgoing communications signals leaving the planet."

Suddenly the virtual globe lit up, hundreds of points of light appearing across it.

"What the hell," Titus said.

"I know, right? I thought, hey, like Doc said, if there's this invading army coming our way, they probably have spies and scouts. So those guys would try to signal back to the mother ship, yeah? Send their spy notes. But this can't be right. That's like seven hundred signals leaving the Earth on a regular basis."

"If I may interrupt," Neal's monotone voice chimed in, startling Emily and Titus both. The surprise caused Emily to standup startled, then sit back down again.

"Do we have a choice?" Titus said.

"Can you at least knock first? I think I may need to change my pants because of you," Emily said.

"What is it, Neal?" Titus said, ignoring Emily's melodramatic response.

"Designation: Whispering, you should be aware that Earth plays host to a large number of embassies for alien cultures, as well as poses as a waypoint for several space-traveling beings."

"Define a large number," Emily said.

"That's ridiculous," Titus said. "Earth is what, the bus stop of the Milky Way?"

"Watch what you call ridiculous, Titus. You're a werewolf. People don't believe in you either," Emily said.

"Look at that screen, Em," he said. "That doesn't seem impossible to you?"

"Listen, Chewie, we just came back from the future. I believe everything now. You could tell me the ghost of Elvis is controlling the body of a Food Network host and I'd be like, yeah, cool, that makes total sense to me," Emily said. "Earth being chockablock full of aliens? Not really a stretch right now."

Titus rubbed his eyes in an almost eerie imitation of Doc's habit. "Okay. Okay. Let's talk parameters. Parameters. How about this. Library? Please narrow those signals down to only the ones that are two-way. A bunch of those have to be Earthlings just yelling into the abyss hoping someone yells back," Titus said.

At that point, roughly half the lights on the virtual Earth went dark.

"Half of those signals get an answer?" Titus yelled, voice cracking.

"Holy carp, Earth is like the Internet provider of the Universe!" Emily said.

"This is crazy," Titus said. "Okay. Again. Parameters. Got it. Library, remove from this search any signals Doc Silence or our predecessors were aware of and deemed non-threatening. Closed cases or whatever."

This time, most of the lights winked out, leaving only five distinct points of light on the map: in northern California, Nevada, in a mountain area in the American Southeast, in the ocean to the East of Florida, and finally one in the South Pacific.

"One of these things is not like the other…" Emily sang.

"Stop. That's a lot of locations," Titus said.

"And one of them is the Bermuda Triangle," Emily said.

Titus stared at the globe.

"Oh come on," he said.

"Right there," Emily said.

"I know," Titus said. "But this is just stupid. Neal, is Doc home?"

"I'm right here," Doc said, walking into the library and throwing his long black coat over a nearby chair. "I was hoping you two would be working on this."

"Are there really over seven hundred aliens living on Earth?" Emily said.

He waved his hand dismissively. "Alien is a relative term.

What've you got?" Doc said.

"Five unexplained two-way signals which had previously been unknown or unaddressed," Titus said.

"Well that one you can discount entirely," Doc said, pointing to the spot in the Pacific.

"Because it's an outlier?" Emily said.

"Because it's a moveable island we've never been able to figure out," Doc said. "We know it pings outer space. It also does some weird stuff with numbers. But it's relatively harmless as far as we can tell."

Emily stared at Doc, hard.

"There's a moveable island in the Pacific Ocean?" Emily said.

"Flying islands too." Doc said. "But most of those are in Europe."

"Would you call the moveable island... lost?"

"Oh no," Titus said. "Emily, can we focus?"

"Are there castaways there? Did their plane crash?" Emily said.

Doc raised one eyebrow at her, playing along. "There may even be a polar bear," he said.

"You're pulling my chain!" Emily said, thrusting and angry finger in his face.

"You watch too much TV," Doc said. "What else do you have."

"The Bermuda Triangle," Titus said, gesturing to Florida.

Doc sighed heavily.

"I hate the Bermuda Triangle. What's left?"

Titus pointed to the remaining three locations.

"Northern Cali, somewhere in the Appalachians, and New Mexico," Titus said.

"That's not New Mexico, that's Nevada—oh my stars and garters is that Area 51?" Emily said.

Doc and Titus exchanged weary looks.

"There is no Area 51. But that's a good spot to get a signal off-world, we know that from experience. We should send a team to investigate," Doc said.

Titus called up the California location, then zoomed in on a digital map. "I know this place. It's the Research Institute for Extra-

Terrestrial Information," he said.

"Nerd," Emily said.

"No, seriously," Titus said. "They're not quacks. Constructed one of the largest signal structures in the world to ping out a welcome message. They're like SETI."

"Even if they're benign, it could be that our enemies are stealing that signal structure to send out messages to their fleet," Doc said. "You and Kate should go talk to them."

Titus nodded. "And the last location?" he asked.

Doc inspected it for a long, pensive moment.

"That one looks familiar to me," Doc said. "I can't place it, but we should investigate."

"We'll be spread pretty thin," Titus said. "I assume Billy snuck off in the middle of the night."

"Yeah," Emily said.

"It's okay. I expected him to," Doc said. "Let's get Jane and Kate up to speed and see if can't find some backup. The five of us are going to be short-staffed and we need to check all three places simultaneously in case they're related—we can't risk spooking the others by hitting them one at a time."

"I'll get Kate," Titus said, standing up. "And I think I know someone we can call for help."

"That's a terrible idea," Emily said.

"I haven't even said anything yet."

"Doesn't matter," Emily said. "I already know who you're going to say, and it is a bad idea. Bad dog, Titus. Bad dog."

CHAPTER 10:
JOURNALISTIC INTEGRITY

Jane hated to admit it, but she found being around Jon Broadstreet incredibly uncomfortable since returning from the future. She understood the reporter wasn't fated for the same horrible end she'd seen in that alternate timeline. They were on a different course here. He'd never infiltrate a world-destroying organization as a spy and die while trying to escape. There were a million other ways the young journalist could meet a bad end, but, Jane thought, at least we can dismiss the one I've seen happen.

But still, she'd witnessed a future version of him die, and she felt sad around the present-day version of him every time they met, now. She longed for the old days when his unrequited crush on her was the main cause of her discomfort. Now during those times when he'd ask Jane out to dinner, her pained expression didn't indicate a lack of interest so much as it reflected a covert attempt to cover up her awkwardness.

And the poor man had no idea.

Today they met on a footbridge that crossed a river cutting through the heart of the City, an area that had, in the old days, been a crime-riddled pathway for illegal smuggling in and out of the metropolis. But before Jane lived here—really, almost before she was born—City officials had labored tirelessly to beautify it, and they'd done a magnificent job. The once grimy and dangerous section had become a walking route and bike path, frequented by joggers and families with strollers, dotted with coffee shops and restaurants with outdoor seating.

Broadstreet showed up with coffee and handed it to Jane as she adjusted the knit cap on her head. He laughed.

"You realize almost everyone who walks by does know who you are, hat or no hat," he said.

"Can you at least pretend my civilian disguise works?" Jane said.

The reporter struck a suddenly serious look, his mouth a hard, straight line.

"I barely recognized you. It's like I'm looking at another person," he said. "You know, in a certain light you kind of resemble someone. An actress or something."

Jane sipped her coffee and leaned against the railing, stealing a quick glance up at the sky. She wondered what was in store for them. Emily ratted Billy out as soon as he left; now everyone knew he was gone. And hadn't said goodbye. Probably for the best, Jane thought. Perhaps saying goodbye is bad luck. The thought of him out there by himself in the blackness of space made her heart hurt. She could do it, or someone like Kate, but Billy couldn't stand being alone for dinner, never mind flying out into the endless sky.

"You've got something on your mind," Broadstreet said.

"I've always got something on my mind," Jane said, shaking off her wandering thoughts.

"Anyone ever tell you that you worry too much?" he said.

She gave him a hard, almost angry look, and then shook her head.

"Can I tell you the truth? Sometimes I worry so much it physically hurts," Jane said. "I'm practically impervious to harm, and I sit here freaking myself out until I'm sick. Normal people don't do this, do they?"

Broadstreet shrugged, then joined her by leaning against the bridge's rail.

"You'd be surprised at how many people do," Broadstreet said. "We live in this big, beautiful, amazing world, and every day all we do is obsess about every little thing. The big picture should be a miracle and instead we're…"

He waved a hand vaguely around, gesturing toward the bustling streets of the City.

"Instead we let all this bog us down," he said. "But who am I to judge. I almost got you coffee with cream instead of milk and practically had a panic attack."

"I still would have drunk it, you know," Jane said.

"Exactly. See what I mean? Why worry about something like that?"

"Because you care," Jane said.

Broadstreet nodded, almost embarrassed.

"I'm not giving you a hard time," Jane said. "I bet you're concerned if you're rude to a stranger in traffic too."

"Happened on the way here," he said.

"I knew it." She studied the young reporter's face, the way that beard he'd been trying to grow for months now almost seemed to be filling in—he had a spot below his jaw line where no hair would come through and it gave him an almost comedic patchy look—and then she reflected on the rumpled aesthetic of his clothes, the way he watched everything around them. It's so unfortunate you keep asking me out, Broadstreet, she thought; if you'd just be normal, we could be good friends, I think.

"So what is today's concern, Solar," Broadstreet asked.

"If there were ever a real emergency, like something that might require people to evacuate calmly, and we got wind of it early—what could you do to help?"

"Me? Like, the press?" Broadstreet said.

"The press, yeah. But starting with you," Jane said.

"You know something I should know about now?"

"Maybe," Jane said. "Yeah. No. Wait. Off the record."

"We're always off the record until you tell me these days," he said. "My bosses would murder me for saying that, but you know it."

Jane looked over her shoulder. The dark water of the river drifted by.

"We're trying to prevent something big," Jane said. "And if we can't…"

Broadstreet's eyes went distant for a moment, deep in thought. He let out a long, frustrated sigh.

"This is where I betray my profession," he said, resigned. "You want to know the truth?"

"Of course."

"You need to control your message," he said. "You make the announcement. Distribute everything you need us to know at the same time, to everyone, immediately. That big old floating fortress of yours has to be able to broadcast a message in large-scale way, yeah?"

"I think so," Jane said.

"Make sure the right people know it's coming. Public safety. Emergency management. Disaster teams. And then do it in your voice," he said. "Because people will listen to you. We'll catch up, but it's going to need to come from you."

"From us?" Jane said. "The team?"

Broadstreet laughed.

"No. From you. I know you don't like to admit it, but you're the one we trust, Solar," he said. "If the worst happens, we're not gonna want to hear it from a werewolf, or a sociopath in some mask, or from a kid who glows, or a blue-haired teenager who talks way too much. People are going to look to a full-fledged hero when something catastrophic occurs, and congratulations, kid—that means you."

"You know how I said I worry about everything and you said I shouldn't?" Jane said.

"I just made it a lot worse, didn't I?" Broadstreet said.

"Yep."

"Sorry," he said.

And together, they watched the river drift by in silent reflection and concern of things far beyond their control.

CHAPTER 11:
A BIT OF BEDLAM

Kate and Titus stepped out onto the roof of a tall, aging apartment building on the edge of the City, the sort of place young professionals cram themselves into right after college graduation. Too grungy to be suburban, too far from the action of the downtown to be high-end, the type of complex ordinary people rent because they have nowhere else to go. Kate kept a space like this on the other side of town, a bolt hole for when she needed to get away from the team, little more than a bed and a closet full of old clothes. Something that was hers and no one else's.

Today, though, they were here on team business, to meet someone who was the furthest thing from the ordinary residents one might find walking around the City. Bedlam, the cyborg who they'd rescued from the Children of the Elder Star long ago, had agreed to meet them here, far from the bustle of the city. She insisted on a rooftop rendezvous because she wanted to see the sky.

Kate gazed at Bedlam and understood why she preferred locations like this. There were very few places someone like Bedlam could stand under an open sky and not draw attention to herself. Her appearance had changed somewhat since their last meeting—she'd helped Kate and Titus spring the rest of the Indestructibles from the Labyrinth prison months before—and she'd been clearly upgrading her cybernetics.

Still, she was a strange sight to behold. Both legs cybernetic replacements from the knee down, powerful machinery that had been slightly streamlined from before, appearing less blatantly robotic from a distance. Bedlam wasn't embarrassed about them, though. She stood waiting for them in a short black skirt, as if daring the world to stare at her mechanical legs.

An entire arm was cybernetic from the shoulder down. At one time clunky and almost unfinished in appearance, with hydraulic parts visible and uncovered, it had since been rebuilt to more closely resemble human musculature, though it still gleamed silver and black, and motors became audible when she moved. Her other arm was robotic below the elbow, but that piece had always been the most elegantly crafted, smooth and silver and nearly human to look at.

When she smiled at the Kate and Titus, the Dancer found herself, as always, taken aback more by the cyborg's face than by her limbs. Her left eye and the area around it had been replaced by cybernetics, running smoothly down her cheek, with her jaw reinforced with metallic parts as well. The transformative work performed on her made it completely impossible for Bedlam to pass for fully human in public. She didn't do much to improve that, either—not only did she proudly keep her legs bare, she wore a tank top with the British flag emblazoned on it, leaving both arms completely visible. Her neon mohawk was gone, but she still shaved her hair down to stubble on the sides and back and kept the top, which she dyed electric orange, swept back dramatically. She wore florescent green lipstick, which made her wild smile even more distracting.

"Ninja Girl and Wolf Boy," she said, reaching a hand out to shake Titus'. "How the hell are you?"

"Thanks for meeting us," Titus said.

Kate found his reaction to the manic cyborg almost as strange as she found the girl's feral demeanor. Titus was comfortable around her, completely at ease, as if they were old friends. He'd explained it to Kate after the fight at the Labyrinth. They'd fought together, a pair of brawlers and berserkers. They came from the same sort of place, where you survived by losing control, where you saw red until the fight was over. He said he understood her.

These two were, in many ways, Kate's polar opposite. But she knew that their team needed both kinds of warriors to win the coming war, berserkers and samurai, wild creatures and Zen.

And despite herself, she did like the cyborg. It was hard not to admire someone who so clearly did not care what the rest of the world thought of her. Not that Kate would ever tell anyone that, of course.

"Where's your boss?" Kate asked.

Bedlam usually traveled with the mercenary Agent Black, who had, in the Indestructibles' earliest days, fought on the opposing side. But Kate had been the only Indestructible to speak to him during that early battle, to look him in the eye, and she respected him as well. Black was a mercenary, but the Dancer could discern honesty in a person's demeanor, and she understood he wasn't a pure villain.

"Black? He still takes jobs he doesn't want me to be a part of," Bedlam said, looking out over the City.

"Working for the bad guys," Titus said, his tone conversational.

Bedlam shrugged.

"Don't know, exactly. But we have to take what we can get. Not like I can walk into an Apollo's Coffee looking like this and ask for a job," Bedlam said.

"You'd probably be a hell of a barista," Titus said.

"You know it," Bedlam said. "Look, I don't want a lecture. Whatever he's out there doing right now, it paid for a lot of my cybernetic work. He's helped me finish the work those Children bastards started on me. I was Humpty Dumpty when you found me."

"You're still doing work together though, yeah?" Titus said.

"Plenty of it," Bedlam said, quirking a dastardly smile at both of them. "I do love making a mess. But some of the… nastier stuff pays better. Also I won't use a gun. That makes a difference."

"Do you even need one?" Titus said.

Bedlam raised her hands up, resigned.

"Perception I guess," she said. "Merc without a gun? Not as scary. Though you drop me into a hot zone and tell me to start breaking things and I'll get the job done for you."

"I'm not sure I really want to know," Titus said.

"No, you don't," Bedlam said. "Then again, you're a weapon of mass destruction yourself, werewolf boy. I bet you could cause some serious havoc if you ever want to take an assignment."

Titus waved his hands dismissively.

"I'm good, thanks," he said.

"You're here to ask me to break things for you again, aren't you," Bedlam said.

"If you're still in the breaking things business," Titus said.

"Sneaking into another prison?" Bedlam said.

"Preventing an alien invasion," Kate interrupted.

Bedlam looked her and shrugged nonchalantly.

"Not the reaction I was expecting," Titus said.

"I'm half-robot and I'm talking to a werewolf. If you told me we were going to ride dragons to go fight the invading aliens, I'd be like, cool, sounds like fun," Bedlam said. "What's flyboy got to do with this? He's your alien expert, isn't he?"

"Straylight's off-world, scouting," Kate said.

Again, Bedlam stared, but more curious this time.

"Off-world. Glow-stick is in outer space," she said.

"Yeah," Titus said. "Trying to figure out what we're up against."

"He is… coming back," Bedlam asked.

"Hopefully," Kate said bluntly.

Bedlam looked back out over the City, chewing on her lip.

"I should hate this world, y'know?" Bedlam said. "Car accident takes half my body; terrible bastards use me as an experiment to put me back together. Can't do anything normal anymore. Can't be normal. I should hate everything about this place."

"But you don't," Kate said.

Bedlam studied her, more with her human eye than the robotic one.

"You've been through some stuff too, haven't you?" Bedlam said. "You're as crazy as I am. You just hide it better."

"She really doesn't hide it as well as you'd think," Titus said.

Kate glared at him, but he smiled back at her, almost laughing.

"What do you think, Bedlam," Kate said. "Ready to put your grownup pants on and become a hero? Or are you content to run around knocking buildings over for fun and profit."

Bedlam rolled her eyes, barking out a hard, frustrated laugh.

"Man I should hate this horrible dump of place," Bedlam said. "But it's all we've got, right? Yeah, I'm in. You need help saving the world, the hell with it, I'm in."

"Glad to have you," Titus said, a big grin on his face.

"What's our first thing? Our first mission? Is that what you heroes call 'em? Missions?" Bedlam said.

"We're going to make sure the bad guys can't talk to each other," Kate said.

"Now that sounds like it involves breaking things," Bedlam said.

"With any luck," Kate said. "With any luck at all."

CHAPTER 12:
DIVISION OF LABOR

Jane watched Emily simultaneously sulk and binge on Wikipedia entries in the control room of the Tower while they waited for Kate and Titus to return. In a way it was impressive—she was absorbing, assessing, and retrieving information from the computer screen with part of her brain while being uncharacteristically petty with another part.

"You, of all people, I don't understand being upset about this," Jane said as Emily scanned through doctored photos of faked alien landings on one of the larger monitors. Doc sat at the conference table as well, feigning meditation. Jane knew he was pretending because he smirked every time Emily said something off the wall.

"All I'm saying is, there's only room on this team for one florescent-haired crazy person," Emily said. "And that's me. The position's filled."

"I would've thought you two would be best friends," Jane said. "You and Bedlam are so much alike."

Emily threw back her head in frustration.

"Don't you see? That's the problem! I'm like a cat. I don't want to be around another cat just like me," Emily said.

"There is nobody just like you," Titus said, entering ahead of Kate and the newly roped-in Bedlam. Jane nodded to the cyborg, who threw back a tough if friendly smirk. They hadn't had much time to talk, but Jane knew Bedlam had taken a beating for them in the breakout from the Labyrinth. She'd earned a place here.

59

"Any word from Billy?" Titus said.

Jane shook her head.

"I don't know if we will," Doc said. "Perhaps if our patient in the infirmary wakes up he can tell us how to communicate with Straylight, but for now, we just have to wait for him to return."

"We should get to work, then," Kate said. She sat in her usual chair and picked up one of the tablets on the table, taking command of the largest monitor in the room and closing Emily's Wikipedia search.

"I was reading that," Emily said.

"And now you're not," Kate said.

Doc ignored the bickering and stood up, taking position in front of the monitor. Kate retrieved a map of the United States with the three spots they needed to investigate marked in red.

"Three locations, three teams of two," Doc said. He looked at Jane for approval. "Sound good?"

"Who should go where?" she said.

Doc quirked an eyebrow.

"I want your input, Doc," Jane said. "You know more of the history of what's going on."

"Okay," he said and tapped the California location. "This organization, the Research Institute for Extra-Terrestrial Information, has been sending signals out to space for a long time. It's a civilian program. Their mission is to make informed, peaceful contact with new species."

"It seems odd that there'd be a civilian organization doing this, knowing what we've learned," Jane said.

"It's always been a moral quandary for us," Doc said. "We realize there's alien life out there. We're friendly with some of it, even. But the less the world knows…"

"Less chance to cause a panic," Titus said.

"Exactly," Doc said.

"It seems sketchy to me," Kate said. "I have trouble believing that's all they want."

"They've also been sending out different signals in recent months," Emily said, chiming in. "Slight variations to the 'we come in

60

peace' message they've broadcast for decades."

"That's why I suggest Kate and Titus head there," Doc said. "You're our detectives. Sniff around, see if they're hiding anything."

"I resent that metaphor," Titus said.

"Sorry," Doc said sheepishly. "Unintentional."

"Dibs on Area 51," Emily said.

"Hang on," Bedlam said, speaking for the first time. "Where's that mark over the Appalachian Mountains? Why does that look vaguely familiar?"

"I was hoping you'd recognize that," Doc said. He motioned to Kate, who zoomed in on the spot. "After you escaped, did you ever do any research on the people who held you captive?"

Bedlam let out a hardy laugh.

"Oh yeah," she said. "I want to find those twisted bastards someday."

Doc smiled, not unkindly.

"I was hoping you might say something like that," he said. "That is the location of an old bolt hole for the Children of the Elder Star. A lab carved into a mountain."

Bedlam looked at Doc and then to Kate and back again.

"That's not the place Black and his squad ran to after you destroyed their island base, is it?" she said.

"It is," Doc said. "And it was supposed to have been empty ever since they evacuated it."

"So who's sending a bloody signal to space from it," Kate asked.

Bedlam looked at Emily, who stared right back at her.

"You can keep Area 51," Bedlam said. "I want to go there."

"Me too," Doc said. "I'm best prepared for any traps the Children might have left behind. Care to join me?"

"Absolutely," Bedlam said through gritted teeth.

Emily slapped her hands on the table.

"Area 51 for me!" she yelled.

"It's not really Area 51, Em," Jane said. "But there's something there, and I'm going to check it out, and your big genius brain is going to come with me to help me figure it out."

"Aces," Emily said. "Field trip."

"Then we have our assignments," Jane said. "Neal?"

"Yes, Designation: Solar," the AI said.

Bedlam's eyes wandered around the room at the sound of Neal's disembodied voice.

"I know you guys explained him to me before, but that is still creepy," Bedlam said.

"I apologize for upsetting you, Designation: Bedlam."

"Neal," Jane said, interrupting. "You will contact us the second you hear anything from Billy, got it?"

"Of course, Designation: Solar."

"Hey Neal?" Titus said.

"Hello, Designation: Whispering," the computer said.

"You should probably ping us if anything troublesome falls from the sky," Titus said.

"I will remain on high alert, Designation: Whispering," Neal said.

"Thanks," Titus said. He looked around the room, as if, Jane thought, he was solving a very long math equation in his mind.

"You okay?" she asked.

"Doc can teleport, and you and Emily can fly," Titus said. "How are Kate and I getting to California?"

Kate stood up dramatically, tapping away at her tablet, sending coordinates and details to the three teams.

"I found something in the landing bay we can use," Kate said.

Titus stared at her. "Found something. In the landing bay," he said.

"Do not be concerned, Designation: Whispering," Neal said. "Designation: Dancer has been approved to operate the vehicle. You will be perfectly safe."

"You always say that," Titus said. "And I'm never fully convinced."

CHAPTER 13:
INSIGNIFICANT

When he and Dude left Earth, Billy thought the journey would be an adventure, flying past planets, dodging meteors, swooping in to check out comets as they passed by.

Turns out, outer space is a vacuum and there's not a lot to see. They almost wiped out a news network's satellite, sure, and Dude had, reluctantly, let Billy take a low-altitude flyby across the surface of the moon, but after that, Billy thought, there wasn't much more than darkness and stars.

It didn't help that Dude's powers kept Billy entirely insulated, too. Not that he was complaining—he'd have died instantly, of course—but he didn't feel any differently than he did on Earth, surrounded by the pale protective shielding that guarded him from injury planet-side.

On the more exciting front, Dude could help them move far faster outside of Earth's atmosphere than he was within it. He explained it to Billy, or at least attempted to, but Billy tuned him out and just kept asking if he could call it hyperspace.

It's just so empty out here, Dude, Billy thought.

That's why your people call it space, and not stuff, Dude said.

Did you just sass me? Billy thought.

It's annoying when someone else does it, isn't it, Dude said.

Billy's disappointment at not seeing Mars—he had asked Dude specifically to find a way for them to fly by the red planet, and the alien refused—was only matched by finding out the Solar System's asteroid belt was mostly empty.

Let me know when we're getting close to the asteroid belt, Billy asked. I'll take out my iPhone and snap a few pictures.

We're already in it, Dude said. *We're passing through right now.*

There are no asteroids, Billy thought.

It's mostly empty. Your Earth fiction paints an inaccurate—

We've flown out past Mars, Billy said. We're further than any human being has ever flown before. And you're telling me there's no asteroids in the asteroid belt?

Perhaps you should listen to Emily more, Dude said. *We're not far from Ceres if you'd like to see the biggest object in the belt...*

No, never mind, Billy thought. This whole trip is ruined for me.

Although if Billy were being honest, the trip itself was ruining the journey for him. Infinitely far from home and helpless, he wondered if this was what drowning felt like.

I ever tell you about the time I almost drowned? Billy thought.

Several times, Dude said.

Billy's family didn't get to the ocean much. They worked too often, spent too much time hammering out an existence to get to the shore. But once, when he was young, they packed up the family car and headed to the beach. Billy, with the bravery that teeters on stupidity all children have, dove into the water, unaware and unfamiliar with how dangerous an undertow can be. He resurfaced far from where he should have been, his back to the shoreline, looking out into the blue and black emptiness of the sea.

And for a split second, he felt completely adrift. Nothing but sky and ocean and the feeling of currents hovering around his ankles. Young Billy Case at the end of the world.

His dad found him, scooped him up in strong arms and carried him to shore, scolding him for wandering off, repeating the word undertow over and over again. Billy kept looking over his father's shoulder, though, at the void, the emptiness beyond him, as if he might tip forward and disappear forever.

Space travel, Billy thought, more to himself than to Dude, is a thousand times worse than that.

His journey with Dude became a cycle of talking too much—

asking questions about astronomy and space travel or just recycling old stories Dude had already heard a thousand times before—and long periods of silence, where human and alien said nothing at all, flying into the black, the infinite sensation of emptiness overwhelming and cold. Time felt out of sorts, something Dude explained had to do with moving as fast as they were.

Y'know, Dude, Billy thought, finally. The least we can do is slow down long enough to let me see one planet. I may not survive this. Think it'd be okay if I get a look at one of 'em before it's all over?

The stars stopped moving, and Billy felt that eerie forward momentum he'd been experiencing cease. Suddenly he was adrift in space, weightless, directionless, staring out into a blanket of stars.

He turned his head, and Saturn rose to great him.

The gas giant overwhelmed his vision, a vast circle of cream and gold. The plant's infamous rings were like grooves on the surface of a vinyl record, hypnotic lines spinning soundlessly before them. Dude had brought them to a stop close to the moon Titan, which hung in space like a lonely globe, cast in silhouette by the Sun.

Billy felt his throat swell. His heart skipped a beat.

This is the most amazing thing I'll ever see in my entire life, Billy thought.

You'd be surprised how many amazing things you'll see, Billy Case, Dude said.

I'm some kid from the City who never even saw stars properly until last week, Billy thought. And now I'm looking at Saturn and it feels so close I could almost reach out and touch it.

Are you alright? Dude asked.

Not even a little bit, Billy said. I am not okay at all. I feel…

Insignificant, Dude suggested.

I feel tiny and meaningless, Billy thought.

That's what… never mind, Dude said. *You are not meaningless. You are going to save your world.*

Yeah, Billy thought. We'll see how that goes.

Billy could sense a change in Dude's demeanor as well. Maybe he was feeling the same sense of astonishment. Maybe he was feeling nostalgic. Billy knew now that Dude had come from the stars, and that he'd been on Earth a long time. Maybe he used to see things like this all the time. Perhaps, under the shadow of all those big, pointless buildings, Dude had forgotten what it was like to be here, looking out onto something too mighty to feel real.

And then both human and alien jerked out of their melancholic reveries as they saw a shadow creep along the far edge of the planet.

Dude, is that... ? Billy thought.

Be cautious, Billy Case, Dude said.

They flew in closer, using the shadow of Titan to hide their blue-white energy signature. Billy felt his vision sharpen in that superhuman way his Straylight powers allowed. This wasn't a single shadow they'd seen moving past Saturn. These were many shadows. Ships. Long, ugly ships, casting irregular silhouettes, barbed and crooked and irrational in their forms.

Billy let himself drift away from the moon, not flying so much as floating on his own momentum, watching the armada. And that was truly what it was, a fleet of warships, aggressive machines, moving surely toward Earth.

They don't look like metal, Dude, Billy thought. They look like muscle and shell. They look alive.

The Nemesis fleet is alive, Billy Case, Dude said. *Their ships are their weapons of war, and they are their children. Their armada is a living, moving hive.*

Billy tried to count the ships, but the darkness and the tight formation they traveled in made it impossible. They were different sizes—huge warships and little scouts, big-bellied carriers and others that didn't look like ships at all.

We have to do something, Dude, Billy thought.

We will. We'll get home and prepare. There is nothing you can do alone here. Not against the entire fleet.

Billy felt a rage building up inside him, and fear. He knew Dude was right.

Okay, Billy thought. How can we do this without being spotted?

I'm plotting a trajectory now, Dude said. *If we use the sun to mask our escape...*

With horrific silence, one of the small, jet fighter-like appendages of the fleet turned slowly toward them.

Don't see us don't see us don't see us, Billy started chanting in his head.

The craft started moving toward them. Two others peeled off the fleet as well, like wasps.

What do we do, Dude? Billy thought, panic rising in his interior dialogue.

We run, Dude said.

CHAPTER 14:
THE ANGRIEST FLOWERS
IN THE WORLD

Titus hated flying.

He'd always hated flying, and the fact that the Indestructibles home base was, basically, a floating block of non-aerodynamic flying saucer didn't help with things. Neither did the frequent trips they took on the Tower's collection of hover-bikes, open-aired flying machines he and Kate had to use to get around when Emily wasn't there to transport them up to the floating headquarters.

So when Kate showed him the vehicle she and Emily found that would get them to California and back without help from one of their more aerial teammates, Titus felt waves of nausea crash over him.

"I'm not flying in that," he said.

"Yes, you are," Kate said, tapping a button and opening the craft up. It was about the size of a large car, and looked like something out of an old sci-fi pulp fiction story—silver metal, not quite streamlined enough to look like it should fly, a bubbled cockpit with seating for two side by side, and a third fold-down seat behind those. The domed glass over the cockpit rose on hinges facing forward to allow them to climb inside onto oddly out-of-date cream-colored pleather seats.

Kate slid comfortably behind what was clearly the pilot's seat. In full Dancer uniform, she wore a pair of sun-canceling goggles she explained would cut down on glare as they flew.

"Do you know how to fly this thing?" Titus said.

"Just get in," Kate said.

Titus sat down in the copilot's seat, buckled himself in, and took a deep breath as the canopy closed.

"You're not going to keep your eyes closed the entire flight, are you?" Kate said.

"Maybe," the werewolf replied.

* * *

Kate never told anyone, but she loved to fly.

Her father had been a hobbyist pilot, renting time in small aircraft on the weekends. On those rare days when she wasn't practicing or rehearsing, he'd take her flying with him, letting her take control of the craft for a little while, teaching her about all the instruments. The older she got, the harder it became to recall her father's voice, but she remembered his hands on hers as they drifted over the landscape and the sense of freedom and joy her father felt when they left the ground.

She missed him. That kind of sadness rarely weighed her down—Kate was nothing if not talented at pushing emotions to the back of her mind—but here, in this cockpit, watching clouds drift lazily below them, she missed her father, and her mother. She longed for the times of doing joyful things.

The Tower was full of old gadgets and machinery none of which the Indestructibles fully understood. Many of these devices were left ignored for the most part—better to not push buttons on alien technology if you don't know what that button did—but Kate and Emily had stumbled across this vehicle months before in storage in the hanger bay the team made frequent us of, under a dusty gold tarp.

Late at night, Kate had talked with Neal, asking the AI, what he knew about it, how it worked, what it was fueled by, and whether she could use it. The AI was a fount of background information, explaining how it had been acquired by one of Doc's teammates early on and used sporadically over the years. With no weapon systems and only room for a few riders, the old team hadn't needed it much, but Henry Winter stored it away carefully just in case.

So Kate took it out for test flights when no one was in the

Tower. The only one who ever caught her was Emily, who seemed, the way Emily always does, to understand what Kate was doing. She kept this all to herself, though she did insist to Kate that they name the aircraft the Indestructicar. Emily found this profoundly funny. Kate never got the joke.

Faster than a conventional airplane, the miniature jet carried Kate and a very stressed out werewolf across the country in a few hours, technology that hadn't been invented yet in this timeline allowing the craft to remain invisible to radar. Kate leaned back, enjoying the sense of weightlessness, the quiet hiss of the machine's propulsion systems, and wished her companion simply could do the same.

"You know, if you fell out of the sky, you'd still heal," Kate said.

Titus looked at her, visibly confused.

"I'm not worried about hitting the ground, I'm worried about the fall itself. That's a lot of time to think about everything," Titus said.

Kate's mouth quirked into a small smile. You and I, she thought, don't need a fall from the sky to think about things too much.

She looked over the latest incarnation of Titus' outfit. He's finally outgrown the hooded sweatshirt he had relied on for so long, though the new look—an army green jacket with a soft, oversized hood, a baggy tank top beneath it revealing his too-thin collarbone and chest, loose-fitting cargo pants that would stretch to fit over his werewolf form if he needed to transform—still didn't look particularly heroic.

"You look like a hobo," Kate said.

"You look like a ninja," Titus said. "Are you sure you should take your eyes off the sky?"

"What am I going to crash into?" Kate said, knowing full well it would upset him.

It was hard to miss the Research Institute for Extra-Terrestrial Information from the sky. The headquarters itself was relatively non-descript, a small brick and glass building the likes of which you see at every office park in the country. But the field of satellite dishes behind the building, including one wider in diameter than the building itself, was a site to be seen. Kate thought they looked like a field of the angriest flowers in the world.

She landed the aircraft, which could set down vertically like a helicopter, in a pair of empty parking spaces in the RIETI lot. Titus sighed heavily when the landing gear connected with the pavement.

"I don't understand you," Kate said. "We've already traveled through time. This, on the other hand, is just flying."

"You're lecturing me about neuroses?" Titus said.

Kate shot him the dirtiest look she'd ever given him.

Titus blanched. "Sorry. I'm snippy. It's the anxiety. Sorry."

She popped the cockpit and stepped outside. Titus followed, trying to catch up.

They entered the lobby and the receptionist, a strangely photogenic young man wearing a checkered shirt, knit tie and dark glasses, looked up.

"Are you kidding me?" he said.

"We're here to see Lester Rice-Bell," Kate said.

"We have an appointment," Titus said. Kate glanced at him. Titus shrugged. "We do."

The receptionist checked a calendar on his desk and shook his head in surprise.

"I… you do. Okay," he said. "Take the elevator to the third floor. I'll let him know you're on the way up."

Titus and Kate stepped on the elevator, the same way normal people who are not dressed for superhero combat do. Titus hit the button for the third floor. They looked at each other again.

"When did normal stuff get weirder than weird stuff?" Titus asked.

"About two years ago," Kate said. The elevator dinged and they stepped off to find Lester Rice-Bell, president of RIETI, waiting for them at the door.

"I have to admit, I never thought I'd have two superheroes show up at my door," the man said. He had a round, friendly face, a body that wasn't so much overweight as soft from inactivity, fair hair cut expensively to hide its thinness on the top of his scalp. He shook Kate's hand first, then Titus'.

Rice-Bell led them into a pleasantly furnished but inexpensive office. Everything about it said well-used and well-loved. Kate soaked in the details. The furniture looked second-hand, or brought from home. The books on the shelves were not just decorative, but read, multiple times. A bookshelf along one wall had framed pictures of what appeared to be historical members of the RIETI staff.

Rice-Bell caught her looking at the photos.

"Some of my predecessors," he said. "We're sentimental. The world's become so strange since they founded RIETI back in the 1950's. I sometimes envy their innocence."

He invited them to sit down. Titus accepted, but Kate continued to wander the office, reading the spines on books and picking up photos to examine them in closer detail.

"Thanks for meeting with us," Titus said. "We're looking into, um, unusual signals being sent into space."

Rice-Bell raised an eyebrow.

"You can't just say something like that to someone who has spent his entire career trying to talk with aliens and then not give me a little bit of detail," he said.

Titus fidgeted a bit in his chair, crossing and uncrossing his legs as if trying to figure out how an adult sits.

"Later? After we've had a chance to follow up on all our leads," Titus said. "This may seem like a strange question but... well we know you've been sending out... friendly messages to space for a long time."

"Since right after World War II, yes," Rice-Bell said. "I know. We sound like quacks. But our philosophy is: it's a self-centered belief to think we're the only ones out there isn't it? There has to be someone else out there, staring up at the sky, wondering if they're alone in the universe."

"So you send out radio signals," Titus said.

"Radio's the wrong term, but yes," Rice-Bell said. "We send out information about ourselves. Our biology. What we breathe. How we think. We send music. Literature. Images. We like to send classical paintings."

"Why bother?" Kate said from across the room. "All these years. Why keep doing it?"

"Because maybe in my lifetime we'll make contact," he said.

"And what if you don't like who answers back?" Kate said.

Rice-Bell's face darkened.

"Why do you say that," he said. "Is there something..."

"I'm just speaking hypothetically," Kate said. "What's the point in sending out all this information if at best they may ignore it, or at worse they may use it against us?"

Titus ran a hand nervously through his hair. "Mr. Rice-Bell," he said.

"Please. Just Lester."

"Lester, has anything strange been happening here lately?" Titus said.

"You're in a building dedicated to finding extra-terrestrial life, son," Rice-Bell said. "Everything we do is strange."

Titus shrugged, silently agreeing.

"Nothing out of the ordinary, though? No misuse of your equipment, unexpected test results?" Titus said.

Rice-Bell laughed.

"Believe me, if something weird happened, we'd not only know it, we'd be celebrating. We spend our lives looking up waiting for someone to say hello. If we heard something, we'd be ecstatic."

"What about unauthorized access of your equipment, though?" Titus said.

Kate crossed the room to look out the window, where the field of satellite dishes were plainly visible, like the strangest crop ever grown.

"That equipment is the reason we exist," Rice-Bell said, suddenly very serious. "No one touches it, fixes it, adjusts it, or looks at it too long without us knowing about it. We can't afford to make a mistake, and we don't have the operating budget to repair it if someone were to tamper with it."

"I assume you've got it under guard at night," Kate said.

"And day," Rice-Bell said. He stood up and joined Kate at the window, pointing out the fencing and cameras along the perimeter. "You might imagine, we're a temptation for pranksters. I'm almost ashamed to tell you how much of our budget goes into security, but people want to see us fail. They think we're just crazy old loonies out in the hills playing science fiction."

"Sorry to hear that, sir," Titus said.

Rice-Bell turned to smile at both of them.

"But we carry on. There are worse jobs than safeguarding a field of postcards from Planet Earth, right?" he said. "Is there anything else I can do for you?"

Titus pulled a plastic card from the pocket of his oversized pants and placed it on the desk.

"If you ever feel like something is amiss—or if you feel threatened in any way—the number on that card will connect you with our team," Titus said.

Rice-Bell laughed again and tucked the card into the top drawer of his desk.

"I appreciate the sentiment," he said. "But I'm still optimistic our first encounter will be a great meeting of the minds, not War of the Worlds."

Titus let out a near-approximation of a laugh, playing along. They shook hands again and let Rice-Bell guide them back to the elevator. Once outside, Titus and Kate shared a look.

"He was lying about everything," Kate said.

"Absolutely," Titus said. "Spinning so many lies his lies were lying."

"We're coming back tonight," Kate said.

"I figured," Titus said. "You get what you needed?"

"I spotted three gaps in their security while looking out his window," she said. "And stole the receptionist's security passkey when he was checking the calendar."

"Great," Titus said. "The sensor in the card I gave him will steal his passwords to anything he logs into while he's in the office."

Kate nodded approvingly, once again unlocking the cockpit to the Indestructicar. She found herself vaguely annoyed for thinking in Emily's terminology.

"So where do you want to get dinner while we wait til dark?" Titus said. "I'm starving."

CHAPTER 15:
THIS IS NOT AREA 51

Jane and Emily landed in the desert as the sun rode low in the sky, bathing everything in pink and gold. Jane turned her face to the sun, almost worshipful, feeling its rays splash onto her skin, her cells drinking it in like water on a hot day. It seemed more potent here, and thus she felt stronger as well, her body recharging as daylight crashed against her skin.

Before them, an abandoned complex spread out, washed in dust and the remnants of mankind, long forgotten in the desert. An old, tall chain link fence had descended into disrepair, fallen in some places, cut open in others, the barbed wire above it pointless and no longer threatening. Low beige buildings dotted the property, windows scratched opaque by time and the elements.

"Okay, now that I've seen it, this is not Area 51," Emily said. "Nothing here screams government facility for holding alien prisoners. It looks like an old gas station."

"You never know," Jane said. She went to tear the gate to the facility open, but Emily beat her to it, shoving it with her bubbles of float hard enough to snap the long-rusted padlock and chain holding it closed.

"I suppose we could've flown over that," Emily said.

Jane shrugged and walked in. No one had been here for a long, long time, she thought. It felt like a corpse, left to mummify in the sunshine.

"What do you think?" Jane said, watching Emily pull her costume goggles down over her eyes against the setting sun. "In one of the buildings?"

Emily made an I don't know face and started walking toward one of the nearest prefab structures. After a few steps she paused, looking down.

"What," Jane said.

Emily stomped her foot. She took another stomping step, then another, then another, and then started jumping up and down, kicking her feet in the sand.

"Any particular reason you're doing that, or have you finally completely glitched out?" Jane said.

Emily turned back to her as she hopped, her goggles now crusted with sand.

"What?" she said.

Then Emily landed with a clang instead of a thud.

The women looked at each other.

"You hear that?" Emily said.

"Yup."

The pair started kicking, looking for the surface below until they found a metal hatch, bigger than a door, the surface scratched and worn by sand and wind.

"Oh, this looks like a fantastic idea," Emily said.

"Going into the hatch?"

"It worked so well on *Lost,*" Emily said.

Jane gestured around her at all the emptiness surrounding them. She squinted at Emily.

"Signal's coming from somewhere," she said.

Emily sighed heavily and threw her head back in resignation.

"Fine. But if there's a Scotsman down there I'm going to panic," Emily said. Again she waved her hand and she bubble-of-floated the hatch open. She and Jane looked down into the gloom hesitantly.

"Age before beauty," Emily said.

Jane sat down on the lip of the hatch, feeling around for steps until she found rungs of a ladder. It occurred to her that using a ladder was a bit ridiculous when you could fly, but for some reason going down into a subterranean lair felt more natural if she had her feet grounded on something, so she climbed like a regular person. Emily did the same, though Jane could sense that Em was using her gravitational powers to take part of her weight, as if afraid she might slip and fall.

When they reached the bottom, they found themselves in a low-slung tunnel system. It reminded Jane of submarines in movies, tight and short with rounded walls. The lights were, creepily, still on in most places, and perhaps more eerily, had burned out in enough spots to create heavy patches of shadow. It smelled slightly rotten inside, like an old drain pipe.

"So I've had this nightmare before," Emily said. "Usually there are xenomorphs in it."

"You watch too many scary movies," Jane said.

"The scary movies aren't why I'm afraid right now," she said.

"Something tries to kill you on a daily basis," Jane said. "I don't know why you insist on watching horror movies all the time."

"Schadenfreude."

"Bless you," Jane said.

They walked side by side down what appeared to be the main tunnel, passing darkened corridors, areas with tipped over chairs, restrooms, even a small kitchen area. Emily inspected the kitchen for clues.

"This place looks used," Emily said.

"I'm sure it was," Jane said.

"No, I mean, it's not spotless, like it hadn't been occupied in a long time. It's not dusty. It's a little cluttered. I'm saying there's been activity here," Emily said.

"How recently?" Jane asked.

Emily shot Jane another "I dunno" look.

"I mean Titus might be able to tell by scent or something, but I couldn't tell you," she said.

Jane tilted her head apologetically and headed back down the main corridor. And then she saw it—a shadow, the size of a person, moving quickly ahead of them, trying to remain in the background.

Jane pointed to the runner, grabbing Emily by the shoulder.

"What!" Emily said, too loudly. Then she saw what Jane was pointing at and started whispering. "Should we chase it?"

Jane was already running at top speed down the hallway, still not comfortable with flying in the enclosed space. She watched the humanoid take a sharp turn, nothing about its shape and movement indicating it was a normal person. Jane took the hard right turn as well and could hear Emily's heavy Doc Martens slapping against the concrete floor behind her.

The creature in front of them led Jane and Emily into a larger area that opened at the end of the hallway, an airy, empty space with little light. The being scuttled further into the shadows, and Jane let one hand burst into flames so that they could see better.

It was just enough illumination to make her regret doing so as they came face to face with a different creature, twelve feet tall and hunched over, its arms long enough to drag along the floor like an ape's. It had one massive yellow eye dominating the center of its head above wide, fanged jaws.

"What the carp is that!" Emily yelled.

Jane came to a stop, moving into a battle-ready stance, and eyeballed the new enemy. For all its alien strangeness, the thing that seemed oddest about it, Jane thought, was the appendage on its chest—something seemed to be latched on there, a cross between an octopus and a crab, segmented and still, both connected to the monster but somehow entirely apart from it.

Just behind the bigger creature, the first critter they'd chased crept forward, an entirely different sort of alien—purple-blue skinned, with too many arms, too many eyes, a mouth like a beak. It too had something attached to its chest, a smaller version of the crab-like thing on its enormous companion.

Jane stepped back to bring herself to Emily's side.

"Em, don't let the little one escape," Jane said.

"And how do you propose I do that?" Emily said.

"If he runs, bubble of float him," Jane said. "I'll take the—"

"Better idea," Emily said. "Wall of slam, dudes!"

Emily shoved her hands forward, knocking both creatures big and small off their feet violently. The flurry of kicking feet and flailing arms would have been funny if not for the complete horror of what they were looking at, Jane thought.

"That didn't do what I thought it would," Emily said.

"I'm actually almost impressed," Jane said, just as both aliens scrambled to their feet. The smaller, purple one made the first move, trying to flee past the heroes before they could catch him.

"Emily!" Jane yelled, but Emily's bubbles of float seemed to be too slow to catch the creature. Jane jumped at him instead, not sure where she should grab, and decided to just throw a punch at his face instead. She connected, hard, but the creature struck right back, grabbing hold of her wrist with one of his too-many hands and punching her right back in the jaw.

"What the... ?" was all Jane could get out before getting punched again. The creature emitted a soft, huffing noise and she was suddenly positive the being was laughing at her.

"I got this!" Emily yelled, but Jane turned back just in time to see the larger alien knock her off her feet, sending the blue-haired girl flying into a nearby wall. The "oof" noise she yelled sounded so painful Jane felt it in her own guts.

"That. Is. It." Emily said. "You one-eyed Rancor-lookin' wannabe, you have messed with the wrong Emily!"

But as Em raised her hands for another wall of slam, the monster scooped her up in one massive paw and held her tight, arms pinned.

"Aw, come on," Emily said as the alien lifted her toward its sharp-toothed mouth.

"No," Jane said, and, stealing a move from Kate's handbook, head-butted her own opponent between its many, many eyes. The purple alien released its grasp on her and Jane kicked the creature in the knee as hard as she could before charging to Emily's rescue.

She leapt into the air, throwing a haymaker at the giant monster's face, connecting with such force she could see its thick, greenish skin ripple with the impact. The monster flung Emily away reflexively, bouncing the poor girl off the wall a second time, as Jane pummeled the creature's enormous face. The beast knocked her back and she could see the appendage latched to its chest glow with a reddish light from within. The monster swiped at her with huge, clawed hands, catching her cape and using it to knock her from the air back to the chamber floor.

The huge creature held its arms out to each side and then

slapped its hands together as if to clap, but caught Jane right in the middle between its palms. The impact rattled her. Jane felt it in her bones as the hands smashed into her from both sides. How strong is this thing? She thought. She'd never been hit like this before, not by a living creature. She saw the thing on its chest glowing brighter and brighter with each attack.

The alien moved in for another swing, and Jane punched upward, a full body uppercut that hammered into the monster's jaw. Broken teeth flew from the monster's mouth as it slammed shut. The giant alien roared in pain and slapped downward at her with an open-palmed hand. Jane caught his hand with hers, a finger in each of her hands, and she tried to stop his attack. Her back arched when her legs pushed back, muscles on fire under the strain.

And then the monster was gone, knocked off his feet, almost taking Jane with him. Emily stood up, hunched over in pain, her hand extended and palm up, aimed at the alien.

"Wall of slam, you filthy animal," Emily said, before falling down onto one knee for balance.

Jane squared off with the monster again as it climbed back to its feet. The thing on its chest was bright red now. She readied herself for another attack.

"Kill it with fire!" Emily said.

"Now is not the time for meme jokes, Em!" Jane said, not realizing until now she was panting from exertion.

"No, the thing on its chest! I think it's powering the alien!" Emily yelled.

Jane smiled a fighter's smile and looked at the alien's one giant yellow eye. She threw her tattered cape aside and ran at the monster, dodging one smashing fist and then another, ducking underneath to grab hold of the thing attached to its chest. It felt almost plantlike under her hands, the texture of rose stems without the thorns, thick with almost no give.

Jane closed her eyes and poured on the fire, letting her hands burst into flames, engulfing her arms up to the elbow. She held on. The monster thrashed and howled, but did not let go, burning away at the strange thing until it blackened and the alien squealed in pain.

The crab-thing hissed and popped like food cooking on a grill, and Jane pushed on the alien's abdomen, using its own body to yank the parasitic element away. The limbs or stalks holding tight to the alien crackled and snapped, and suddenly Jane was holding a dead, grotesque thing, some alien parasite corpse, and the bigger, host alien was wailing, smashing its fists into the ground, gasping and roaring.

Jane threw it away and looked for the smaller, purple alien. Emily was staggering back to her feet and pointing at the corridor toward the outside world.

They nodded to each other and started running as best they could, following a trail of bluish blood the monster had left behind.

"Thanks for trying to stop it from getting away," Jane said.

"Did I or did I not figure out how to stop the bigger one?" Emily said.

When they passed the kitchen at a run, the purple alien jumped out, smashing Jane with an entire table clutched in its many arms. She fell to the floor, half-stunned, as Emily tried to bubble of float the monster away. It used one of its remaining free hands to knock Emily into the wall and headed for the escape hatch, climbing the runs with nauseating speed.

Jane wobbled back to her feet and gave up running, flying down the tight corridor instead, up into the daylight, arms at her side to burst free of the underground tunnel. The sky had changed; the salmon-colored sunset gone, replaced by storm clouds, heavy, black, threatening clouds covered the sky. The purple creature was running, its gait uneven and mind-bendingly weird. Jane flew after it, tackling the being as it ran, but it seemed to understand that she knew its secret and batted her hands away with eerie precision as she tried to grab the parasitic attachment on its chest. It took hold of each of her wrists with vice-like strength and threw a barrage of punches, preventing Jane from getting her own attacks in.

"Emily, help!" she said, but it wasn't Emily who answered her. Instead, a bolt of lightning lanced out from the darkening sky, striking the purple alien with conscious precision. One bolt shocked the creature enough to cause it to release its grip, and as Jane fell back, she pointed at the creature's chest.

"Hit that thing!" she yelled, knowing exactly where help had come from. Another bolt of lightning struck, brightening up the sky in a flash of white. When Jane's vision cleared, the alien lay squirming in the sand, arms going in different directions, the parasite on its chest a burned and blackened mess.

Valerie Snow drifted out of the sky, her skin the color of the dark clouds above, eyes glowing the blue of lightning. Her long hair drifted on the wind like it had a mind of its own.

"Did we kill it?" Valerie said softly, watching with profound sadness as the alien suffered.

"I hope so," Emily said, staggering to catch up, a huge bruise growing on the side of her face.

Jane walked up to the ailing creature, pulled the parasite from its chest, and watched as it struggled and flailed. She looked at the half-formed creature in her hand and wondered how much of what just happened was controlled by the dead thing she held.

"It can't breathe," Jane said. She looked back at the hatch, positive the bigger alien was suffering the same fate. "The parasites let them breathe here. They're suffocating."

"What can we do to help?" Valerie said.

Help. It was a funny word, Jane thought, considering how hard both aliens had just tried to hurt them. But she knelt down in the sand, picked up the purple being and carried it back to the hatch. Jane was sure there was nothing she could find to save its life.

She knew she shouldn't care. But she was tired of death and had grown weary of seeing living creatures dying. It hurt her heart to have it happen in front of her yet again. She found herself singing the "Parting Glass" under her breath as she carried the alien back to the underground base, and fought back a wave of sadness as it stopped breathing in her arms.

"Emily, check the base to see what they were broadcasting their messages on," Jane said, remaining composed and steady. "We should try to figure out what they were telling the fleet."

"You okay?" Emily said, uncharacteristically gentle in her tone.

"Not at all," Jane said. "But we carry on."

CHAPTER 16:
WHAT THE CHILDREN KNEW

oc Silence and Bedlam stepped out of a portal on the side of the mountain as if materializing from nothing. Doc watched the young cyborg to judge her reaction to the teleportation spell he'd cast, not out of cruelty, but because so many people react so poorly to this method of travel the first time.

A little pale around the edges, but otherwise fine, Bedlam looked back at him with a half-crazed smile.

"Compensators in my headgear," she said, tapping the metal on the side of her head. "Prevents motion sickness."

"Aren't you lucky," he said, smiling back at her.

"Yeah, Doc," she said as they started walking further up the mountain, a craggy, moss-covered expanse that felt so isolated as to be on another world. "Whenever I look at myself in the mirror, I think—that's a lucky person right there."

Perhaps a quarter mile on, they came across a huge set of doors, palatial in size but incredibly ordinary in design—nothing fancier than reinforced garage doors.

Doc closed his eyes and listened. The air was cool and damp, the wind whistling a quiet tune as it cascaded through the mountain. They felt very alone.

"Want me to break it down?" Bedlam said, approaching the set of doors.

"No need," Doc said. He spoke in the language of magic, uttering the name of the door, its true name, as all doors have. The gateway swung open with a low creak.

"Aren't you fancy," Bedlam said.

"Whenever I look in the mirror I think—that's a fancy person right there," Doc said.

Bedlam smirked.

"I see what you did there," she said, pulling the door open the rest of the way and stepping inside.

Inside smelled like a battle between disinfectant and swamp gas, a steadfast one-two punch of sterile and earthy. Bedlam grimaced and walked inside. Doc followed close behind, calling up a variety of spells to be ready at the back of his mind.

"Lights are on. Anyone home?" Bedlam said, gesturing to the huge halogen lights turning the guts of the mountain into a brightly lit chamber. The area in front of them was enormous, like an aircraft hangar, with high ceilings and smooth, paved floors.

On the far side, a small door stood closed, leading out of the hanger. Next to one of those doors was a body, a backpack on one side, a rifle on the other. Doc and Bedlam walked slowly across the hanger to the corpse, their feet clanking softly against the floor.

"What the hell happened to him?" Bedlam said.

The man had been grievously injured, burn marks scoring his face and arms. Where he wasn't burned, he'd been scratched, as if by claws. A thin sheen of sweat covered his undamaged skin.

Doc crouched down to get a better look. The head tilted back in his direction and the eyes opened.

"You," the body said.

Bedlam cursed.

Doc just waited.

"I was hoping it'd be you."

"You seem to know who I am," Doc said. "But I'm at a loss for who you are."

The body struggled to sit up more, clearly not as dead as they first thought. The man patted his pockets weakly until he found a pack of cigarettes. With relish and care, he placed a cigarette between his lips. Doc snapped his fingers and a small wick of flame appeared on the tip of his pointer finger. He held it out in front of the wounded man so he could light his smoke.

"All these years," the man said, coughing as he inhaled his cigarette. Doc felt Bedlam lean in close over his shoulder. "We knew all about you, Doc Silence. Whether it was with your collection of

84

misfit toys or band of merry men, we've always known about you."

"What were you doing here?" Doc said.

The man leaned back, struggling to swallow.

"Can you believe some of us were actually serious?" the man said. "Most of us, most of us, we played the game, we picked the name to scare people, we pretended to be a cult. But we just wanted money. We wanted power. We wanted to rule through fear."

"The Children of the Elder Star?" Doc said.

The man nodded.

"That name," the man said. "We were a bunch of men in suits, Silence. The Children... it was marketing."

"But not for all of you," Doc said, suddenly piecing things together. The cave—he'd known this was a place the Children of the Elder Star used as a lab during their recent experiments. They'd owned the space for years, though left it mostly unused. Agent Black and Rose and their operatives used it briefly as a staging area, but not long. Doc could sense that his nemesis and friend, the Lady Natasha Grey, had been here as well—her spells still hung on the air like fading perfume. But what was here now?

The dying man laughed, a barking, scratchy huff.

"Maybe it was their idea all along," he said. "Recruit wealthy megalomaniacs and play the role of supernatural cultists. But they... some of these idiots meant it. They want this world consumed in fire. Something coming from the stars."

"What happened here," Doc said again.

"The experiments," the man said. "The board thought... the board thought they were exactly what we said they were. Weapons."

"We were weapons," Bedlam said. Doc heard her robotic hands hum as she clenched and unclenched her fists. "We still are, the ones you didn't kill."

"That's what we thought," the man said. "But these others... these others were trying to build a better *host*."

Before Doc could react, Bedlam grabbed the dying man by his shirt and slammed him against the wall.

"Host for what?" Bedlam said, powerful cybernetic arms holding the grown man's body aloft. A thin runner of blood trickled down his fingertip and splashed on the floor.

"I came here to..." the dying man started laughing again, almost hysterically. "I came here to *fire* them. Isn't that ridiculous? I came here to fire them... "

"A host for what?" Bedlam yelled again, slamming the man against the wall again.

He just laughed, though, choking on his own saliva, and Bedlam let him drop to the floor. She looked at Doc, and he saw in her eyes real fear for the first time.

"What the hell is going on?" Bedlam said.

Doc held out a hand to quiet her. Again, he tilted his head to listen. Breathing. Footsteps. Something was coming. Doc muttered another incantation, a summoning spell, and a long silver sword appeared in his left hand. He held it toward the floor, ready.

Bedlam's infuriated expression faded for a split second when she saw what he'd done.

"Did you just make a flippin' sword appear in your hand?" Bedlam asked. "Forget it. Forget it. What is this guy saying? They were building us to be hosts for something?"

The door creaked open, sending Doc and Bedlam into combat stances, Bedlam on the balls of her robotic feet like a boxer, Doc with one hand outstretched and glowing with magical energy, the other with sword at the ready.

The man who walked through the door had, at some point, been completely ordinary. Average height, medium build, a face you might walk by in a crowd. But now he was anything but ordinary. His skin had turned grayish green, cracked and split with scales. That bland face had become monstrous, with strange protrusions pushing out from his cheekbones and jawline. His hair had clearly been falling out, the remnants long and brittle.

Clinging to his chest was the worst of his transformation, though—some sort of parasite, as wide as the man's ribcage, claw-like appendages wrapped around his shoulders, chest, and neck to hold on. The parasite glowed red from within with a rhythm like a heartbeat.

"We wanted to be ready for when they arrive," the transformed man said. His gait was staggering and uneven, but his movements implied great strength. His arms, though sickly in pallor, twitched with bizarre power, the veins and musculature clearly defined.

Doc shook his head at Bedlam, asking her to wait. The cyborg's robotic limbs whined as she prepared to attack, but she held back.

"All this time we figured you were just power-hungry villains," Doc said. "I'm impressed, whoever you are. A cult pretending to be a business pretending to be a cult."

"Oh, our brothers in arms didn't know either," the man said, walking sideways to position himself better away from the door. Doc and Bedlam followed suit, trying to stay on either side of him. "Only a handful of us knew the truth. The others weren't ready for it. They couldn't handle looking into the face of eternity."

"And you could?" Doc said.

"We were chosen by the Elder Star," the man said. He smiled and outstretched his powerful arms.

"This guy is completely nuts, right?" Bedlam said.

Doc didn't answer. So many questions, he thought. So many questions I need answers to before we have to kill him.

"Why create new host bodies?" Doc said. "What were you doing with the experiments?"

"We told our blind colleagues we were building an army," the man said, a blissful smile on his face. The alien parasite on his chest glowed brighter. He placed a hand lovingly on the creature. "But our friends from the Elder Star, they not only grant powers to those they chose. They consume it. We wanted to give them more powerful bodies to consume. Bodies that would give them wondrous gifts."

"Didn't want all the toys for yourselves, then?" Bedlam said.

"You misunderstand," the man said. He looked sadly at his fallen colleague on the floor, who stared back up with exhausted, pained eyes. "You were supposed to be a gift, so that they might let us all live. We were trying to save the world."

"Oh you are so full of..." Bedlam said.

"You thought you could buy them off?" Doc said. "Give them gifts and they what, let you keep the world when they're done with it?"

"We wanted them to love us," the man said. "But you stole our gifts for them, Doctor Silence. You have always stood in our way. I wonder though. What might they do with the body of a magician? What gifts might you give them when they arrive?"

Before Doc could answer, Bedlam charged in, her patience spent. She moved with blinding speed, a blur of metal arms punching the man in his face, the thudding of her fists like a drumbeat.

The man laughed and threw her aside. Doc heard her cursing even after she crashed into a nearby wall, angrier than hurt.

The man charged at Doc, that uneven gait disappearing as he launched into an attack. Doc sidestepped him, slashing upward with the sword he'd conjured. He felt the blade connect with flesh, tearing into the man's side below the elbow. Blood poured out, too dark to be human blood, and Doc watched in horror as the gash sealed itself back up in front of him. The man smiled as the wound healed.

"I told you, they grant us mighty gifts," the man said. Then the smile shrank on his face as Doc heard the heavy pounding of metal feet running. Doc ducked and Bedlam flew over him, her entire body built into a single haymaker, her fist slamming into the possessed man's mouth.

"A host?" she said, punching him so hard and so fast Doc saw teeth fly loose. "I was going to be a host? Do you know how long it took me to get over knowing I was just going to be a weapon and now I have to deal with this? I'm going to need so much therapy!"

She got in three or for more good punches before the man tossed her aside again. He shook off the blows, running a too-long tongue across bloodied lips.

Doc let his sword drop to the ground. Fine, he thought. If you heal that fast, let's see what happens if I cauterize your wounds...

He held his hands at his side and remembered the words to a spell as old as magic. The first one any young magician wants to learn, and the first one he's warned to be careful with. A simple spell, known to all, held dear by wizards since the first time a shaman brought light on a dark night to his tribe.

Doc Silence aimed his palm at the possessed man and a fireball shot forth from nothing, a gout of flame that splashed into the man's chest, burning the parasite there, cooking it with unnatural heat. Both the possessed man and the creature latched to his chest cried out, mirrored squeals of pain and terror. The parasite body shook in a spasm, clamping down so hard on its host body Doc could hear ribs breaking. And then the parasite let go, the gripping appendages going limp, and it fell to the ground, twitching slowly as the life left it.

Its human host fell backward, burned, terrified, the agony written plain across his face.

"You..." the man said. Doc stood over him, waiting.

"How many more of you are here? What else have you done? What did you tell them?" Doc said. "We need answers from you."

The man just smiled, pain clear across his face, and rested his burnt hands where the parasite had been. Doc heard the hiss of his sword being lifted from the ground, and glanced over to see Bedlam lifting it up. She came to stand over the fallen enemy and pressed the tip of the sword against the man's neck.

Doc put a hand on her metallic wrist, and she hesitated. The man passed away, as though his body failed under the strain of his own transformation, with a blind smile on his face.

"I'll tell you what I know," the first man they'd found said. Doc had almost forgotten him, lying on the ground, looking like half a corpse himself.

"You made me," Bedlam said. She flexed her robotic fingers aggressively. "Give me one reason why I shouldn't pop your head off your shoulders right now."

"I'll give you two," the man croaked. "One: without us, you're a vegetable and invalid in a hospital somewhere, and because of us you're standing beside a superhero."

Bedlam scowled at Doc. He kept his expression blank, wanting the cyborg to make her own choice.

"And two?" she said.

"That bastard on the ground over there tried to kill me, and my own..." he paused, catching his beleaguered breath. "And my own colleagues left me here to die. Don't do the same to me, and I'll tell you everything the Children knew."

CHAPTER 17:
WEREWOLVES AND WINDOWS

Kate and Titus returned to the RIETI building under cover of darkness, parking their aircraft in a field a mile away. He seemed legitimately concerned someone would try to steal it.

"What if our getaway car isn't there when we need it?" he said as they crouched in a blind spot in the facility's security cameras, just beyond the sea of satellite dishes.

"Do you know how to fly it?" Kate said.

"No," Titus said.

"Then why would you think some teenager out for an evening stroll is going to be able to climb inside and fly away in it?" Kate said.

Titus glared at her.

"Don't taunt me with your logic, devil-woman," he said.

"You've been spending too much time with Emily," Kate said, punctuating the comment by breaking out into a run. He followed close behind. They maneuvered their way carefully across the field, perfectly timing their sprints based on the movement of security cameras Kate had absorbed earlier in the day. Getting to the building was the easy part, she thought. It was a matter of timing. But they couldn't just walk in the front door, not even with the stolen passkey they had. So Kate decided they'd try a trick they'd used once before.

Arriving alongside the building and pausing in a shadowed corner, Titus shook his head and shrugged off his coat, handing it to Kate.

"This is twice you've convinced me to help you breaking and

entering," Titus said.

"Won't be the last time, either," she said, watching, as she always does, with mild fascination as he transformed from skinny human boy to massive werewolf. Metamorphosis complete, Kate hopped onto his back, wrapping her arms around his thick neck, and Titus leapt along the side of the building, huge paws grasping at windowsills and ledges to haul both of them up to the fourth floor and then onto the roof. At the very top, Kate peered over the ledge, checking for rooftop security cameras. As she suspected, a building this isolated focused its security on outside intrusions, assuming no one would be able to get close enough to get up to the roof.

They scurried over and Kate handed Titus' jacket back to him as he transformed back.

"We left a flying machine a mile away and you just had me climb us up onto a roof," Titus said.

Kate threw one of her patented dirty looks at him.

"Which we would have had trouble live-parking on a roof," he continued.

Kate kept staring.

"And might have been seen on camera—want me to tear that door open for you?" Titus said, altering the topic of conversation and gesturing at the door leading to the stairs into the building.

"I've got it," Kate said, swiping the stolen security card through a reader. The light on the reader blinked green, and they stepped inside.

The moved quickly to the third floor. Kate remembered exactly where Lester Rice-Bell's office had been. The building itself was empty, offices dim, doors left casually open. One office remained lit, though.

"He's still here," Titus said.

Kate nodded. They approached the door and walked in together.

Lester Rice-Bell sat at his desk, his back to them, unmoving. He remained in his dark, ill-fitting business suit, hands on his knees, head up.

Titus approached the desk cautiously.

"Mr. Rice-Bell?" he said.

91

"I knew you'd come back," the man said, his voice stronger than before. Stranger. He still did not move, though, nor turn back to face them. "I knew you couldn't resist."

"What are you talking about—" Titus said, putting a hand on Rice-Bell's shoulder across the desk. Moving with inhuman speed, the older man grabbed Titus' arm and threw him, as if he weighed almost nothing, through the window behind the desk. Titus' body smashed through the glass with a horrific thump and crash, and Kate watched as her companion plummeted into the night sky.

Lester Rice-Bell stood up to his full height then, turning to face Kate. His shirt and tie had been undone, and underneath them, she saw an eerie, spider-like thing clinging to his chest, segmented, crablike legs holding on like a child. It pulsed a deep, patient red.

Kate smiled.

"Not quite the reaction I was expecting from someone who just watched me throw her friend out a window," Rice-Bell said.

"He'll be fine," Kate said, clenching her hands into fists. "And you have no idea how much I've been wanting to hit someone."

Rice-Bell looked quizzically as Kate launched herself across the room, using his own desk for leverage to leap into the air and kick him in the face. She felt her tungsten-capped boot smash into his cheekbone. The man staggered, hunching over, but rose again to his full height and laughed.

"My turn," he said, picking up the desk with both hands and swinging it at her like a club. Kate dove onto the floor, the table passing over her harmlessly, though its contents—pens, laptop, family photos—poured down, pounding onto her shoulders like rain.

The desk out of the way, Kate spun herself to kick Rice-Bell in the knee, connecting hard where the joint was most easily damaged. His leg buckled and he dropped the desk—again, just barely missing Kate—but seemed otherwise unhurt.

She scurried back a few steps, looking at Rice-Bell's grossly bent knee, his lacerated and crushed cheekbone. Both healed visibly in front of her, mending as he walked limping toward her.

She looked around the room, surveying potential improvised weapons. Good. *This means I don't have to feel bad if I hit him* with...

One of the fallen objects from Rice-Bell's desk rolled past her. A glass ball with a family photo trapped inside, heavy, round, and exactly the right size to fit in her hand. She picked it up and almost laughed.

"You don't have any powers, do you," Rice-Bell said. "That's disappointing. I was hoping for—"

Before the man could finish, Kate pushed herself up using all the strength in her legs and reared her throwing hand back, the weighty glass globe held like a softball. But instead of throwing it, using the same motion, she brought the sphere down on Rice-Bell's face, dead between the eyes. Kate felt the thrum of glass against skull reverberate all the way up her arm into her shoulder. Her fingers went numb. The light in Rice-Bell's eyes flickered.

Blindly, he lashed out, catching Kate with an outstretched arm and knocking her against bookshelves. Kate reached up and found some sort of award, a wood and metal statue attached to a marble base, and weaved her way in closer, horrified as she watched the man's nose reform itself back to its original shape. She swung the trophy at Rice-Bell, who smirked as he side-stepped her, dodging a blow to the face.

Instead, the trophy connected with the thing attached to Rice-Bell's chest, the marble base hooking grotesquely where the parasitic creature met the man's skin. Disgusted, Kate tugged on it, instinctually putting one booted foot against the alien creature. The corner of the award's base scrapped wetly against the parasite's flesh. Rice-Bell screamed.

He batted her away again, yanking the trophy free, his face becoming less human, a mask of rage. His skin seemed to be changing color, too, growing almost jaundiced, bruised bags forming under his eyes.

Seeing an opening, Kate moved in again, throwing a barrage of punches and kicks at Rice-Bell's head and throat while hammering at the parasite with her knee. This seemed to only enrage him more, and Rice-Bell caught her, one unexpectedly strong hand gripping her shoulder, the other grabbing her upper arm.

She kicked him three times in the groin, aiming her tungsten-capped boot with brutal precision. Pain flickered behind Rice-Bell's rage-filled eyes, but his grip only tightened.

And then, over his shoulder, Kate saw a very angry werewolf climb in through the broken window, breathing heavily, fangs bared.

"Took you long enough," she said.

Rice-Bell turned his head just quick enough to be watching when Titus pounced on him, claws flashing lightning quick, shredding the man's upper body. Rice-Bell released Kate instinctually, dropping her to the floor. She watched as his body knitted back together incredibly swiftly under Titus' rampaging attacks, his pale hands dug fingers into Titus' neck as the werewolf clamped jaws down on the man's shoulder and shook him like a dog with a toy. Rice-Bell pushed back, shoving Titus toward the window again.

"The thing on his chest, Titus!" Kate yelled, wondering how far buried her companion's rational mind was. She knew Titus had more and more control over his feral werewolf aspect, but she also realized trauma made it more difficult to reel the wolf back in, and he had just fallen three stories through a window. She might be talking to a furry brick wall right now.

The werewolf looked at her for a split second, confused, and Rice-Bell took advantage of the pause to head butt Titus in the face. Titus roared, more out of anger than pain, and reached back with one clawed hand to plunge it into the creature on the man's chest, sinking talons deep into its flesh. The result was almost comical in its vileness—Rice-Bell began shaking, his body trying to pull back and away from the werewolf, while Titus' claws were trapped, leaving the werewolf shaking his arm like a child trying to free itself from a bug stuck to its hand.

Finally, Titus—or the wolf itself? Kate saw a dark, inhuman logic in his eyes as he made his next move—reached down with his other hand and dug those claws in as well, pulling the parasite apart in two directions. The bug-like thing began to split in half, cracking like an eggshell, strange, blackish blood welling out with the density of syrup.

Titus roared triumphantly and tore the parasite entirely in half, throwing it away to either side. Kate grimaced as the halves of the creature landed with wet thumps. Rice-Bell collapsed to the ground, his body shaking, mouth moving like a fish pulled from the water.

She ran across the room, sliding on her knees to the fallen man's side. Kate grabbed his head in both hands.

"What do you know?" she said. "Tell us what you were doing!"

The man stared at her like he was seeing her for the first time, gasping. He reached out toward the debris they'd knocked on the floor. At first Kate thought he was trying to grab his laptop, but she saw something else, a nondescript box, dark wood and smooth, something you'd hide keepsakes in. He pointed at that, then grabbed her hand, gripping it tightly, looking into her eyes.

As she watched the life leaving Rice-Bell's body, she heard Titus reverting to human form behind her, his breathing changing from the deep, monstrous hum of the werewolf to his own pained and labored breaths.

"Tell me I didn't just kill that man?" Titus said, kneeling down beside Kate. Titus looked at his hands, covered in the viscous blood of the parasite, and made a face as if he might gag.

"You didn't," Kate said. She pointed at the still squirming remnants. "That thing did. All you did was break its hold on him."

Titus sat down, tried to wipe the sweat from his face, but caught himself before smearing alien blood all over his forehead. He rubbed his face against his bare shoulder instead, ineffectually.

Kate picked up the box Rice-Bell had been gesturing to and opened it up. Inside there were handwritten letters on yellow legal paper. She closed the box and tucked it under her arm.

Titus gestured around at the chaos of the room, eyes wide.

"What are we going to do about this?" he said.

"Call the Department on the flight home to come in and do a thorough sweep," Kate said. She absorbed the full scope of the mess incredulously. "And then we figure out what was so important about these notes."

CHAPTER 18:
DOGFIGHT

Billy felt Dude kick up the speed as three Nemesis fighters chased him just outside Saturn's atmosphere.

Running had seemed like the smart option at the beginning, but the ships were fast, almost as fast as Straylight could fly, and with three pursuers, dodging was getting more and more difficult.

The ships behind him were silent and swift, chitin-like armor gleaming in the light of stars. So far, they hadn't fired at him, but Billy knew it was just a matter of time.

Then something flew past him, a pellet the size of a human head.

What was that, Billy thought.

Projectile, Dude said. *An oversized bullet.*

They can use bullets in space? Billy thought, dodging another sphere.

No friction, Dude said. *If they launch it hard enough, it'll just keep going until it hits something...*

Billy soared down closer to the planet, tugged by its gravity, the vastness of the gas giant feeling like the deepest water he'd ever seen. Another bullet swung past him and disappeared, and he found himself suddenly angry.

What are you doing, Billy Case? Dude said.

Billy didn't answer, banking up away from the planet's atmosphere, creating a dramatic arc of light, using his greater speed to advantage. Suddenly above the three alien fighters, he held out his hands toward the center ship and fired duel blasts of blue-white light

96

into its shell. To his surprise, the blasts tore right through the surface of the ship, red-black fuel spilling out of the gaping hole he'd created. He fired again with both hands, and the fighter seemed to be cut adrift, tilting and falling slowly toward Saturn.

Well that worked, Billy thought.

There was a reason I didn't want to fight them, Dude said. *Don't get cocky.*

Before Billy could demand follow-up information from that statement, the two remaining fighters turned toward him, amped up their speed, and took evasive action to dodge Billy's light-blasts.

Okay, okay, bad move, Billy thought, returning to his escape plan, kicking up his own velocity to avoid the two ships.

He aimed for Saturn's glowing rings, hearing Dude's voice yelling at him not to fly through the ice and dust that made up the rings. Billy banked left rather than fly through the rings themselves, skirted the fast-moving debris and hoped the fighters wouldn't be able to maneuver, and be forced to crash into the dust storm. Instead, they kept up with his moves and, spinning skillfully, maintained their sights on him, flying in a complex pattern to limit his options for escaping.

Then an alarmingly familiar reddish bolt of light hummed past him, terrifyingly close.

Tell me that wasn't a null gun! Billy thought, thinking of the weapon he'd encountered twice now that had been designed to kick Luminae like Dude out of their host body temporarily.

The weapon was deadly effective on Earth where it could be used to cut off Billy's connection to Dude when he was in danger, or even when flying. Here in space, Billy assumed he'd be dead in seconds without Dude's powers protecting him from the vacuum.

I told you there was a reason I wanted us to run, Dude said, calmly enough to make Billy mad at him.

Next time, lead with 'they have null guns,' Billy thought. That should be your first fricken' comment.

Who do you think invented the null gun? Dude said as together they evaded another blast. Now both fighters were firing null guns at them, intuitively trying to fire where Billy would be rather than where he was, cutting off all his escape routes.

History lesson later, Billy said. New plan.

No, Dude said, reading Billy's mind and clearly disagreeing with his plan.

Got a better one? Billy thought, feeling another null gun blast sizzle past his ear.

No, Dude repeated, and Billy felt the alien relent in his argument.

If this doesn't work, Billy said, steeling himself to perform one of the stupider actions he'd ever done, I had a lot of fun being your partner.

Stop talking and do it, Dude said.

Billy smiled despite the danger and hit the virtual breaks, coming to a dead stop. The lack of motion seemed to confuse both fighters, whose next shots were very far off the mark.

Billy turned and flew full speed at the nose of one fighter. The ship balked a bit, as if unsure how to react to the suicidal move by its target. Billy could see the reddish light of the null gun warming but not firing. Somewhere inside that ship, the pilot or gunner didn't know how to respond to its target flying straight toward it.

That hesitation lasted until Billy smashed straight through the nose of the ship, a hammer through a piñata, Dude's protective energy shield acting as armor against the impact. Together they gutted the fighter, which all but exploded on impact.

Billy whooped silently.

We did it! Told you that would work, he thought.

But shaking off the impact had half-blinded him, caught up in the muck and debris of the torn-apart ship. As his vision cleared, the worse possible sight faced him. The third and final fighter waited like an aimed pistol, null gun warming to fire, with Billy dead to rights in front of it.

I've made a mistake, Billy said.

Yes, we have, Dude said.

Billy tensed, hoping he could blast the fighter before the null gun went off, more than certain he wouldn't be fast enough, and found himself thinking in strange, fleeting thoughts, at least I made arrangements for the dog…

And then the third fighter exploded, a powerful blast of blue-white light not unlike Billy's own energy signature tearing through it like a spear.

Billy startled at the explosion like he'd been electrocuted.

What the hell was that! Billy said. He felt waves of emotion coming from Dude, in the way they shared each other's moods. Dude gave off a sense of unexpected happiness and relief.

That was help, Dude said.

The source of the explosion flew at them, his energy signature also that same white-blue glow Straylight gave off. The man himself couldn't have been more different, though—older, a stark white beard, his male pattern baldness awkwardly long and unkempt and stark white as well. His eyes glowed the same way Billy's did when exerting significant power from Dude.

The man spoke to Billy, but in the vacuum of space, he couldn't hear the words. It wasn't hard to lip read though: "get in the ship," the man said.

"What ship?" Billy said, knowing his own words wouldn't carry.

The man sneered at him and grabbed Billy's arm. He pointed just past him at a ship, maybe twice as long as a city bus and twice as wide as well, materializing in front of him, parts of the ship fading from invisible to visible.

"You have a cloaked space ship?" Billy mouthed, incredulous.

The man didn't answer, but instead shoved Billy into an airlock forcibly and slammed the door behind him. Billy felt the room's makeup change, oxygen filling it, the vacuum of space being replaced by a metallic but welcome familiar breathability.

"Ship, re-engage cloak," the man said.

Billy's mouth hung open, his ears ringing after listening to the first human words he'd heard in so much time.

The newcomer rolled his eyes. "Close your mouth. What were you doing engaging them?"

"What I'm usually doing. Trying not to die," Billy said.

The man tugged on his beard, agitated. Then, threw up his hands. "I'm too old for this. I'm too old to deal with this," he said.

"There's a good age to deal with an alien invasion?" Billy said.

"Because I was thinking I'm probably too young to deal with it, myself."

The older man paused, squinting at Billy, still agitated, but de-escalating.

"I'm Billy, by the way. Thanks for saving my life." He extended a hand.

The older man took it. "You're him, aren't you?" he said. "The new Straylight."

Billy squinted back at the older man in almost an identical expression.

"Yeah..." he said, drawing out the syllable. "And you are..."

"I'm Suresh," the man said, putting a hand on his chest. "But we—my Luminae and I—we're... we're Horizon."

I knew it was him, Dude said in Billy's head. Again, waves of happiness flooded his mind.

"Dude said he knew it was you," Billy said. "We thought you died."

"You call the Straylight Dude," the man said, not phrasing it as a question.

Billy looked at his feet, suddenly embarrassed.

"It's an informal thing. He hates it."

The older man burst into a raspy, powerful laugh, so hard he bent at the waist, one hand on his knee, the other holding his belly.

"You call him Dude," Suresh said, tears running down his face. "Oh it's almost worth finding you out here just to learn that. Oh, thank you, you strange little boy. I haven't laughed in years."

"Well," Billy said, starting to chuckle himself as the man's infectious laughter continued. "What did my predecessor call him?"

Suresh started to speak but the words caught in his throat. He coughed and choked, and this somehow seemed to make him laugh even harder.

Tell him not to tell you, Dude said.

"Dude says not to tell me," Billy said.

The man roared again.

"He called him Moneypenny!" Suresh said, barely able to contain himself.

100

"Moneypenny?" Billy said, visibly entertained.

I don't want to talk about it, Dude said.

Suresh pulled himself together, wiping his eyes. His expression grew more serious when he looked Billy over as if really seeing him for the first time.

"We have to talk, Billy," Suresh said. "We have a lot to discuss and there's not much time. We've got a stupid little world to save."

"We do," Billy said.

"Then let's speak quickly," Suresh said.

CHAPTER 19:
A COMPLETE AND UTTER FAILURE

Agent Black sat in a run-down bar in Montreal and waited for his contact to arrive. He liked this city, liked its energy. The older he got, the more he wished that the weirdness of his visible cybernetic implants didn't make going out casually to have a drink in the city virtually impossible. For the past few decades, he'd seen most beautiful and entertaining cities from the gutter up and it wore on him sometimes. He understood why some of his peers, particularly the ones with less human-looking cyborg alterations, spent their entire lives on the battlefield. In a warzone, nobody stares at you because your eye glows red in the dark, or your arm is made of silvery metal.

A woman, wearing sunglasses and a decorative scarf, walked in alone. She moved with the confidence of a trained warrior. Black instantly knew this was his contact. He raised a hand, holding up two fingers. She joined him at his booth. He'd ordered a pitcher of beer when he'd arrived, and poured her a glass, sliding it across the table.

She took off her sunglasses, and Black had to fight back laughter.

"Rumor had it you were dead," Black said.

The former Department agent and mercenary operative known as Prevention set her glasses down on the table between them and took a sip of her beer. She looked tanned, healthy, not like someone who had failed an unnamed employer and whom the mercenary community believed had been marked for death. That was the word on the street, anyway—she'd been paid for years to infiltrate the

Department, to change it from the inside, and when she'd failed to contain the Indestructibles not too long ago she'd disappeared entirely. There were rumors who her benefactors had been, but nothing substantive, and usually when an agent blows an operation that significant and that long in the making, it spells a death warrant.

Instead, here she was, staring back at him and smiling.

"That's the rumor I had hoped for; I'm glad to hear it," she said.

"If you're looking for help getting away from whoever you were working for, I'm not it," Black said. "I won't tell anyone I saw you, but I don't want any trouble."

The operative laughed at Black's words.

He found himself confused, and suddenly irritated with her.

"Didn't anyone ever wonder why I wasn't assigned to kill the Indestructibles?" she asked. "I reined in three of their most powerful members. Tried to manipulate them. But didn't kill any of them."

"My sidekick tells me you stripped one of powers and tried to kill the vigilante," Black said.

"Temporarily depowered the alien, yes, but that was to assist me in manipulating the other two," she said. "And the original plan wasn't to kill the Dancer, but she got on my nerves. It's true, I may have been a little overzealous toward the end there. She's incredibly irritating."

Black nodded slightly. The Dancer had an ability to get a rise out of the wrong people.

"So what are you saying? Your gig was to hire them?" Black said.

"My job was to get the Department ready for something big," she said. "I was never fully briefed. They wanted an insider to take the assets of the Department and make the organization as ruthless and war-ready as possible. And when Doc Silence went and recruited a bunch of children capable of operating on massive power scale, they became assets I was to acquire as well. I was coercive, but never put them in danger."

"I heard the stories, Prevention," Black said. "Don't kid yourself. There was a lot of danger involved."

"Did anyone tell you it was that little blue-haired lunatic who released a bunch of our prisoners?" she said. "And please, skip the

103

code names. Call me Laura. What *is* your first name, anyway?"

"Agent," Black said.

"Very funny," the woman said, taking another sip of her beer.

"So that whole thing. Kidnapping three super-powered kids, nearly losing the Labyrinth—thanks for that, by the way, there's about twenty guys locked up in there who want to kill me, so I appreciate you almost having a complete prison break—and then having an all-out battle in the prison was on purpose?" Black said.

"Oh no, it was a complete and utter failure," Laura said. "A catastrophic screw up. I thought I was dead the minute I left the premises. I sat in a hotel room for a week and waited to die."

Now Black was curious. He'd had some failures himself, but he'd always made sure he was never the singular go-to field agent. He was muscle, not planning, because he didn't want to be in the position where, if everything went wrong, it all fell back on him.

"Clearly you didn't die," Black said.

"I told you, my employers wanted the Department ready for something huge," Laura said. "And while my original mission parameters went pear-shaped, the incident did net what my employers desired."

"A more active, battle-ready Department and a team of super-powered individuals on high alert for trouble," Black said.

"Exactly. My employers wanted them under their control, but if they couldn't be controlled, they were at least primed to react to what we knew was coming," Laura said.

"Are you going to tell me what your employers were so worried about that they hired you to try to commandeer an entire government agency and super-team?" Black asked.

The agent previously known as Prevention pointed up into the sky.

"Several years ago, my employers learned of a potential alien invasion," she said. "And while they are not... as you might suspect... entirely altruistic in what they do, it is beneficial for them to have a world that has not been invaded by aliens."

"Hard to run a profitable business if your planet is a smoking husk, I suppose," Black said.

"You're taking news of a pending alien invasion with particular calm, Agent Black."

He shrugged dismissively.

"You and I come from the same place," Black said. "The things we've seen... War is war. We're all going to die in violence someday. Whether that's by stupid, bigoted countries throwing nuclear warheads at each other or goblins from outer space, it's all the same."

"It's not my intention to die in violence," Laura said. "And I also don't intend to botch two contracts in a row."

"Oh really," Black said. He refilled her glass. "So what exactly do you need me for, call-me-Laura?"

"How'd you like to work on the side of the angels for once," she said.

"I don't want Bedlam involved," Black said. "I don't want her on your employer's radar, whoever they are."

"She's already involved," Laura said. "I have eyes on the Indestructibles, and they tell me she was seen with them yesterday."

Black sighed and sipped his beer, feigning irritation. Part of him, some strange little place where fatherly pride might have lived in another lifetime, fluttered with unexpected happiness. He'd hoped, all along, that somehow Bedlam could avoid simply becoming a younger version of himself, but he had no idea how to prevent that—she couldn't live a normal life, couldn't just walk into society and be treated with ordinary kindness, and he knew that she'd been built as a weapon of war. For her every path involved violence, and he had wondered, and hoped, she might find a way to turn out better than he had. Maybe time with those strange kids in their floating Tower would help her figure that out.

Something else flickered inside him as well. Sadness. He wanted much more for Bedlam, but he knew anywhere better would be far away from him. Maybe that's why she hadn't told him yet. He felt no anger, but something else instead, a sense of loneliness he'd never had need or use for before.

He eyed the woman across from him again.

"So what are you asking me to do?" he said.

"Those kids are going to be the world's first line of defense, for better or for worse," Laura said. "And that means they're going to need help."

"And how do you propose a couple of aging mercenaries do that?" he asked.

"How would you feel about helping me liberate an entire arsenal of alien technology?" Laura said.

Black raised his beer, and she joined him. They clinked glasses.

"No one will ever say we lived dull lives, will they?" Black said.

"You're lucky," Laura said. "I can sense you hope she never follows in your footsteps, but at least you've got someone who'll remember you when you're gone."

Black downed his beer in one long sip and set the glass down.

"That's assuming we're victorious," he said. "Let's go help these kids win a war."

CHAPTER 20:
WHAT HAPPENED TO YOU?

Doc and Bedlam sat in the control room, waiting for the others to return, their silence strangely comfortable. Doc let the cyborg be within herself, glancing over occasionally to watch her eyes flicking around the room processing. He liked her, enjoyed her confidence, but was also worried—she'd experienced a very different trauma from those the Indestructibles had suffered in their early experiences, and he was curious how she processed it all. She was certainly a different character than the one they met on that small island a year or so ago. Despite her foul mouth and intense attitude, there was a maturity to her, an adult level of self-awareness his team was still developing. In some ways she reminded Doc of Kate. Hardened by the world, long before she should have to be so tough.

"This is messed up, Doc," she said, finally.

"It is," he said.

"I accepted a long time ago that how this all came about was screwed up. Even made some peace with it," Bedlam said. "I mean I wasn't going to live after—it was an accident—"

"—That cost you your arms and legs," Doc said quietly.

"Yeah. It was a stupid… it doesn't matter. An accident. I was a lump of meat in a hospital bed. Gone. You know that? I knew I was gone. Knew I was dead," Bedlam said.

"Did you see the other side?" Doc asked.

He wasn't mocking her. He'd been to the other side of death, as a tourist, as an explorer. Not everyone goes to the same place, but there were, he had learned, more than one thing humanity sees when life ends. Sometimes it is oblivion, and sometimes, it is something else.

"I'm not sure," Bedlam said. "But I do know what it's like to feel yourself go cold. I know that much."

"And then you didn't die," Doc said.

"New and improved me," Bedlam said. "And I've spent a lot of time thinking about that, reflecting on what these idiots did to me, and after a while I thought—hey, I'm still here, right? I'm still me. Not the off the shelf version of me, but whatever they had planned the end result was I'm still here. So I thought—I can forgive them for that. Doctor Frankenstein was a heel too, but that doesn't diminish the humanity of the monster he made."

"That's a powerful analogy there, Bedlam," Doc said.

The cyborg and the magician locked eyes for a long moment, his face peaceful and welcoming, hers hard and taut.

"You want me to say I'm not a monster," she asked him. "Too bad. I am."

Doc shook his head.

"We all are," Doc said. "Someday I'll tell you why my eyes glow and you'll know—we're all monsters in some way or another. It's what you do with what comes next that counts. "

The young cyborg almost smiled. Doc settled for the slight loosening of the lines around her mouth as a sign he'd said something right. She looked back down at the table.

"Now I have to try to make peace with the idea they were going to install an alien in my body," she said. "Grr. That doctor in front of your name wouldn't happen to indicate you're a psychotherapist, would it?"

"I didn't even finish college," Doc said.

Bedlam looked at him to try to figure out if he was kidding or not and then, finally, burst into laughter.

"You didn't, did you?" she said.

"Nope," Doc said, just as the other two pairs of heroes converged at the door, nearly simultaneously, everyone looking like they'd had a very bad day. Worst of the lot was Titus, covered in scratches and bruises and wearing different clothes than he'd left in, and Emily, sporting a huge black eye and split lip, along with a bump on her forehead that looked angry and painful.

"What happened to you?" Titus and Emily asked each other.

"Got thrown out a third-story window," Titus said.

"Punched in the face by a twelve-foot-tall alien," Emily said.

Kate and Jane followed them in, Kate looking roughed up but otherwise well, Jane with the last remnants of her torn cape flapping off one shoulder. They looked at each other without saying a word and sat down, Kate placed a dark plastic bag on the floor beside her.

"I just thought of something," Titus said, gingerly sitting down. "Emily, have you ever been hit the entire time we've been doing this?"

"Hit by what," Emily said.

"A fist. A laser. A falling rock. Anything," Titus said.

Emily pondered this for a minute.

"Nope," she said.

"Wait," Jane said, leaning forward in her chair. "You really haven't, have you?"

"I got hit with some sort of decorative office supplies when rescuing Billy in the Labyrinth," Emily said. "I think I got concussed one time. That's about it."

"I've lost enough blood to stock a Red Cross drive and Emily's been concussed once," Titus said.

"You have magical healing abilities," Emily said. "Don't whine."

"You guys know it still hurts when I get beat up, right?" Titus said. "Healing factor does not mean impervious to pain. It actually feels like falling out a three-story window. And 'he'll be better soon' is not funny, Kate."

Kate seemed suddenly a lot more invested in the conversation than she had been a moment before.

"You heard that?" she said.

"Super hearing to go with my super healing," Titus said.

"Just stating a fact," Kate said. She reached down beside her and dropped the plastic bag she'd brought in onto the table.

"We found this," she said. "What did everyone else find?"

"Hang on," Emily said, interrupting. Kate shot her a dirty look. Emily ignored it. "On the subject of me not pulling my weight in getting beat up like everyone else. I want to learn how to fight."

"How have you not learned to fight yet?" Bedlam asked. "You're on a superhero team and you don't know how?"

"I hang out in the back behind all these meatshields and make bubbles of float like a civilized person," Emily said. "I have not, until now, needed to do much punching. I am, however, sick of that noise. Someone's going to teach me how to kick some butt. I demand it."

"I'll teach you," Kate said. The entire room went quiet.

"*You'll* teach me?" Emily said.

"Why wouldn't I?" Kate said. "The more competent you are the less we have to worry about your safety in the battlefield. It's to our advantage to not have you running around like a declawed kitten in a combat situation."

A very loud laugh escaped from Jane's lips. "Sorry." She caught herself. "I think we're all a little concussed. Can we debrief?" she said.

Doc stood up, rubbing his eyes beneath his glasses.

"We've encountered something interesting," Doc said. "It appears our old enemies, the Children of the Elder Star, have been infiltrated from within. These aliens have taken control of a number of members and have tried subverting their plans to the advantage of the approaching invasion."

"They were making host bodies to give to the aliens when they get here," Bedlam blurted out. "Me. I was supposed to be a host body. All of the experiments were."

"That was the plan all along?" Jane said. "That's why they made Project Valkyrie?"

"Not exactly," Doc said. "Oddly enough, according to the captive member of the Children Bedlam and I just dropped off at the Labyrinth, most of their leadership still thinks they're just a run of the mill organization bent on world domination for greed and profit. They were unaware until recently that they'd been infiltrated. Which, under less terrifying circumstances, would be hilarious to me given how vile they are as a group in general."

110

"So if you thought turning teenagers into science experiments to be weapons of mass destruction wasn't evil enough, imagine those kids were going to be used as extra special host bodies for mind-controlling aliens," Bedlam said.

Kate spoke next, gesturing to the bag.

"That's what remains of what was controlling Lester Rice-Bell, president of RIETI," Kate said.

"Who is currently in a coma," Titus said. "Removing that... parasite... that thing nearly killed him, but he almost killed us while it was still attached."

"How was he able to pass for normal?" Bedlam asked. "Our guy had a parasite, too, but he was all misshapen. His skin was changing."

Kate produced a stack of yellow legal paper from a pouch on her belt.

"Before he fell unconscious, Rice-Bell pointed to a box containing these," she said. "Titus read them on the flight back."

"Apparently Rice-Bell was only recently, um, infested," Titus said. "These were his notes from the past few months. It sounds like the parasite might have been working its way up the chain of command at RIETI. Rice-Bell took notes on different employees acting strangely, off kilter, unauthorized use of their radio equipment, people coming and going at odd hours. These notes ended about a month ago."

"The time the parasite most likely took him over," Doc said. "I wish I knew more about these things. It might be that the parasite changes the host gradually over time and Rice-Bell hadn't begun experiencing the full effects yet."

"Or maybe the parasite didn't need him to be stronger, and so wasn't changing his physiognomy," Kate said.

"Ours did know he was being hunted," Doc said. "Perhaps the parasite started pumping him up for a fight?"

Doc turned to Jane next.

"What did you find?" he asked.

"Two more parasitic entities, just like yours," Jane said. "But the hosts couldn't have been human."

She described the odd creatures they fought, both giant and

multi-limbed.

"Whatever they were, they were strong," Jane said. "And those parasite things seemed to be providing them other powers. Speed, healing."

"I wonder if those were host bodies they brought with them from outer space, or if they found them here," Emily said. "You told us there are already a lot of aliens inhabiting the Earth, right?"

Doc exhaled deeply.

"I don't know. It might be worth asking Neal to research and find out if they match any descriptions of aliens we've encountered before," he said.

"Whatever they were, that was the welcoming committee," Jane said. "They'd set themselves up with a little bunker in the desert. Like they expected company."

Doc sat back down again, feeling older and more tired than he had in a long time.

"I just wish we knew more," Doc said. "The former Straylight and his partner Horizon were so quiet about this though. They rarely talked about it. We never got the full story out of them."

"I might be able to help with that," an unfamiliar, metallic voice said.

Standing in the doorway, holding onto the frame for support, stood the alien Billy, Jane, and Emily had discovered fallen from the sky. His scaled skin dry and cracked, his huge eyes dull and exhausted, he spoke English slow and deliberately, without a noticeable accent.

"My name is Seng," he said.

Titus stood up and helped him to a chair.

"I would like to help prevent your world from dying," the alien said.

CHAPTER 21:
WHERE HORIZON WENT

Billy watched in wonder as the plant-like Nemesis vessels drifted by, almost close enough to touch, just outside the windows of Suresh's ship. The little ship itself hummed with a mechanical life, a sort of sterile white noise that made it feel somehow even more quiet than ordinary silence.

"So this stealth technology thing really works, huh?" Billy said.

Suresh joined him by the window, handing him a cup of what the older man claimed was coffee generated by the ship's kitchen. It looked like coffee, it smelled like coffee, but Billy thought the closest approximate flavor it compared to was ear wax.

"Most of the time," Suresh said. "Depends on who you're trying to hide from. There's a lot of species out there, and not everyone perceives reality the same way. Fortunately the crews of those ships use mostly the same senses we do, both naturally and technologically."

"So you just… found this ship?" Billy asked. The entire craft was white and chrome, like something out of a particularly pleasant view of the future.

"Our solar system is either very lucky or very unfortunate," Suresh said. "A lot of things pass through here. Ships, debris, explorers. Some might say we're positioned somewhere that attracts attention, but others, more philosophically, think Earth is somehow, I don't know. Important. That it's fated for things. And that fate draws others here."

113

"Like this ship," Billy said.

"I suppose," Suresh said. "The occupants died long before I found it. And I only found it because, in case your Dude hasn't explained to you, the Luminae perceive things not only through their hosts' senses, but through light. So Horizon and I were able to find this invisible ship just drifting out by Neptune. Derelict. And we made it home."

Billy kept his eyes on the Nemesis fleet, amazed at how they lacked uniformity. It was as if each ship were not built so much as they were grown, with all the different variations a living thing might take on as it developed. The ships had personalities, and flaws, quirks and strengths. Some were more similar than others—the little fighter-style craft often looked very much alike—but each one had its own singular personality.

"So what did the others tell you of me, then, Mr. Case," Suresh said, sipping his coffee.

"Doc only said you went to the stars," Billy admitted. "He doesn't talk much about any of the old team. Only when we need to know things."

"Do you think he's deliberately keeping you in the dark?" Suresh said.

Billy shook his head.

"I think he doesn't want to speak ill of people, actually," Billy said. "Because he said all of you, himself included, just gave up on being heroes."

Suresh walked closer to the windows and watched the enemy armada floating by, relentless and silent.

"And Straylight? What does he have to tell you about me?" Suresh said.

Dude had been strangely quiet since they came on board. Though Billy could sense him busily doing something in the back of his head. He suspected Dude was having a private conversation with Suresh's Luminae right now, in whatever silent language they shared.

"He talks about you and my predecessor as being good people," Billy said. "But he's always kept a lot to himself. He says sometimes it's better to not know too much about those who came before."

Suresh turned his back on the window to look directly at Billy.

"Have they disgusted you yet?" Suresh said.

"Kate's gym bag is vile," Billy said.

"Not your teammates,' Suresh said. "Humanity. Have they let you down yet?"

Billy thought about their imprisonment not long ago, about having his connection to Dude severed. He thought about what he'd seen the Children of the Elder Star doing to kids just like him, in labs, under the knife. He thought about a future they had to save from destruction because of human behavior and hubris. He thought of all the little crimes they'd stopped as a team, all the awful things they'd seen, all the darkness, all the tragedy.

"Not yet," Billy said instead.

The old man smiled a broad, white-toothed smile.

"They made me so angry," Suresh said. "Nigel and I—Nigel was Straylight before you, you know, the finest living being I have ever known—we became heroes years before Doc Silence and the rest. The Luminae keep you young, they keep you strong. But when Doc and the others started to appear, and that fool magician suggested we band together and make the world a finer place… it was nice to be a part of something. Among other heroes. But the weariness was already growing in me, even then."

"Weariness about what?" Billy said.

"The darkness in humanity," Suresh said. "It's like trying to stop a flood. You plug a hole, you divert the water, but it always finds a way to keep coming, it pools at your feet. And grows and grows and grows. No matter how hard you try, humans always find a way to be awful to each other."

"You must've been so much fun at parties," Billy said.

Suresh laughed again.

"I wasn't that bad until they killed my friend," Suresh said. "Nigel, an optimist, could laugh it off. He witnessed all the same awful things I did, but somehow… As long as we worked together, I could overlook it. But when he died, that was the last straw for me. I left."

"Because you didn't think humans deserved to be saved," Billy said.

Billy felt a glimmer behind his eyes, sensing Dude rejoining the conversation.

Horizon and Straylight were partners, Dude said. *We've always chosen complimentary hosts, humans we knew would want to work together, who could feed each other's courage. But Nigel and Suresh were different. We found them as boys. Friends. They grew up together. They did not know a world in which the other didn't exist. We sometimes chose our partners so that one could learn from the other, but the timing, the circumstances... we thought these two boys, together, would be good stewards for the world.*

How did Nigel die, Dude? Billy thought.

Dude hesitated. Billy could feel his discomfort.

I deserve to know, Billy thought.

You do, Dude said. *He died because Nigel was a good man, and he trusted the wrong person, at the wrong time. And it cost him his life.*

Is that person he trusted standing right in front of me? Billy thought.

No, Dude said. *But Horizon blamed himself. Which he shouldn't. Because...*

Because what, Dude? Billy thought.

Because the blame is on me, Dude said. *I failed him. If anyone is to blame for your predecessor's death, it was my incompetence.*

Billy's breath caught in his throat. It hadn't occurred to him—how had this not occurred to me? He thought—that Dude had to be there at the time of this Nigel guy's death. Nigel was Dude's host. Dude would have felt the loss as it happened.

Before Billy could pull on that thread, Suresh spoke.

"He's telling you about us, isn't he?" Suresh said, folding his arms across his chest.

"Not nearly enough," Billy thought.

Suresh glanced over his shoulder out the window again, staring at the fleet.

"It doesn't much matter anymore, I suppose," Suresh said. "The world I'd spent my not inconsiderably long life protecting let my brother and friend die like a cow at a slaughterhouse and I couldn't do it anymore. To hell with humanity, I said. To hell with planet

Earth. Let the Nemesis come. That place would deserve it."

"But you're still here," Billy said.

Suresh unfolded his arms, made a vague gesture toward the Sun and, Billy supposed, toward Earth as well.

"I couldn't do it," he said. "I had to leave, to get away. It wasn't possible for me to look humanity in the face anymore. But... I love my home, son, love that stupid, ignorant little ball of dirt. I couldn't be there, but found it difficult to leave. And when we found this ship..."

"You've been here the whole time," Billy said reverently.

"Watching. Waiting."

"So you didn't give up," Billy said. "You just needed some space."

"You're a lot kinder to me than I am to myself."

"I dunno, voluntary exile to beyond the asteroid belt seems pretty harsh on yourself, man, not gonna lie," Billy said.

"It hasn't been so bad," Suresh said, sounding suddenly tired. "Travelers pass through. I've helped a few stranded vessels. Fought off some space pirates. Watched a lot of streaming video."

"What?" Billy said.

"This ship is able to tap into Earth media," Suresh said. "Streaming video and eBooks saved my sanity."

Billy looked at the wild hair and overgrown beard on Suresh's face and frowned.

"Wouldn't go that far," Billy said, joining him by the window. He tried again to get a count of the vessels slowly flying by. "So what's our next move? You and me, taking out the whole fleet? Go back to Earth as heroes, have a parade?"

"I can't tell if that's youth speaking, or legitimate delusions of grandeur," Suresh said.

"Snark," Billy said. "The word you're looking for is snark."

"Well, my sarcastic young friend, you're going home," Suresh said. "We're going to stealthily move far enough away so you've got a clean run back to Earth without being spotted."

"And you're going to go finish watching the complete series of *Fringe* and leave us to all die a horrible death," Billy said.

"No," Suresh said, voice calm, not taking the bait. "I'm going to find you some help."

"Help?" Billy said. "What, you going to call in the Starfleet or something?"

Suresh looked at him with eyes Billy suddenly realized had seen far more combat than he had in his young life. Hard eyes, ready for a fight.

"There's help out there if you need it," Suresh said. "I'll be back, and, fates willing, I won't be alone."

CHAPTER 22:
WHERE MONSTERS COME FROM

The chieftain used to remember his name.

He recalled many things from his life before the invasion, before he was kidnapped by this terrible armada; though, with each passing day, those memories became foggier and foggier. He reflected on the times with his wife, their litter of children, and a pre-technological world, with high trees, and clear skies, and bloody battles between nomadic tribes.

Finally, he remembered being a warrior.

Here, aboard this starship, the cold emptiness of space all around, his home world felt like a dream. It was a dream, in any way that mattered, he thought. Gone, a desiccated husk of a world, eaten alive by these creatures, the Devourers, as his people had come to call them, and all that was left behind—every ally, loved one, mountain and tree—gone with it.

The chieftain had not forgotten pain. Perpetual pain. His life had been one of battle and blood, and every waking moment there were aches—old injuries, hardened scar tissue, even just the heartache of growing old in a world where every day was a struggle. He hurt because he had been a warrior, and he hurt because he had lived.

This thing on his chest, this parasite, it took away the pain. He did not feel hurt, cold, or warmth. Yet it was not true numbness, not precisely, but it was a barrenness, an absence of feeling, a disconnect between his body and his mind.

Disoriented and completely separated from his actions, it was as he viewed himself from afar.

His brother walked by, in a slow, aimless shuffle, recognizable in the dark by the cracked and broken horn growing from the left side of his head. They did not speak to each other any longer. They'd tried, at first, but the parasites sent waves of agony through them, as if to stop them from communicating. Now they stared at each other with dimming yellow eyes. *My brother,* the chieftain thought, his heart breaking at the emptiness he saw in that green, scarred face. *The mightiest of us. The strongest. Reduced to cattle. Like me.*

There were others here, as well, not just from the chieftain's planet, a menagerie of freaks and monsters, reptilian and furred, six-limbed and twelve, things that walked on two legs and things that moved on many. All seemed dim and distant, wearing these decorations of flesh on their chests. There was a strength to them, though, and the chieftain had come to realize this was what they all had in common—the Devourers kept the strongest from each world they destroyed, enslaved them, making them their own warriors and servants, leaving the rest behind when the world no longer had anything left to feed them.

But even this dull life was not forever. He could see the cycle. The strong become stronger, but then, like everything else the Devourers touched, they would be consumed, worn down, undone by the monstrous touch of these creatures. They were many when the Devourers took the chieftain's world, dozens of warriors captured, but their numbers dwindled, disappeared, fed into the machinery of this place.

At least the numbness kept the worst of it away. *Suffering is not noble,* he thought. *Suffering is not brave. Not like this. Not in this place.*

Sometimes he dreamed—or perhaps it was something else, a hallucination, a prophetic vision—of his wife, or his children, or his home. His tribe, his entire people, did not marry for love, nor did they have children for love. Everything was for the betterment of the tribe, to ensure survival, and all activity and efforts were directed toward that one goal, to be stronger, to be more powerful.

But when he dreamed, and envisioned the hollow outlines of his wife's cheeks, when he saw the yet-unscarred skin of his newborn son, held in his hand like a toy, he remembered love. Even in the battle to be strong, love will find a way to exist. Love is born where lives intersect.

He missed his wife and his many children. In the darkness, he silently recited their names. It became more difficult with each day, though. He wondered if that meant he was fading. If he would soon be fed to this infernal machine and discarded like a bone picked-clean.

All I wanted was a warrior's death, he thought, sitting in the darkness, the silence around him oppressive and deafening. A blade in my hand, face to face with some grim beast, and we would know, that creature and I, that we would fight, and one of us, or both of us, would die in that place. I just wanted to die on my feet. Brave. To feel my death, fang or claw opening my veins. I hoped to smell the wilderness of my home world once more before oblivion came for me.

This is no death, the chieftain thinks. He tries to recall his father's face, his first battle. These things slip around the edge of his consciousness like tiny fish. He looks once more at his brother, lumbering and heavy-limbed, and wonders if he could free him, if they could free each other. Perhaps together they could find a way home.

Except home is gone, he reminds himself—broken-hearted that he'd forgotten. There's no home to go back to. Only this waiting, this cold passivity, this horror clinging to his chest, filling him with strength and devouring his spirit.

He closed his eyes and wished for oblivion, hoping, on the other side of that darkness, his family might be there waiting for him.

CHAPTER 23:
AN ELEMENTAL FORCE

Jane monitored the faces around the table as much as she watched the alien reveal his story. How he'd crossed the stars as a messenger to their world, to try to get here in time for Earth to prepare. Seng was clearly exhausted; the act of speaking alone seemed to take all his effort, and he frequently paused to cough, or to grimace and hold his ribs in pain.

Doc, of course, listened intently, quietly, taking everything in from behind those red glasses. Emily leaned forward, fascinated— this is what she dreams about, Jane knew, science fiction as reality, aliens and spaceships and everything strange. Titus wore a mask of worry, which, Jane understood, would mirror her own. We're the caretakers she thought, the watchers. She knew the werewolf would have a gnawing sensation in his stomach, fear and concern and anxiety chewing away at him.

Bedlam, the newcomer, looked blatantly overwhelmed. With each new fact Seng uttered, her mouth would drop open, often with some vile combination of curse words that even turned Emily's head a few times.

And then there was Kate. Unfazed, unconcerned, all business, listening and plotting. Jane wasn't sure what she could be planning— this was so far beyond anything they'd done before, after all—but there she was. Fearless and ready for a fight.

"Okay, so what I don't understand," Emily said, resting her chin on one hand thoughtfully, "is what they want?"

"I think Seng is saying that they want to eat our world," Titus said.

"I mean big picture wise," Emily said. "It has to lead to

something, right? Can't just drift from world to world, munch munch munch burp, moving on, forever and ever, right?"

Seng made a strange gesture with his hand. Jane realized as he performed it that it seemed to indicate agreement.

"This is something the beings your world calls the Luminae have pondered for ages," Seng said. "Because they, like we, demand a purpose to things. We want—"

"—A reason," Kate said.

Seng bowed his head to her.

"But from what we have seen, from all the battles, all the dead worlds, we think they are..." Seng tilted his head as the Luminae sharing his body the way Dude shared Billy's helped him find the words he was looking for. ". . . an elemental force. They simply exist, and this is simply what they do."

"That. Is messed. Up," Bedlam said.

"So what do we do about a force of nature?" Jane said. "Have they ever been defeated before?"

"There have been worlds where the Nemesis have been driven off," Seng said. "Not many, but it is not unheard of."

"Well that's good. What are we talking about, a twenty-five percent chance of survival?" Emily said.

"We can recall... perhaps three or four incursions when the Nemesis fleet has been repelled," Seng said.

"Okay then, never mind, we're screwed," Emily said.

"Well, they're already here," Titus said. "Whatever that means."

"Fortunately," Seng said, "what you've encountered are only seedlings. They grant power, and they do the bidding of the fleet, but they are stoppable, as you've shown."

"If those are hardly a threat, I want to know more about what's coming for us," Kate said. "Because if those are the average foot soldier we'll be dealing with, we're going to need more help."

"Your main concern is to keep the seed ships off your world," Seng said.

"Oh, that sounds fantastic," Bedlam said. "Seed ships. Let me guess, they crash and thousands of those things we fought come crawling out like baby spiders and start taking people over."

Seng looked at her as if she'd taken the words out of his mouth.

Bedlam's eyes widened. "Tell me I'm wrong. Tell me I'm wrong, man, I don't want to be right," she said.

He looked around the room, his alien expression unreadable.

"The seed ships are their..." again, Jane watched as the alien conversed with its Luminae symbiote for the right word. "You would call them their terraforming device."

"I have no idea what that word means," Bedlam said.

"You need to read more," Emily said.

"You need a punch in the mouth," Bedlam said.

"You both need to shut up," Kate said. "If one of those seed ships lands, how long do we have? Can we stop the process once it starts?"

Seng stared at Kate with huge, unblinking eyes.

"It would be recommended that this not happen," he said.

"What about Billy?" Jane said. "What are the chances he's already dead? We sent him up there to investigate."

"If the Straylight did not choose to engage the fleet alone, he should be able to outrun them," Seng said.

"Like you did?" Emily said.

"I was ambushed," the alien responded, not taking the bait in Emily's taunt.

Doc spoke next, and everyone, even Kate, turned to listen.

"Then we need to make sure these seed ships don't get here," Doc said. "I'm going to go scare up some help for us. Emily, you and I are going to head over to the Labyrinth. I hate to admit it but they might have something there that might help you if we have to go toe to toe with these things again."

"Field trip!" Emily said.

Doc looked at Jane.

"I'll come with you," Jane said. "I'm kind of curious what they might have for all of us."

"And the rest of us?" Titus said.

"Eyes on the sky, Titus," Doc said. "Let's hope we hear from Billy soon."

CHAPTER 24:
THE TOY BOX

Henry Winter met them at the gates of the Labyrinth, smiling broadly as he leaned on his cane. He led Doc, Jane, and Emily inside with the light playfulness of a millionaire showing off his bungalow. You'd never know, Jane thought, that he had been a prisoner here himself for almost a decade.

The trauma was still fresh enough in her own mind that she felt an electric creep of anxiety crawl up her spine just by walking inside. From the sour look on Emily's face, Jane guessed the younger girl felt the same way.

"I can't believe I'm saying this," Doc said. "But we need to get a look at that item you showed me the other day."

Winter's face displayed genuine surprise.

"I thought…" he said.

"We're dealing with an alien invasion," Doc said. "I'm trusting you to tell us the truth about what it does."

Winter nodded solemnly.

"Of course. You know I wouldn't lie about something like this," he said.

"Something like what?" Emily said, an edge to her voice. She was dancing around as she waited for the men to finish talking, indicating she was either getting very bored or had to pee.

"Come on down to the toy box," Winter said. "I'll show you what we've got."

The toy box was what Winter had taken to calling the lab where he'd once been put to work developing tools for the Department under Prevention's watch. An open room littered with tables and half-built inventions, it looked like a mad genius' workshop. They walked past what had to be several prototypes of the armored suit Winter used to wear when he was a hero like they were, a dismantled "null gun," the type of weapon that had been employed to knock Dude out of Billy's body, and other, more esoteric items Jane couldn't quite place.

And then they saw the man who could have destroyed the future, puttering away at a work station.

Keaton Bohr. The scientist who, in another timeline, turned Emily into a battery to power weapons of war, had somehow tinkered too much with Emily's powers and turned her into a world-destroying bomb, and who, in the end, found nothing left for himself but death and oblivion. Jane had a difficult time looking at him. It was because of him the future versions of herself and Emily from that other timeline were dead, why that version of Billy was dead, why that other world was a cataclysmic disaster.

None of those things would come to pass here, they hoped. When they returned to their own timeline they had two options—put Bohr down to prevent him from making the same mistakes, or target the genius he clearly possessed in better pursuits. And so the Department took him in, and told him to make a better world.

It turned out a genius is a genius, and given the right tools and the right motivation, Keaton Bohr stood a chance of redeeming himself in this timeline, of being a hero and not a villain, or at least, Jane thought, building a better battery. Leaving the world a better place for having been in it. Which is all anyone should really strive to do in life.

But still, when she looked at him—this mousy man with his lank hair and glasses, looking so gleeful and proud in front of his inventions—it was hard not to see the man who played a huge part in ending an entire timeline. She wanted to be more gracious than hating a man for what he had not yet done, but it was hard to forgive him for the things she'd seen.

Emily barely looked at him. Somehow, his reaction to Emily

ignoring him broke the tension, because Keaton clearly wanted to be liked, and could not understand why she seemed so bent on giving him the cold shoulder. Jane, at least, made an attempt at being polite.

"I was tinkering with the suits the Department developed based on the kinetic-energy powered armor confiscated from that young drug dealer," Keaton said. "The Distribution suits."

Jane actually smiled a bit at that—Distribution, a low-level supervillain and all around sleaze—was the target of the Indestructibles' first mission together. It was a disaster. A successful disaster in that they apprehended him, but, as Billy liked to say when they talked about that first fight, they were like kids in a bouncy castle, not superheroes.

"Yeah, I didn't do too well against those," Emily said, picking up a mass of wires and circuit boards which Henry Winter promptly removed from her hands and placed back down on the countertop.

"Because they absorbed the kinetic energy you used against them, right?" Keaton said. "You used some sort of reversion of your floating spheres—"

"Bubbles of float, yo," Emily corrected.

"Bubbles of float," Keaton continued. "And turned it into an outgoing kinetic force."

"A wall of slam," Emily once again corrected. "Dude, this isn't hard to remember. I use very small words."

"Speaking of your wall of slam," Winter said. "I've been meaning to ask. When I took over, I had a structural analysis performed taking a look at the whole Labyrinth, and I found several locations on the detention level where entire sections of wall looked as if it has been moved forward several inches, doing severe damage to the integrity of the—"

"So you were saying something about my bubbles of float?" Emily interrupted.

Winter looked at Jane and winked.

Jane just offered him a wide-eyed expression—lying had never been Jane's specialty, and she'd been right there when Emily, pitching a fit, moved an entire prison wall with her mind.

"I understand you have trouble with precision," Keaton said.

"Not true," Emily said. "I can pick your nose with a bubble of float."

"But with your… offensive abilities?" Keaton said.

"I call it wall of slam for a reason," Emily said.

Keaton pulled a black plastic cover off an object that had been sitting on the worktable and drew out a metallic glove, robotic and segmented like armor.

"This might help," Keaton said.

"We've discussed," Doc said. "Nothing that draws power from her."

Winter waved a hand reassuringly.

"All this does is let her point that wall of slam with more precision," Winter said. "It lets her concentrate it into a smaller wall. One the size of her hand. Like a long-distance punch."

Emily picked the glove up and promptly slid it on. Everyone at the worktable, including Jane, took an involuntary step away from her.

"You guys are such wimps," Emily said. "So this'll let me basically…"

Emily aimed the glove at a glass beaker on another table and flexed her fingers. The beaker shattered.

"It's a wallop of smash!" Emily said.

"Those beakers actually cost money, y'know," Winter said.

"Wallop?" Jane said.

"Ha ha," Emily said dramatically. "I have my own Infinity—"

"No," Jane said.

"Power glo—"

"I think that one's taken too, Emily," Jane said.

"My own Iron F—"

"Taken," Jane said.

"I call it the gravity glove," Keaton said.

Emily gave him a sidelong glare, pursing her lips.

"It pains me to say this, but I like it," Emily said.

Jane had removed the earpiece she and the others used to stay in touch, but she heard it chirp from where she'd looped it on her belt. She tucked it back into her left ear.

"Jane, get the others on the line," Kate said.

Jane motioned for Doc and Emily to join in.

"What do you have, Kate?" Doc said.

Titus answered instead.

"We've got some kind of message going back and forth," Titus said. "It's coming from the RIETI institute. Either there was another sleeper agent we missed, or they got wind of Rice-Bell being taken out and sent someone to finish the job."

"Do we know what it's saying?" Jane said.

"We can't be a hundred percent sure, but Neal thinks it's landing coordinates," Titus said.

"Oh, awesome," Emily said.

"And what does Neal think those coordinates are?" Jane said.

"Hey Titus, what's this thing?" Bedlam's voice chimed in.

Jane heard Titus ask Neal to zoom in on something, and then all three of them, Titus, Kate, and Bedlam, started swearing at the same time in a cacophony of curse words. Together, they covered a huge expanse of foul language in just a few seconds.

"Well that sounds fantastic," Emily said.

"Yeah, it's landing coordinates," Titus said.

"We've got something inbound," Kate said. "It hasn't come through the atmosphere yet but it's definitely some sort of craft."

Doc and Jane exchanged a look.

"Send us the location," Doc said. "Can the three of you get there in case they make it to the surface?"

"Already on our way, boss," Titus said.

"Okay. Jane and I are going to try to keep it from landing," Doc said.

"And I'm just going to watch?" Emily said.

"You are going to practice with that thing," Doc said.

"The heck with that," Emily said. "What better way to practice than on actual bad guys, I mean seriously Doc. There another one of these?"

"The other isn't fully operational yet," Keaton said.

"Want me to suit up?" Winter said.

Doc shook his head.

"No, you get your people ready in case this is the big one," Doc said. "Kate, Titus, we'll see you there."

"How are we going to get there before them?" Emily said.

Doc waved a hand, and a purplish sphere of emptiness appeared on front of them. On the other side was nothing but blue sky.

"Through the looking glass," Jane said. She waved at Henry Winter and stepped past Doc, through the portal and into the waiting sky.

CHAPTER 25:
AERIAL COMBAT

Emily stepped through Doc's portal and immediately started plummeting toward the ground. Catching herself abruptly in a bubble of float, she looked for Jane, and found her, as she often did, basking in the direct light of the sun, her skin glittering like a diamond as she absorbed its energy, eyes closed, an involuntary smile on her face. Jane's hair seemed to come alive, dancing flames trailing behind her as she readied herself for a fight.

Doc flew more like Emily, less speed and more drift, his long coat hanging behind him, fluttering on the breeze. She couldn't hear his words, but all around him, symbols made of light appeared and disappeared, spells coming to life as he prepared. It occurred to Emily she'd never really seen Doc let loose in a battle before. She'd watched him do amazing things, turn entire buildings into dust or butterflies, but she wondered what he would do if he didn't have to hold back. Real magic, Emily thought. I want to see colossal magic.

The glove on her hand felt heavy and constricting, her own palm-sweat began to gross her out almost immediately.

With her non-gloved hand, she tucked her earpiece more firmly into her ear. Jane's voice was the first she heard.

"I count three incoming," Jane said.

"Three what?" Emily said.

Doc pointed. Asteroids or ships, Emily couldn't tell, but three objects were earthbound, burning orange in the atmosphere, flying in formation.

131

"Where's Bruce Willis when you need him," Emily said. "Or Ben Affleck, I'd settle for Affleck at this point…"

Doc hushed her and started saying something in a language that never existed, words that sounded like falling snow and breaking icicles. Emily watched as he made a series of gestures with his hands, then pointed at the falling objects.

The air below them flashed with blue light, and a bird the size of an airplane appeared—not an actual one, Emily realized, but some sort of golem made of ice, a frozen phoenix on a collision course with the burning objects. The bird flew upward, smashing headlong into the lead ship with a deafening bang, and the air filled with steam.

The center object—looking more like a ship than an asteroid, though its exterior had an organic, almost plant-like shell to it— began to fall off course, swerving away from the other two vessels after the impact. Jane dove towards it, leaving a trail of flame behind her, throwing a fiery haymaker at the ship's hide. Its armor cracked under Jane's assault.

"My turn," Emily said. She aimed her gloved hand at one of the falling ships and willed a wall of slam at it. She felt the familiar feeling of vertigo as her powers emanated outward, but instead of the entire ship being knocked off course, she saw a hole punch right through it, sending cracks and splits all around the circumference of the cylindrical main body of the ship. Emily pushed again, aiming at the back end of the ship, and this time not only did she punch a hole straight through the carapace, the initial cracks widened, cutting the craft in two. Both halves fell toward the earth, tumbling out of control.

"Why aren't they defending themselves?" Doc said.

"Because they are intimidated by our awesomeness," Emily said.

"I think I know why!" Jane said, her voice rising. Emily banked left to get a better look at where the solar-powered girl was, and saw her bracing herself with her legs against the side of the ship she'd attacked so that her hands were free to fight off two of the bug-like parasites they'd seen on the aliens she and Emily fought in the desert.

Emily swooped in to try to help, but turned back when she saw Jane use her own powers to light her hands on fire, setting the two parasites aflame.

"This isn't an attack, this is reinforcements," Doc muttered. "Emily…"

"You got it, Doc," she said, knowing exactly what Doc meant. Emily held out her hand, the one without the gravity glove, and aimed it at the last, undamaged ship. Engulfing it in a bubble of float, she watched as the ship stopped falling toward the ground and instead began to drift lazily in the air.

"One," Emily said. "Jane, head's up—"

She turned her attention to Jane's target just in time to see something big—another alien, seven or eight feet tall, held tight by one of the parasites on his chest—jump out of the hole Jane had made in the ship's armor and tackle her, sending both spiraling into the open air.

"Are you kidding me!" Emily yelled as she watched Jane fall, exchanging mighty punches back and forth with the alien host. The creature seemed to understand it needed to hold onto her to avoid plummeting into the ground, and kept one hand clenched on Jane's shoulder while the heroine threw brutally powerful punches into the alien's belly.

"Doc?"

Knowing Jane would survive the fall—or hoping, at least, given she's really the only actual indestructible Indestructible—Emily turned her attention back onto the falling ship Jane had broken open. She pointed her other hand toward this craft and slowed its descent as well, holding one starship with each hand.

Bubbles of float, bubbles of float, I can make more I swear, she thought, looking at the rapidly descending halves of the ship she'd broken in two.

In her mind, she shifted the two ships she had bubbled into the palm of one hand, holding them aloft with the gravity glove hand while pointing the other at one half of the falling ship. She reached out, envisioning a third bubble around the falling craft, watching as it started to spin and drop.

"Doc, little overwhelmed here," Emily said.

He muttered something in that strange, mythic language again, the sky opened below them in a perfect circle of fiery light.

Emily swore. "What is *that*?" she said.

"Pocket dimension," Doc said.

"You're kidding me? Did you seriously just conjure up a *bag of holding*?"

"Can we talk about this later?"

"Dude, you made a pocket dimension while we're just floating here?"

"Emily, please bubble of float those ships into that circle if you don't mind," Doc said. "Holding that gateway open is harder than it looks."

Emily deposited the half-ship over the golden ring of fire and released it, letting the cylindrical shape fall through. It did not emerge on the other side, but rather disappeared into nothingness.

"Please tell me I can get one of these for the next time I clean my room," Emily said.

"Em!"

"Working!" she said. Emily dropped the undamaged ship into the dimensional rift wholesale, releasing the bubble of float dramatically. "Bullseye!"

She maneuvered the damaged ship over the pocket dimension, splitting her attention as she searched for the other falling half of the broken vessel, which spun alarmingly close to Doc.

"Hey Doc, on your right, "Emily said.

"Thanks, I'll—"

Before he could finish his sentence, another parasite-controlled monster, this one with boney, membranous wings, crept out from the inside and launched itself at the magician, tackling him mid-air.

Doc tumbled into the air with the alien wrapping its arms around him.

Emily watched in awe as the wizard and the alien plummeted toward the ground. The action startled her so much she accidentally let go of the ship Jane had damaged, and she turned her attention back to the now free-falling ship in horror.

"Mistakes have been made!" Emily said, not sure if anyone could hear her.

And, almost as if she planned it, the ship plopped daintily into the pocket dimension just as the glowing ring disappeared.

"Hey hey! Look what I did!" Emily said. "Wait. Where is…"

Emily looked around, unable to spot the remaining half-ship she hadn't been able to capture. It was too far for her to catch by the time she saw it.

"Um, Titus?" Emily said.

"What the heck is going on up there?" Titus said.

"Stuff and things," she said. "Where are you?"

"On the ground watching something big and creepy falling right at us."

"Can you…?"

"On it. Where's Doc?"

"Um. You may need to help me find him, too," Emily said.

CHAPTER 26:
I KNOW WHAT THEY
SMELL LIKE

Kate stood with Titus and Bedlam as the broken starship crashed into the ground in the fields outside the RIETI institute, leaving a huge crater and kicking up a cloud of dust and dirt at least a hundred feet high.

As a unit, the trio approached the crater carefully, as if all three refused to let one of the others be the first over the edge.

"Think anything's alive down there?" Bedlam said.

"Yeah, there's something alive," Titus said.

"How can you tell?" Kate said, afraid she already knew the answer.

"I know what they smell like now," Titus said, touching his nose.

"When you say things like that, I'm mystified why I still find you attractive," Kate said.

"You think that's tough, try being crazy about you whenever you bring your gym bag to the Tower after a workout when I've got a super-human sense of smell," Titus said.

Kate almost, almost ignored the quip, but turned one quick but brutal dirty look his way.

"Wow," Bedlam said, just watching the two of them. "Just... wow."

"So if something is alive in there, we should—" Kate said, when, with a sort speed normally reserved for horror movie jump-scares, a small arachnid shape scrambled up over the edge of the crater and darted between her and Titus, skittering with blurred legs toward the RIETI institute's main building. Kate watched in awe as the parasite—clearly one of the creatures that had latched onto Rice-Bell and the others—made it at least a hundred yards away before they could even regain their footing.

"Son of a—!" Bedlam yelled

Kate glanced at Titus, who was already throwing off his hoodie and starting to transform.

"On it," he said, and leapt into action, fluidly transforming from human to werewolf, loping like the predatory creature he was and ran down the small alien being. She realized he'd really come a long way since they first met—he'd been like Bambi in that monstrous body before, loose-limbed and clumsy, and now he moved like a killing machine.

And once he was out of sight, the crater rumbled again, and something inhuman wailed from within it. Kate turned to Bedlam, who looked back at her with a resigned frown.

"Whatever that was, I guarantee you it'll be something that would've been easier to deal with if we had a werewolf with us," Bedlam said.

Kate reached down to her belt and pulled open a pouch. She withdrew two identical objects—like brass knuckles, but reflective black, with a power source built into the grip and a button near the thumb. She slid one on each hand, clenched her fist, and hit the activation button on both, feeling the hum of electricity buzz across her knuckles.

The toys she'd found over the past year in the Tower just kept getting better, she thought. Taser knuckles? I'll take two.

She and Bedlam waited for whatever had howled from within the crater to show its face. Then, partially obscured by the dust and grime of the crash, a tall, egg-like shape rose up on a stalk, appearing like the bud of a flower before blooming. It turned to face them, and split down the middle was a mouth rowed with shark-like teeth.

"If that thing says 'feed me Seymour' I'm legitimately going to freak out," Bedlam said.

"Steady," Kate said, flexing her fingers.

Other stalks rose, one, two, three, four, moving like spider legs, reaching for them.

"Oh good, evil flower has arms," Bedlam said. "You know what would make me feel better?"

"If we still had our werewolf with us?" Kate said.

"Yeah," Bedlam said. "You want me go first?"

"No," Kate said. "I want to see if this thing can take a punch."

* * *

Titus lost sight of the parasite before he reached the main entrance of the institute. Given the choice between slowing down or smashing through, he chose the latter, knocking the door off the hinges and letting the thick glass shatter, his silver fur protecting him, mostly, from the shards. A quick glance showed the little alien creature had done something similar, breaking a smaller hole in the exit.

Titus huffed, catching the creature's scent, and ran down the left-hand corridor to the emergency staircase. The door had not been damaged, and in the back of his mind where his human thoughts hung out while Titus let the monster take over, he wondered how the spider-like thing had managed to open the door like that without hands.

The trail led him not to the third floor, where he expected—back to Rice-Bell's office—but rather to the second floor, where he hadn't been before. This floor was dark, lit only by windows, humming with machinery as computers tracked the signals coming in from the field of satellite dishes outside. Titus slunk in, using his arms for balance like a gorilla, listening, waiting for the alien parasite to appear.

Instead, the solitary shape of a young man in an expensive yellow dress shirt and navy pants stood by a computer. The receptionist they'd met the day before. Only it wasn't just the receptionist he saw. The young man turned to reveal a parasite latched onto his chest, small rivulets of blood showing through the front of his shirt.

138

"I... I should be scared," the young man said. "I'm looking at a monster and I should be frightened. There's this thing... I think it's eating me. I should be devastated. But I'm not. Isn't that strange? I'm not afraid."

Titus moved in closer, cocking his head, eyes on the young man's every movement.

"We just sent a signal out," the man said. "We. We? I did. I pushed the buttons. I sent the signal. I didn't understand it. It was just sounds. No message, no images. I don't know what it said. I don't know how to work these machines, not really. I'm just the receptionist. What am I doing up here?"

Titus sized the man up. How does this work? Titus wondered. Does he gain all the alien's strength right away? Did it need time to build up? He still seems partially in control—if I kill the parasite, is it too late to save the human?

"You should look out behind you," the receptionist said.

Titus heard the scurrying of insectoid feet and spun around, catching sight another parasite as it launched itself into the air, legs outstretched as if to grab onto him. The werewolf snatched it up in one hand and, in a singular movement of animal fury, smashed the creature against the floor, up and down, again and again, blackish blood spraying out as he crushed it. Roaring, he dug his claws into the parasite and ripped it apart, the werewolf part of his brain in a blind red rage at the idea of being taken the way this young man had been. No one enslaves me, Titus could feel the wolf's emotions screaming, as it tore the alien parasite limb from limb.

Footsteps rang against the floor as the receptionist ran. Leaving the ravaged corpse of the parasite where it died, Titus pursued the fleeing young man, pounced on him, bringing him down like a deer. The man shoved him, far stronger than he should have been, but not nearly as powerful as Rice-Bell had been. He's not at full strength yet, Titus thought. Not completely gone.

Titus shoved the receptionist against a wall, hearing ribs cracking, grimacing internally as the poor man's head bounced off the plaster. With his other clawed hand, Titus dug into the parasite's flesh, rending and tearing. Both human and alien squealed in pain, the parasite sounding like a lobster lowered into boiling water. Its legs spasmed, releasing the young man, dropping him onto the floor. The alien thrashed and howled, but Titus tore it apart as he had the other, black ichor poured out. He dropped the body onto the carpet and leaned in, muzzle dangerously close to the receptionist's face.

The receptionist opened his eyes. He screamed. Not in pain, but in perfect human terror at being nose to nose with a three-hundred-pound werewolf, breathing hot air onto his skin.

Perhaps he'll live, Titus thought. Maybe I made it in time.

* * *

This entire situation is going all wrong, Kate thought, dodging thrashing vines and desperately trying not to get eaten by the giant Venus fly trap that had emerged from the crashed ship. She danced around the plant-creature's waving arms, snapping off electrified punches if it got too close, her movements quick and graceful but in the end, useless at putting the creature down.

Bedlam, in a way almost comedic, had been unable to dodge the grasping vines and was now hanging from one by her foot, kicking so hard Kate could hear her cyborg parts whining as they moved. On the upside, hanging in the air also gave Bedlam a good vantage point to throw thunderous punches at the plant-creature's jaws. Those punches were doing some kind of damage, the jaw didn't hang right anymore, as if coming unhinged, and the shards of alien teeth littered the ground like confetti.

Kate extended herself in a smooth leap over an outreaching vine, tumbling out of range. She heard Bedlam cursing.

"Let me go, let me go, let me go, let me go," the cyborg said, punctuating each repeated phrase with a punch. The vine holding her listed at an awkward angle, and Kate's mouth fell open as she watched the alien suddenly release its grip on Bedlam and drop her twenty feet to the ground. The cyborg hit the dirt with an ugly bang, but her response seemed to indicate she wasn't hurt too badly.

"I hate my life!" Bedlam said, lying still with both arms held up in the air in a tantrum.

Kate jumped up onto one of the vines, using it for leverage, dancing her way along the length of it to get close enough to throw a series of electrified punches at the base of the creature's main stalk. This seemed to only anger it, however, as the Venus flytrap head turned its attention from Bedlam onto Kate.

Kate bounced back, looking at the core of the creature, and realized it was never intended to move. It had no legs, no means of propulsion. Why send a stationary creature like this on an intergalactic journey? What was the purpose?

As Kate pliéd over another swiping vine, she heard Emily's voice crackle in her earpiece.

"Hey Dancer," Emily said.

"Not right now," Kate said.

"No seriously Dancer I need you to move."

"I am moving," she said.

"Kate, dude, get your butt out of there for a second, I have an idea," Emily said.

"No ideas," she said.

"Bedlam?" Emily said.

"What, what, what!" Bedlam said, throwing punches at the plant's vines as they tried to drag her back into the air.

"I need you to move too."

"Why?" Bedlam said.

"Just get away from the thing! Away from the thing! Listen to Auntie Emily and get away from the thing!"

Kate, suddenly not trusting anything Emily might have in mind, sprinted out of range of the creature's vines. Bedlam did the same, tripping over vines multiple times, falling down onto her hands and knees and then half-running, half-crawling away.

"What could she possibly—" Bedlam said.

And then a delivery van landed on top of the alien Venus flytrap with a sickening thud, exploding in a cloud of frozen food products.

Kate tried to say something in reaction, but just deactivated her taser-knuckles and put her hands on her hips, admiring Emily's culinary carnage.

"Audrey II, you are now Audrey Goo," Emily said, drifting down out of the sky to stand next to Kate.

"I don't even know how to react to what I just saw," Bedlam said.

" 'Thank you' works," Emily said. "I also accept gift cards."

It was Titus' turn to chime in over the earpiece.

"What was that bang?" he asked, clearly back in his human form.

"Emily dropped a meat delivery truck onto a... never mind," Kate said. "Are you whole?"

"What? Yeah. I'm fine," Titus said. "There was more than one parasite here though, something weird is going on. Where are Doc and Jane?"

"Oh no," Emily said.

"Titus, we're going to need your help immediately," Kate said.

"Why?"

Kate wrinkled her nose.

"We need you to track Doc and Jane for us," she said.

* * *

The foursome stuck together in their search, following a once-again wolfed-out Titus as he ran across the hillside behind the RIETI institute on Doc's trail. The fight had begun to catch up to Kate. She was feeling the bruises in her arms and legs, a tightening in her back from being thrown about. Emily struggled to keep up, and Kate found herself hanging back a little, as if to stay side by side with the younger team member.

There are times I hate being human, she thought, watching the tirelessness of Titus and Bedlam a few yards ahead of them.

They found Doc on the edge of a wooded area. The grass all around him had been scorched and blackened. His glasses were gone. He held a sword in one hand—where he got a sword out here, Kate was almost afraid to imagine—which he had thrust into the chest of the muscular alien on the ground in front of him. As they approached, he put one foot on the creature's torso, where another parasite had latched on, and yanked the sword out of both host and parasite in one pull.

142

Doc turned his head as he heard them approaching and his left hand lit up in blue flames. His eyes became balls of indigo fire as well, a rare image without his red glasses to hide them. He looked tired, and older than he usually did, and very angry. Recognizing them immediately, he tossed his sword to the ground, where the tip of the blade pierced the earth and stayed upright.

He wiped his hands on his pants, caught his breath, and looked them up and down, clearly searching for injuries.

"Well, magic works on them," Doc said, his lip curling in disgust.

"Was that a question?" Emily said.

Doc looked at her impatiently, but his face, as always, immediately softened.

"I honestly didn't know," Doc said. "Magic is funny. It can be the most powerful thing in the universe, but when it decides not to work..."

"Are you okay?" Titus said.

Doc looked himself over. His clothes were scorched and covered in blood and dirt. Kate realized they hadn't ever seen him after a fight before. He was so quiet, so gentle, it was easy to forget that he was as much a warrior as any of them were, and had been fighting terrible things longer than many of them had been alive.

Instead of answering Titus' question, Doc countered with one of his own. "Where's Jane?" he said.

"Right here," came Jane's voice from the forested area behind Doc. Seconds later, she appeared. Jane looked as worse for wear as he did, a bruise growing on one side of her face, dirt and leaves in her hair and stuck to her uniform, which had been trashed as well. One whole sleeve had been ripped off at the shoulder, revealing scratches on her upper arm. Her cape was gone. She'd lost a boot.

And yet, she was dragging a still-breathing alien body behind her.

"Is that what I think it is," Kate said, not asking.

Jane threw the unconscious creature onto the ground between them. Its parasite was still whole as well, its plantlike carapace rising and falling with shallow breaths.

"That," Jane said. "Is a captive."

"Why didn't you just burn the parasite off?" Emily said. "Like a tick? Seems like you might have saved yourself a little trouble. Or at least, y'know... not lost your shoe?"

Jane wobbled a bit on her feet. Doc leaned in, put an arm around her waist, and she draped an arm over his shoulder for support.

"Two reasons," she said, eyes bleary like a boxer's after a long fight. "One, I want answers."

"Well, I mean, we can try. Maybe see if he speaks Esperanto or something," Emily said.

"And two: I am so tired of killing things," Jane said. "I wanted to try at least once to talk to these creatures before we have to go to war with them."

Doc looked at the two bodies, one living, one dead. He turned his gaze off into the distance. At first, he seemed to be staring at nothing, but Kate watched his expression, and saw something there. Anger, and very targeted anger at that. Doc Silence was focusing on something very specific, Kate knew. What are you looking at, Doc? She wondered. Or who?

"Let's make sure he's locked up tight," Doc said, turning his attention once more to the alien on the ground. "He may not want to talk, but you're right. It's worth a try."

CHAPTER 27:
NOT MADE OF CHEESE

I never believed I'd have a reason to say this, Billy thought as the Earth grew blue and bright in the sky, but I'm so happy to see my home planet again.

Everyone likes to go home, Dude said.

Well, this wasn't exactly a pleasure cruise, Billy mused. Also I've been wearing the same clothes for like a week. I can't wait to shower.

Between them and home, the moon hung shadowy and gray, disconcertingly big in Billy's vision. Close enough to touch.

Hey Dude. Can we swing by the moon and look at the American flag there?

You realize we're trying to save your home planet from destruction, Dude said.

Yeah, I know. But when am I going to do this again? Can we just drive by? I won't even get out of the car, just roll down the window.

We are not in a car, Billy Case.

I'm speaking metaphorically. Please? Billy pleaded. Come on, it'll be fast.

As always, Billy could sense Dude's reaction like a temperature shift as the alien acquiesced.

We can't go looking for the flag, but there's no harm in flying in lower on our way by, Dude said.

Billy smirked, banking in like a landing airplane, arms outstretched, as they flew in for a closer look. Billy found himself marveling at how complex the surface was, more uneven and varied

145

than he expected. He thought it might be like a beach, just gray sand untouched by tide or footprints.

Hey, it's not made of cheese after all.

Do you have any concept of how ridiculous that old myth is? Dude said.

I always figured if the moon was made of cheese I didn't want to see the cow involved in making it, Billy thought. He dove in closer, reaching out, almost touching the surface of the moon with his fingertips, but resisted, as if afraid to leave a mark on the untouched surface there.

What if I wrote my name? In the dust. 'Billy Case was here.'

That would be extremely mature of you, Dude said. *Truly a legacy to leave behind with pride.*

I kinda feel like I should take a scoop of moon dust home. Emily would like that. I could put it in a mason jar for her, be all crafty like.

I don't believe there's any rule against taking dust from the moon, Dude said.

Are you approving petty larceny?

I see no harm in it.

Billy found himself strangely put off by Dude's lack of protest. Maybe we've been alone for too many days straight. I haven't had the opportunity to annoy anyone else for too long and he's giving up.

Billy let himself coast a bit, drifting in the low-gravity of the moon, suddenly very annoyed he never put pockets on his uniform.

I didn't think this through, Billy thought.

Now you know why I didn't argue with you, Dude said.

Billy was about to fire off a weak retort when he saw something drifting nearby. Spherical, it looked like a miniature moon itself, but shiny, reflecting the light of the sun off the curve of its surface.

What's that? Billy said.

Before Dude could answer, Billy flew up toward it, taking a wide, playful arc to get a full view of the object. Maybe it was something left behind by a space mission. Or a satellite that wandered off too far. Something cool.

He coasted in closer and saw that its surface was essentially clear, like a bubble, with an oily sheen to it. Inside Billy could see something twitching, spasming like a dog kicking its leg as it dreamed. Billy scooted in even closer. Inside the bubble were piles of crablike legs or plant stalks, segmented, pale green, too tangled to count.

What the… Billy thought.

Don't touch that, Dude said.

What is it? Billy said.

Please don't touch—

Billy ran his fingers along the surface of the bubble.

The bubble burst.

And suddenly the entire nest of things inside sprang to life.

I have made a mistake! Billy tried to yell in the silence of space as a half-dozen creatures the size of small dogs reached for him, looking like a cross between enormous crabs and potted spider-plants.

Shoot them! Dude said.

I can shoot them? Billy silently yelled.

Just shoot them!

Instinctually, Billy blasted one of the creatures with a burst of energy from his hand, sundering the thing and sending globes of blackish fluid into the vacuum around them.

What are these things Dude? Billy yelled. He could feel his vocal cords trying to create sound, scratching in a silent scream. The remaining alien creatures grabbed at him. One engulfed his hand, but he unleashed another blast of light and the critter fell away. Another took hold of his leg, and one more wrapped claws around his throat. Holding the limb as it pressed down on his neck, he found himself wondering, simultaneously—can I suffocate in space? And can I hurt myself with my own light blasts? Billy was shocked when Dude answered both questions, reading his mind.

You can't hurt yourself with your own light blasts, and yes, you can suffocate if one of these things chokes you to death, but they don't want to kill you.

Billy, unable to form the words to question how Dude knew this or what the creatures wanted to do if *not* kill him, seized the one around his neck and fired with both hands. The grip around his throat tightened and released, and he threw the spidery thing away.

Then he looked up at the burst bubble they'd emerged from and watched more scrambling out like tarantulas made from flower stems.

Oh you gotta be kidding me, Billy thought, trying to shake one creature off his leg while another latched onto his upper arm. The newly hatched aliens joined them, attacking with the blind aggression of insects.

Dude, what do I do, what do I do Dude.

Starburst, Dude said.

What? Billy said. We're talking about candy now? Candy will kill them?

You need to send a light blast out from your entire body, Dude said. *Every direction at once.*

I can do that? Billy thought.

Yes, you can.

And you're only mentioning this now?

Focus, Billy Case.

I'm focusing on the fact that you keep me in the dark about all the most awesome things I can do until I need to do them and can't.

Pull yourself together, Dude said.

I'm not hysterical! I'm perfectly calm! Billy thought.

I mean literally you fool! Fetal position!

Oh, Billy thought, curling up into a ball as the little aliens pig-piled onto him. This is seriously the weirdest most awkward thing I have ever...

Gather all your strength up into yourself, Dude said. *Center it. Let it build up in your chest.*

I have no idea what you're talking about, Billy thought, but he clenched his limbs in, tightened his chest muscles, gritted his teeth, trying to pull all the tension and fear into his belly. He'd started to glow brighter, and Billy could feel his powers humming inside his bones like electricity.

Now let go, Dude said.

Not knowing what else to do, Billy flung his arms and legs out violently. Not sure what else to say, he silently screamed.

Cowabunga! Kiai! Billy tried to yell. He knew no one would hear it, but it somehow felt better to try.

Dude's advice worked; instead of a single burst of light from his hands as he usually used, a vast explosion of luminosity flared out all around him, brightening up the darkness. Billy felt the tangled limbs of the small aliens not just loosen but break away, releasing him immediately. All around him, the bug-plants drifted motionless and lifeless, destroyed by his blast of energy.

Hey, that worked, Billy thought, automatically nudging himself away from the bodies of the creatures and toward Earth.

He felt incredibly tired suddenly, the urge to sleep landing on him with the weight of a sledgehammer. When was the last time I slept? he thought, feeling control over his flight fading. His limbs felt loose and bendy, his vision blurry. He struggled to focus on anything—flying, looking for straggler aliens, anything.

I should get home, Billy thought, even the speech in his mind slurring. He pointed his body toward Earth and tried to kick up the speed. I'll get Em some moon dust 'nother time.

You should rest to recover from the fight, Dude suggested.

You afraid I'm going to fall asleep at the wheel? Billy thought. How much farther do we have to go anyway?

Two hundred thirty-eight thousand, nine hundred miles, Dude said.

Oh I got this, Billy thought. He pushed all his strength into propelling himself toward Earth. His vision swam. He felt vaguely nauseous. Dude's voice sounded hollow in his head.

Please do be careful, Billy Case.

Don't worry, Dude, Billy thought. I know a short cut.

Flying faster and faster, the stars began to swim around him, and Billy Case, like a trucker on the last leg of a long journey, gritted his teeth to stay conscious, with home close and bright right in front of him.

CHAPTER 28:
INTERLUDE: SWORDS HAVE NAMES

Emily found Doc sitting by himself in a hallway of the Labyrinth, head tilted back as if asleep. She could never tell if he was sleeping or not with those glasses—he'd found a replacement pair somewhere between the battle and now—and of course his tendency to be so still. She wondered if it was some meditation thing he did, or if he just napped a lot and pretended he was doing something else.

The team had brought their prisoner to the Labyrinth immediately, Emily holding the unconscious and enormous alien in a bubble of float to contain him the entire way. They'd deposited the captive in one of the strongest cells in the prison, a room designed to hold powerful superhuman threats. No one was sure if the room would be strong enough to contain him, but so far, so good, Emily thought. The building was still standing.

She sat down next to Doc, deliberately picking the chair closest to him. Her feet didn't reach the floor, so she kicked them back and forth, her oversized Doc Martens clunk heavily against the legs of the chair.

"What's up, Doc?" she said. She did refrain from launching into her full *Bugs Bunny* imitation.

He did not turn back to look at her but responded softly. "Hello, Emily."

"I have a question for you."

"Go right ahead," Doc said, his head still tilted back as if out of exhaustion. Emily wondered if the fight earlier had taken a lot out of him somehow.

"That sword you conjured up out of nowhere. What is it?"

"A sword."

"No, I mean," Emily said. "Is it a sword? Or is it a capital S Sword?"

"I don't follow you."

"Does it have a name is what I'm asking. Is it famous."

"Maybe," Doc said. "Would it matter if it was?"

"Is it Glamdring?"

"No."

"Orcrist?" Emily said.

"No."

"The Sword of Gryffindor?"

"No," Doc said.

"The Singing Sword? The Master Sword?"

"No and no," Doc said, his tone continuing to be calm, tired, and monotonous.

"Stormbringer?"

"What? No," Doc said.

"Longclaw?"

"No."

"Sikanda?"

This one brought a smirk to Doc's lips, but he shook his head.

"No, it's not Sikanda."

"The Vorpal Sword!"

"Snicker snack," Doc said.

"Am I right?" Emily said.

"No," Doc said.

"Dangit," Emily said. "Well it can't be Excalibur, that's ridiculous."

Doc raised an eyebrow from behind his glasses at Emily. She tilted her chin questioningly.

"You're putting me on, Doc Silence," Emily said.

He made a tiny gesture with his hand and then pointed to the chair next to Emily. Sitting there comfortably in an old leather scabbard sat Doc's sword. The hilt was simple, in a dark, almost blue metal, the grip wrapped in oiled leather. The scabbard held no adornments, just a sturdy home for a sturdy blade.

Emily picked it up.

"Careful with that," he said. "Sharp."

"Seriously. What is this sword called?" Emily said.

They were interrupted but the rhythmic thumping of Henry Winter's cane as he strode down the hallway toward them. Doc stood up and pointed at his old friend, who was accompanied on his right by Keaton Bohr.

"You," he said. "Get your coat."

"You look terrible," Henry said.

"I know," Doc said. "Coat. Now."

"Where we going?" Henry said.

"You and I are off to see an old friend."

"Can't you bring someone else?" Henry said, looking sheepish. Emily eyeballed him as she sat down in her chair, cradling the sword. "And why does she have a sword? That thing looks like Braveheart's claymore in her hands. It's as tall as she is."

"That's my sword, she's holding it, and you're getting your coat," Doc said.

"Bring Sam. Bring Alley Hawk!"

"Sam isn't up to it, and Alley Hawk's gone radio silent since he captured the Vermin King," Doc said. "Kate's been checking in on him. You're up, sunshine. Coat."

Henry sighed, shoulders sagging dramatically.

"Fine. Is he still… " Henry trailed off.

"Bring a warm coat," Doc said.

As the two older heroes argued, Bohr gestured to Emily and to the glove she still wore.

"How did that work out for you?" he said.

Emily turned her gauntlet-encrusted hand back and forth a few times, inspecting it.

"Could use some adjustments, but it got the job done. Ka-blammo," she said.

Bohr held out his hand and she pulled the glove off and handed it to him. He flipped open a control panel near the wrist and studied it. "We might have some better options for you if you—"

Before Bohr could finish, Doc interrupted.

"Em, Henry and I have to step out. Tell Jane to stay on high alert in case the prisoner decides to try to escape," he said. "I know she wants to try to reason with them, but I don't want anyone taking any chances."

"You realize you just asked the least responsible team member to rein in the most responsible team member, right?" Emily said.

"Desperate times call for desperate measures," Doc said. "We'll be back."

He shot Bohr a vaguely threatening look.

"We can talk tech when we get back. Not before," Doc said.

Henry waved an apologetic hand at Bohr, seemingly to say—do as he says, sorry.

Doc turned back to Henry.

"Coat."

Henry sighed heavily again.

"Office. Fine. It's in my office."

The two veteran heroes walked away, leaving Emily standing beside Bohr in the hall.

"Hey Doc, you forgot your..." Emily started to say, then held up her empty hands. The sword had disappeared. "Curses. Foiled again."

She smirked at the suddenly anxiety-riddled Bohr.

"You said you had other toys I could test out?" she said.

"That man scares me," Bohr said.

"Doc? He's a teddy bear," Emily said.

Bohr just blinked nervously at her.

"Fine," Emily said. "Gimme my glove back. I need to go tell our best-behaved Indestructible to behave herself."

CHAPTER 29:
GOOD COP, BAD COP

Kate watched Jane from the shadow of a half-opened door in the Labyrinth's detention area. Jane had pulled a pair of sweatpants with the Department's log on the leg over the leotard of her battered uniform and replaced her one remaining boot with a pair of inmate-issue socks, then sat in front of a set of monitors, cameras trained on their captive in his holding cell.

The massive creature sat perfectly still, curled up on the floor with his knees pulled to his chest. The parasite clinging to him seemed to breathe at a different rate than the host body did, both creatures inhaling and exhaling slowly. The host's eyes barely blinked as he stared at the door of his cell. He looked like a warrior, whatever he had been in his previous life, before being enslaved by the Nemesis parasite—craggy brow, scars across his entire upper body, a chipped fang visible in his jutting lower jaw. It made sense, Kate thought; if the Children of the Elder Star were working, knowingly or not, to build better host bodies for these aliens, it would be logical that they took with them from previous worlds they'd destroyed the strongest and most resilient examples of those species. Kate envisioned the approaching fleet filled with a rainbow of aliens, all the most violent and powerful versions of their civilizations. All coming here, prepared to battle.

As much as I love a good fight, Kate thought, I really don't want to see them get here.

Kate pushed the door open the rest of the way.

Jane didn't turn to greet her.

"Hello, Kate," she said. "You could've come in five minutes ago."

"You knew I was there?" Kate said.

"My super-senses are getting stronger," Jane said. "I could hear your heartbeat."

"That's… disconcerting," she said.

"Try realizing you can hear individual heartbeats and then we can talk about things being disconcerting," Jane said. She finally turned her eyes to Kate. "How are you?"

"How am I?"

"We've hardly had a chance to say hello to each other since you came back," Jane said. "I missed you."

"Nobody misses me," Kate said.

"Well, it was weirder without you here," she said.

"That sounds more accurate," Kate said. She tapped one of the monitors. "Has he done anything?"

"Nothing at all," she said. "I can't tell if he's catatonic, he's meditating, or he's trying to put us into a false sense of security so we'll make a mistake…"

"We should talk to him," Kate said.

Jane gave Kate a doubtful look.

"I don't think he speaks English," Jane said.

"I speak four languages."

"Or French or Japanese or… what's the fourth one?" Jane said.

"Spanish."

"Or Spanish," Jane said.

"What's the worst that can happen?" Kate said. "He attacks and kills one of us? Let's speak to him."

Jane paused as if she were going to say no, but she got up out of her chair and headed for the door.

"If this goes at sixes and sevens I'm telling everyone it was your idea," Jane said.

"Why wouldn't you?" Kate said. "It *was* my idea."

* * *

The cell holding the alien prisoner was larger than most in the Labyrinth. One of the technicians had made an off-handed comment when the team brought the creature in about this cell being "designed especially for" something or someone, but Henry Winter made a gesture across his own throat at the tech and the young man went silent. Kate wondered what threat it had originally been crafted for, and if it was, in fact, strong enough to hold the being now locked inside.

The door she and Jane used to enter, however, was still normal sized. It opened with a heavy thud, letting the greenish interior light spill out. Next to the entrance, a Labyrinth guard who had introduced himself as Two-Ton Tony warned them to make for the exit if things seemed to be getting out of control and they'd pump the room full of anesthetic gas.

The alien inside, however, seemed anything but out of control.

Tall enough that sitting on the floor he was nearly at the same level as both Kate and Jane, the creature did not react as the women walked up to him, not even with his eyes. Kate observed those organs with curiosity. Funny that we both have eyes, she thought. Not that we can see, or that we have optical organs, but that we have two spheres, in our heads, pointed forward, to observe the universe with. It seemed like a stretch that human and alien would be so similar. But then Jane had described the aliens she and Emily fought in the desert who hadn't been nearly as human-like, and the parasites themselves were so strange they didn't seem to fit firmly into a category of animal or vegetable, and had no outward indications of how they took in information around them. Maybe the Nemesis creatures preferred to find aliens who were like humans. Maybe they sought those species out specifically.

Kate waited for some sign from those eyes. They certainly did not look human. Yellowish, and made up of rows of circles inside rather than a single iris, Kate found herself curious what the design differences meant. Did he see dozens of her? Did those circles provide some sort of extrasensory peripheral vision? Or were they just cosmetic? The art of biology?

Jane knelt in front of the alien to better look at him.

"I don't know what you can hear and what you can understand," Jane said. "But I want to talk with you. I want to communicate with you. Is there any part of you inside there who understands me?"

The alien remained impassive, unmoving.

"We don't want war. We just want to be left in peace. Is there anything we can do to make that happen?" Jane said, again with no response.

Kate wanted to judge her, to be annoyed by her desire to talk with this killing machine, but she found herself strangely inspired by it. Someone still needs to have a little bit of hope, Kate thought. I certainly don't have any. But this is Jane's job. To be the best of us. To look for that one remaining peaceful option. But Kate studied this creature's skin, the scars, the thick knuckles of its fists, and saw a being who had been through many battles long before the Nemesis fleet destroyed his world. This was a warrior. There was no surrender there. Kate imagined that his world, much like her own, refused to go quietly into oblivion. She thought about what it would be like to be like him, to be taken over, to have some alien parasite commanding her every move.

She'd shared her mind with the Straylight entity for a little while, and Billy's Dude, while pushy and judgmental, had not been controlling. Never did Kate feel like she was no longer in charge. But these aliens... they looked defeated. They were like domesticated beasts.

She thought, at least a little bit, that she might understand them.

"You wish to be free," Kate said quietly. The alien didn't react, but she continued. "These monsters put a yoke on you and won't let go. I imagine this is worse than dying. You would have rather died fighting them than become a part of them. I understand that."

The parasite twitched. And for the first time, the alien host blinked. No other movement, no other reaction, just a blink. But Kate could tell he was listening.

"I'm sure you don't understand my words, but I bet that creature on your chest is translating my tone. And I'll say this. We'll set you free when this is over," Kate said. "I promise you that. Whether it's true freedom or just an honorable death, we'll do everything we can to help you."

The alien blinked once more. The parasite pulsated faster, beginning to glow red inside, just slightly, softly.

"We might want to step outside," Jane said.

Kate nodded.

"I know you can't help us," Kate said, not moving as Jane stood up and put a hand on her shoulder. Out of the corner of her eye, Kate saw Jane gesture to the cameras that Tony should open the door for them. "But if we survive this, I'll make sure you don't have to suffer any longer."

The creature's entire body shivered, just once, as if it caught a chill. Jane pulled gently on Kate's arm, and Kate allowed herself to be led out of the cell. She looked back once and saw the alien's bright yellow eyes watching her. No longer blank, she thought. There was something there, behind them, some thought, some intelligence. Maybe it understood what she said. Or maybe the creature just found her voice annoying. Kate didn't know. She realized she never would.

Kate and Jane stepped outside the cell and, as the heavy door closed with a loud metallic thud, Kate felt tension she didn't know she'd had release across her back and shoulder.

"What just happened in there?" Jane said.

"I have no idea," Kate said.

"Well, something *you* said got its attention," she said.

Kate shrugged, noncommittal.

"We'll try again later," Jane said.

Kate nodded. Before she could answer, their earpieces chirped simultaneously, Neal's voice filling their heads.

"Designation: Solar, are you available?" Neal said.

Kate and Jane exchanged a worried glance. They'd had the AI monitoring the skies for another incursion, and neither wanted to face a second round of enemy ships.

"Go ahead, Neal. Is it another attack?" Jane said.

"I do not believe so, Designation: Solar," Neal said. "I have picked up something you should be aware of however."

"Don't keep us in suspense, Neal," Jane said.

"Something is entering the atmosphere right now," Neal said. "I at first thought it was just a small meteor, but I noticed a unique energy signature."

"Neal, spit it out," Jane said.

"The signature matches that of a Luminae, specifically Designation: Straylight," Neal said. "But the object is not responding to my requests to identify itself. I suggest someone investigate."

"Billy is falling out of the sky right now?" Jane said, her voice rising.

"That is entirely possible, Designation: Solar," Neal said.

"Where?" Jane said, her expression incredulous. She waved a perfunctory, polite goodbye to Tony at the controls of the cell and started walking away. Kate followed, curious.

"The object, should it continue on its current course, should crash in... well, the City's downtown district," Neal said, sounding almost amused.

"I'm on my way," Jane said. "Emily, are you online?"

Emily's voice crackled in the earpieces.

"Where are you? I'm over near the cafeteria. Nobody knows where you are."

"I'm heading up to the surface. Meet me there. Hurry," Jane said.

"OMW," Emily said.

Jane shot Kate a worried look. Kate read everything there in the other woman's eyes—fear, concern, and most of all, a distinct request: do not go back inside the cell without me.

"Go," Kate said.

Jane nodded and broke into a run, her hair turning to flames behind her.

CHAPTER 30:
TRUST/FALL

To someone on the ground, walking through the City, they might have looked up into the sky and seen a shooting star cutting across the twilight, a white streak of light hurtling toward the earth, silent and harmless.

Turning to the left, they might then see something even more unusual, a streak of fire, its trajectory putting it on a collision course with the shooting star. A meteor, burning up in the atmosphere? Something more nefarious? What were these things falling from the sky?

The ball of fire, of course, was Jane, fist extended in flight, her eyes never wavering from the falling form she knew to be Billy. She could hear Titus on the earpiece trying to get Billy to respond, saying his name over and over again, receiving no response. He plummeted in a steady arc, not his usual playful darting about, and the closer Jane got, the more she thought the worse was happening. Why was he falling? Was he dead? Unconscious?

"Come on, Billy Case, wake up," Jane said.

She poured on the speed, getting close enough to make out Billy's shape within the ball of light. His limbs dangled loose, his shoulders slumping forward, head lolling against his chest. She pushed herself even faster. Now she could see the looseness of his hands, his closed eyes. Falling. Straylight was in free fall.

"This game again, is it?" Jane said, aiming herself at the prone hero in front of her.

"What was that?" Titus said into her earpiece, but Jane ignored him. She focused on one place: Billy's wrist, somewhere to grab hold of, to keep him from crashing. What would happen if he hit the ground? Jane thought? Would his shields hold, or would the impact kill him? Would the crash hurt anyone there in the City? What if he hit something explosive?

Closer now, almost there, her hand outstretched, fingers extended, but he was falling so fast...

"Em, where are you," Jane said.

"Where are you?" Emily responded through the earpiece.

"In the air, above the downtown," Jane said, gritting her teeth as she reached for Billy and missed.

"Are you serious?"

"Em I need some help here," Jane said.

"I'm moving as fast as I can!" Emily said.

Jane knew she was on her own, picturing Emily's tugboat-like flight puttering toward them. Once more she willed herself faster, felt a burst of fire explode forth from her feet, and she was there, reaching Billy, grabbing hold, catching his forearm in her grip. She lifted, feeling the tug of his weight against her shoulder, feeling his body shudder as it stopped falling too suddenly, his bright white aura mixing with the gold of her flames.

She felt his hand grab hold of her wrist in response and looked down.

His face was gaunt and hollow, the color under his eyes bruised. There were broken blood vessels across his cheeks. But he was smiling.

"Hey, you," he said weakly.

"Look what I found," Jane said.

"You caught me," Billy said.

"Just returning the favor," Jane said.

"Pretty good aim considering I just fell from the moon, I think," Billy said. "I think my shoulder's dislocated."

"I did that," Jane said, swerving around to start flying them back toward the Labyrinth. "You find what you were looking for out there?"

"Jane," Billy said. "The stuff I saw out there."

"Good? Bad?"

"Everything," he said, still dangling from Jane's grip. "Good, bad, and everything in between."

CHAPTER 31:
EMPATHY EMILY

Bedlam couldn't believe she was getting bored already. Couple of near death experiences, fight a few aliens, and suddenly some hours in a quiet, secure location and she was ready to start climbing the walls.

So she paced the Labyrinth, wandering wherever the signs and corridors would take her. She spent a little time looking over research with Titus, but then they got wind that Straylight was in trouble and everyone scrambled into action.

So Bedlam hung around. Alone.

Not quite part of the team yet, am I? she thought.

She decided to head down to the infirmary, where she'd heard Jane had taken Billy after the rescue. Might as well get a look at him, see how things went. She was curious what he'd come across.

When she got there, though, Emily sat in the waiting area, arms folded, as if expecting her.

"Hello, Bedlam," Emily said.

"Hello," she said, echoing her melodramatic tone.

"I thought I might see you here," Emily said, with cartoonish suspicion.

"Oh really," Bedlam said. "You a detective now?"

Emily did a spot-on impersonation of Benedict Cumberbatch's accent as Sherlock Holmes.

"Consulting detective," she quoted. "Only one in the world. I invented the job."

"You are so weird," Bedlam said.

"We have to talk," she said.

163

"About what?"

"About the Billy thing," Emily said.

"What Billy thing. There's no Billy thing."

Emily patted the seat next to her. Bedlam, resigned, sat down.

"Look, we're just going to bomb the Bechdel Test right now, but I'm just going to say it: Billy has had a crush on you for like more than a year and I don't want to see you mess with him in any way," Emily said.

"Are you seriously calling dibs or something?" she said

"What? Huh? No! Oh. No, not at all," Emily said. "Billy's not my type. I'm—no. He's my best friend, though, and I do not truck with people messing with him."

"Why do you think I'm going to mess with him?" Bedlam said.

"Because you strike me as the type of person who messes with people," Emily said.

"This from you. I've hung out with you approximately twice and all you do is mess with people," Bedlam said.

Emily growled.

"I'm just saying. He's sensitive. Don't toy with his heart or whatever," she said.

"You realize he and I have never actually had a conversation outside of either beating the hell out of each other or breaking him out of prison, right?"

"… I thought he asked you out to coffee," Emily said.

"Apparently, we've all been really, really busy or something," Bedlam said. She studied the younger girl, in her mismatched uniform and blue hair and bravado. Her annoyance drained away. "Look, I don't know him at all, okay? I barely know any of you. It's funny to joke that he has a crush on me but it's like having a crush on a cartoon character. We're not real people to each other."

"Not yet," Emily said.

"Right, not yet," Bedlam said. "Do I think he's a good-looking kid? Yeah, I think he's a good-looking kid. I'm a little weirded out that he's got an alien living in his brain, but half my body is made out of car parts so who am I to judge anyone else for their quirks? I don't get why you're so freaked out about this."

164

"He's a profoundly sad guy," Emily said, not making eye contact. "I'm just concerned about him is all. He's my best friend and I don't like worrying about him, and I can't protect him against things like crushes. Aliens I can help with. Monsters? Sure. A crush? Nope."

Bedlam leaned back against the wall behind her. She could hear the servos in her limbs humming. Most of the time she could tune it out, but sometimes all she heard was her cyborg pieces and it drove her insane, some sort of white noise endurance test.

"Trust me, he's not the only profoundly sad person around," Bedlam said. "I get the impression there's two more of us right now in this stupid waiting room."

Emily stopped staring at the floor and faced Bedlam.

"Yeah," she said, her eyes shiny and big.

"A tough life, isn't it?" Bedlam said.

"I'm pretty sure there's no other kind of life than a tough one," Emily said.

"That's pretty deep for a lunatic," she said.

"I get that a lot," Emily said and popped up out of her chair. "I'm going to go see if he's awake yet. You want to come with me?"

"Not afraid I'm going to walk in there and pull his heart out, 'Temple of Doom' style?"

"Can we pretend we never had that part of the conversation?" Emily said.

Bedlam laughed.

"Fine," she said, standing up. "Sure, I'll come with you. And hey?"

"Hey what," Emily said.

"What is your type, anyway?" Bedlam said.

Emily made a face and wagged her hands in the air.

"Wouldn't you like to know?" she said, laughing. "C'mon. Let's go freak Billy out. He doesn't know you're here."

CHAPTER 32:
THE GOD ON THE ISLAND

Doc Silence and Henry Winter materialized on a snowy island, gray mist hanging all around them like a sad song. Henry immediately turned up his collar and grimaced as his cane sank into the snow.

"Could've warned me I needed to bring a hat," he said.

Doc ignored him.

Henry walked to the edge of the island, and where water should have been, he found nothing but open air, a drop into foggy gray nothingness. He kicked a clump of snow over the edge and watched it fall away into the mist.

"This place goes against everything I believe in," Henry said.

"You traveled through a magical portal to get here," Doc said. "You going to pull the scientist card on me right now?"

Doc started to walk away, but slowly, allowing Henry to limp along and catch up.

"It's just... it's an island in the sky, Doc," Henry said. "Even you have to question why it doesn't fall."

"Magic," Doc said, smirking. Henry hit him on the shin with his cane. "Watch it or I'll make that cane evaporate."

"Ha ha," Henry said.

They came across a campsite, logs in a semi-circle covered in snow, a fire pit burned down and blackened, cool and damp. On the far side of the camp there stood a cave, ringed with snow like a frozen mouth, too dark to see inside.

166

"We really need to ask him to help?" Henry said.

"I'm not about to throw these kids into space and possibly to their death and still allow his royal highness to sit in a cave and ignore us," Doc said. "I refuse."

"You do all the talking, then," Henry said. "He never liked me."

"He never liked any of us," Doc said. "But that's not relevant now."

Doc strode around the dead campfire, throwing a fireball from his hand into the pit, setting it ablaze. He pulled a bottle of what looked like red wine out of his coat—Henry wondered briefly if there had been a hidden pocket inside, or if Doc conjured the bottle from thin air as well—uncorked it with a twist of his wrist, and took a sip.

"Korthos of Aramaias, the Truthbringer, the Dragon's Son! Get your sorry backside out here and talk to me. It's Doc."

No sound came from the cave. Doc rattled the bottle. Henry could hear the booze lurching around inside.

"Come on, Kevin, get out here. I want to talk to you," Doc said. "I have mead."

"Go away, wizard. I want none of what you're selling," a booming voice rumbled from within the cave. "And don't call me Kevin."

"I'm certainly not calling some petulant child hiding in a cave the Dragon's Son," Doc said. "You want to be treated with respect, start acting like you deserve it."

Henry's breath caught in his throat. Snow fell in light flecks, catching on Doc's dark coat. Finally, a shape appeared at the mouth of the cave—a man, seemingly made of nothing but writhing muscles. He was shirtless and wearing an armored kilt below the waist, his hair, the dark blue of early morning sky, belt-length and braided to hang over one shoulder. His beard, the same dark blue, was also long and elaborately braided and framed a face that was something both human and not, as if he were from another place and time, carved out of the ancient ancestors of humanity. He was both handsome and horrible to look at, a wonderment of violence. In his hand he held a halberd taller than he stood, its blade black as oil.

"Hi, Kevin," Doc said.

Henry cringed again. That name. Doc was taunting him. Goading him.

"You have come to my island uninvited, magician. You best have a better reason than a bottle of sour mead," the massive man said, snatching the bottle from Doc's hand and drinking half of it in one long drag.

"You know that fight you've always wanted? The one where you can finally prove yourself? Well it's coming," Doc said. "I thought you might like to know."

"I'm done with fighting for your world," Korthos said. He spat into the fire.

Henry heard the saliva sizzle there. For the first time, the huge man seemed to notice him.

"I see you brought the tinker with his soft money-counting hands."

"Good to see you too, Korthos," Henry said.

The warrior shot Doc a disdainful look.

"Even the tinker knows to call me by my proper name," he said.

"I'll call you what I want to, Kevin. Until you prove to me you deserve all those honorifics after your name."

"I have fought wars on a dozen planes. By your side and alone. I have murdered tyrants and killed monsters from across dimensions. I deserve—"

"If you deserved respect you wouldn't have to ask for it," Doc said. "All I know is you came up here to your little island and ignored your home world for years and now that it needs you again you're still sitting here, what, playing dice games all by yourself?"

The warrior rose to his full height. Somehow, Henry thought, the silence was worse than the bluster.

"What are your 'years' to me," Korthos said. "I am of time unending."

"And what good has that done you?" Doc said. "You used to have purpose. Now you're just the son of a dead god from a religion no living human except myself has ever even heard of. Instead of honoring your fallen pantheon, you retired. I hope the fishing is marvelous here on your little floating island."

"How dare you speak of my family like that?" Korthos said. "I am—"

"You're what, Kevin? What?" Doc said. "A god? You're a demigod. And you used to be a hero. You used to be a fine, wonderful hero. And now you're either lazy or cowardly, and neither of those things look good on you up here."

Henry's stomach became a pit of acid. He could feel the anger emanating off Korthos like static electricity.

"I will not be spoken to like this! Not by some petty charlatan hedge wizard who—"

Doc pulled off his glasses, his eyes flaring in bright purple flames. Their light reflected off the snow, turning the campsite into a violet hellish nightmare.

"I am Doctor Silence, last Silver Wizard of the Council Prime, holder of the Seven Flames. The Eye of All Things Points to me. I am Demon Blooded, High General in the Army of the Dreamless, First Mage of the Nightmare Kingdom, the Flame of the Forgotten Way. And by all my names Korthos Truthbringer... I. Will. Speak. To. You... however I bloody well want to."

Henry Winter stared with his mouth hanging wide open as the wizard and the warrior stood like statues, eyes locked in a battle of wills.

The bottom of the bottle of mead cracked and fell away, spilling the remains into the snow like black blood. Doc spoke softly then.

"You forgot to pour a draught for your fallen brothers, Kevin," Doc said. "If you remembered who you were, you would have done that first."

The monstrous man looked at the empty, broken bottle in his hands with an unreadable expression. He no longer made eye contact with Doc.

"Consider what I said, Korthos Aramaias," Doc said. "There's a war coming. It would be a better war if you were on our side once more."

With that, Doc stormed away, leaving Korthos illuminated by the firelight, still staring at the empty bottle.

Henry waved at him weakly. "It was good to see you again, man," he said, hobbling away quickly. "Um. Sorry about the mess." Then, he scurried along, catching up to Doc, who was walking with long, angry strides toward the shore of the floating island.

"What the hell was that!" Henry said.

"It was properly motivating him to stop pouting," Doc said.

"And all those names? Were you just making stuff up at the end?"

Doc stopped, put his glasses back on his face, and smirked at Henry. "I might have made a few of them up, yeah."

"You really are a charlatan, aren't you?" Henry said.

"All magicians are, by degrees," Doc said. He let out a deep sigh of relief, and Henry could see the wizard had been terrified the entire time, his whole body bound up in fear and tension.

"If you were just going to do all that, why even bring me?" Henry said.

"You were here in case it didn't work and he decided to chop my fool head off," Doc said. "I figured you could at least stall him long enough for us to teleport out of there."

"And if I couldn't?" Henry said.

"Well, if nothing else, I wanted a witness if he killed me," Doc said.

Henry exhaled his own sigh of relief as Doc opened a portal home.

"Do you think it worked?" he asked.

"No idea," Doc said. "I guess we'll find out if he shows up."

CHAPTER 33:
HIDDEN TREASURES

revention—or Laura, as Agent Black kept reminding himself she wanted to be called now, I guess we're on a first name basis—parked their Land Rover in a seemingly desolate place under the North Dakota sky. They hadn't seen another human being for hours, not on the road nor on the dirt path they'd taken to get here. If she hadn't been so chatty, Black would've thought Laura had been leading him out to the middle of nowhere to kill him.

She gestured at a rocky outcropping fifty yards away.

"There's our destination," she said.

Black gave it a once-over, letting his cybernetic eye run a complete scan on the area. No abnormalities, nothing particularly threatening, no hidden soldiers or guns as far as he could tell. Just a rock in the middle of nowhere.

He reached down and loosened the gun on his hip. Laura noticed.

"So you're a shooter, huh?" Laura said. "Gunman."

"Yeah," Agent Black said, checking his weapon for the tenth time, studying it, looking for flaws in the machine.

"You must love guns."

"The opposite," Black said. "To tell you the truth, I hate guns. I absolutely hate them."

"Is that so?" Laura said. "Seems counterintuitive for how you've made your living."

"Maybe," Black said, drawing the gun and shifting the weight of his massive pistol back and forth between his hands. "But here's the thing. I can take this device, this ignorant tool, and aim it at another living being and pull the trigger—push one button, really—and a nugget of metal will fly hundreds of yards away and punch through that person's eye and end their life. And that's it. That life is over. There's no taking it back. There's no changing your mind. One button. One life."

"But you're a trained killer," Laura said. "This is your profession. That's the tool of your chosen profession. A blacksmith doesn't hate a hammer."

"But that's the point, Laura," Black said. "Any ignorant bastard can pick up a gun and end a life. They're not the tools of an artisan. Most of them are made so you can hand them to terrified kid on a battlefield and tell him to aim it in the right direction and fire. Anybody can do what I do."

"Not as well as you do it," Laura said.

Black held the gun with his metal hand, tightened his grip on the specialized padding, watched as the weapon interfaced with his cybernetics. Ammunition counts, wind fluctuations, distance to target, all manner of information flowed into his false eye, feeding his head's up display, telling him better ways to kill. He put the gun back down.

"No, not as well as I do it," Black said. "But does it matter? A bullet's a bullet. Death is death. And guns are so easy. That's why I hate them."

"How many men have you killed, Agent?" Laura asked.

"Not as many as you'd think," he said.

"Really?" Laura said, her lips quirking into a half smile.

"Honestly," Black said. "Because fear is more useful than murder. More often than not, my job is to instill fear, so I don't have to shoot anyone. I'm hired as a deterrent to violence, not as a spark to it."

"And here I thought you were just a big scary guy with a gun," Laura thought.

"Then my reputation has done its job," Black said. "The less often I have to pull the trigger, the happier I am."

Laura nodded. She unbuckled her seatbelt and slid a jacket on in her seat.

172

"What about you?" Black said. "You have telepathic powers. Or at least that's what your file says. What's your ethical stance on those?"

Laura thought about her life when she was known as Prevention—someone who, if her reputation were even half-true, had a history of telepathic interrogation and mind wipes—turned her eyes out over the hood of the truck and paused.

"I wasn't given my powers," she said, leaning back in her seat. "I was born with them. And it took a long time to learn how to not accidentally invade the minds around me. You'd think being a mind reader would be tantalizing, but it's as invasive for the telepath as it is for the person whose mind you read."

"So you don't go around just reading peoples' minds like browsing a magazine in line at the supermarket?"

"Deciphering someone's mind is like going into a stranger's home," she said. "It's uncomfortable. It puts you ill at ease. You don't know where anything is. You feel like you don't belong."

"Then how'd you get into this line of work?" Black asked. "If you don't like it."

"If there isn't much work for a guy with a metal arm," she said, "how much normal employment do you think there is for a telepath?"

"We do what we have to," Black said.

Laura nodded. She slid out of the vehicle, and Black followed her.

The sensors in Black's cybernetic implants picked up on it before his eyes did, a hidden door carved into the ground where the rocky outcropping began. Laura knelt down beside it and brushed away the dirt until she found a small hatch. Flipping it open, she entered a code into a keypad.

"Give me a hand with this," she said, indicating a pair of handles in the dirt. They each grabbed hold of one and lifted. Inside, a darkened staircase led deeper into the earth.

"You're kidding me," Black said.

"You know the Department had this place out here when I came onboard?" she said. "Just locked up and abandoned. So I used it. Off the books."

"Off the books," Black repeated. Suddenly his speculation that she'd driven him out here to kill him didn't seem so farfetched.

"Yeah," she said, heading down into the dark. Black followed her, his cyborg eyes kicking up the light to make up for the shadows. At the bottom of the stairs, he could hear Laura feeling around for a light switch.

"What is it, a bunker?" he asked. Maybe the plan is to hide out until the invasion hits, he thought. Wasn't the best plan in the world; he'd seen worse.

Laura found the lights and instantly the entire space was illuminated. It was roughly the size of a football field, and filled with an array of contraptions and vehicles, some of which were easily identifiable, others which straddled the line between machine and modern art.

"I started stockpiling things the Department found," Laura said. "Not everything, but if I could divert something that might be useful someday, I moved it here. I thought this might be a good place to look for some toys."

Black stared at one vehicle in particular, a dark cylinder that could have been a submarine. But no, those engines were designed for flight. This was an airship.

"I thought you brought me along as your shooter," Black said.

Laura smirked.

"I heard a rumor that the same cybernetics that connect to that fancy gun of yours also lets you interface with other technology," she said.

It was Black's turn to raise an eyebrow.

"Maybe," he said.

"Well, some of these machines respond to telepathic control," Laura said. "But a bunch of them need a cybernetic interface to operate. I was thinking you might want to give it a shot."

Black looked around at the huge warehouse full of oddities, some clearly weapons of war, others more elegant, indiscernible in design.

"Beats shooting people," he said.

174

CHAPTER 34:
WELCOME HOME, FLYBOY

Billy woke in a bed he wasn't familiar with, staring into tubes of light turned dim. He moved a little, shifting his shoulders, feeling pain across his whole body. Nothing broken, he thought. Just tired. Beat. One big bruise.

Dude? He thought.

Good to have you back, the symbiote said.

How long was I out?

About one hundred and fifty thousand miles, give or take, Dude said. *You didn't miss much.*

Billy squirmed, the bed creaked beneath him. He blinked his eyes a few times until he could focus on something: Titus, in human form, sitting in a chair with his feet up, a comic book in his hands. The werewolf folded the comic and set it aside.

"Welcome back, flyboy," Titus said. "Rough trip?"

"Ugh," Billy moaned. "Where am I?"

"Jane brought you to the Tower," Titus said. "She figured Neal would know what to do more than anyone at a regular hospital."

"Why would I need a hospital?"

"Because you fell out of the sky and passed out," Titus said.

"Jane caught me?" Billy said.

"Yep," Titus said. "She's probably never going to let you forget it, either."

Billy waved a hand dismissively.

"We do that. It's our thing."

175

"What?" Jane said, entering the room.

Billy noticed she was wearing sweatpants and carrying his dog. She plopped Watson on the bed and the terrier licked his nose and eyes.

"Nice pants," he said. "Easy buddy. Watch the mouth."

"At least I'm wearing pants," Jane said.

This was the awkward point. Beneath the blankets, Billy wasn't wearing any clothes.

"How did this happen?" he said.

"You and I shall never, ever speak about who got you into that hospital bed," Titus said. "We're never going to acknowledge it. I've seen things…"

"Stop," Billy said.

Jane pulled up a chair and sat down.

"You up for talking about what you found out there?" she asked.

"I was until you guys pointed out I'm not wearing pants," Billy said.

"You're not wearing any pants?" a new voice said.

It took Billy a moment to realize who it was.

"Oh come on," Billy said, seeing Bedlam framed in the doorway.

"Good to see you too, flyboy," Bedlam said. She leaned against the wall and crossed her arms.

"Is everyone going to come into my room?" he asked.

"Emily for some reason thought we should get you a pizza, so she's stepped out," Jane said.

"And Kate's doing something at the Labyrinth," Titus said. Jane gave him a puzzled look. "She didn't say."

"And your friend the alien is resting," Jane said.

"Dude is right here," Billy said, tapping his head.

"The other one who crashed. His name is Seng, by the way," Jane said.

"And why's Bedlam here?" Billy said. "Not that it isn't… wonderful to see you. You're always welcome, but I mean you weren't here when I left and…"

"I'm want to help," Bedlam said. "Heard you guys needed a bruiser."

"Well," Billy said, smiling awkwardly at the cyborg, "It's good to see you again."

"So what you got for us?" Jane said. "I hate to be pushy—"

"—But we're running short on time," Titus said. "While you were gone we rooted out a few spies for the Nemesis fleet."

Billy nodded.

"Doesn't surprise me," he said. "They're close. They're in the solar system. I have no idea how long—"

Less than a week, Dude said.

"Okay, Dude says they're less than a week away," Billy said.

"What about numbers?" Jane asked. "Did you get a solid count of how many ships we're talking about?"

"A lot," Billy said.

"Is that a metric or an Imperial measurement?" Bedlam asked.

Billy pointed at her. "It's more than a Smoot," he said.

Three seed ships. One brain ship. At least a dozen independently controlled cruisers. Unsure how many attack ships and fighters, Dude said.

"Three seed ships. One brain ship. At least a dozen independently controlled cruisers. Unsure how many attack ships and fighters," Billy repeated exactly.

"So Dude counted and you didn't?" Titus said.

Billy shrugged.

Thanks? He thought, silently.

I knew you weren't going to do it, Dude said. *One of us had to take responsibility.*

"It would be helpful if we knew what those ships were capable of," Jane said.

I can help explain, if you think you can translate, Dude said.

"I can talk us through it," Billy said.

"Good," Jane said.

"Also, I met Horizon out there!" Billy said.

"Horizon as in the other Luminae guy who used to be on Doc's team?" Titus said.

"Yeah!" Billy said. "He's kind of nuts. Long story."

Jane smiled and touched his shoulder.

"It's good to have you back," she said. "We thought we lost you."

"Really?" Billy said.

"I had complete faith you'd make it back," Titus said.

"Thanks," he said.

"Just kidding—totally thought the aliens got you," the werewolf said, bursting into laughter. He stood up and tossed a pile of clothes onto the bed. "We'll let you get back on your feet."

Billy nodded in thanks and watched his friends shuffle out of the room. The dog stayed with him, curled up at his side. Billy scratched behind his ear.

"Hey Billy," Jane said, standing by the door after Titus and Bedlam had left.

"Yeah?"

"What are the chances they'll talk with us?" she asked. "Do you think we can find a peaceful solution?"

Billy grimaced and looked at the dog. He thought about the relentlessness of the larval creatures that had attacked him near the moon; of the brutality of the attack fighters Suresh had saved him from.

"I don't think so," he said. Nerves crept through his guts. He felt terrible saying it out loud—especially to Jane—who Billy knew abhorred destruction when a better solution could be found. "I'm sorry."

She dipped her chin, acknowledging what he said.

"I thought so," she said. "We'll be in the command center when you're feeling up to it."

"Okay," Billy said. He watched her leave and the door closing behind her.

What do you think, Dude? Has anyone ever made peace with these things? He thought.

Billy Case, before we met the Nemesis, my people were harbingers of peace. In the history of our existence we parlayed for peace and for hundreds of years tried to make them stop. We never made war.

So that's a 'no', Billy thought soberly.

One can always try again, Dude said. *If one is optimistic.*

CHAPTER 35:
I'D LIKE TO TRY

Kate walked onto the landing platform the Indestructibles used as their aerial front door to the Tower. Jane stood alone near the edge and looked out across the cityscape. Her hair flamed in the early morning sunlight, at odds with the ruined uniform she hadn't bothered changing out of and her borrowed sweatpants. Still, Kate thought, while standing there in her bare feet and pajamas, she looked more like a superhero than any of the rest of them.

"You look like you're thinking bad thoughts," Kate said.

Weariness settled into the corners of Jane's eyes.

"I have a stupid idea. Nobody's going to like it," Jane said.

"You'll do it anyway," Kate said.

"Will I?"

"Yes," Kate said. "Whatever it is, you should do it."

"You don't even know what it is."

"Your worst decisions are better than our *best* decisions," Kate said.

"I want to try to talk to them," Jane said. "I want to find a solution that doesn't involve us going to war."

"That's a terrible idea," Kate said.

"I know."

"Jane, as far as we know, they have no interest in talking. They're just looking at our planet as a meal."

"I know," Jane repeated. "It seems so wasteful. People will die."

Kate paused for a moment thinking, then inhaled sharply. "You know what I would do?" she said.

Jane raised an eyebrow. "Do I want to?"

"I wouldn't offer them peace," Kate said. "I'd walk in and state their terms for surrender."

"And you said my idea was terrible," Jane said.

"No," Kate said, holding up a finger. "To ask for peace is to appear weak. But if you were to walk in and tell them that going to war with us is the worst possible thing they could do—if you said in no uncertain terms that we will be the end of them if they try…"

"You're telling me I should bluff," Jane said.

Kate's mouth broke into a grin.

"It's not bluffing if you believe it," Kate said.

"You're really insane, aren't you?" Jane said.

Kate shrugged and handed Jane a tablet she'd been holding. On the screen was a map.

"What's this?" Jane said.

"Remember how Titus told us another signal was sent during our fight with those ships yesterday?"

Jane rubbed her eyes, the gesture almost an exact replica of Doc's habit when he was tired.

"That was yesterday?" she said. "Yeah, I remember."

"Neal snagged it. It took him time to decode it, but he figured things out," Kate said.

"Coordinates," Jane said.

Kate gestured to the screen.

"Something is there," Kate said. "Has to be."

"We should go check it out," Jane said.

Kate shook her head. "Let me go in quiet," she said. "Maybe we can catch them by surprise."

Jane gave her an indignant look.

"Are you saying Emily and I aren't quiet?"

"Your hair's on fire."

"I'm kidding," Jane said. "Okay. Yeah. Not alone though?"

"I'll bring Titus," Kate said.

"And Bedlam."

Kate could tell Jane expected her to protest, but it made sense—

if things went poorly, it'd be good to have the extra pair of fighting hands available.

"Sure. If she's willing," Kate said. "I'd like to leave immediately."

Jane returned her gaze to the City.

"Billy says they're less than a week away," she said. "Sooner is better."

Jane handed the tablet back to Kate and wrinkled her nose.

"I really feel like I have no idea what we're doing," Jane said. "Do you know where Doc went?"

"I saw Emily. She said he went to get us some help," Kate said.

"Help," Jane said. "Who's left to call?"

Kate shrugged. She turned to leave, but stopped herself.

"Don't go flying off to try to be an ambassador for the entire planet without speaking with him first," Kate said.

"Doc'll say no," Jane said. "You think it's a stupid idea?"

Kate pursed her lips and looked away.

"At this point, all that remain are stupid ideas," she said. "Just be careful."

"You too."

CHAPTER 36:
WHERE WE COME FROM

illy couldn't tell if Dude's powers helped him recover faster from his injuries or if he was just incredibly bored, but it didn't take long for him to drag himself out of bed and go wandering. The clothes Titus left him were ridiculously comfortable after having spent several days in his uniform.

"No wonder he wears yoga pants and a hoodie all the time," Billy said.

We can always change our uniform choice, Dude said. *You were the one who wanted to look like a comic book character.*

Billy shuffled down the hallway, his legs unexpectedly stiff and uncertain. Confused at first, until he realized he hadn't walked for several days. His limbs weren't used to bearing his own weight. His powers righted his internal compass and strengthened his balance.

"Thanks, Dude," he said, knowing the alien was working to get him back to a hundred percent as each new little weird problem arose.

This is what we do, Dude said. *When my previous hosts and I traveled between worlds, I'd need to help them adjust for different gravity or atmosphere so they can breathe. Let me do my job.*

"I appreciate it," Billy said.

I don't think you've ever said that before, Dude said.

"Don't get used to it," Billy said.

Billy stopped by one of the other quasi-hospital rooms, somewhat amazed how little time they'd spent in this part of the

Tower. The interior of the place was so irrationally big, he thought. There were days he was convinced it was twice as large inside than out.

He peeked into a room and saw Seng, the other Luminae host, sitting on the bed, eyes closed as if asleep.

Then Billy edged out quietly, afraid he'd wake him.

"Come back, young one," Seng said in a strangely echoing voice. Billy wondered if that was the way his voice box was designed, or if the echo was some side effect of having his own Luminae translate his words into English for him.

"Didn't want to disturb you," Billy said.

"It's never a disturbance to speak with one of my brothers," the alien said. He opened his eyes and gestured for Billy to come forward.

"I'm... glad you made it," Billy said. "I was worried the crash killed you."

"I'm sure you've noticed we're a little more difficult to kill than most," Seng said. "You went to meet the Nemesis fleet. Tell me what you saw."

Billy described the dark, bug-like ships, the chase, the encounter with Suresh.

"So our other brother still lives," Seng said. "He no longer speaks to any of us."

"Did he talk to you before?" Billy said. "I've never had a conversation with another one of our kind."

"Sometimes we leave our worlds, the ones we're supposed to protect," Seng said. "He's not the first of us to give up hope. Believe it or not, your species is not the first to drive a Luminae to despair."

"We seem to be pretty good in that role," Billy said.

Seng shrugged.

"I haven't been here long," he said. "So I can't say. But usually when we have to move on—whether the world is destroyed or it simply can't be saved—we do reach out. Your Luminae wouldn't have needed to talk to his brothers if he felt secure here."

I did feel we were secure, Dude said. *I'm unhappy with myself for not anticipating this invasion sooner.*

183

Billy mentioned his encounter with the egg-thing near the moon, describing the fight and how he escaped. "What was that thing?"

"Sometimes, the Nemesis identify a world to consume and then send scouts. These scouts often bring eggs. The first round of warriors for the battle ahead," Seng said.

"Did I… I mean, were they babies? They hatched in front of me. Did I kill a bunch of babies?"

Seng shook his head. The human gesture seemed creepy and out of place on him.

"You shouldn't feel guilty about anything you do to defend your home, but you're young, and you haven't lost a world yet," Seng said. "So I understand. But the… you call them parasites?"

"The grabby things. Yeah."

"The parasites are an extension of the consciousness of the mind-ship," Seng said. "To kill one is…"

Seng held out his hand and wiggled his fingers.

"To chop off a digit. You aren't ending a life. You're simply maiming a threat."

"Not super reassuring," Billy said.

"You chop off a finger from a monster who can regrow its hand whenever it wants to," Seng said.

"That's disgusting," Billy said.

Seng shrugged again.

"I apologize for my lack of manners. I don't know your language customs. My companion can only translate my words for me," Seng said.

Billy threw up his hands. "No need to apologize. I've heard worse," he said.

Billy peered at the alien's face, saw the old scars there, wounds that his Luminae hadn't been able to heal.

"You came here to warn us," Billy said. "But where were you before? What happened?"

Seng remained silent for a long moment, almost as if he hadn't heard Billy's question. Billy could tell, that the alien was having a conversation with his own symbiote. Were they getting their stories straight? Figuring out a lie? Determining their own truth?

"We couldn't save my home world," Seng said finally. "We did our best. But the Nemesis proved to be too much."

Billy felt his chest constrict, a cold fear seeped up the back of his neck and down his limbs.

"They destroyed your world," he said.

Seng's voice grew quiet as he spoke next. Sometimes, he paused to say things in another language, some dialect that sounded like water rushing over sand.

"Our world was just the kind they like best," Seng said. "An ocean world. A well cared for world. The Nemesis like blue worlds. Ones teaming with life for them to consume."

"You fought back?" Billy said.

"We tried," Seng said. "But… it was never a military world. And not aimed toward the stars. We tried to warn them. That we were too happy. Too complacent. Your world, is it an angry place?"

Billy almost laughed. He would have cracked if his mind wasn't reeling from the image of an entire world eaten alive by that fleet he'd seen.

"We've got some anger issues," Billy said instead.

"Good," Seng said. "I thought our hope would have saved us, but I think it only made us unprepared. Perhaps your world will be able to harness your anger. If you can use it like a weapon…"

"Most times we use it on each other," Billy admitted. "We're good at that."

Seng made a soft clicking noise.

Dude told Billy that the noise was equivalent to a sigh.

"Maybe this is just another world that deserves to be ended," Seng said.

"You believe that?" Billy said.

Seng turned his eyes to the door of his room and looked out into the hallway.

"I have met your allies," Seng said.

"They're a little odd," Billy said.

"But they are… you have something we lacked," Seng said.

"Crazy people in costumes?"

"Heroes," Seng said. "My brother and I stood alone against the fleet. We did our best. But my people weren't ready. We had no heroes."

Billy thought about Jane's question. If the Nemesis fleet could be reasoned with. The hero who wanted peace. He felt a gnawing in his stomach, acid roiled inside. Poor Jane, he thought. Someday I want her to be right. Someday I'd like her to discover that finer world she's always searching for. It won't be this time, will it Dude?

Thousands of years, Billy Case, Dude said. *We have tried. I promise you. We have tried.*

"Well, heroes we got," Billy said. "You think we should fight?"

"I think you should," Seng said. "And I will join you."

Billy almost smiled, but then realized he needed one more answer.

"What happened to your brother, Seng?" he asked.

"He gave his life to buy me time," Seng said. "So that I could find the next world, and give them a chance."

"He must've been pretty brave," Billy said.

"The bravest ever known," Seng said. "I'll battle with you, but I fight for him."

CHAPTER 37:
A PART OF THE MACHINE

The chieftain walked slowly through a long corridor—a vein in the mothership of the fleet—down dark, fibrous walls lit from within by a naturally occurring, pale red glow. For some reason the weight of the parasite on his chest felt heavier today. Perhaps his body was finally breaking down, the end was in sight and this farce of a life was almost over.

That parasite connected him to the fleet and so he felt the movement of the other ships around them. The fighter craft, like wasps, almost able to think for themselves, acted as living drones to guard the mind-ship. The silent seed-ships moved at the behest and command of the mothership, where the Council of Thought resided. The chieftain had seen the council a few times, withered bodies halfway between tree trunk and corpse, stood suspended in the dark, manipulating the fleet from afar. He'd never witnessed one of the council move, though he'd watched others of their kind. The final stage of the species' evolution constituted a life cycle that took them from immobile plant thing to mummified telepathic god, shuffling around in the dark, commandeering their vessels of war.

The chieftain used to wonder how these creatures functioned, how they progressed from birth to death. They didn't seem to die, he noted. Just remained part of the machine, part of the monster, always hungry, consistently moving forward. He used to care. Not anymore. The hum of the ship's heartbeat numbed and hypnotized him—if not literally at least figuratively—and made the passage of time rhythmic and droning, on and on as the catapulted into the endless black.

The strange creatures also saddled with the multi-legged parasites once made him anxious. They made no sense, their alien biology illogical and endlessly weird. The creatures with two faces, the asymmetrical ones who seemed to go in three directions at once, the winged beasts who had, when first brought onboard, seemed so constricted, so panicked to be without an open sky.

Such was life here on the brain-ship, the central nervous system of the fleet. The fleet itself loomed as one beast. The brain-ship its head, the seed-ships its hands that would reach down and tear open this new world with hungry fingers, the warships acting as mighty legs thundering forward toward their next victim, and the buzzing outriders like little sharp teeth and claws for gutting their enemies.

He could almost respect it, if not for what it did to him, to his people, to the world he never appreciated until it was gone. His world was for conquering, the chieftain thought. Fighting petty wars—stupid mortal barbarians killing each other—over a rock in space. But it was all we knew, and everything we had, and we were too selfish and violent to realize we were wasting what little time remained. There was no defeating this fleet. Seed-ships plunged into the soil of his home world like a knife into sand, changing and tormenting everything they touched, dark sorcery about to bring the apocalypse. He could not regret losing that war. There is always someone stronger than you are, faster, willing to commit atrocities you are not.

But not taking advantage of the time we had, the chieftain thought, that is what I regret. Because we believed we had all the time in the world. Until our world disappeared.

He continued to walk aimlessly through the veins of the brain-ship, restless and lonely. He dreamed of home, of the dead, of everything he loved and would never see again.

CHAPTER 38:
A CHAMBER FULL OF THE DEAD

This feels terribly familiar," Titus said softly over Kate's shoulder. They looked at the low-slung building in front of them, surrounded by electrified fences and barbed wire. The structure itself wasn't enormous, but they knew from past experience that any one they needed to break into had a decent chance of being bigger on the inside.

It didn't appear well-guarded. Armed men patrolled, but compared to super-powered symbiotic aliens, humans with guns didn't seem like quite as much of a barrier.

"Do we knock on the front door?" Bedlam said.

Hunkered down in a wooded area just beyond the fence, a twenty-five-foot clearing stood between the trio and the fence itself. The one gate they'd spotted had the most security: four guards and too much light for stealth.

"I can make that jump," Titus said.

"That's a fifteen-foot fence," Kate said. "You sure?"

Titus grinned. It pained Kate to realize that the best adjective for his smile at that moment was, in fact, wolfish. Emily would gloat about that.

"We've cleared higher," he said. "I can do it with you on my back."

Bedlam raised an eyebrow.

Kate shot her a dirty look.

"Not saying a thing," Bedlam said. "I can clear that height too,

189

though. I just need a running start."

"We'll go over first and knock out the patrol coming around," Kate said. "Then you follow."

Bedlam nodded and shimmied to the edge of the clearing. Titus exhaled and smoothly transformed from human to werewolf, his silvery fur luminous in the dark. He looked at Kate with those strange yellow eyes. She always wondered how close to the surface he was when he transformed, and how much the monster was in control. Titus crouched down so Kate could hop onto his back. Gripping his torso with her legs, she threw one arm over his shoulder, leaving her other hand free in case she needed it.

With surprising grace, Titus ran forward, his loping gait covered the distance of the clearing in two or three strides. She felt his entire core tighten as he leapt into the air, easily soaring over the electrified fence. They landed without a sound on the other side, just the soft crush of claws through dirt and a feint 'huff' as the werewolf exhaled. Like a flawless machine, Kate and Titus went to work, Kate slid from his back and ran into the dark so she could sneak up behind the patrol they knew would soon pass by. Titus jumped again, this time batting at a tall light, bathing the area in shadows when the bulb softly broke.

Kate rushed up behind the two guards on patrol as they came around the edge of the building. Both had tensed when they saw the light had been extinguished. Kate punched him with one of her taser-knuckle devices and the first man had no idea what hit him. She pounced on the second man and wrapped an arm around his neck before pulling him to the ground until he passed out. Both men subdued, Titus appeared beside her and together they dragged the guards along the ground and further into the shadows.

A less graceful thump trembled though the dirt.

Kate saw Bedlam on one knee, looking over at her sheepishly. Sparks flew from the section of the fence she jumped over.

"I tripped," she said, her eyes full of wild energy.

Kate shook her head and pointed toward the main building inside the compound. All three ran toward it. Titus and Bedlam made clear moves to kick in the closest door, but Kate waved them off, and quickly examined the digital lock on the door. She produced a security key card she'd taken from the guard she'd knocked out.

"Kicking it in would've been more fun," Bedlam said.

Kate shrugged and zipped the card through the scanner. The door unlocked with a metallic clunk. Bedlam pushed it open.

Inside, the building consisted of a wide-open space, bathed in soft blue-green light. Large crates obscured their view of the main area. Titus leapt up on top of the crates, as always moving with deceptive grace. Kate walked left into the dark, Bedlam right. Kate slid along the crates until she found a spot where she could slip between them easily to see what might be waiting.

What she found nearly made her heart stop.

Two long horizontal rows of glass tubes, each large enough to hold an adult human, were lined up down the center of the building. Each was hooked up to dozens of monitors. The machines presented no immediate indication what purpose they served. Lights blinked in red, green, and blue. Lit from within by ghostly blue light, the tubes themselves were filled with dense fluid, thicker than water. A human body floated still and unmoving in each. Most had been modified in some way, limbs or eyes or hands, some sort of robotic addition or, in even stranger cases, inhuman parts seemingly surgically attached where ordinary limbs or organs once resided.

Kate stepped out from behind the crates and walked up to the nearest tube. A young man, eyes open, stared blankly ahead. She watched his chest and saw no movement, no hint of breathing.

"I'm going to kill them," Bedlam said softly as she, too, emerged from the shadows.

Kate glanced up at the rafters and looked for Titus in the dark, but she couldn't see him. "You know what this is?" she said.

"I should," Bedlam said. "I was in one for six months."

Kate locked eyes with Bedlam.

The cyborg turned away and walked up to one of the glass chambers in the other row, this one containing a teen-aged girl.

"This is how they stored me, while they were grafting on all these parts," Bedlam said. "It felt like a dream."

She looked back over her shoulder at Kate.

"I didn't know if it was a hallucination or a nightmare," she said. "The light, the cold… it's so cold inside there."

"Does this mean these kids are alive?" Kate said. She examined the machinery attached to the cylinders, trying to find any indication of vital signs or status.

"They're not breathing," Bedlam said. She placed one cyborg hand against the glass, her metal fingers clinking as they touched it. "I remember breathing. It's like… breathing Jell-O. Too thick, slow moving, it fills up your lungs. I remember…"

"And I remember you," a voice said from the darkness.

Kate stepped back, took shelter behind one of the tubes, hoping to find the source of the voice.

A man emerged from the darkness, well-kept, dressed in a dark suit, his collar loosened. He stood standing on a landing at the top of a flight of stairs. Too far way for Kate to reach, out of range of her throwing weapons. He looked tired, feverish. "You were the one who survived. Our great success."

"Who the hell are you?" Bedlam said, standing her ground in the middle of the warehouse-like chamber.

The man shot them a pristine white smile.

"I am… Well, I suppose I was one of the Children of the Elder Star," the man said. He was leaning on something, Kate saw. A cane? She couldn't make it out in the shadows.

"Past-tense?" Kate yelled from her hiding spot. "We heard about some dissension in the ranks."

"There's always been dissension. That's what the Children are, con artists pretending to be a billion-dollar enterprise pretending to be cultists," he said. "Liars. All of them. Except me and my brothers. We were the true believers."

"You believed something was coming from the stars," Kate said.

"We knew," the man said. "Do you know how difficult it was to play along with all their petty earthly scheming when we realized the world was coming to an end? Who cares about money and influence when your planet's demise is set to an egg timer?"

"You made us," Bedlam said.

"Made you?" the man said. Kate stole a glance at him. He hadn't moved from his perch, but he also appeared alone. No backup, and no parasite on his chest. Somehow that made it worse, Kate thought—the others they'd fought had been enslaved by the parasitic creatures. This man seemed to be betraying their planet entirely voluntarily.

"You know, we had nothing to do with you at first," he said. "One of the others thought building weapons out of half-dead teenagers posed as a good investment. They thought we'd get better PR if we had doomsday weapons."

"But you wanted us to be..." Bedlam began.

"Oh, we'd still like you to be host bodies," the man said. "But beggars can't be choosers. If the ones who lived couldn't be controlled, well..."

He made a grand gesture towards the rows of seemingly dead people in their tubes.

"After you escaped we realized that we could enhance cadavers just as easily," he said. "More so, because they wouldn't think for themselves and escape. So we took our leftover dead and turned them into a little squadron of hosts for our loving gods when they arrive."

"You what?" Bedlam said.

"Bargaining chips," the man said. "Do you know what they do to worlds? The only way to survive is to make yourself useful in anticipation of their arrival. To sell your soul to them. Otherwise you're just food in the machine."

"And you think you can bargain your life with... these poor kids?" Bedlam said.

"We wanted a place in the machine," the man said. "They keep the strong ones. The ones they can use. And everything else is just dust and food. You would have been a great gift, Bedlam. You and the others. It's so funny to think how small-minded my colleagues were. You were just a weapon to them. Something to break things. My brothers and I knew you weren't a sledgehammer. You were a gift."

Kate mulled her arsenal over in her mind. Smoke bombs, throwing tasers, the gauntlets. A grappling hook. Little paralytic darts she could use to take him out if she were able to get close enough. She glanced around the room again, wondering where Titus went to.

"You did this to me," Bedlam said, fury growing in her voice.

"Oh come now. You were practically a corpse," the man said. "I've read your file. Did you want to live as half a person? Is that the life you wanted? We made you better!"

"I should have had a choice," Bedlam said.

"So ungrateful," the man said. "Then again your file did say you were a head case."

Bedlam took a step forward.

"Uh-uh," The man said. He raised the thing he'd been leaning on—not a cane, Kate realized, a weapon of some kind—and pointed it at Bedlam. "Trust me. We built you. We know what it takes to shut you down."

Kate made a move, but the man shouted her name.

"Dancer! We know all about you too," he said. "You might be ruthless enough to let me kill your little robot friend in order to get to me. We've always admired that about you. The cutthroat one in that little group of yours. But I'm willing to take the shot. It's up to you what happens next."

"It's up to me," Bedlam said.

Kate heard the control in her tone cracking.

"I'm tired of other people deciding if I live or die."

"Too bad," the man said playfully. "Don't worry, this machine will only destroy your brain. You'll be added to the bodies we offer when they arrive."

The man started to pull the trigger, but he never got to take the shot. Three hundred pounds of werewolf dropped from the rafters onto him, a mass of silver brutality, claws flashed and mouth roared when it tore the weapon from the suited man's grasp.

"Alive, Titus!" Kate yelled, running out from behind her hiding place.

Titus raised the man into the air, held him by both arms, and growled in his face, fangs as long as knives flashed in the blue light of the chamber.

Doors on both sides of the room slammed open. Guards poured

in. Before anyone could say a word, they opened fire with short, angry machine guns. Kate winced. She saw more than one bullet hit Titus' body, but knew he'd recover. When she watched the explosion of blood tear through the mystery man's body though, she knew he was gone. Stray bullets riddled his frame. Titus roared again, then tossed the limp mystery man aside. He pounced onto the nearest group of guards. Kate couldn't see what happened next in the shadows, but the screams of strangers told her Titus was winning.

She threw a smoke grenade at the second set of guards, watching as it burst against an armored chest. She closed her eyes and threw another device, a flash bang, blinding them. In seconds she was kicking knees until they bent in the wrong direction, snapping an elbow over her shoulder, feeling a nose crumple beneath her palm.

And then there was no noise but the hum of machinery and moans of broken men.

The smoke cleared and Kate let her eyes adjust. Bedlam still stood in the center of the room, arms hanging at her side, her chrome cyborg parts and bright orange hair glowing in the blue light.

"This could've been me," she said to herself.

Titus dropped down from the second level, hobbling a bit, blood stained his fur. Kate knew he would wait to transform back. He healed faster as a monster than he did as a human.

"If I hadn't pulled through. They would've stuck me in one of these jars and just kept me," Bedlam said. "Just in case they needed spare parts."

Bedlam spun in a slow, deliberate circle, taking in the entire room, looking at each of the tubes one by one.

"We have to destroy them, don't we?" she said.

"If they're still alive, we could save them," Kate said.

Bedlam found a control console between two of the center tubes. She touched a few keys and a screen lit up. Kate joined her at the terminal. Hospital-style monitors showed the vital signs of the bodies. Nothing but temperatures and electrical currents. No signs of life. No heartbeats. No blood pressure.

"This should have been me," Bedlam said.

"It's too late to change that," Kate said. "So you can either quit or make the best of what you have."

Bedlam glared at her but said nothing.

"Titus, did you see a generator anywhere from above," Kate said softly.

Bedlam connected eyes with her and nodded gently.

Titus pointed toward the back wall and limped over. Kate and Bedlam followed him. Against the back wall stood a machine, tall and vaguely designed, humming louder than anything else in the room.

Kate and Titus stepped back.

Bedlam walked up to it. She paused, almost as if in prayer. And then she punched the generator. Again and again, she slammed her cyborg fists, tearing the guts from it, sending sparks and parts flying. She screamed, primal pain and anguish, something dark and lonely and terrifying and scared. Titus still in werewolf form, turned his back to let her rage. He knew also what that feral energy felt like.

Kate simply watched the destruction, the loss of control, the way each strike was like a heartbeat and each piece torn away a shard of that same heart.

One by one, the tubes of blue light flickered and winked out. They were left alone in the dark. Kate felt Titus' hand, now human, then his arm, grip hers. She wanted to pull away, but she let him take her hand and held on tightly herself. They left Bedlam to sob in the darkness for as long as she needed. To mourn for the dead, and to mourn for herself.

CHAPTER 39: BOOKS OF SECRETS

Doc Silence stood hunched over his desk, piles of books, some written in languages older than humanity itself, opened haphazardly and spilled on top of each other. They included books of magic and secrets, tomes written by wise men and mad ones, by gods and monsters, by wizards and priests.

In these books, Doc once thought, were the answers to everything. But tonight, they seemed to be just stacks of paper. Kindling for a world on the edge of burning.

He picked up a small book, bound in blue, its pages so papery thin as to appear made of mist. He set this aside in favor of a massive tome, so big it required both hands to lift safely. This one he'd stolen from a demon king, in another world, when Doc behaved bravely, yet stupidly and did foolish things without worrying who they might hurt.

None of them revealed the secrets he wanted. None of them offered the answers he sought.

Well, he thought. You don't possess all the books in the universe. The answer might be out there in some other wizard's library. Or maybe there just wasn't an answer this time. No secret spell, no weapon to turn toward the sky and save them.

He wondered if there had been beings like him living on the other worlds the Nemesis fleet had destroyed. Magicians who waved their fingers at the sky and caused things to change. Men these aliens defeated simply through relentless force. Magic was not Earth's alone, he knew. It weaved its web across all things.

"Haven't seen you hit the books in a long time." Jane stood in the doorway to Doc's suite. She leaned against the frame. Out of her costume, she wore the sort of clothes she'd first dressed in when she arrived in the Tower, jeans and a plain white tee under a checkered shirt, two sizes too big, old canvas sneakers on her feet. She'd pulled her hair back into a ponytail, but it still glowed with the reddish light of a low flame.

"Haven't had to," Doc said.

"Thought you knew everything."

"Fate has a way of reminding you that you can't possibly know everything," Doc said. He set the book down and sat on the edge of his desk, folding his arms across his chest. Jane stared at his arms, and Doc remembered how rarely she saw the mystical tattoos that covered most of his upper body. His long coat hung over the back of a chair, leaving his arms bare from his short sleeves down.

"What are you looking for?" she asked.

"Answers," Doc said. "I can't help wondering if there's a spell, some big bang I can conjure to stop them. All these books, spells, theories, and it just feels like a collection of parlor tricks when I really need something more powerful."

"You got us," Jane said. "How much more powerful you need?"

"Something potent enough so I don't have to take you up there with me," Doc said.

Jane tucked her hands in her pockets, bounced the heel of her right shoe against the toe of her left rhythmically. She didn't look like a hero then, in the dim light, her eyes cast to the floor. She looked young and like someone who deserved a chance to grow up normal and happy. Doc wondered if he'd stolen that from her, if bringing her to the Tower eliminated her chances at living an ordinary life. She was born extraordinary. Fate had something in store for her from the moment she took her first breath.

That isn't fair, Doc thought. It's a cruel and selfish world that thrusts so much power and responsibility on someone so young. We did our best, first the Hawkins and then Doc himself, to give Jane a chance to be happy. But people like her never stood a chance. They would always and forever be asked to place the weight of the world on their shoulders so others wouldn't have to.

Doc had loved in his life. Family, friends, partners. Despite living in the darkness and looking up at the world from the most shadowy of places, he had always loved. But there was no living being he cared more about in his entire strange and inconsistent life. Everything good Doc had in him he'd given to make sure Jane grew up to be a hero. *If I've done anything right in this world*, he pondered, *it is that I haven't failed her yet.*

"What are you looking at?" Jane asked.

"Just thinking."

"About?"

"I'm going to have to borrow a few more books," he said and scooped up his jacket from the back of the chair.

"You're going to her, aren't you?" Jane said.

"Natasha has books I don't," he said.

Jane gave a disapproving glare.

"Don't make any deals with the devil," she said.

Doc waved his hand dismissively.

"I gave up dealing with devils years ago," Doc said. "Bad for your health."

Then they shared a short, honest, comfortable laugh. They really hadn't laughed much in recent months, Doc thought. They'd seen too many dark things, been through too much.

"Hey," Jane said.

"What?" Doc said.

Jane threw her arms around him in a hug. She radiated warmth, like stone on a sunny day. The solar-powered girl. Doc hugged her back; guilt gnawed at his belly. The worst of things always came down to them, he knew. The others had faced down terrible threats, but in the end, there was so much Jane and Doc did to protect their friends and each other, to keep the monsters at bay. He brought them all together, he taught them to save the world, but even now, even knowing and trusting his protégés, even with all his faith in them, there was nothing he wouldn't do to save them.

"We're all going to come back from this," Jane said.

"Yeah," Doc said. He knew his tone was unconvincing.

"Fine," Jane said. "I'll be optimistic for both of us. That's always been my job, hasn't it?"

CHAPTER 40:
LET'S NOT LEAD WITH THAT

Billy almost had a chance to knock on the door to Emily's room but, in spite of the fact she was wearing enormous headphones and being overly engrossed in something on the computer, she spoke up.

"I know you're there, Billy Case," she said. "Since when do you knock?"

He shrugged and entered the room. Surprisingly spare for a geek culture hoarder like Emily, but like all the Indestructibles, she tended to keep truly personal effects elsewhere. All of them were, in some way, afraid the base would someday be attacked and didn't want too much of their personal lives on display here. Billy visited Emily's room back at her mother's house. She was certainly not, by nature, this tidy.

He flopped down on the bed and looked up at the ceiling.

"Things going that well, sunshine?" Emily said.

"I leave for a little while and I find out we've been secretly invaded for what, years? You guys almost die a few times, and now I get to be the harbinger of death when I try to describe just how bad the fleet was when I found it," Billy said. "Yeah, things are going south."

Emily spun around in the chair and tossed her earphones on a desk.

"So you met the other guy? Horizon?"

"Met, yeah. Can't say we had much time to talk," Billy said. "I'm halfway between impressed because he didn't really abandon Earth and terrified because he seems like he kind of had a massive mental breakdown and went to become a hermit out near Jupiter."

"But," Emily said, holding up a finger. "You got to see Jupiter."

"Saturn, actually," Billy said. "We zipped past the other planets on the way there. Dude wouldn't let me sightsee."

We did, in fact, have more important things to do, Dude said.

"I know," Billy said.

"Was that to me or him?" Emily said.

"Him," Billy said.

"But right. You saw Saturn. The planet. How was that?"

"Amazing," Billy said.

"I knew it would be!" Emily said, palpable glee in her voice.

"The whole thing made me feel so… insignificant. The universe is so big, Em. We're these little specks of dust and we think we're the center of the universe but we're just…"

"What was the best part?" Emily said.

"The rings of Saturn," Billy said. "Before the fleet spotted me and I almost died. The rings were the most beautiful thing I've ever seen."

Emily shot him a dirty look.

"What, are you seriously fishing for a compliment right now?"

"I'm just busting on you," she said, laughing. "If we survive this, can we go out there? I don't care how."

"I don't know. I have no idea how we'd get you out there," Billy said. "Dude lets me not need to breathe in space. You'd need… y'know. Help."

We'll find a way, Dude said softly.

"Really?" Billy said.

You need to actually survive the coming invasion, but if we all do, we'll figure it out.

"Is Dude offering to be our tour guide?" Emily said.

"Something like that," Billy said. "I think he's incentivizing us to survive."

"All right then, let's not die," Emily said. "Sidebar: I think we need to alert the public."

"That sounds like a terrible, terrible idea."

"Not if we craft an appropriate press release," Emily said. "Like, for instance, how would you describe the fleet?"

"It's this nightmarish green-black thing, like living space ships. They're halfway between bugs and plants and they might be immortal. Nothing about them makes sense in a human, logical way. You look and then it's hard to remember what you saw because they don't seem real."

"That sounds positively Lovecraftian," Emily said.

"Let's not lead with that in the press release," Billy said. He put his hands out in front of him as if laying out a headline on a newspaper page. "Breaking News: Lovecraftian alien body snatchers to invade Earth, film at eleven."

"Can we call them Shoggoths?"

"Seriously?"

"Gugs?"

"Now you're just making words up," Billy said.

"Trust me, these are the least weird names in Lovecraft stories," Emily said. "Changing gears, what about slitheens?"

"What?"

"Oods? Mindflayers?"

"How about we just call them aliens," Billy said.

"Fine, but that's boring," Emily said. "We have a chance to come up with something original. The gargleflargs. The poofniddles. The vormaghasts."

"Are you seriously just throwing syllables together and hoping they stick?" Billy asked.

"I am 'writing,'" she said. "Don't stifle my creativity, Billy Case."

He exhaled and sat up abruptly.

"Who would we tell, anyway? Can't trust the media not to blow this out of proportion," he said.

"We're being invaded by aliens," Emily said. "I believe it is literally impossible to blow this out of proportion."

"But still," Billy said. "Full-blown panic in the streets won't help."

"Might be fun, though," Emily said.

"Panic in the streets is fun?" Billy said.

Emily shrugged insolently.

"You're such an anarchist," Billy said.

"But you missed me when I was gone," Emily said.

"Sure did."

"Glad you didn't die in space, Billy Case," Emily said.

"Me too," Billy said. "Cause now I can die on Earth instead."

"It's that bad up there, huh," Emily said, spinning her desk chair back and forth aimlessly, then letting herself spin all the way around one time.

He shook his head in silence.

CHAPTER 41:
WE'RE KILLING OURSELVES

Jane waited in the landing bay for the returning Kate and company, watching as the trio climbed out of the little vehicle they'd used to run their most recent mission. If things hadn't been so dire—and if Kate hadn't stepped off the craft looking fit to murder someone—it would have been funny to see all three of them squeezed into one little flying machine, but they'd clearly been in a fight, and that alone swallowed up any humor Jane might have found in it all.

Kate stormed toward her, pulling her cowl down so it hung like a hood off the back of her uniform. She punched the nearest wall.

"Lunatics," Kate said, slamming it again. "Lunatics. We've got an alien invasion force and there are actual human beings willing to sell us out because they think these things are some kind of religion. Our own people. We're killing ourselves, Jane."

"What happened?" Jane asked.

Titus, as always looking worse for wear but simultaneously the least upset of the three, explained.

"Hosts," he said. "We found another one of the traitors of the Children of the Elder Star with a facility full of host-bodies for the aliens."

Kate slapped the wall a third time.

"How do we win when our own species seems incapable of not destroying itself voluntarily?" she said.

"Are you okay?" Jane said.

Covered in soot, Bedlam brought up the rear, small cuts evident on her face and the exposed skin of her arms. She had a sense of sadness to her. Something changed.

"Bedlam?" Jane said.

The cyborg shook her head. She walked over to the wall where Kate had been venting her frustrations and leaned against it, casting her eyes at her feet.

"Do we need to go back there?" Jane asked.

Kate, who was pacing back and forth, paused and said, "It's taken care of. But now I'm wondering how many more of these places exist. They're here building armies of host bodies for those parasite creatures to use."

"Were they... powered? Like us? If this was one of the members of the Children of the Elder Star..." Jane asked.

"They'd been modified, but they weren't actually alive," Titus said softly. "They were amplified bodies. Kept in some sort of suspended animation."

"So for our aliens to use a host body they don't even have to be living," Kate said.

"Do we know that for sure?" Jane said. After Kate gave her a frustrated shrug, she looked to Titus for confirmation.

"It may have just been an experiment," he said.

Kate ran her gloved hands through her hair and made a low, frustrated growling sound.

"I... I am a misanthrope on a good day, guys," she said. "You know this. I see something like this and I feel a little justified."

Kate stormed off, leaving the rest of the group behind. Titus and Jane exchanged a look; Titus nodded his head and then gestured for Jane to follow her down the hall. Assuming Titus knew who Kate needed to talk to more, Jane took his advice and ran to catch up.

"You okay?" Jane said.

Kate stopped walking; her shoulders slumped.

"I don't know how we beat this," Kate said. "I'm just a person. Just an ordinary person. I can't keep this up. Not against something like this."

"Yes you can," Jane said.

"No, I mean—we've fought monsters," Kate said. "We've fought evil people before. But we're what, six, seven people against... it's not the odds, Jane. It's the relentlessness. We keep hitting them and they don't stop."

Jane smiled.

"Well now you know what it's like to fight you," she said.

Kate glared at her like she'd said the most ridiculous thing in the world, but then she almost—almost—cracked a smile.

"It was tough on Bedlam," Kate said.

Jane frowned.

For Kate to say something about another person's emotional state was rare; it must have been truly awful for her to bring it up.

"How was it on the two of you, though?" Jane asked. "I can't remember the last time I've seen you this rattled."

Kate sighed and peeled off her fighting gloves, tucking them into her belt.

"I've always hated wasting my time. What we saw tonight," Kate said. "Could be a waste of our time."

Jane leaned against the wall, folding her arms across her chest.

"Why do you do all this, Kate?"

"What?" Kate asked.

"Why are you a hero?" Jane said. "You were doing this before any of us were. There on your own in leotard and painted-on mask fighting muggers months before Doc found you. Why?"

"To be better," Kate said.

"Why else."

"Because I didn't want anyone else to go through what I went through," Kate said.

Jane nodded.

"Has that changed?"

Kate didn't answer, and simply looked back at her silently.

"Do yourself a favor," Jane said. "Go down to the streets. Do what you do. Jump around on rooftops. Go watch the ballet. The Third Symphony of Gustav Mahler is playing at the City Performing Arts Center."

"You expect me to sit through a show," Kate said.

"It's the end of the world again," Jane said. "You should see one last ballet just in case."

Kate let out a soft grunting noise that might have been an assent to Jane's suggestion and started to walk away. She turned back.

"Thanks, Jane."

"This is what I'm here for," Jane said.

"No, it isn't," Kate said. "But thank you anyway."

* * *

Titus sat down next to Bedlam and allowed her to ignore him for a few minutes. She smelled like burnt electronics, his superhuman senses able to pick out the specific parts of the machine she'd torn apart, copper wiring and steel plates, circuit boards and solder.

"You want to talk about what happened?" he asked.

Bedlam refused to answer at first.

Titus didn't press. He leaned his head against the wall and closed his eyes.

"I don't know why I lived," Bedlam said finally.

Titus kept his eyes closed, listening to the strange and no longer completely human beating of her heart.

"After the accident. I was like them, I think. I should've been dead." She hesitated, took a deep breath and exhaled anxiously. "One of the scientists in the lab where they put me back together, I remember him talking to one of the others, and he said, he was amazed at the trauma the human body can endure," Bedlam said. "In some ways we're these fragile little flowers, yet in others, the trials and tribulations we can withstand… it's not fair. Not fair at all. Sometimes surviving is suffering."

"But you're alive, and you *are* extraordinary," Titus said.

"And I can't go out in public," Bedlam said. "But that's not what's bothering me. It's that… those people in the jars down there, those bodies. They got to leave. To die. And they left fair and square. Their turn on the ride is over."

Titus nodded and watched as Bedlam's face screwed up into a heartbreaking mask of sadness.

"They died. That's okay. That's how it works. And they weren't going to suffer anymore. They could rest. Because it was over."

"And those people wanted to bring them back," Titus said.

"Yes," Bedlam answered. "How dare they. How dare they drag those poor people back. What if they remembered how they died? What if they were trapped in there somehow, just, hurting and remembering?"

"It sounded like they were just corpses," Titus said. "Whatever it was inside them, whoever they were had long since gone. It is horrible, that they were being desecrated in that way, but I don't think they were still present."

"How do we know?" Bedlam said. "I was dead too for a few minutes. I came back. And I didn't want to."

"You didn't?"

Bedlam looked at her feet again, not answering. Finally she returned her gaze to Titus.

"You know what my last thought was? As the accident was happening? I was just happy to get off the ride. I was okay with what was taking place."

"And then you came back," Titus said.

"And I was angry. I've been so angry. I make the best of it, but…"

"You hide it well," Titus said.

"That's what people like me do, Titus," Bedlam said, a tiny smile flickering across her lips. "We cover it up really well."

"It won't help if I tell you we're glad you're here with us, will it?" he said.

Bedlam shook her head.

"It doesn't hurt to hear it," Bedlam said. "But you understand? Why it doesn't help?"

"I do," Titus said.

Bedlam studied his face.

"You've been there too, haven't you," Bedlam said. "Sad little werewolf."

"Sad little boy, but yeah," Titus said. "I've been there."

They both looked away, sitting in companionable quiet for a

while. Titus broke the silence.

"I don't know if it's ever going to offer real consolation or not, but they were dead, Bedlam. Those bodies. They were really and truly gone," he said.

"You know that?"

Titus tapped his nose with his finger.

"The downside to being a freak," he said. "I would have known if they were alive."

"That doesn't fix everything but... it makes it a little easier to take, I guess."

"Little victories, Bedlam," Titus said.

"I guess so," she said.

CHAPTER 42:
MAGICIANS AND THEIR BOOKS

oc walked up the path to the Lady's current home, a modernized castle she'd settled into on the Spanish coast. He was surprised she hadn't moved on already. She rarely stayed in one place long, flitting about this world and others as if on permanent vacation.

He knocked on the door, pleasantly surprised when, for the second time, Natasha answered it herself.

"Look who darkens my doorstep," she said. "Good morning, my little Doctor."

"You're still here."

"I like it," Natasha said. "And it's been a long time since I've liked it anywhere. I'd prefer to enjoy the feeling for a bit."

Leading him through the foyer into a sitting room, she gestured for him to take up a spot on one of the burgundy couches. Natasha sat across from him and folded her legs. She appeared to be a wealthy woman on vacation, linen pants, a soft white shirt, her hair slicked back as if she'd just been swimming. The apparent normalcy of it boggled Doc's mind.

"I can't get over this," he said.

"What's *this*?"

"You. Not trying to take over the world."

"I never wanted to take over the world, you know that," Natasha said. "I just prefer things my way."

"Well, it's nice to see you relaxed. Which makes my visit even worse."

"That sounds ominous," she said.

Natasha gestured with one hand and a tray with a teapot and two cups floated into the room. Despite all her outward affectations of normalcy, the Lady Natasha Grey was still one of the most powerful magicians on Earth. Of course she'd continue to use air elementals to do her cooking and cleaning for her. She'd have it no other way.

"What brings you to my humble hideaway?" the Lady said. "Since you've already warned me I won't like the reason, you might as well spill it."

"Ever have one of those moments when you realize just how strange your life has been?" Doc said, sipping his tea. Ginger lemon. Of course. "You get used to it after a while, the strangeness. We're magicians. We've seen just about all the weird things we could possibly imagine. And then you travel to your friend's home and say: there's an alien invasion happening and I need your help."

Natasha raised both eyebrows and held the cup in front of her mouth without taking a sip.

"Part of me is genuinely surprised that it hasn't happened before now," she said. "I'm caught off-guard."

"I wondered if you already knew," Doc said.

"I'm retired, darling. I don't even watch the evening news let alone gaze to the stars for approaching enemies," she said. "You and yours are, I assume, preparing to stop it."

"Trying," Doc said. "It's a lot. I'm worried."

"You're always worried. That's what you've always done," she said. "Doc Silence, magician and professional worrier."

"You really knew nothing about this?"

"You're thinking I had something to do with it?" Natasha asked.

"No, you've always steered clear of aliens," Doc said.

Natasha laughed.

"Speaking of surreal phrases," she said. "So why come to me?"

Doc rubbed his eyes behind his glasses, and squinted.

"I need something to cast at their fleet. A spell. Anything. I could use a hammer, Natasha," Doc said.

"All the knowledge at your disposal and you don't have what you're looking for?"

"I have a lot," Doc said. "I can do a great deal. But I just..."

"You've never really gone to war," Natasha said.

"No. No I haven't," Doc said.

Natasha set her cup aside, stood up, and motioned for Doc to follow her. They walked down one of the ancient stone corridors of the castle until the space opened up into a library, bookshelves rose two stories high, natural light spilled in through tall, stained glass windows.

"So this is where all the books in the world went," Doc said.

He approached the nearest stack and ran a finger along the spines of the books. They were in all languages, mortal and not, bound in fanciful skins. Some felt warm to the touch, as if alive, others ice cold. Some hummed with strange energy and still others called out to him, begging to be opened, malignant intelligence hiding inside.

"The most dangerous library in the world," Natasha said. "Or I like to think so. I've bargained for centuries to build this library."

"It's not really here, is it," Doc said.

Natasha spread her arms out.

"This room? It's here. But it's not *only* here," she said. "You know that old trick."

"I have a similar set up with my own library," he said.

Natasha reached up toward the ceiling and motioned with her hand. A single book slid from the top shelf and floated down to her gently. She caught it in both hands.

"Magicians and our books," she said, thumbing through the tome she'd pulled from the shelf. She let go and it drifted back up to its previous home. She reached for another and a second floated down. This time, she nodded as she opened it. Bound in gray leather, like an elephant's skin, its pages were dotted with red ink or blood.

Natasha handed the book to Doc. He flipped through it and saw fire spells and schematic designs for siege engines that could not possibly be built in this dimension.

"I took that from a battle mage in another plane where life is eternal war," she said. "I was there bartering other goods, because a place made of perpetual destruction rarely learns how to make things not related to warfare, so I marked up the price of my magic astronomically. I never had much use for a book like this, but I thought, it never hurts to know more about anything. So I took it."

"Just a book of hellmagic sitting on your shelf for a few decades," Doc said.

"Pretty much. I never turn down a book of magic, Doc. Somewhere on these shelves there's a book of cooking magic written by gnomes. I've never lifted a finger in the kitchen my entire long life but why not learn how to make cupcakes that help you travel between realities?"

"Must be delightful cupcakes," Doc said.

"I can't say. Never made them," she said.

Doc closed the book and turned it over in his hands.

"There's some dark things in there, Doctor Silence," Natasha said.

"You and I both realize I'm no stranger to dark magic," he said.

"Yes, but I know you've become averse to it," the Lady said. "I don't need to warn you that what you do with the contents of that book cannot be undone."

"Thanks for the warning," he said, tucking the book inside his coat.

"So you haven't asked me," Natasha said.

"What?" Doc said.

"If I'll help you."

Doc smiled at his own nemesis, oldest friend, and teacher, the one who brought out the best and worst in all that he did. At the end of the world, it always came down to the two of them. There was a unique kind of magic in that.

"I think you like this world," Doc said.

"Maybe I do," Natasha said, smiling.

"I suspect I don't have to ask you to help. I think if things get dark enough, you'd rather fight to save it than pack up your library and move to another world."

"I do have that option," Natasha said.

"I know."

"So do you," Natasha said. "Could come with me. We've done it before."

"In theory, yeah," Doc said. "But in practice…"

"In practice this is our home," Natasha said. "I may be ruthless, Doctor, but I do understand."

"So do I have to ask?" Doc said.

Natasha straightened his coat for him and touched his face.

"I make no promises," she said. "But I do have to admit… I like it here."

CHAPTER 43: THE INTERVIEW

Jane asked Broadstreet to find a place where they could talk without pedestrians walking by. They'd done okay in the past, quiet coffee shops or paths in the City's parks, but this time, she wanted to make sure no one could overhear them. Broadstreet seemed put off at first—not upset, just confused.

"Well the newsroom is out. It's a building layered in gossips," he said. "Best location I can think of is the rooftop of my apartment building."

"Your neighbors don't use it?" Jane asked.

"Not if I lock the door while I'm up there," Broadstreet said, giving her the address.

Jane sometimes wondered if she was the only person in the City who could find her way around from above. She knew all the streets, despite never having to walk them, but that came from perspective—she'd been staring down at the roadways and alleys for years, a literal bird's eye view of the metropolis. Even still, she had to look up where the reporter lived to be sure. Apparently, with his journalist's salary, he couldn't afford very nice accommodations. She found his apartment building in a rundown part of the City, a place no one had gentrified yet, filled with too many people per apartment, all living paycheck to paycheck.

Dressed in jeans and a college sweatshirt, Broadstreet waited on the roof. She'd called him on his day off, but as always, he made time to see her. He was reliable that way.

"So how much lower has your opinion of me dropped now that you know where I live?" he asked.

"Why would I think less of you because of where you live in town?" she asked.

Broadstreet chuckled.

"You don't spend a lot of time around regular people, do you?" he said.

"The answer to that question is 'no time,' " Jane said.

Broadstreet gestured out over the City like a celebrity showing off his penthouse.

"But look at this view! You can almost see downtown if it weren't for the deteriorating billboards over there," he said. "But why the secrecy? Bad news, I assume."

"I need a favor," Jane said.

Broadstreet cocked his head.

"Well that's new," he said.

"If I gave you something, could you sit on it until the right time to release the information?" Jane asked. She paced, anxiety giving her the jitters, making her unable to sit still.

"This is that thing you were hinting at the other day," he said.

"Yeah," Jane said.

"How bad could it be? Are we being invaded by aliens or something?" Broadstreet said, smiling.

Jane stared at him.

The smile faded slowly from Broadstreet's face.

"We are?"

"Ayup," Jane said.

He sat down on the lip of the building, suddenly looking very green.

"That's upsetting," he said.

"Ayup," Jane said.

"Okay," Broadstreet said. "So what are you doing? Giving me the story? You want me to write something and then have it ready for when you need to start an evacuation or something? I mean, my bosses would absolutely murder me if they knew I sat on something like this for a few days but you can trust me to…"

"I need you to record something," Jane said, interrupting. "You told me last time we talked, that we should control the message, and that it should come from me," Jane said.

"That's right," Broadstreet said.

"Well, I'm giving you that message. All I'm asking is that you hold off on broadcasting it until the right moment," Jane said.

"Why not do it yourself? That Tower of yours has to have transmitter capabilities," Broadstreet said.

"It does," Jane said. "But there's a pretty good chance I won't be here when the word needs to go out."

"That sounds ominous," Broadstreet said. "So if you're not here and I'm sitting on your announcement, how am I going to know when to release it?"

Jane grimaced and looked out over the City. It wasn't difficult, she thought, to picture it under attack. Her imagination started to kick up and she wondered where the aliens would strike first, where they'd cause the most destruction. How they'd tear the City apart. It didn't help that she'd seen the City in ruins during their trip to the future not long ago. She had witnessed firsthand what sort of damage could be done. This world is remarkably fragile.

"You'll know," Jane said softly. "Trust me."

"This is when it dawns on me that I'm a terrible reporter," Broadstreet said. "My peers would be chomping at the bit for this. They'd lie and promise you they'd embargo your information and then leak it the first second they could."

"That doesn't make you a bad reporter, it makes you a good person.... A friend," she said.

"They always warn you not to become friends with your sources," Broadstreet said.

"There's probably a rule about constantly asking them out, too," Jane said.

"Yeah," Broadstreet said. "I feel pretty bad about that now."

"Don't," Jane said, smiling. "It's okay."

Broadstreet laughed at himself, shaking his head.

"See? A crackerjack journalist would have figured out how to get you to spill everything about this invasion and already would be running back to the newsroom to scoop the competition, and I'm standing here worrying about whether or not you'll be okay," Broadstreet said. "You'll be alright. You're always okay."

Jane shrugged. She hadn't thought much about it, really, whether they'd succeed in fending off the invasion. These things are easier if you don't think much about it. Easier to face certain death if you don't put a lot of reflection into it.

"Again, with the ominous," Broadsteet said.

"Sorry," Jane said.

"So what do we do? Should I take notes? Is this a formal interview?"

"Do you have a video camera?" Jane said.

"Wait—you're letting me record you?" Broadstreet said.

"You told me the message should come from me," Jane said. "I'm taking your advice."

Broadstreet gave her another worried look but picked up his messenger bag and pulled out a first-generation digital camera. He showed it to her apologetically.

"Cheap execs won't let us upgrade our equipment," he said.

"Will it work?" Jane said.

"It'll get the job done," he said. "You'll make your statement and I just… publish it when the time is right?"

"Yes," Jane said. "In every format possible. You're going to want the world to hear this."

"The other papers and networks will pick it up the second I release it," Broadstreet said.

"That's okay. We want to maximize reach," Jane said.

He adjusted the settings on the camera without ever really taking his attention off Jane.

Jane exhaled nervously. She'd done interviews before, with Broadstreet and others, but she'd avoided being on camera as much as possible. She hated the sound of her voice, the hollow and low tones she heard when played back.

"Are you ready to start?" he said.

Jane sighed heavily, her stomach fluttered with nerves. She'd been practicing what to say for days now, ever since they last spoke. She would never be more prepared, yet she also felt she would never truly be ready either.

"Now's as good a time as any," Jane said.

"Should I record an intro?" Broadstreet said.

Jane shrugged again. "I have no idea," she said.

"I'll just do a quick intro for context," Broadstreet said. "Nothing self-aggrandizing."

"You really are a terrible reporter," Jane said, laughing a little.

"I know," Broadstreet said, setting up the camera on a table left behind by one of the other tenants. He pressed record and then jumped in front of it.

"This is Jon Broadstreet of the *City Guardian*. I am here with Solar, leader of the superhuman team the Indestructibles. Solar has requested the opportunity to speak directly to you, the viewers, about a topic of utmost importance. What she has to say will speak for itself. I think it best if I leave the rest up to her. Solar?"

Broadstreet stepped aside and picked up the camera, and held it steady. Jane looked to Broadstreet, who gestured with his face to direct her attention to the lens.

"My name is Solar," she said. "I apologize for the cryptic nature of this message, but I ask everyone watching to listen carefully..."

CHAPTER 44: AWKWARD

Billy entered the control center and set a mug of coffee down in front of Bedlam. In the room by herself, her head placed in her hands, she looked tired and unexpectedly sad.

The coffee cup clinked against the tabletop and she looked up. "You," she said.

"Of all the flying saucers on all the planets on all the worlds, you had to walk into mine," Billy said, offering an awkward smile.

"That's the cheesiest thing I've ever heard in my life. Ever."

"Wasn't sure what to lead with," Billy said. "Since we've never had a normal conversation before."

"And this is normal?" Bedlam said. She nodded at the empty chair next to her.

Billy slid into his chair. "And how've you been?"

"Oh, y'know. Not too bad. Mostly going to the mall with Suzie and Amy, looking forward to senior prom," she said.

"What did you think of McGillicuddy's math exam? Brutal, huh?" Billy said.

"Oh man," she said. "The worst."

They laughed. The sound of their voices echoed in the oddly quiet Tower. Little footsteps clicked across the floor and Watson arrived, the tiny dog jumped into Billy's lap. He scratched at the dog's chin absently.

"Do normal people have conversations like that?" Bedlam said. "I still can't believe you have a dog that fits in a purse."

"He doesn't ride in a purse, and they talk that way on TV, so it has to be true," Billy said. "I went to real normal regular person schools for most of my life, y'know."

"Me too," Bedlam said. She offered her hand to Watson, who sniffed it suspiciously, then licked her metal fingertips. "It's not as if we've never been normal."

"Well, I wouldn't have called myself normal at the time," Billy said.

"Me either," Bedlam said. "We never did have that date we joked about."

"It's remarkably difficult to find time for the movies when you're a superhero," Billy said. "Did you hear we traveled through time?"

"A little something about that," Bedlam said. "On a scale of one to ten, was it more, less, or equal to the amount of fun *Back to the Future* seemed to be?"

"I'd rate it as *Days of Future Past*," Billy said. "With a side of the *Terminator* thrown in."

"Sounds like a party."

"Oh it was," Billy said.

Bedlam sighed and sipped her coffee.

"Like we could've gone to the movies," she said. "Look at us. Your eyes glow like Christmas lights and I've got more metal in my body than a Jeep Cherokee. Normal lives are not in the cards for us, Mr. Straylight."

"Doesn't mean we can't try," Billy said. "Though it might be easier to act like we're normal people if we had normal names. I don't actually know your real name."

"Maybe Bedlam is my birth name," Bedlam said. "Maybe my parents hated me."

"You don't have to tell me," Billy said. He paused for a few seconds, realizing how quiet Dude had been the past few minutes. He could sense the alien there in his mind, but withdrawn. Giving him privacy, Billy realized. He couldn't explain how the alien was able to accomplish it, but somehow Dude had pulled down a virtual curtain in his mind, leaving him alone with his thoughts, and with this strange and sad girl.

"Slippery slope, that," Bedlam said. "I tell you my first name, then we have to treat each other like actual people… "

"You know my real name," Billy said.

"That's because your teammates are horrible, horrible, horrible about using codenames. I know *all* your real names. You never stop saying them," Bedlam said.

"And yours is?" Billy said.

"I'm actually pretty good at aliases," Bedlam said.

"You don't like it, do you?" Billy said.

Bedlam shot him a dirty look.

"What?" she said.

"You're not refusing to tell me your first name because you're being secretive. You hate it," Billy said.

"Listen, William Byron Case, just because everybody knows your secret-not-secret identity…"

"Who told you my middle name!" Billy said.

"Give you three guesses and the first two don't count," Bedlam said.

"Emily. It's always Emily," Billy said.

"Of course," Bedlam said.

He scowled. "This isn't fair."

They locked eyes for a minute, the silence turned from charming to awkward and back to charming.

"I know what you're thinking," Bedlam said.

"And?"

"You want to tell me I have a pretty eye," Bedlam said.

Billy's jaw dropped.

Bedlam laughed, a straight on, filled-with-happiness laugh.

"Do you have any idea how long I've sat on that joke?" she said.

"That's so inappropriate!" Billy said.

"Not if I say it," Bedlam said. "Come on, what's the upside of having a cyborg eye if you can't tell that joke."

Billy joined in her laughter. He put his head down on the table, his ears turned red with embarrassment. Then, he raised his eyes back up at her

"I really do think you're pretty," Billy said.

"You're pretty too, flyboy," Bedlam said. "It's not much to go on though, is it? Thinking we're pretty."

"Not really," he said.

"How do normal people do this stuff?" Bedlam said. "How do regular people make friends? Meet people? I forgot how to do it. All I know is weird now."

"Forget normal," Billy said. "I hated it. Did you like those days?"

Bedlam's face softened, her expression becoming almost distant.

"I wasn't a happy normal person," she said. "There are days I hate this. Hate being this thing. Can't stand what I look like and who I've become. But you know something funny? I have more happy days now than unhappy ones."

"Being able to punch through brick walls must help with the unhappy days," Billy said.

"Destruction therapy," Bedlam said. "It works. I highly recommend it."

They both sipped their coffee, didn't speak, didn't seem to feel the need and to speak. I've had worse days, Billy thought. I really have.

"Hey listen," Bedlam said. "If we get through this alien invasion thing, I'm taking you out."

"You're taking me?" Billy said.

"Yeah. I know a junkyard where they let me break old cars for fun. You're coming with me and smashing some stuff. Group therapy."

Billy smirked and thought back to the night Doc found him. He remembered Dude chastising him for being destructive and shooting tin cans with light beams.

"You do know how to make a guy feel special," Billy said.

"Is that a no?"

"It's a yes," Billy said.

The duo laughed again, awkward and unsure, yet warm and welcome. Bedlam's mouth broke into a grin. For just a moment, she looked shy.

"Kimberly," Bedlam said.

"What?" Billy asked.

"Before all this," Bedlam said. "My name is Kimberly."

"Never in a million years would I have guessed Kimberly," he said.

"Try not to tell everyone," she said. "I'd like to do a slightly better job at the secret identity stuff than you guys do."

Billy offered her a mock salute. "Aye aye, Bedlam," he said. "Can I call you Kimberly though?"

"Let's hang out a little bit more first."

"Okay," Billy said.

Abruptly, their conversation was interrupted by the monotone voice of Neal coming through the room's speakers.

"I beg your pardon, Designation: Straylight," Neal said. "But there is an incoming call from Sam Barren. Shall I patch it through?"

Billy looked up at the ceiling to Neal's disembodied voice, his face a wrinkled mask of annoyance.

"Is there anyone else who can take the call?" he said.

"Designation: Solar and Designation: Dancer are both off-site and you are sitting in the control center. You seemed like the logical choice. Mr. Barren said: 'I guess Straylight will do.'"

"Well that's a resounding endorsement," Billy said. He shrugged apologetically at Bedlam.

"I'm beginning to see why we never met up before," she said.

Sam Barren's face appeared, oversized, on the main screen.

"Hey, kid," Sam said.

"So you calling with bad news, worse news, or really awful news?" Billy asked.

"Considering I just got a call from NASA asking if the Department knew anything about the unidentified objects someone just saw with one of their deep space telescopes, I'm going to call it really awful news," Sam said. "Where's the rest of the gang?"

"Everywhere," Billy said, running a nervous hand through his hair. "I'll put out the call and get them back here."

CHAPTER 45:
THE TOOLS AT MY DISPOSAL

Kate saw the surprise on Henry Winter's face when she stopped him in the hall at the Labyrinth. The older hero stopped dead in his tracks, leaned back and thumped his cane against the floor.

"You look like someone on a mission," he said, glancing back and forth between Kate and her mostly unwanted tagalong, Emily. How Kate allowed herself to be talked into taking Emily with her she'll never know, yet here the odd couple stood, waiting on the director of the Department.

"We need things, Henry," Emily said, folding her arms across her chest.

"Okay then," he said. "Step into my office."

Winter led them just around the corner to his private office, the smaller one he maintained at the Labyrinth when he didn't need to be in Washington or on the road. He sat down and waited for the two young heroes to join him, a pair of empty chairs stood unused in front of him. Neither girl took advantage of them.

"So we're in a rush, I take it," he said.

"I need the Distribution suit," Kate said.

"The what?"

"The suit the Department took off Elliott Smoot back after our first mission," Kate said. "I know it ended up here, because before you were director someone reverse-engineered it to make their own versions."

The Distribution suit was a strangely high-tech bodysuit used by a local drug dealer the Indestructibles had apprehended very early on in their careers. It absorbed kinetic energy, then redistributed it back, empowering the wearer, thus essentially granting limited protection and a sort of temporary super strength.

"I know the Department reverse-engineered it," Winter said. "I was a captive here then. I actually led the team who did the work."

"So you know where the suit is," Kate said.

"I can do you one better," Winter said. "Would you rather one of the improved suits? I can just give you one of those. Do you really want the sweat-stained original we got from Smoot? That guy was extremely sweaty."

Kate fired one of her impenetrable stares at him.

"I don't have time to learn a whole new fighting technique," she said. "I don't need the latest fancy tech. I just want the kinetic redistribution."

"Didn't realize you were a tech person," Winter said, his tone curious, not judgmental.

"I use the tools I have at my disposal," Kate said. "You of all people should understand that."

Winter chuckled softly, nodding in agreement.

"Understand it and approve it," he said. "I can get you a replica suit. No bells and whistles, just a straight reconstruction in your size. Trust me, I worked on the design—you want one that fits properly to maximize the effectiveness. Baggy won't do."

Kate bowed her head slightly in gratitude.

"And you?" Winter said, turning to Emily. "What do you want from Santa this Christmas?"

"I liked that glove you gave me," Emily said.

"I'm glad. Be sure to thank Dr. Bohr for that though," Winter said.

"I need more," Emily said.

"More gloves? Did you break the first one?"

"What? No," Emily said. "The glove is fine. But it's not going to do me any good in outer space."

Winter turned his eyes to Kate, who raised one eyebrow

imperiously.

"You're going to need something... to help you fight in outer space," Winter said.

"I'm sorry," Emily said. "I didn't realize you were suffering hearing loss issues. I always forget how old you guys are."

"I'm not—my hearing's just fine!" Winter said. "I didn't think you'd... never mind. You need to fight in space."

"I do indeedy," Emily said.

Henry Winter glanced back and forth between the two women a few times, hesitating.

"You have a bad idea, don't you?" Emily said.

"No I don't," Winter said.

"Yes, you do," Kate said. "Show us."

Winter ran a hand through his hair anxiously.

"Oh, this is such a terrible idea," he said. "Look, it's something I've been working on for years, okay? I built it for me. But I could never figure out how to make it all work. And then we realized... the main problem is it's just too heavy."

"You're talking gibberish," Emily said. "We broke his brain."

"No, no," Winter said. "Look, it's easier if I just show you the project."

He picked up a tablet off the desk and tinkered with it to retrieve a set of schematics. Kate leaned over the table, watching as different projects streamed across the screen. When Winter found what he was looking for, he opened a set of photos and handed the device to Emily. Kate intercepted though, taking a look first. Emily stood uncomfortably close to Kate and peered at the screen as well.

"Oh. My. Frelling..." Emily said.

"No," Kate said.

"Heck yes!" Emily said.

"That, Entropy Emily, is going to be a last resort," Winter said. "Okay? I only showed it to you in case things get so bad that we need to throw the kitchen sink at these aliens to stop them. If it turns out they're delicate daisies that wilt under an angry glare, there's no way I'm letting you use that."

"You realize you've just put me in a position *hoping* I need to use that, right?" Emily said.

"All the options available to us," Winter said. "Right, Dancer?"

Kate frowned.

"Within reason," she said, watching the insanity on the screen one more time before handing it back to Winter.

Emily and Kate both startled when Billy's voice came through their earpieces simultaneously.

"Where are you guys?" Billy said.

"You need to be more specific, Billy," Emily said, shooting an apologetic expression at Winter.

"You. I mean you. And Kate. Solar's not answering her radio either," Billy said. "Sam says we've got bad news."

"We're here with Henry Winter right now, Straylight. Go ahead," Kate said

Billy made a series of confused noises on the other end of the line.

"What are you doing? Never mind. Just get back to the Tower ASAP," Billy said.

Winter gestured to his computer.

"I heard that. I'll patch Sam in," Winter said.

"We'll conference call in," Kate said.

"I hate you just a little bit for saying that out loud," Billy said.

Emily tuned Billy out and returned her attention to Winter.

"I'm going to need that thing," she said.

"I already regret bringing it up," he said.

Emily winked at him.

"Too bad," she said. "No backsies."

CHAPTER 46:
THE STOCKPILE

"I've seen a lot of weird things in my time," Agent Black said, while hunched over the control panel searching for alien aircraft. "But this place is something else."

The former Prevention surveyed their haul. Weapons, machines, and inexplicable apparatuses, an arsenal and a lab. They'd moved a few items closer to the exit of the old Department bunker, but the place seemed to go on forever, a graveyard of strange tech.

"The Department comes into contact with all things unexplainable," Laura said. "This isn't even a drop in the bucket of what's been locked away."

"Still," Black said. "It had to be tough to gather all this technology without being noticed."

Laura examined a rig, not unlike a rifle, silver with deep indigo spheres that glowed along the barrel.

"I had a long time to get myself in just the right spots," she said. "Requesting the key assignments, showing an aptitude for the project."

"Your Jedi mind tricks didn't hurt, either," Black said.

"Being able to poke around in someone's mind to find out what they knew and what answers they wanted me to say helped, yeah," she said. "It's easier to give the correct answer if you know the question before it's asked."

"I can't imagine how you got into the espionage business with those powers," Black said sarcastically. He picked up a melee weapon, like a kendo stick; it hummed and sang when he moved it.

Laura shrugged. She'd risen quickly up the ladder in the Department's organizations, in part because of her telepathic powers, but also because she knew how to work people in more traditional ways. Even in an organization full of secret agents, she knew how to push the buttons and make friends.

"Did anyone ever find out you were doing this?" Black said.

"I covered my tracks pretty well," Laura said. "Made certain reports disappear. Greased a few palms. And for those who didn't want to cooperate, it wasn't difficult to nip and tuck their memories a bit to make sure they had no recollection this base existed. Then it was simply a matter of 'officially' boarding up the location and boom—secret war chest."

"Just in case the Earth was ever invaded," Black said.

"My employers tell me they always knew the invasion would happen," she said.

"But you didn't," Black said.

"How often have you taken money from someone no questions asked?" Laura said.

Black made a noncommittal movement of his head.

"I was doing as they asked. Stockpile alien weapons and get the Department ready to be militarized. Recruit and retain any superhumans who stepped up and appeared useful," she said. "Honesty I thought I was working on a coup."

"I never liked coups," Black said.

"They have their plusses and minuses."

The two mercenaries shared a professional-humor laugh. Only a couple of hired guns like us can find coups funny, she thought.

Black gestured at the room full of devices.

"So what do we do with all of these?" he said. "I don't imagine you and I are going to use them all."

"How many people do you think you'd need to turn this arsenal into something useful?" Laura said.

"Me?" Black surveyed the room, his cyborg eye whirring as it took in data. "I don't build armies."

"You build teams," Laura said.

"If you're asking me a serious question, I'd get ten good fighters—perhaps an even dozen," Black said. "Hand-pick them for their skills and set them up with the sort of tech they can make the most out of. There's more here than I'd use, but better to have a smaller number of tools in the hands of the right talent than to just start handing out laser cannons to yokels."

"How long would it take you to put a team like that together?" Laura said.

Black turned that cyborg eye onto her instead of the tech.

"Depends," Black said. "My type of people don't work for charity."

"I have a very generous budget," Laura said.

"It would have to be considering we're confronting what could be an extinction event," Black said.

"Bonuses if they survive," Laura said. "And really shouldn't saving the world be enough to motivate them? If we all die, what does it matter?"

"Exactly," Black said. "Maybe they don't want to stick their neck out and would rather hope we get lucky with those super-kids."

Laura smiled.

"Something tells me you could find the right men and women for the job if I asked you to," she said.

"Are you asking?" Black said. "And what about you? Don't you know people?"

"I'm a burned double agent who infiltrated a government agency," Laura said. "My reputation isn't stellar on either side of the espionage community. The good guys hate me and the bad guys don't trust me."

"How the hell did I end up working with you then?" Black said.

"So what do you say. Make a few phone calls?" she said.

Black stood up and looked around the room, as if determining what he'd need from whom to make the best use of the equipment.

"I'll get you people if you're paying," Black said. "We survive this, we're all going to have a big laugh over helping save the world."

"Takes all kinds," Laura said.

"And what are you going to do while I'm tracking down

mercenaries with hearts of gold?"

Laura pointed to a section of the bunker where she'd gathered a very specific set of items.

"I need to try to find a way to get a few things to those super-kids to help them out," Laura said.

"Didn't you incarcerate three of them a while back?" Black said.

"Unfortunate, isn't it?" Laura said. "I'll just have to get creative with my delivery method."

CHAPTER 47:
GODS OLD AND NEW

Jane and Doc met in mid-air. As both hero and magician flew back to the Tower, Jane eyed the book tucked under his arm.

"I thought you were teleporting instead of flying these days," she said.

Doc smiled.

"Maybe I just wanted to see the City from above today," Doc said. "You never know when this view will be your last."

"It's easy to forget that," Jane said. The City, in all its grubby glory, really had become her second home since joining the team, her place in the world.

Once again, she checked out the book Doc carried.

"That looks like it's made of poison," she said.

A twist of disgust on his face he said, "Might as well be. But it might help us in the coming battle."

They drew closer to the Tower and Jane said, "What's in it?"

"War magic. I never needed war magic before."

"I've seen you cast spells like weapons, though," she said.

He nodded.

"I've cast harmful spells before, or even aggressive ones, but this type of magic is larger scale," he said. "The damage it causes is more profound, as is the cost to the caster, and the harm it does the world. There's a reason I never use it. But if we're at the point of perish or die…"

"What do you mean, cost to the caster?" Jane said, squinting at

Doc with worry. Her mentor had a self-sacrificing streak. She had no desire to see him martyred again.

"Nothing I haven't dealt with before, Jane," he said. "Don't worry."

"Worrying is my job."

Doc grinned.

"I know," he said. "Where were you just now?"

"Not like you to pry," Jane said.

"Just curious. You don't have to answer."

"Where did you go to get that book?"

Doc frowned and glanced down.

"You went to her for help, didn't you?" Jane said.

"You really want to know?"

"Why does it always come back to her?"

"Because Natasha has been here a long time, Jane," Doc said. "She'll always know things I don't. And sometimes you have to ask for help, even if that means going to people who otherwise oppose you."

Jane's lip curled into a slight snarl.

"I don't like her," Jane said.

They arced toward the entrance of the Tower, but Doc grabbed Jane's wrist before she spotted what caught his attention. Two figures, standing guard outside the landing bay, one man, one woman.

"That's Valerie," Jane said, seeing the sentient hurricane's distinctive cloud-like skin.

The other figure looked familiar to Jane, but she couldn't quite place him. Deep blue hair, braided down his back, with an equally well-crafted long beard. He wore armor that looked archaic and unearthly, also in deep blue, and held a staff in one hand, tipped with a razor-sharp axe head. The stranger and Valerie stood in mid-air, watching their approach.

"Well look at that," Doc said.

"Who's the guy?" Jane asked.

"If we're lucky, he's our backup."

He picked up speed a little and Jane followed suit until they both

235

hovered in front of the newcomers.

"Val," Jane said, floating over to put arms around the sentient storm. Valerie, always a little shy and awkward, hugged her back, her arms cool as mist.

"I've come to help," she said. "I'm ready."

"We're glad to have you," Jane said. "Your timing is perfect."

The powerfully built man stared at Jane, his eyes like polished black stones, before addressing Doc.

"You shamed me, Doctor. I will not soon forget this," the man said.

"Did I shame you into action?" Doc said, fighting off a bemused smirk.

The monstrously large man ignored the question and pointed one thick, scarred arm at Jane.

"Is this your little sun god?" the man said.

"Hi. I can speak for myself. I'm Solar. And you are?"

"I am—" the man started, but Doc cut him off.

"This is Korthos," Doc said. "He has a lot of names. Let's keep it simple for now."

"Korthos of Aramaias, the Truthbringer, last son of—" Korthos started, and Doc stopped him again.

"It's nice to see you face to face again, Val," Doc said to the storm, who floated patiently beside them.

"I'm sorry I don't come around much," she said, delicately offering her hand to Doc.

Jane couldn't help but smile a bit, the four of them, flaying, floating in the sky, making introductions as if at a dinner party.

"A sun goddess and the sky herself on your side, Doctor," Korthos said in his booming voice. "Look at how you gather greatness around you. And with me, you'll be unstoppable."

Doc and Jane exchanged looks. He mouthed the word 'sorry.'

"We're up against something pretty unstoppable, big guy," Doc said. "But we're glad to have you along."

Billy's voice chirped in Jane's ear. "Jane? Where you at? We've got news. Never mind, I see you on the security camera. Who the heck is He-Man and why is he flying outside our door?"

"Long story," Jane said. "We'll be right in."

CHAPTER 48:
TAKING STOCK OF THE SITUATION

itus hung back and watched as the latest additions to their menagerie walked in. Valerie, he recognized—though he was surprised to see her indoors—and to say she walked was really a misnomer, as her feet, bare and the color of rain clouds, hardly seemed to touch the ground. She actually held hands with Jane, who appeared to be whisper encouraging words, reassuring her that being indoors was safe for all of them.

Then the other guy walked in.

Titus had seen pictures of Korthos the Truthbringer in the Tower, and also while growing up and watching Doc's team on television, so he thought he knew what the man looked like, but in the same room, he seemed to be at least as large as Titus was in werewolf form, muscles piled on muscles. He smelled like war, smoke and fire along with the faint hint of blood. Mixing with the way Val turned the room into a cool spring storm, Titus felt suddenly overwhelmed.

Emily, of course, spoke first.

"It's like Conan the Barbarian mind-melded with a samurai," she said, far louder than anyone felt comfortable with.

Korthos stared at the monitor, looking into Emily's eyes.

She stared right back at him.

This went on for a few seconds, stretching out for a disconcertingly long time, and then Emily winked.

Korthos burst out laughing.

"The fairy child has guts, Silence," Korthos said. "I like that one!"

Sam sighed heavily on screen. The soft noise was enough to draw everyone's attention his way, though. "Are we done?" he said. "Because I have a report to make."

"Go ahead," Jane said, sitting down at the long table.

"So we started getting reports that the fleet was visible to NASA, and sure enough, not long after, we had civilian groups reporting they could see something strange via telescope," Sam said. "They're still far enough out that you need some real equipment to know what you're looking at, but—"

"—But they're close enough for people to know something's on the way," Billy said. "Sorry guys. Either we miscalculated or it took me longer to get home than I thought it did. I lost track of time out there."

Seng, the alien with powers identical to Billy's, who had joined them in the control center chimed in. "They are nothing if not adaptable," Seng said. "It's possible they've learned how to travel faster recently. Often, they absorb into their system powers or technology from the worlds they devour.

"Whatever or however they've been able to accomplish it, we've moved up our timetable," Kate said from her position on screen. "We need tactics."

"I plan on calling in Starfleet to help out," Emily said. "And possibly also the Rebel Alliance. I volunteer for Red Squadron."

"Earth has a star fleet?" Korthos said. "I've been away too long."

"She's being... never mind," Billy said. "No, we don't have a star fleet."

"Right now what we have is four of us capable of taking the fight to them before they break through the atmosphere," Doc said. "Jane, your powers do allow you to not require oxygen in space. Billy, have you recovered?"

"Yes," Billy said, pausing. "Maybe ninety percent. But I'm good."

"You'll have me as well," Seng said, sharing a nod with Billy.

"Five, then. Korthos and I can also fight in outer space."

"What about us land-locked grunts?" asked Bedlam.

"We're going to miss some," Billy said. "It's inevitable. The fleet is enormous. We can't get them all."

"So you'll be here on Earth to fight the ones who do make it through," Jane said.

"I'd rather put our full efforts into making sure none of them get to the planet," Kate said.

"I know, Kate," Jane said. "But unless you're proposing a boarding party—"

"I'm proposing a boarding party," Kate said.

Jane looked at Titus, who shrugged.

"I agree with her this time. I'd rather be up there fighting them on their own turf than down here where our own people are at risk," he said.

"We'll draw up some options," Doc said. "For certain, Valerie, you'll stay here planet-side. Your ability to control the weather only works if there's an atmosphere to control, and we've clearly seen lightning is very effective on their soldiers."

"Happily," Val said.

"And keep in mind the Department will bring the military up to speed," Winter said. "But from what I've seen, if we can keep the fighting off-planet—"

"—The more lives we'll save," Jane said. "Which is why I'm going ahead of all of you to try to talk to them."

An involuntary response caused Titus to bolt upright in his chair and when he looked around, he saw he wasn't the only one. The group grew strangely quiet, but every single one of them wore some expression of shock or surprise, all except Korthos and Kate, who simply stared at her. Even Val's storm-colored eyes had opened wider.

"That's the dumbest thing I've ever heard anyone say—ever," Emily said.

"Jane, I get what you're trying to do, but you can't take them on alone," Billy said. "I saw them. It's too much. I'm not even sure all of us working together will be able to do it."

"I'm not planning to do battle with them. I'm going to try to reason with them," Jane said.

"For millennia the Nemesis have marched onward, devouring worlds," Seng said. "I tell you, the Luminae were a peaceful people before all this happened. We've tried every way to negotiate with them. They don't listen."

"You're not really traveling up there to negotiate, are you?" Kate said softly.

Jane smiled. "I'll try. But if they won't listen, at least I can buy the rest of you some time to prepare," she said.

"You're going to get yourself killed," Billy said.

Jane winked. "No I'm not. I'm Indestructible," she said.

Doc regarded her from behind his red lenses, his face emotionless.

"You're not talking me out of it, Doc."

"I know," he said. "So you and I are going to talk about the extent of your powers and I'm going to give you something to make sure you get back here to us in one piece."

"Okay," Jane said.

"Don't leave without speaking with me," Doc said.

"Okay," she repeated, softer.

"Everyone, we've got very little time. Go do what you have to do. See your families. Be safe, and come back soon." Doc turned and walked out, gesturing for Korthos to follow.

Titus stood up, but, as the big monitor blinked out, Jane caught his attention.

"Hang a minute," she said.

He sat back down, trading confused glances with Billy, who left with Bedlam and Valerie.

When she was sure they were alone, Jane spoke.

"If I don't come back, they're going to turn to you," she said.

"You're coming back," Titus said.

"If I don't."

"They'll look to Doc and Kate," he said. "Not me."

"No," Jane said, her voice just a hint above a whisper. "Kate is a strategist, not a leader. And Doc... you and I know he won't be okay if I don't come home."

Titus shook his head. Doc didn't play favorites among them, but everyone knew Jane was the one Indestructible he was closest to. Despite his unflappable demeanor, Doc would be devastated without Jane.

"Why me, then?" Titus said.

"We saw who you became in the future," Jane said. "We shared leadership. We were partners. You know you can take command."

"You're asking the guy with crippling self-doubt to lead this group?" Titus said. "You're out of your fool mind. Even more than I thought you were when you announced that you hoped to parlay with these aliens."

"You've come a long way, Titus Whispering," Jane said. "You more than all of us. You remember that first time we met?"

"You knocked me out in the middle of the forest," he said.

"You were out of control. Scared. Angry. Dangerous," Jane said. "And now look at you."

"I'm still a monster, Jane," Titus said.

"No," Jane said. "You like to pretend you're just a monster. I know you do. It's easier that way. It sets the bar lower. But even your own people know you're destined for something grander than to simply be a monster. So if they need something more from you…"

Titus ran his hands along the edge of the table nervously, then made eye contact with Jane.

"You know I'll take care of them," he said.

"I know. I better go talk with Doc."

"You better come home," Titus said. "Just because I said I'll take care of them doesn't mean I want your job."

CHAPTER 49:
SOME GREAT BEAST

From a distance, the fleet might appear as one single entity, a writhing, shimmering plant, extending outward with stalks and spiked leaves. The closer you crept—though few survived a closer inspection—an onlooker would see ships, each unique, the fleet like a monstrous garden, living machines great and small, all moving with a singular purpose, walking like an angry god across a deathly silent galaxy.

No one knows where the Nemesis fleet—the name given to it by the Luminae centuries ago—originally came from. It's been said that once, a historian had tried to communicate with the fleet's brain-ship, its core, and asked what the creatures called their own species.

"We" was the response.

Over the centuries, planets fought back. Some battled well. The Nemesis fleet lost many ships, like fingers from a hand, or more aptly, like hairs from a head. The fleet grew more ships, tearing apart the living matter of inhabited worlds and turning that substance into extensions of itself.

And like some great beast shuffling off to be born, the fleet would move on, looking for its next meal.

To call it a fleet was, in many ways, not accurate. Alien philosophers and scientists had pointed out over the years it is not composed of ships and commanded by a hive-like mind, with only very specific parts of the whole able to act with true autonomy. It did resemble a fleet, with its little fighters and its mother ships, but these were living creatures, extensions of a greater biological presence, depending on and supporting each other like organs and cells.

It became a swarm of locusts, moving as one creature, feeding one hunger, pursuing one relentless goal.

While no one knows where or how the Nemesis fleet came to be, survivors of their attacks have long speculated about its origins. Some claim it was a biological weapon, created by some ancient race, destroyed by their own creation, the fleet's first meal and victim. Others wonder if it began as a singular creature, eating its home world until all its resources were gone, and then took to the stars for more. Still others suggested it was a disease, a cancerous growth, forever multiplying and destroying, death through biology.

The more esoteric sort saw something darker in it. The remorseless hunger of the creatures making up the fleet felt demonic to them, the fleet itself some sort of hell-spawned devil.

But few worlds that encountered the fleet had time for such speculation. Planets which had not yet taken to the stars, for whom the arrival of the Nemesis fleet marked both their first and last encounter with an alien species. These beings soon watched the stars blacked out in the night sky, or saw the shadow of a great beast rumble in front of their sun, and all they had time for was terror and death.

The deaths of these worlds silenced those philosophers who sometimes spoke up, among the Luminae and others, and postulated that the fleet was some sort of immune system for the cosmos, a natural thing, destroying worlds that no longer served a purpose, cutting off dead limbs from the tree of life. And some worlds destroyed by the fleet were in fact dark and horrible places, where the living committed atrocities upon each other all the while citing culture and courage. There were even times the Luminae wanted the Nemesis fleet to take those worlds.

But others were just babies in the blanket of the universe, young children beneath stars they had not yet named, innocent of what occurs in the galaxy above them. When the fleet took one of those worlds, it snuffed out all its potential. All its hope.

These were the fears of Straylight and of Horizon, and of all their human partners, looking up in the night sky, waiting and watching. Wondering if their world, their home, would be one that never reached for the sky, one that died in ignorance, or one that, through violence and brutality, seemed to earn the cold and silent wrath of the Nemesis fleet.

And in quiet moments, both Luminae would pray that, like a swimmer who never senses the shark that brushes under his feet in the ocean and returns to shore blind to the danger he had been susceptible to, the fleet would swim by an unaware Earth in favor of a different meal.

But Earth glowed blue and bright in the crosshairs of the fleet, the singular attention of the vast many-mouthed beast. This planet had been prepared by children of the fleet sent ahead to scout, to make ready, to find the things they would want to keep and the things it should consume. They travel a great distance on their journey to this world.

Hungry, it was unstoppable and more than ready.

CHAPTER 50:
ALL IN ONE PLACE

Some day, Billy thought, I'll figure out why I still get nervous when knocking on my own parents' door.

He rapped his knuckles softly. Staring up from shin-level, Watson gave him a disapproving look.

He knows what I'm doing, Dude, Billy thought.

Of course he does. Canines are particularly perceptive Earth creatures.

He knows what I'm doing and he's giving me the guilty eyes, Billy thought.

You say that like you've never done the same thing to me.

I can't look you in the eyes! Billy thought.

You have, in fact, looked in the mirror, making sad puppy dog eyes, to try to manipulate me in the past, Billy Case. Don't act like you haven't.

A potential argument was quickly adverted by Billy's mom yelling from inside.

"Are you seriously knocking on the door? Just come in! What is wrong with you. I've failed as a parent," she said.

"I just want to announce my arrival," Billy said, opening the screen door and letting Watson take the lead. The little dog charged forward, hitting the end of his leash, straining against the harness. Billy unclipped him and the terrier sprint deeper into the house.

"Announce your arrival," Lori Case said, walking into the living room from the kitchen.

"Hey, I don't know what you guys are up to when I'm not here," Billy said.

"Oh you wouldn't believe the things we do," Lori said.

"Mom!" Billy said, appalled.

She just smirked.

His father walked in, looked at the dog, glanced up at Billy, then down at the dog again, before returning his eyes to his son.

"Is that an overnight bag you have in your hand?" Al Case said.

"Maybe."

"An overnight bag for your dog?" Al said.

"Don't judge me," Billy said.

"I'm your father, I'll judge all I want," Al said. "Your dog has a *Star Wars* themed overnight bag."

"Emily wanted him to have a *Hello Kitty* bag for irony's sake, but I vetoed that," Billy said.

"Somehow, that would have been better."

"I'm guessing you have your dog and the bag because..." his mom said.

"Yeah, things are about to get bad. I'll feel better if he's here with you guys," Billy said.

Watson whined. Al sat down on the couch. The dog leapt into his lap and curled up comfortably.

"You've been in bad spots before," his father said. "Are you just being melodramatic, or should we be concerned?"

Billy shrugged. "Your only son is a superhero. I'd rather you not worry, but I don't think anyone would blame you at this point."

"Where's Emily?" his mother asked.

"She's checking in on Melinda," Billy said. "You guys still have Sam Barren's number?"

"On the fridge," Lori said.

"I'm serious about calling him if you need help. He knows you have his contact information, so don't be shy about it."

"You really think I'm going to be shy about anything?" Al Case said.

Billy smiled.

"So this is where I say I'm really sorry about not growing up to take over the hardware store for you," Billy said.

Al laughed.

"Are you kidding? I was going to sell it to pay for my retirement anyway. You were never going to inherit the business."

"What?" Billy said.

"He's kidding!" Lori said, shooting Al a dirty look.

"Are you sure?" Billy said.

"I'm always kidding," Al said. "Your mother blames your sass mouth on me, you know."

"Apple, tree," she said.

"Besides, if you do what you seem to be planning on doing, it'll be because of you and your friends I'll still have a store to care about next week," Al said.

"Yeah," Billy said, looking at his parents and his silly little dog coiled on his father's lap. "If we don't blow it, maybe everyone will get to keep their normal lives."

"And if you do blow it?" his father said.

"Well, I don't think anyone will have the time to complain about our collective incompetence," Billy said.

CHAPTER 51:
THE TALISMAN

Jane opened up the storage closet in her room and pulled out a drawer resting along the bottom of the space. Inside lay shirts sweaters, and winter clothes she rarely needed, because her powers caused her to run so hot most of the time that the cold never bothered her. She'd wear warm clothes to fit in, winter coats and scarves and wool hats, but the same elements that allowed her to create fire with her hands also kept the chill away from her skin. And so she had drawers full of nice clothes during the winter months she never really bothered with.

Folded neatly on top of these sweaters and flannel shirts was something else entirely: the uniform of her future self, the older, wiser Solar she'd met when the team traveled into an alternate future.

In that timeline she hadn't survived the final battle and sacrificed herself to save the world from an out of control version of Emily. The remaining teammates had given Jane her older self's spare uniform as a keepsake. A white bodysuit framed in black on the sleeves, chest, and back, with a golden sunburst emblem on the front, it stood as a far cry from her usual costume, the red and gold outfit, complete with cape and skirt designed to be a nod to an earlier and more innocent sort of hero.

The Jane in that dark future had been more utilitarian, and the black and white felt more symbolic of a world on the verge of collapse.

The suit they'd given her on that occasion had never been worn.

An old spare costume, held onto—just in case—and tucked away for safe-keeping. The future heroes thought Jane might like it, in case she ever had a need to be inspired.

She kicked off her shoes and undressed, pulling on the black and white costume carefully. She was surprised when it fit perfectly, though, she mused, that should be the least surprising thing in the world. It seemed strange to be in a one-piece, and she felt somewhat incomplete without her cape as well, but she looked in the mirror; the simple colors of the suit contrasted with the flame-like nature of her hair and she did, in fact, feel inspired. It was as if she were seeing that future version of herself, who'd been so brave and self-sacrificing.

Emily revealed during their time in that dark tomorrow that she had seen only one Jane. A hero.

She turned and headed down the hallway, seeking out Doc's lair. She found him mulling over that strange book he'd obtained from the Lady.

"Find anything good?" she asked.

Doc placed a silk bookmark on the page and closed it.

"There are spells in there that I never want to see cast on this planet," Doc said.

"Good thing you're going to practice them in outer space, huh?" Jane said.

Doc folded his arms across his chest and leaned back on his table.

"You're determined to do this, aren't you?"

"I think I can buy us some time," Jane said. "And believe I can sneak in and out of there safely. If I can get them talking..."

"We don't know if they'll even understand you, but... I get it. You meet with them, maybe you can assess what their defenses are," Doc said. "I'd like to go with you."

"You and I both know it'll be easier if things go bad for me to just punch my way out," Jane said. "And If I'm captured you'll come save me."

"Our track record has you rescuing me a lot more than me saving you, Jane," Doc said.

"Well then, you owe me," Jane said.

Doc pushed himself away from the table and went over to another part of the room, covered in trinkets and small magical items. Emily called it costume jewelry, but Jane had, over the years, seen Doc use these items like magical tools, conduits for arcane powers. Doc called them shortcuts and talismans. He picked one up, a golden pendant on a thin chain, a large opal dominated the center of the circular design.

"Take this with you," Doc said.

"Parting gift?" Jane asked.

"No," Doc said. "A get out of jail free card."

He turned the item over in his hands a few times then gave it to Jane. Cool to the touch, strange runes covered the metal.

"Do I talk into it?"

"I meant to make one for Billy before he left, actually, but he took off before I could put the materials together," Doc said. "Lucky for us, I had time to finish it without you sneaking off."

Jane ran her thumb over the opal, trying to figure out how to activate it.

"You crush it," Doc said.

"I crush it?"

He nodded.

"If things go bad, you crush that opal in your hand. It contains a teleportation spell. One use. A free ride home," Doc said.

"A teleportation spell," Jane said.

"Simple as that. If you break that stone, the spell will activate. I've set it to bring the user back to Earth."

"Here, in the Tower?" Jane asked.

He shook his head.

"I didn't know what might happen to the Tower, if we have to move it or ground it. You'll appear in the Labyrinth parking lot."

"That is so not the homecoming I want if I have to use this thing," Jane said.

"It's the one place I know where you'll have allies and that won't go floating away somewhere," Doc said.

"The parking lot?"

"You'd rather it be inside?"

251

"No," Jane said. "Parking lot works."

"Plus just in case you're... hurt in any way. You'll be near help."

"I want to give you a hard time for being such a pessimist about this, but you're being too thoughtful about what could go wrong," Jane said.

Doc opened his arms graciously. "It's what I'm here for," he said.

Jane wrapped him in a hug.

"You'll get everyone ready?" Jane said as he returned her embrace.

"Of course. And you'll be careful."

"Sure," Jane said. "What possibly could go wrong, flying directly at an invading alien army?"

"I can't imagine," Doc said.

Jane stepped back. They stared at each other for a long moment.

"This never gets easier," Doc said. "When I brought you all together, I thought I'd eventually just come to understand you're all good at what you do, and you know what you're doing, and you'll all be safe."

"But then we wouldn't have you worrying about us all the time," Jane said. "And frankly, as the resident worrier around here, it's nice to know someone else is in a state of perpetual anxiety as well."

Doc took the pendant from Jane's hand and draped it over her head

"Don't forget that," he said. "You leaving now?"

"There's not a lot of time for dawdling," Jane said.

"Walk you to the landing bay?"

"You better."

She took his hand.

Doc looked down at their entwined fingers, his expression confused, sad and nostalgic all at once.

Jane beamed a smile, doing her very best to fake as much confidence as possible.

"This is what you taught me to do, Doc," Jane said.

"I know," he said. "It's just... sometimes I wonder if I did too good a job."

CHAPTER 52:
BEAUTY IN THIS WORLD

Kate sat in the dark and watched the second movement of the Third Symphony of Gustav Mahler at the City Performing Arts Center. Professional dancers swam across the stage with the strength of Olympic athletes and the weightlessness of butterflies. She sometimes wondered what it would have been like to grow up to be one of them, the way her life had been intended once upon a time. But on this reflection, like on most things, Kate had grown incapable of dwelling. It just was not in her nature to regret anymore. Regretting, she thought, was a loss of control over a small piece of yourself.

Titus sat next to her, his luminous golden eyes reflected the stage lights back like an animal's. This she could not get used to. Sometimes, while in the dark, she'd see his eyes before she saw him, two glowing spheres in the blackness, reminding her that he was not human, that they were not the same.

But he held her hand anyway, and that was okay.

Jane gave them the tickets before she left for outer space. Kate didn't want to take them.

"Why are you doing this?" she asked, looking at the tickets Jane handed her as if they were written in another language.

"Because it's the end of the world again, and you should see one more ballet just in case, I told you this already," Jane said.

"But why give me tickets?" Kate asked.

"Just go to the theater and sit with your boyfriend and recharge," Jane said, her smile never wavering.

"I hate when you call him my boyfriend," Kate said.

"Kate Miller, can't you just for one moment relax and enjoy the fact that someone in this world loves you?" Jane said.

"No," Kate said. "I have… a really hard time with this."

There was no anger in Jane's voice during the exchange. She truly did want Kate to find happiness. Whether through Titus or on her own. Some days Kate wondered if this was on some sort of list of goals Jane kept for herself.

The problem, Kate realized, was that she never even tried to be happy. Maybe she could, if she wanted to. She understood Titus suffered from clinical depression. They'd talked about it. He'd been in treatment, quietly, for a long time and eventually discovered that it was a particularly common trait in werewolves, that something inherent in their nature led to a tendency toward depression. But he knew how to be happy. Sitting with him, while taking in the spectacle of the show, joy graced his face. He reveled in something beautiful despite knowing nothing about it.

Kate leaned back and turned her full attention to the stage, the way the dancers mirrored each other, the finesse, style and power of their actions. She was struck by how much of their movements seemed like her own, how much dance remained a part of her despite the violence of her life. As a child, she had danced like a fighter, and as an adult, she fought like a dancer, and the two were forever intertwined in her life.

She released Titus' hand to flex her fingers. Sometimes, the pain caught up to her. Not the pain from her crime fighting days—though there were certainly enough injuries to haunt her there. But the injuries from the car crash, the result of an attempted carjacking that cost Kate her parents and her dancing career, those injuries welled up in the dark, in old bone breaks and scar tissue. Though in nearly constant pain since the accident, she got up, every day, and danced, and fought, time and time again.

She watched dancers on the stage, who did not go out at night to live a life of violence, and she realized that in many ways she got involved in all the dangerous things so that somewhere, each night, other people could dance in peace. Other people could create something beautiful, the sort of beautiful thing her body no longer felt capable of doing. She carried the pain silently so that no one else would have to.

I'll need to thank Jane for these tickets, she thought. Her mind drifted as the show came to a close, to where her friend might be, out there in the night sky alone.

Titus and Kate slowly made their way out of the theater, "like normal people," the werewolf whispered in her ear, though Kate knew he joked to avoid pondering things they were both already thinking about, like how this could be the last time they did something like this together. They possessed a strong sense of the consequences of the risks they both took, and they had an unspoken agreement not to talk about how any day might be their last. Still, with the strains of music resonating in their ears and worry in their hearts, it felt more real tonight. When Titus slipped an arm around Kate's waist, something she normally shied away from in public, she didn't pull away, instead leaning in and wrapping her arm around him as well. It caught Titus off-guard. The look he gave her unmasked his surprise. She glanced at him and realized just how terrible she was at saying anything at all, and even here, arm and arm, she still never seemed to find the words to tell him what was on her mind.

I wish you spoke dance, Kate thought, reflecting on the pure emotion of the performance. I could use it like sign language to tell you how I felt about all the things I never say. About every single thing. Instead you stand, waiting for me to reveal things I never will.

"I could help with that," a familiar voice said from an alley. Kate and Titus immediately launched into defensive positions, stepping apart to flank the newcomer, Titus already sliding out of his coat to transform.

Then a woman they both thought they'd never see again stepped out from the shadows.

"Prevention," Kate said, snarling.

"I'm going by my first name now, but that's fine," the woman said. "And I mean it. I'm a telepath. I heard all those complicated dilemmas bouncing around in that dark thing you call a brain, Dancer. And I could translate for you."

"Give me one reason why I shouldn't knock you out right now,"

Kate said.

"I'm here to help, not start a fight. Calm down," Laura, the former Prevention said.

"You kidnapped my friends and tried to kill me," Kate said. "And you're here to help?"

"I came to you exactly for this reason," Laura said. "Because you have the most reason to distrust me. I wanted the person I contacted to be suspicious."

"Well, we're suspicious," Titus said.

Laura removed an envelope from inside her coat and put it on the ground slowly.

"Inside's a list with information about a stockpile of tools you'll want to fight the invasion," Laura said.

"What do you know about it?" Kate said.

"Probably as much as you do, maybe more. I've been working to prevent it all along. None of us knew that, but it's true."

"You're full of garbage," Titus said.

"Take that envelope to the Department. Have Sam Barren look up what's in there. It'll help them to help you," Laura said.

"You think you're just going to drop this on us and walk away?" Titus said.

"Let her go," Kate said.

"I knew you of all people would understand," the former Prevention said. "You know it's not personal, don't you?"

Kate said nothing and watched the telepathic agent drift back into the shadows.

"Don't think this settles things between us," Kate said.

Prevention, Laura, shrugged.

"My fight's not with you anymore," she said, pointing up into the sky. "In a lot of ways it never was. Just give that to Sam. Tell him it's all their gear anyway. I just put it away for safe keeping."

Prevention disappeared. Kate held out a hand, to stop Titus from pursuing.

"We're really going to just let her walk away?" he said, staring at the empty space where the former agent had just stood.

"It's the end of the world, Titus," Kate said. "If ever there was a

256

time for strange allegiances, it's now."

CHAPTER 53:
THE STRANGE MACHINE

Henry Winter limped into his office, looking at a text message from Sam that simply said "we have to talk." Winter found himself strongly considering hitting an old man. "We have to talk." About what? Is he quitting? Having digestive problems? He couldn't possibly give slightly more detail than this?

"When did the old man get so good at being vague," Winter muttered, sitting down at his desk dramatically and reaching for the phone.

"They say that talking to yourself is a sign of insanity, but I don't believe it," Entropy Emily said, standing in the corner looking at the bookshelf lining the office wall. Winter's whole body shook in surprise, not having seen her on his way in. "I talk to myself all the time."

"Why didn't you tell me you were here!" he said. "Are you trying to give me a heart attack?"

"Don't be ridiculous," Emily said. "That only happens in the movies."

"I don't... you can't just... why are you here, Emily?"

"You're going to teach me how to use that strange machine you showed me and Kate before," Emily said.

"You're not touching that machine unless there are no other options," Winter said.

Emily crossed the room and sat down in one of the chairs across from Henry Winter. She crossed her legs and steepled her fingers.

"We're days away from an alien invasion, we're outmanned and outgunned. I'd call that having no other options. Obi-Wan Kenobi, I'm your only hope. Show me how to use the machine."

"Emily," Winter said.

"Don't Emily me, Henry Winter," Emily said. "I saw the look on your face. You are dying. Dying. Dying to show me how to work that thing. You want to see it in action. You're a crazy inventor guy. Watching your creations destroy stuff is how you sleep better at night."

"I don't know what you're talking about," Winter said.

"You built that thing for yourself, huh," Emily said.

"Huh?"

"You did! You built it for yourself. Are you not showing me because you wish you were using it instead?" Emily said.

Winter stared.

Emily belly laughed. "I knew it. The second I saw it I realized you built that thing for yourself," she said.

"Why would you think that?"

Emily smirked.

"It's got the same color palette as—"

"Fine, fine, yeah, I built it for myself and it never worked. And yeah, I think Dr. Bohr is right and you'll be able to manipulate it using your bubbles of float, but you are not supposed to be allowed to use it yet," Winter said.

Emily leaned in conspiratorially.

"You ever seen it working?"

Winter shook his head.

"Not once?"

Winter shook his head again.

"Wanna go see if your plan will work?"

He shook his head a third time.

Emily stared, waiting.

Winter threw his hands up in the air.

"Fine, fine! I admit it! I'm dying to see if it'll work. I'm dying to. Why do you do this stuff?"

"Because I can," Emily said.

"Doc's going to kill me," Winter said.

"That's okay," Emily said. "There's a fair to moderate chance the whole world will be dead in a few days anyway. The least we can do is have some fun first, right?"

CHAPTER 54:
SPY GAMES

So Agent Prevention just showed up in the street and gave you the location to a forgotten warehouse where a bunch of our stuff has been stashed?" Sam Barren said while standing in a hallway of the administrative wing of the Labyrinth.

"That's what happened," Titus said.

Kate folded her arms and leaned against the wall.

"We'll go retrieve the items," she said.

"No," Sam said. "No, we got this. If a Department field team can't go pick up items we recovered ourselves over the past ten years and lost, we don't really deserve our jobs. We'll take care of this and see if there's anything in the inventory we can use."

Sam thumbed through the file Kate had given him, grumbling under his breath.

"Well, she certainly made us look stupid for years," Sam said. "I suppose we shouldn't be surprised that she'd pop up one more time to make us appear like fools again."

"She said the people who hired her had this in mind all along," Titus said. "That she was there to get the Department ready for an invasion."

Sam sniffed and smoothed his mustache.

"Well I'll say this much," Sam said. "When I retired, the Department was like a giant detective agency. We were investigators, we were researchers... agents, certainly, and we knew how to defend ourselves, but we were really a covert sort of thing. Prevention turned the Department into a fighting force. I can't say I was happy about the idea of my old company being militarized, but that would make sense—she made the Department much more of an armed service than an agency."

"You think she's telling the truth?" Kate said.

"I don't know anymore," Sam said. "I can't say that I trust her. But we've seen some things the past few years, haven't we?"

Kate nodded.

"The Children of the Elder Star were infiltrated by people who wanted to promote the invasion," Kate said. "It's not a huge stretch to think that an opposing force might try to infiltrate the Department to do the opposite."

Sam grunted and closed the folder aggressively.

"This is too much cloak and dagger garbage, and I was a professional government agent most of my adult life," he said. He shook his head and turned back to Kate. "Any word from our friend?"

"Alley Hawk is still laid up," Kate said. "Vermin King almost killed him."

Her quasi-mentor and fellow vigilante without superpowers had dropped off the grid weeks back after recapturing his arch enemy. His allies had complete confidence he would recover, but still, everyone concerned. His injuries were severe. "No word on your end, then?" she said.

"We're keeping an eye out," Sam said. "He always disappeared when he needed to. And he always came back."

Kate made a sound in the back of her throat. She didn't have the time to worry about Alley Hawk, but she was worried nonetheless.

"I'll put a team together to check out this bunker," Sam said. "With its space-junk. You know, this is a clerical screw up."

"Clerical?" Titus said.

"Paperwork. We collected all this junk. If we'd kept better track of it…" Sam said.

The sound of Billy's voice in Kate and Titus' earpieces cut them off.

"Guys," Billy said.

"Way to be formal, Billy," Titus said.

"No time," he said. "We've got a thing. There's a ship coming in fast, one of the Nemesis fleet ships, it looks like a gunship or something."

"On our way," Kate said. "What's the trajectory?"

"It's headed right for the City. Where are you?"

"At the Labyrinth. We'll move out," Titus said.

"It's worse," Billy said. "Neal has detected that the fleet is within striking distance of the planet."

"What?" Titus said.

"It's starting," Billy said. "They're here."

CHAPTER 55:
AS ABOVE, SO BELOW

Billy, Bedlam, Seng, Doc, Valkyrie and Korthos watched the monitor, a split screen in the control room. On one side, they saw the brightly glowing shell of the attack ship heading for the City, on a collision course for downtown.

But on the other screen was a feed from an Earth satellite pointing out into space. And there, in the distance, they spied the writhing monstrosity that was the Nemesis fleet.

"We've got to head up there," Doc said.

The first ship is a distraction, Dude said in Billy's ear. *They want us to pay attention to a small ground force so that we're not prepared for the rest of the fleet. We got lucky spotting them.*

"Dude says this is a distraction," he repeated. He couldn't stop staring at Doc.

Doc sent an irritated expression in Billy's direction.

"What?" Doc said.

"I'm sorry, I'm just trying to adjust to… you," Billy said.

Doc had swapped out his usual jeans and long black coat for a form-fitting costume, a black and gray suit with a long black cape, a full mask hung around his neck. The suit had been treated for the vacuum of space, and Billy understood Doc's reasons for swapping his outfit, but seeing their mentor dressed basically in spandex, in the face of an alien invasion, was profoundly disturbing to him.

"This is really your biggest concern right now?" Doc said.

"Hey man, you're wearing tights. It *is* disturbing," Bedlam said.

Korthos, let out a rumbling laugh. "I profess, when you stopped wearing that getup in the early days I was supremely relieved," he said.

"Forget it," Doc said. "Battle plan. Kate, are you online?"

"We're both here," Kate said.

"Where's Emily?" Billy said.

"I'm listening!" Emily said, her location still a mystery.

"What are you doing, Em? This is kind of important right now," Billy said.

"I'll be there when you need me, cupcake, cool your jets," Emily's disembodied voice said.

"The plan," Doc said. "Bedlam, you'll rendezvous with Kate and Titus and handle the ground assault. We expect that ship is going to dump some foot soldiers on the City and we need them neutralized."

"Got it," Bedlam said.

Doc turned an eye to Val, who watched him with a gentle, neutral expression.

"Are you up for this?" Doc said.

"I will be," Val said.

"Okay. Your powers are only going to be effective here with an atmosphere to work with, so you'll be air support for Kate's team. Are you comfortable with that?"

Val's eyes glowed a deep, electric blue.

"This is my world," she said. "I'll do anything you need."

"The storm goddess will be fine," Korthos said, stroking his midnight-blue beard. "I see a warrior in her."

"Right," Billy said. "Thanks for the color commentary, Beowulf. The rest of us are heading up into space?"

"We'll be the first line of defense," Doc said. "You all must hold back for my signal. I've got something big planned and can only do it once. But hopefully it'll start us on the right foot."

"I'll anxiously await your performance, war wizard," Korthos said.

"Seriously, this guy," Billy said.

Korthos shot him a vile look.

Billy smiled sheepishly back.

"I can provide some advice as we head up," Seng said. "I engaged the fleet once before. I couldn't stop them, but I know some of their weak points, and a few of their tactics."

"What should we be looking for, Seng?" Doc asked the alien.

Seng walked up to the screen and pointed to some of the larger structures visible in the blurry video of the fleet.

"The fighters will provide cover, but we need to stop the seed-ships," he said, pointing to the spear-like machines. "If those make Earthfall, they will immediately begin to terraform the planet. The destruction they'll cause in hours may be more than the planet can recover from even if we're able to defeat the entire fleet."

"Which is unlikely," Billy said.

"Aren't you a ball of sunshine today," Bedlam said.

"We shall be victorious, little shiny one," Korthos said, thumping his chest. "Fear not!"

Billy found himself staring blankly at the warrior god, completely unsure how to respond.

"Is there some sort of mother ship you could hit?" Kate's voice chimed in. "Cut the head off the beast?"

Seng gestured to one central shape, bigger than the rest, its features unclear.

"This. Their brain-ship. All others receive orders from it," Seng said.

But we'll never get close enough, Dude said. *We're better off focusing on the seed ships first.*

"Dude's being a pessimist and says we'll never hit it," Billy said.

"Straylight is correct," Seng said. "Every ship in that feet will die to protect the brain-ship."

"So we know our first targets," Doc said. "Billy, Seng, you're the fastest. You'll run interference after my alpha strike. Korthos?"

"I shall break everything in my sight," Korthos said. "My axe will—"

"Right, Korthos smash," Emily said, cutting him off.

Korthos looked around the room for her. "Distance makes you brave, little sprite," he said.

"You're wearing a kilt," Emily said. "You're automatically ten points less scary dressed like that."

Korthos fumed but said nothing.

Billy almost laughed at the idea of Emily shutting the big guy down with a jab. But then he remembered something. "What about Jane?" he asked.

"She's out there somewhere," Doc said, his voice strained with worry. "We just have to hope she's close enough to help."

"And not dead," Emily said solemnly.

No one spoke.

Emily broke the silence.

"What? Nobody else was thinking it? I don't know about you guys but after our time travel thing it's like all I *can* think about."

As if on cue, a new and welcome voice interrupted the meeting. Billy felt a smile of relief break out on his face, but seeing the look of pure joy on Doc made him feel even better.

"Indestructibles," Jane's voice said through the speakers. "I'm back. Mission failure. They're not stopping, and they're closer than we thought."

"Jane?" Billy said. "We know they're close—they're already here."

CHAPTER 56:
AMONG THE STARS

The night she left Earth, the same night Kate and Titus had their run-in with Prevention, Jane flew straight up into the sky and beyond, leaving the Earth behind. She felt the atmosphere cling to her, like a hand pleading with her to stay. But a few moments later, as if passing through a soap bubble, she crossed beyond the stratosphere and felt, for the first time, the unadulterated rays of the sun splash against her skin.

Can I, she'd asked Doc, long ago, before the invasion, before the future, when she was young, and testing her limits. Doc answered: the sun will sustain you. You don't need to breathe, or to eat. You are a child of the sun as much as a child of the Earth.

She asked questions about distances and speed, and things she never really wanted to know the answers to. Something about how, in space, she would be so much faster, some theory Henry Winter had about the friction or drag of the atmosphere, the energy loss of forced combustion. None of it was of consequence. All that mattered, Jane thought, was that she could fly into space, fast and true, into the black.

Neal had helped her plot a course, given her a device, now strapped to her wrist, to assist her in finding the Nemesis fleet. She looked at the sun, watching her like a guardian, a mother, her loving light spilled down on her. And then she flew onward, past the moon, the electromagnetic sounds of space singing in her ears like the songs of some alien world.

As she left her planet behind, a blanket of profound loneliness enveloped Jane. So distracted, she did not see the shadowy shape move from behind the moon and creep, silent and prowling, toward the planet.

* * *

The fleet waited for her in the distance as if it knew she was coming, as if it were a single entity, calmly prepared for her arrival. The ships hung suspended in space like modern art, shell-like armor and irregular shapes turning the fleet into a garden of nightmares. She could discern the seed-ships, like javelins, a trio of spears pointed toward Earth, studded with nests of living terraforming machinery. Other ships, barbed and cruel-looking, drifted near the seed-ships, bodyguards against attack, looking like deep sea fish on the offensive.

And poised in the center of the sea of living machines was the brain-ship, the central nervous system of the fleet, staring at her with an eyeless face.

Fighters took notice of her, while she drifted in close and then zipping by them to get a closer look, like wasps protectively buzzing and hovering around their nest. Jane did her best to ignore them, not flinching when one craft flew in too close, and then floating around another that stopped in front of her to block her path.

The brain-ship, the mother ship, turned its attention on her, a cavernous mouth opening as Jane drew close. Inside that mouth, more fighters sat unmoving, strapped into the system through black cabling. Were they resting? Is this where new drones were born? Jane couldn't tell. It looked like a nursery for hornets.

She entered this strange landing bay but did not touch down. Instead, Jane flew, a few inches off the surface, deeper into the vessel, into the shadows, until she came to a place where the walls glowed red and illuminated her way.

Monsters waited for her there, strange aliens with shapes like nightmares. They did not speak, a parasitic creature latched on to each, controlling its movements, controlling its thoughts. These possessed creatures parted as she approached, guiding her inside the brain-ship but not touching her, keeping a respectful, almost reverent distance.

She gazed into each creature's eyes, but only found blankness there, an empty void. Though not in all of them. A few looked at her with a sort of desperation, a helplessness, a pleading request for something, for help, for release. And others displayed a cruel malevolence, something horrible, something hungry, something wanting.

She journeyed deeper into the ship, through pathways like veins, wet and shining corridors, the ground like muscle beneath her heels. It was someone's vision of hell in here, she thought. Somewhere in history or literature a poet had envisioned the afterlife like this, an endlessly dark world, lit in red luminance, demonic and alien beings staring at you from the shadows.

She arrived in a chamber, where more of the varied and strange aliens stood in a circle, parasites glowing brightly on their chests.

Jane waited. No one moved, no one spoke. Just a room of oddities, staring at each other with multifaceted vision, eyes almost human and eyes like some other organ entirely.

"I come representing my world," she said. "I want to speak with you about a peaceful resolution."

The monsters simply watched in silence.

"I know you can understand me," she said calmly. "We realize you take information from us through your scouts. You can speak our languages. Your servants taunted us with it."

The silence was deafening. Jane wondered if this were a wasted trip. Then one of the creatures began to speak, a being with dark green skin, ornate horns growing out of its head, skin covered in scars.

"We know your words," the creature said in a voice that seemed like it had never formed a complete sentence before in its life. The creature's vocal chords sounded more accustomed to screaming, roaring and barking orders. Not this docile discussion about surrender.

"So speak with me," Jane said. "What would it take to turn you away. To bargain for my planet's life."

The alien who spoke paused, eyes growing distant. It occurred to Jane that he was not the one truly speaking—but a conduit for a mind elsewhere on the ship, or elsewhere on the fleet, controlling him through the vile thing latched on to his chest.

"You think we are evil," the alien said.

"I don't know anything about you," Jane said. "Help me understand."

Again, the alien paused, waiting for a signal. And then: laughter.

The sound chilled Jane to her guts. Her stomach churn with acid. It was the laugh of a demon.

"You think we are conquerors. You believe us to be greedy," the creature said. "But we are not always the scourge the creatures of light think we are."

"How so?" Jane said, keeping herself loose and ready to move if they attacked her.

"We eat the cancers of the universe," the creature said. "Is that the word in your tongue? Cancers? We eat the rotten places; the ones that will bring destruction and death."

"You're saying you… eat evil worlds?" Jane asked.

Again, a thoughtful delay from the speaker.

"It is our role. You think we are a cancer ourselves, don't you? But we are a carrion creature. We eat the rotten things. The poisons. We wipe the slate clean."

"You can't tell me the Luminae's world was a cancer. All the good they do. All the nobility they have. You can't expect me to believe that," Jane said.

The speaker waited for a signal, and turned its head side to side in an awkward parody of the human gesture.

"No, no, no, they were not poison," the creature said. "But we must eat some worlds to sustain our strength, so that we can devour others that need to die. Some muscle must be sacrificed to excise the disease."

"It sounds to me like you're eating everything in your path, good or bad," Jane said. "It seems as if you're making excuses for your gluttony."

The speaker inhaled sharply, bearing sharp yellow teeth.

"We take what we need," it said. "From good worlds and bad. This body I use as a conduit to speak to you. We took him from his world because he represented the best of it. We took him to save him, to incorporate some small part of that now dead place. We do not obliterate. We retain. We save."

"You enslave," Jane said.

"That is a matter of… perspective," the voice said.

Jane's curiosity about who really was using this barbarian-like alien to speak grew stronger.

"So where do we fall on your skewed scale of right and wrong?" Jane said. "Are we a cancer? Or are we special?"

The creature laughed its haunting chuckle again.

"Your world is… unique," the speaker said. "Do you know this? Your world. Your capacity for right and wrong. We have never seen anything like it in all our millennia. You are both the light in the darkness, and the poison in the vein. Your… humanity. If you ever reached the stars, you would ruin everything you touched."

"But we're not just poison?" Jane asked, curious.

"You also have a remarkable capacity for good," the creature said. "You have strength unlike anything we've ever seen. And your world is filled with wonders."

"I doubt you've ever seen a better place," Jane said.

The creature slapped its hands together loudly. Jane watched as the being stood up, nearly seven feet tall, body covered in keloid scars and bone spurs.

"Never in such variety. The creatures of light, the Luminae you call them, their wonder is uniform. Their power is uniform. But your little blue stone, your tiny little world… filled to the brim with wonders. With monsters. With gods. Your world will feed us very well. The variety. We can smell it. We have long waited for an entity like yours. We will never be the same."

"So there's no talking you out of it?" Jane said.

"Nothing has ever stopped us," the speaker said. "We are one. We are might. We are hungry. And we want your world. Your nobility, your savagery, your fear and cowardice and heroism and love. Your world will be the most delicious thing we have ever encountered."

"We won't let you take us," Jane said.

"So you say," the being said. "But you will. We sent our scouts ahead of us. We know what we'll take from you. And we know we must devour the rest. We can never let your people go to the stars."

"We'll stop you," Jane said.

"You'll help us," the creature said. Out of the shadows, one of the parasites skittered forward, a clumsy, quick spider, swaying on its feet as if afraid to stop moving. "You'll join us now, ambassador. We will welcome you into the fold. We wish to know you. We want to have you here with us in the sky."

The parasite pounced, arms outstretched, ready to latch onto Jane and take her mind from her. Jane was prepared, though, and caught the springing creature with one hand. Unhesitating, Jane ignited that hand in a burst of flames and a bright flash of light left the creature exhaling like a lobster cooking in its own skin.

"We know about you as well," Jane said. "And we will not go quietly."

More parasites clattered out of the darkness, hovering around the speaker like guard dogs, hissing and aggressive. They launched themselves at Jane, but she flared her flame powers, sending a burst of fire out around her. Those in the blast radius blackened and shriveled, then dropped to the floor like dead spiders, finger-like limbs curled into loose fists.

The room smelled like burnt flesh, the mindless parasites squealing as superheated air killed them from the inside.

Now, some of the other aliens, the possessed hulking brutes all around her, started to rise from their chairs.

"Such a little trick you have," the beings all said at once, like a chant. "Your little trick, your insignificant little trick."

"I am powered by our star itself, and I tell you true: you will not take my world from me."

One of the unspeaking alien hosts swung a massive, bony fist at her. Jane stepped aside, using the momentum to smash the being's arm over her shoulder, the popping of bone against flesh almost unbearable to watch.

"You think you've won, but you've already lost," the being said. "You never found all our spies. You never learned all our tricks. We have been planning your demise for a very long time, and our warriors strike right now."

"Well then," Jane said, backing away from the slow onslaught of captive warriors. "You won't like when I do this."

She reached up to her neck and snapped the cord of the pedant Doc had given her.

"Feeling victorious, aren't you," Jane said.

"It is our natural state," the speaker said, his peers closing in on her from all sides, a dozen massive, scarred warriors with unknown abilities and physiologies. Jane thought she could stop them on her own, sure, but in such tight quarters, in unknown capacity…

"You'll forgive me if I steal this one from you," she said. She crushed the pendant in her hand, feeling the opal in the center of it split and sever.

The mother-ship chamber glowed blue and white for a moment.

And where Jane once stood, nothing remained.

* * *

Jane reappeared outside the Labyrinth in a flash of light, the air smelled like strange particles of space, nausea and confusion settled in her belly like motion sickness. She fell onto one knee, resting, more shaken by Doc's teleportation spell than by what transpired on the alien ship.

"Oh, Doc, why didn't you warn me it would feel like this," Jane said, shaking. She touched the earpiece she wore and spoke. "Indestructibles. I'm back. Mission failure. They're not stopping, and they're closer than we thought."

"Jane?" Billy's voice said, sounding strained. "We know they're close—they're already here."

"What?" Jane said. But she looked out to the horizon and saw parts of the City smoking and on fire. "No."

"We're getting this first wave under control," Billy said. "They sent some sort of attack ship—oh, no."

"What, Billy?" Jane said, already heading for the city.

"Look up."

She turned her eyes to the sky. It resembled a painting, something abstract crafted on a plane of blue, but there, pale and ghostly in the sky, the first view of the Nemesis fleet had become visible, a small shape beyond the daylight moon.

"The whole fleet is here," Jane said.

Kate's voice chimed in next, sounding winded and strained.

"We've got this. Get the flyers ready. Do what you have to do, Jane."

Jane nodded, knowing no one would see her. Somehow the gesture felt comforting.

"I'm on my way," Jane said. "We'll head up together."

CHAPTER 57:
THE BATTLE OF THE CITY

Kate watched the attack ship hover in the air above the City's downtown. It fired red bursts of light at the buildings and sent shards of glass and powdered concrete raining down onto the streets below. The ship hung low, perhaps three stories up, a lump of shiny, beetle-like armor.

She got closer and saw a hatch opening in the flying insect's guts. Shapes formed there, living creatures, and soon they leapt to the ground. Hulking things, varied in shape and form, with the only thing in common the omnipresent parasite latched onto their chests.

The aliens split up and headed in all directions, leaving their vessel to continue their destructive path. Two of them marched right for her. Kate tapped a button on her belt and the Distribution suit hummed to life.

The first creature, a four-legged thing with a face shaped like a bay leaf, reached her first. Though the beast had no eyes, it knew exactly where she was, and galloped toward her like some sort of nightmarish centaur. Kate jumped, sent a knee into what she assumed was its guts. The shot had no effect—his "chest," or whatever the thickly padded surface was she had just kicked, had almost no give to it. Before she could strike again, the alien backhanded Kate sending her sprawling across the street. The blow rattled her teeth.

The Distribution suit whirred louder. Kate smiled viciously and ran back towards the alien, her ears still ringing from his initial blow.

He punched again, but this time she let it graze her, allowing the suit to pick up more kinetic energy. Before he took another swing, Kate hit him with a full body, from-her-feet haymaker. The suit fed the punch, sending a kinetic burst through her tungsten-tipped gauntlet when it connected with the parasite on the alien's chest. Host and symbiote lurched backward from the force of the blow, then tumbled, crashing hard and loud into a parked car.

Kate instantly smelled gasoline. She covered her eyes just before the car blew up, engulfing the alien in a feeble cry.

Please tell me the car was empty, Kate thought, tell me there wasn't anyone in it.

The second alien arrived next and smashed Kate's back with two arm-like appendages. The suit absorbed the energy, but she felt the punch across her ribs, her heart pounding at the sudden pain zapping across her body. She punched the bear-shaped creature in what she thought looked like a kneecap. She'd guessed right, and the monster toppled over awkwardly as its leg gave way to pain.

"What was that?" Titus said through Kate's earpiece.

"Blew up a car," Kate said.

"I thought we were gonna keep collateral damage to a—"

"—Better than knocking him into a convenience store, Titus," she said. "That was a BMW, in case you're wondering."

"Wasn't wondering," he said. "You okay?"

Kate didn't answer. She stole a glance at the car—no human bodies inside, just the burned-up corpse of the alien. Kate intentionally let the bear-like creature hit her a few times, blocking the blows with her forearms, absorbing more kinetic energy. She ducked under another swing, punched what seemed to be an elbow—again a good guess—and felt connective tissue and bone crumple under her up-swinging fist. Finally, she head-butted the creature in the nose, hoping to stun him.

Instead, she stunned *herself*. Her brain rang at the impact. The alien brushed its nose, now streaming with clear fluid. It grabbed hold of her, preventing Kate from getting in a good punch, then knocked her to the ground, before dragging her by her ankle toward its toothy mouth.

Something sharp grazed her hip. She looked down and saw a piece of twisted metal from the car wreck laying on the pavement, long and almost flat, like a sword without a hilt. She snatched it up in her gloved hands, and when the alien pulled her close enough, she stabbed downward—not at the alien itself, but into the parasite, plunging the makeshift weapon inside the crablike creature's body. The parasite shuddered and squealed, a high-pitched whine of pain, then blackish blood poured out from where she'd injured it.

A few seconds later, the parasite's shiny, spider-like limbs loosened, and the creature slid off the chest of its host alien. The bear-shaped creature watched this all unfold, its attack on Kate over, and when the parasite hit the ground, a dead lump of plant-like flesh, it then fell to one knee.

Kate scurried to her feet, prepared to fight, but the alien was finished. It simply looked at its chest where the parasite had just been. Its skin looked burned and infected, raw and painful. The alien placed one squat hand on the wound, and then turned to look at Kate, who readied herself to throw another punch.

With no human features, the creature's face bore no resemblance to anything that might display emotion. Yet Kate saw in its expression something. Relief? Maybe gratefulness? Definitely a flicker of serenity. It reached out to her with its other hand, slowly, almost thoughtfully, then fell to the ground, unconscious or dead. Kate couldn't tell.

She stood over the unmoving body for a moment, the sounds of terror and destruction all around her suddenly absent. And then, sure the alien would not stand up again, she ran down the street, looking for her next opponent.

* * *

Bedlam understood what she was.

Somewhere deep in the parts of her brain that had never been human, the commands were all there. The code. The instructions. The Children of the Elder Star had created her to be a weapon of mass destruction. She was designed with pure malicious intent, to be dropped into an urban environment and to cause pure, unadulterated chaos. Her name was Bedlam for a reason. She possessed the tools to cause untold mayhem, especially in an enclosed, heavily populated environment.

That was what I was made to be, Bedlam thought, but that's not who I am.

She ran down a major street in the City's downtown, faster than a car, her cyborg legs carrying her with the grace and speed of a hurdler, her feet thudding against pavement, cracking and tearing it.

She saw one of the creatures the attack ship had dropped on them, a hunched beast with spines along its back and huge, glowing red eyes—fifteen feet of rage with a parasite clinging to its collarbone. It turned to face her, and she ran faster. The alien, seeing her challenge, plodded directly forward, ready to meet the cyborg head-on.

I'm not a weapon, Bedlam thought, seeing her next move. The targeting computer in her brain identified what she needed— something to strike this charging monster with.

She slammed on the breaks, metal heels digging into the asphalt, and then reached down to grab hold of a parked car.

Without stopping or losing momentum, Bedlam lifted it off the street, and hoped the frame of the car would hold together while she spun it.

The huge alien upon her, Bedlam completed the twisting arc of her attack and swung the entire car like a baseball bat. The back end slammed into the alien's face, knocking the massive creature flat. It hung there for a moment, limbs loose, head thrown backward, before slamming into the street.

"Home run, Bedlam," she said, admiring her handiwork.

The alien coughed and started climbing back to its feet.

"Dammit!" she said, hefting the car and slamming it down on the creature once more for good measure. The bumper fell off in her hands, and Bedlam watched the car roll off the alien and, oddly, land back on its wheels. She made a mental note to look into the brand. Clearly it deserved a high crash test rating.

The alien sat up, still taller than Bedlam even while sitting on its haunches. She looked once more at the bumper in her hands and then reared back, taking aim at the parasite on the being's chest. She swung.

Not a pretty sight, but a perfect swing—the bumper connected with and caught the parasite, hooking into the mindless thing's shell-like carapace. Bedlam's inhuman strength kept the bumper moving forward, and suddenly the parasite was disconnecting from the host body, tearing away, its limbs ripping off like a bug's. The body bounced down the street, pouring black fluid as is rolled, legs fell away, looking disturbing, like something you might eat at a seafood restaurant.

The light went out in the host creature's eyes, its long, powerful limbs spasmed, before falling onto its back and shuddering into unconsciousness.

"Got one," Bedlam said into her earpiece. "How many did we say we saw?"

"Neal spotted about twenty," Titus said.

Bedlam sighed, tossing the bumper aside.

"Back to work then, I guess," she said, once again sprinting toward the action.

* * *

Titus let the fleeing residents run past him. He walked through them, almost invisible, bumping shoulders with strangers, helping an older man up as he staggered to his knees, catching a woman running with her child before she fell. A few blocks away, the ship rained destruction down on the streets, and below it, monstrous foot soldiers pursued the citizens like predators, striking them down as they went.

Titus started moving faster. The crowd pushing into him was relentless, as scared men and women screamed and looked for an escape. Drowning, he couldn't get through them. He heard explosions in the distance, some sort of enormous bang from the direction Bedlam was headed. Too many people, too much noise, he couldn't see...

The monster inside him told him what to do. And, as Titus was often afraid to admit, the monster was right.

He threw his hooded sweatshirt on the ground and willed himself to transform. It hurt, it would always hurt, this violent shifting of cells and molecules, no matter how good he got at it, no matter how smooth he made it seem. He fell to one knee, letting the pain subside. Suddenly he smelled the skin and sweat of aliens, of every single City dweller around him. He listened to heartbeats and distant screaming.

And the people around him began to scream as well, terrified when a three-hundred-pound werewolf suddenly took shape beside them. The crowds ran even faster away from him, but Titus charged toward the oncoming aliens. One looked like a crocodile on long limbs, another like a hairless bat. Both had controlling parasites attached to them, turning them into biological weapons.

Titus broke free from the throng of humanity and roared at the aliens, who stared him down with deadly silence. The three monsters—alligator, bat, werewolf—circled each other, sizing each other up.

The bat-like alien moved first, lunging at Titus with bony, oversized arms. Titus bounced back, out of reach, but heard the reptilian creature make its move to attack him. The werewolf lashed out with a clawed foot. Talons sank deeply into the creature's parasitic partner and drew gobs of blood. The alligator-alien gasped and hissed before taking a quick step back, clutching the parasite as if to hold in the pouring blood.

The bat-thing attacked again. Claws pierced the muscle of Titus' shoulder. The werewolf roared in pain and surprise, and the alligator-thing took advantage of his distraction to snap with massive, toothy jaws, catching Titus' forearm.

The hurt shoved a nail into Titus' brain, making him angry, to feel out of control. The bat-creature piled on, bony limbs bruised Titus' body as the creature flailed. Titus felt his control slipping and his fear building. His heart thundered, a wet beat in his ears. And then the beast took over.

He barely registered what happened next. Jaws clamped down on the bat-thing's neck, dragging him away, the attack caused the alien to forget its assault and to instead focus on staying alive. Titus shook him like a dog toy and the bat-alien cried out in agony.

The alligator-alien opened its mouth and adjusted its toothy grip on Titus' flesh. The momentary release was all Titus needed to turn his attention on that creature, raking his claws up its belly and sinking them into the softer meat of the parasite's body. Titus dug in his long talons like a child tears into clay, squeezing and ripping. The reptilian alien grew limp and started to convulse, and then the werewolf shoved him away.

The bat-creature clutched its throat, limped towards him, not willing to give up, ready to fight to the death. Somewhere in the back of Titus' mind, his human side felt pity and regret for this warrior from another world. He realized it was hopeless, that these creatures ended up destroyed by their melding with the parasites, but still, to have journeyed across galaxies only to perish on the streets of a faraway city…

Still, the monster remained in charge, and the monster had no mercy. With blinding speed, the werewolf leapt at the wounded alien, not attacking the creature's body, but at the parasite controlling it, slashing downward with all his claws, gutting the bug-plant hybrid, two swipes down, two across, delivering death.

The bat creature fell forward, landing in the werewolf's arms. Monster to monster, they locked eyes. The beast within the wolf recognized only fallen prey, while Titus, watching, witnessing, saw something else. He saw relief. He saw a feral warrior ready to die.

And then it died, another victim of the Nemesis fleet, another tool discarded.

Titus roared, his voice echoing in the emptying streets of the City, and he raged on, looking for another battle.

CHAPTER 58:
PRESIDENT SOME DAY

You could see the fleet from Earth.

If I don't die, Jon Broadstreet thought, looking up at the blue sky above the City, watching strange shapes, pale and uncomfortably close, hanging there like the moon, this will be my lead in the story.

Nearby, smoke rose. He heard the terrified rumble of humanity and saw the humped back of the aircraft that had crept out of the sky and into their midst, a shelled slug of a thing, created fear wherever it turned.

Broadstreet held his laptop in front of him and watched the screen as Jane's recorded message went live. When she told him that he'd know, that she wouldn't have to tell him it was time to release the recording, he believed her, but he'd no idea she meant it would be this obvious. The City, under attack, suffered a direct assault. Why here, Broadstreet wondered, scanning the Internet and his professional resources for news of attacks in New York or London, Paris or Beijing. Nothing, though, just here, in the City, a single, calculated strike. Monsters at the gates.

Broadstreet had prepped the file to release immediately, on multiple video-sharing sites, and through his own publication's pages. His professional conscience stood at odds with his moral compass— he realized it represented the scoop to end all scoops, the sort of first report that made careers and saved newspapers, but he believed he should have shared it with everyone immediately. No, he thought, it'll be okay—it's the information age, you've put it online, every one of your colleagues and competitors will share it within seconds. It will be ubiquitous. Everyone will see it. Everyone needs to.

It took half a second for the video to go live on the paper's website before his editor called him. Broadstreet's phone buzzed in his pocket.

"How long have you had this video?" his editor, a beleaguered and underpaid battering ram of a journalist with the unfortunate name of Butch Dancy, sounded more bewildered than angry.

"Just got it," Broadstreet lied.

"Next time you want to lie, don't show me a video from an overcast day and tell me you just shot it when the sun is out," Butch said. "I'm sometimes smarter than you are."

"I know," Broadstreet said.

"Doesn't matter. Where are you?" Butch said.

"On the roof of my building. I can see the smoke downtown," Broadstreet said. For once he was happy to live so far on the outskirts of the City. He could make out the destruction and see the smoke, yet he felt like he was watching a movie.

"Can you get downtown," Butch said.

Tempted—at least momentarily—to tell his boss to get lost, Broadstreet then thought about the Indestructibles—maybe Jane, maybe just her friends, but people younger than he was were risking their lives without a second thought for their own safety.

"I can try," Broadstreet said.

"You know the players. Get the rest of the story," Butch said. "And don't get yourself killed."

"OK. I'll try not to boss."

"And Broadstreet," Butch said.

"Yeah?"

"Good job with the video. Did you wordsmith her at all?"

"That would be unethical," Broadstreet said. "That's all her."

"This kid could be president someday," Butch said.

"Yeah," Broadstreet said, looking at the black smoke continue to rise from the City's center. "We have to make sure we still have a world left after this before we can start cracking jokes like that."

"Well," his boss said, sounding tired and more than a little afraid. "Let's hope we do."

Broadstreet hung up, then put his hands in his pockets. He pensively gazed at the City, where he'd been born, where he'd grown up, where he'd wanted to become a storyteller and newsman. We all play our parts, I guess, he thought.

He started to close his laptop, but paused, and pressed play on Solar's video one more time.

His own face appeared first, the impromptu opening made him feel self-conscious and unprofessional and amateur.

Broadstreet watched as he stepped away, remembering how he'd crossed behind the camera to zoom in, framing the shot around Solar's head and shoulders. The clouds on the day they'd met made her open-flame colored hair seem brighter, more supernatural.

"My name is Solar, of the Indestructibles," she said. "I apologize for the cryptic nature of this message, but I ask that everyone watching this listen carefully."

On screen, Solar did not immediately brim with confidence. She looked exactly like what she was—a young woman with far more responsibility thrown onto her shoulders than any one person deserved, facing things nobody could be prepared for, whether they had superpowers or not.

"We deal with impossible things all the time, and today is one of those days when one such impossible thing is about to happen. It sounds ridiculous to say it, believe me. But we will soon find ourselves under attack by an invading force. There's no better phrasing to make it less strange."

Solar sighed on screen, brushed her hair from her eyes.

"An alien fleet is coming here. To Earth. And its mission is not one of good intentions."

Solar took a beat, looking into the camera. Broadstreet cringed at his camerawork—he had adjusted the lens and zoomed in closer to focus more on her eyes. She noticed the camera moving and fixed her gaze.

"I know. I know. It's impossible to believe. But it's my hope that you'll never have to see this message, and we'll stop them before they ever arrive. No matter what, we're here for you. We'll be your first line of defense. Those of us who are able will fly into space to fight for you. The others will be here on the ground waiting to protect you. This is our promise."

Solar looked beyond the camera. Broadstreet remembered that moment, when she broke character, gazing at him as if to ask: have I said enough? Have I covered everything? He found himself doing the same thing now as he had when Solar stood right in front of him. He shook his head, regretting that there was nothing at all he could do to make this easier for her.

"We may not make it back. But that comes with the job. And we need to ask something from you. When and if this comes to a head, and the battle comes to our planet, we need you to be good to each other. Help your neighbors. Be kind to those who need someone to lean on. There will be dark days ahead, and only you can make them less so. They're coming to take our world—let's show them that we think this is a place worth holding onto."

Solar exhaled deeply.

"So for now, this is Solar, signing off for the Indestructibles. I hope to see you tomorrow, safe and sound."

The video played out and the screen went dark. Broadstreet closed the laptop and headed downstairs. In the apartment hallways, he heard rushed conversations, the sounds of people packing, the voices of fear. Would they listen? Broadstreet couldn't be sure. When we needed each other most, humanity had a tendency to turn on itself. Maybe not this time, he thought. He headed out into the street in the direction of trouble instead of fleeing from it. He held his camera and notepad firmly in hand.

Maybe not this time.

CHAPTER 59:
TO SCAR THE ARMADA

Doc Silence had been to space before.

All of them had, really, to varying degrees. Some took the journey in stride. Others hated it. In their younger days when they left Earth Doc hadn't been a fan. Traveling between dimensions felt natural to him. Space, however, seemed more like science, and science was too logical to play well with the finger paint style of magic Doc employed.

Sitting cross-legged in the vacuum of space, his old, lightly armored hero uniform fit clingy and tight. Doc gazed out into the darkness, Earth behind him, or below him—that's the thing, he thought, there's no up and down here—and watched the approaching alien fleet growing large and monstrous before him, moving quickly toward his home.

"How you doin' out there, Doc?" Billy's voice said in his ear.

"I hate space," Doc said.

"You should see Saturn. It'll change your opinion of things," he said.

Doc smiled. Billy's sojourn into the beyond seemed to have given him some perspective. He was curious to see how the young hero evolved after all of this, provided they survived the onslaught.

"I always liked Pluto better," Doc said.

"You would." Billy said.

"Might I inquire, are we discussing a pantheon or planets in this discussion?" Korthos' rumbling voice said. He didn't sound right;

Doc suspected the immortal had put the earpiece in backward, something he had been prone to do in their youth.

"Planets, big guy," Doc said. "You ready for your part?"

"I shall rain destruction down upon—"

"You're ready," Doc said.

And so am I, Doc thought, running through the patterns and manipulations he'd need to perform to make this spell work. It was war magic, hard magic, creating something out of almost nothing. Doc wasn't looking forward to it, but, he thought, if it worked, he could at least push their enemies back on their heels a bit before they got to Earth.

He turned his burning purple eyes toward the fleet and held out his hands, muttering inside his mask—sealed by both science and magic to let Doc speak in the vacuum of space—the words to the spell he needed to cast. This was war poetry he spoke, evoking old gods and warriors of myth and song. It was a poem of fire and blood, of fury and revenge, of death, pure mortality, a weapon intended to leave a bloody, ragged scar across an entire army.

The space in front of the fleet lit up into a razor-straight line of bright golden glow as wide as a horizon, becoming a tripwire of light and heat.

The fleet passed across that line like a foot crossing a threshold, and the trap was sprung.

A crisscrossed barrier of radiant netting leapt into existence, directly in front of the fleet, its ships moving too quickly to avoid passing through it. It resembled a fisherman's net, but the ships were not trapped so much as severed, their hulls splitting like cheese through a metal wire, no, through an infinite number of wires, crumbling and splintering, exploding in fire and whatever bloodlike fuel the ships used to sustain themselves.

Immediately, the rest of the armada took evasive action, banking up and above or down and below the barrier where Doc's limitations prevented him from making the trap any larger. He sensed the fear and panic as the fleet felt the loss of its numbers, the spell triggering feedback into his mind, letting him know exactly how much death he'd caused. This is the price of war magic, he thought, and why its practitioners are the way they are. You either need to have no conscience at all, or the ability to sacrifice yourself to the greater cause, to experience such horror over and over again. He hated it. Nauseous, his skin began to crawl and tears welled up in his eyes even as he knew these enemies were the ones bent on destroying his world.

Doc fought off these gruesome feelings and prepared another spell. He unfolded his legs from lotus position and moved his arms in a smooth, slow arc, speaking the phrases of another war spell, one of pain and destruction, not a poem now but a war cry, one that demanded the death of enemies. He felt oily and awful saying the words, greasy thoughts poured across his lips like a bad meal, but the spell worked as a red whip of light formed from his hand, and, in the distance, a remote representation of that weapon he'd conjured in his palm. He lashed out with the whip, and the distant version, a massive thing, moved as if wielded by a giant, carving a swath through the fleet, splitting warships in two, scattering fighters. A dreadnaught positioned itself to become a martyr for one of the spear-like seed ships, and crumbled under the cracking scourge.

Once again, the cries of pain echoed from spell to caster, traveling down Doc's arm like a heart attack. His fingers grew cold, his pulse spiked, and his body reacted in cataclysm to the violence it caused.

Doc reached into his mind, searching for another spell, trying to find more to give, something else he could throw at the oncoming alien fleet. But his thoughts, like lightning bugs, danced in the dark, without pattern and completely beyond his control.

"That's it," Doc said, his voice cracked and rough.

"What. The hell. Was that?" Billy said.

"A mighty strike, my old friend," Korthos said, his voice ridiculously energized by the display of destruction.

And then, Jane. "Are you okay, Doc?"

"I'll be fine," he said. "Go get them. I'll join you in a minute."

Doc's chest spasmed. Not a heart attack, but an electric jolt of pain as his body rejected the dark magic's feedback. He bit back the hurt, realizing his microphone was live.

"We could see that from the ground," Kate said.

"Good," Doc said, his breathing ragged. "That means it worked."

His consciousness faded and he fought to remain awake and an unexpected question rose from his cloudy mind: Where was Emily?

CHAPTER 60:
A SKY FULL OF HEROES

Billy watched the firestorm of Doc's spells explode in the distance. The brightness caused his eyes to water and left echoes in his vision.

Well that was intense, he thought, watching the armada scatter, its spiraling, tightly woven pattern broken by Doc's trap. Tiny fighters spun, out of formation and out of control, as heavy warships took evasive action. The central figures, the three big spires they called seed ships, still flanked the biggest vessel, the brain-ship.

Before the fleet could fully reconstitute itself, the rest of the team launched an attack of its own. Billy laughed, remembering a scene from *Braveheart*, or any other battle scenario where a group of lunatics took on a much larger force. To his left, crazy Korthos flew, pointing that ridiculous axe on a stick weapon of his, somehow making sound in space, contrary to scientific principles Emily had drilled into Billy's head. Nothing Korthos did should be possible, he realized, but then again, Doc said much of the big barbarian's powers came from old, old magic—they shouldn't expect it to make sense.

Still, watching a guy in a kilt with dark blue hair screaming a war cry in space as he charged against insurmountable forces was pretty funny.

To his right, Seng flew in stoic silence, the alien and Billy's fellow Luminae host entity grimly seeking revenge for the world he lost. Billy hadn't realized just how much what happened to him and Dude in the future had changed them both until he watched a normal

Luminae at work. We really do glow brighter, Billy thought. And fly faster. Everything is amped up.

It's true, Dude said. *Our power is nearly doubled, Billy Case. I don't know what else might have been effected by this but…*

I'll take being extra fast and extra strong, Billy thought. I don't see how that's a bad thing right now.

Billy caught a flash of flaming light out of the corner of his eye and saw Jane streaking into the sky like a fireball, gaining on them.

"Good to have you back, boss," he said. "Always you and me flying around at the end of the world, isn't it?"

"Wouldn't have it any other way, Straylight," Jane said. "We'll need to thin out some of those attack fighters to get close enough to the seed ships."

"Got it," Billy said. "Seng and I will engage the fighters since we're fastest. Korthos?"

"To victory my young friends!" Korthos yelled. "We shall give them no quarter!"

"Yeah, okay, um. But can you take on the warships?"

The demigod raged ahead. Billy's jaw dropped when he watched Korthos point his axe at the fleet. A bolt of energy lanced out of the edge, crashing into one of the closest enemy ships and split it in half. Korthos roared again and dove into the crowds of Nemesis vessels, swinging his axe in huge, broad strikes, half-dance, half-berserker rage.

"So I guess we're improvising?" Billy said.

He dove into the fray, conscious that Seng flanked him and had been watching his back. Billy, far more confident than he'd been with his first encounter with the fleet out near Saturn, went on the offensive, easily dodging blasts of light from cannons mounted on the enemy ships, moving with incredible speed and agility. He zipped past one fighter, and before it could bank to attack him, Billy fired a light-bolt through its armor, making it glow from the inside as the blast gutted the organic machine.

He felt like bird of prey. Or maybe a dolphin. Something fast, moving smoothly through this alien environment, as if this were exactly where he belonged.

I'm good at this, Billy thought.

This is what we've waited our whole lives to do, Dude said. The alien sounded focused, but not stressed.

How are you holding up with all this extra power? Billy thought.

I don't know how long it'll last, but let's enjoy it. We're cutting through these ships like they're nothing.

Billy certainly enjoyed it. He took out two more fighters with quick blasts to their hull, and when a bigger craft, a twisted thing larger than the wasp-like fighters but not a full-fledged warship, drifted up to block his path, Billy felt a surge of power from Dude and rammed his way through it like a bullet. He risked a glance over his shoulder to witness it splitting apart at the seams.

"I'm a cannonball," Billy said.

I said enjoy it, don't revel in it, Dude said.

But Billy was off, not slowing down, smashing through the shells of fighters too slow to get out of his way, leaving a wake of destruction in his path.

"I love being a superhero," Billy said, joyfully flying through the battlefield, arms outstretched like wings.

He watched in the distance as Korthos, barely visible in the chaos, fought maniacally, gutting ships like fish with his axe. The more he destroyed, the more the ships seemed to swarm him, trying to stop his devastating onslaught.

Billy attracted a bit of a following as well, with ships pursuing him, barely able to keep pace. They fired null guns and suddenly Billy refocused. It was one thing to smash his way through regular fighters. But he needed to watch out for those that had been outfitted specifically to kill Luminae hosts.

"Head's up, Seng," Billy said into his radio. "Null guns."

"Nothing you just said made sense, Earthling, but I think I know what you're trying to tell me," the alien responded.

"Hey," Jane's voice chirped in. Billy spun around, trying to locate her in the chaos of the fight. She set a warship on fire, her arm outstretched and spewing flames like a dragon's maw. "Speaking of people who love being superheroes, where's Emily?"

"Em?" Billy said. "You out there, kid? How's things on the

ground?"

"On my way," Emily said.

Billy surveyed the carnage, his stomach sank as he spied the seed ships drawing close but flanked by more attack ships than he could count.

"Not that I'll turn down the assist, but Em, you can't breathe up here like the rest of us, I don't know what you're planning—"

"—Oh Billy baby have I got a surprise for you," Emily said. "You're going to be so jealous you're gonna puke."

Billy wanted to be annoyed, but the truth was, now he really, really wanted to know what his best friend had up her sleeve.

"If you have an X-Wing I'm going to be so mad," he said.

"Even better," she said.

And then Billy saw it. He didn't want to believe it, but there it was.

A giant robot, monstrous and cartoonish, rose out of the Earth's atmosphere.

Not simply a giant robot, Billy thought—it resembled the sort of machine that nearly killed him in the future, something out of an anime, a big mecha-thing with exaggerated human proportions, arms a little too long, shoulders a little too wide, feet lit up with rocket boosters, its face an impassive helmet studded with antennae.

The robot was painted in blue and glossy white, the signature colors Henry Winter wore on his armor as the hero Coldwall. In fact, the scheme itself looked entirely like Henry's old armor, blue boots, chest, and gloves, white piping, bright spots of red on the hands, feet, and face. But hastily spray-painted on the mech's front in black was the unmistakable trifold image of Entropy Emily's nuclear fallout symbol, the one she wore on the chest of her own uniform.

"Are you freaking kidding me, Emily? Are you serious?" Billy yelled.

"I have a giant robot Billy. Look look look! I have a giant robot!" Emily yelled, her voice causing everyone's earpieces to squeal with feedback.

"Do we even want to know where you got that?" Jane said, sounding somewhere between tired and incredibly amused.

"And more to the point—do you know what you're doing with it?" Billy said.

Instead of talking, the robot attacked, sweeping one giant arm in a huge arc through space, swatting two or three fighters with such force that they spun off into the black. The other arm swung as well, capturing a fighter and grabbing hold, crushing it between giant metal fingers. A warship turned to attack, but the robot held out its palm, and, though Billy couldn't see it—Emily's powers shimmered in the air a bit like heat on pavement, but in space, they were imperceptible—the warship was struck by what had to be one of Emily's Walls of Slam, caving the vessel in.

"This is amazing!" Emily yelled.

That is the most terrifying thing I have ever seen, Dude said. *And I say this knowing we're actively fighting the Nemesis fleet.*

"How are you even doing all of this?" Billy said.

"It's a long story," Emily said. "So… who do I smash next?"

CHAPTER 61:
THE LONG STORY

You've got a giant robot," a surprised Emily said to Henry Winter the morning before the attack. Hours later she would join the rest of her team in space piloting the three-story high suit of armor standing in front of her.

"Technically, it's a giant armored suit, but I guess robot works," Winter said. The two of them were standing in a hidden silo beneath the Labyrinth, an area where, for years, Henry Winter had been locked up by Prevention and forced to design new technology for her more militarized version of the Department.

"Besides the obvious answer, which is, 'because if you can have a giant robot, you build a giant robot,' why, um, do you have this thing?" Emily asked.

Winter tapped the foot of the machine with his cane.

"Remember my story? That I was the superhero Coldwall, and used mechanized suits designed for security and crowd control when I served with Doc?"

"I grew up in the Internet age," Emily said. "I Googled everything about you."

"Except the fact I have a giant robot suit," Winter said.

"Everyone is entitled to some secrets," Emily said.

"So I had different variations of the suit," Winter explained. "Underwater, deep space, fire-proof models—versions that were built to be more maneuverable while flying, versus the more heavily armored types for big battles."

"And this is the one you wore when you were cosplaying Voltron?" Emily said.

"My last big project," he said. "I always knew we'd confront something big again. You've seen the giant mole monster that we hid under the Tower? That wasn't the only giant monster we ever faced."

"So you built this… to fight ginormous creatures?"

"It's a prototype," Winter said. "I actually wanted something bigger."

"Just in case Godzilla ever attacked."

"You joke, but…There are some huge things out there, Emily," Winter said.

"You sure this isn't just because you watched a lot of anime growing up?" Emily asked. She walked up to the giant mech's leg and rapped her knuckles on its shin.

"Well, like you stated," Winter said. "The real reason to build a giant robot is because if you can build one…"

"You do it," Emily said. "So why's it down here?"

Winter sighed and put a hand affectionately on the robot's metal leg.

"It's heavy. It's impossible to build this thing to be quick and mobile. It's just not feasible to be equipped with that kind of armor and weight and make it maneuverable," Winter said. "It can go very fast in one direction with boosters, but then you're carrying rocket fuel, so you're essentially driving a bomb."

"We saw giant robots in the future," Emily said. "They were pretty quick."

"They were also—"

"—Powered by me," Emily said.

"So Doc told me," Winter said. "Which is why we never showed you this before."

"Are you asking me to drive this thing? Because I've seen what happens when my powers are misused. I won't be at fault for the apocalypse," Emily said. She stared longingly at the robot. "But maybe just this once…"

"No," Winter said.

"It's funny. We recruited Keaton Bohr because we didn't want him to develop dangerous theories that would put you in harm's way. But you know what he figured out?" he said.

"How to put me at risk?"

"That you wouldn't need to power this thing," Winter said. "You'd be a puppeteer and not the battery. You've learned to control gravity at a very precise level."

Emily belly laughed.

"Sure, if you think so," she said.

Winter shook his head disapprovingly. "You're sloppy when you don't pay attention, which is all the time," he said. "I've seen the footage. You're better than you let yourself be."

"Footage? You watched footage?"

"Of all of you," Winter said. "Believe it or not, all, five of you could use more training. You're still young. And while you think I'm an old fart, I did the same job you did for a very long time, and I made a lot of mistakes so you don't have to."

"I'm judging you so hard right now," Emily said.

"Fine, judge me," Henry Winter said, sniffing in mock insult. "If you don't want to drive the suit you don't have to."

Emily slapped him on the arm.

"I'm driving this suit if I have to kill someone to do it," Emily said, her eyes huge with excitement. "I want to drive a mech. This is a lifelong dream. Do you have any idea how much I want to do this?"

Winter let out a boisterous, giddy laugh.

"Suit up. We'll get you in the cockpit," Winter said. "If I'm telling the truth, I've wanted to see this bird fly for years now. I'm as psyched as you are."

* * *

Emily returned to the silo where the robot waited for her. She wore a jumpsuit designed to maximize her ability to work the controls and to let her seal herself in should the cockpit lose air. She was appalled to find Winter waiting in a lighter version of his Coldwall armor. It wasn't a full suit, more like select pieces, a chest plate and gauntlets, a helmet in his hands.

"Why are you also suited up," Emily said, deadpan.

"You're going to need a copilot," Winter said.

"You lie."

"If something breaks in space, are you going to be able to fix it?"

Emily stared him down, then acquiesced.

"Okay fine. But you are copilot. *Co*-pilot. Not pilot."

"I wouldn't have it any other way," Winter said. "Look up."

Emily followed his gesture and felt her little heart grow three sizes too big. Sure, it was sloppy and rushed, but there, in dark paint on the chest of the giant robot, was her nuclear fallout symbol. *Her* symbol. Her robot.

"I think you're just about my new favorite person," Emily said.

"You really do weave back and forth pretty violently with your moods, don't you?" Winter said.

"It's my specialty," Emily said. "Okay Stacker Pentecost, show me how to run this thing."

He led her to a ladder, but Emily skipped climbing and bubble of floated herself up to a cockpit, located in the head of the machine. She hopped in, pulling the helmet she found there over her head. Winter, with his bum leg, followed slowly up the ladder, and when he got to the platform, he plugged Emily's suit into a few cables to monitor her vitals, and ensured that her helmet was sealed. Then he pointed to the controls.

"For any other pilot, you'd need these," he said. "But I want you to—"

Emily reached out with a bubble of float and took hold of the robot's arm. She thought about it in the same way she would think about moving her own and rotated the shoulder, bent at the elbow. Suddenly, one huge metal hand was held out in front of both of them. She wriggled the fingers.

"Can you do that with two arms at once?" Winter asked.

Emily repeated the endeavor with the other arm. She waved them back and forth like she was putting on a puppet show.

"Emily, I'm so disappointed in how much you've held back with your powers until now I almost want to throw you out of the cockpit," Winter said.

"I just need proper motivation," Emily said. "Trick me into working to my potential."

She made one of the hands wave coyly at Winter. He couldn't help laughing.

"You're not getting into the cockpit with me, are you?" Emily said, looking around at the cramped space, even for her.

"No, there's an engineer's chamber in the chest," Winter said. "So try not to get me killed."

"I make no promises," Emily said.

"I heard that about you," Winter said. "So here's the deal. Bohr will be here in the lab, trouble shooting. He'll look for indications the suit is in the red, or if either of us is in distress. He'll help me if we run into any mechanical problems that I can fix when we're in battle."

"This is nuts," Emily said. "Are we staying on Earth or going up into space?"

"I wanted the suit environmentally sealed for undersea duties or outer space," Winter said, tapping the armor on the head of the vehicle. "And we've said all along if we can keep the fleet from reaching the planet, we stand a better chance of winning, so…"

"I'm going to be flying a giant mech in space against an alien invasion," Emily said. "This, Henry Winter, is the greatest day of my life."

"Let's hope it's not your last," he said. "How about a test drive?"

Emily turned her helmeted head at Winter and pounded her little fist against the console.

"Get thee to engineering, Scotty! We have a world to save."

* * *

Emily had done a lot of fun things in her life. But none of those involved a giant robot, so she would put 'learning to drive a mech' into her top three life experiences.

She and Winter took the vehicle out, via an underground tunnel beneath the Labyrinth, and traveled to an unused and abandoned industrial park located outside the City. Emily knew someone, somewhere, had to have seen them. But the Department blocked off the area quietly to keep gawkers away, and three stories was not too enormous, so walking between old mill buildings didn't leave them overly exposed.

But still. I'm piloting a giant robot, Emily thought. I'm a Gundam. Battletech. Mechwarrior. Best day of my life.

Also, Winter explained, he and Bohr had rigged the hands of the robot to let her use her walls of slam like the gloves they'd loaned her earlier. Though definitely not precise, they helped her focus her powers while she used bubbles of float to control the vehicle's limbs.

She wasn't crazy about needing to concentrate to keep the suit balanced, but a benefit of controlling gravity was that when she fell, a quick bubble of float would catch her and put her right back on her feet again. Henry told her it would be easier in outer space, when her self-created artificial gravity would be used strictly to move, not to maintain equilibrium.

"Does she have a name?" Emily said.

"What?" Winter said from his unseen compartment inside the robot.

"The suit?" Emily said. "Gipsy Danger? Blue Destiny? Hellbringer? Something?"

"You're the pilot, you pick."

"Can we call it Hideaki?" she said.

"I… guess?" Winter said. "Why?"

"He's one of the creators of Neon Genesis Evangelion—y'know. Oh, never mind. Trust me. Hideaki is a good name."

Winter laughed.

"We'll call the robot Hideaki," he said.

Emily was almost disappointed when their communicators beeped at the same time with an incoming call from the Tower. They both understood what the call could mean. Emily wasn't ready to stop playing yet. Although, she thought, if it was time for action…

"Go for Emily," she said, activating her headset. "I'm listening."

* * *

And now, in the present moment, Emily moved with shocking grace through outer space, controlling Hideaki like an expert. She realized what she was doing—mimicking with her bubbles of float the sort of movements she'd watched Kate perform thousands of times, sweeping kicks, powerful punches, forever in motion, causing destruction with each swing and step.

Imitation is the sincerest form of flattery, Emily thought. She wished Kate could be here to witness her giant robot impersonation of the dancer.

But listening to Billy yell "Are you kidding me!" into her headset was reward enough.

Emily saw him—a bright white streak tearing through enemy ships in the distance.

"This is what you get for taunting me in the future, Billy Case," Emily said, knocking another fighter out of the sky.

"Listen up," Jane said, cutting them both off. "The seed ships are on the move."

Emily turned the giant robot's head to scan the center of the fleet as the seed ships—strange terraforming vehicles designed to tear into the planet like a spade into a garden—started breaking away from the brain ship.

"Three of them, three of us," Emily said. "Sounds like a party."

Without waiting for her orders, she picked one of the missile-like seed ships and used a bubble of float to throw herself at it.

"Cowabunga, dude," she said, having more fun than she'd ever experienced in her entire life.

CHAPTER 62:
CHILD OF THE SUN

Jane dodged another enemy fighter, punching it as they crossed paths and sending it spiraling out of control. Another flew directly at her, laser-like energy blasts fired away, but she backed up and kicked the nose of the craft when they met, shattering its bug-like armor.

She stole a look at Emily and her giant robot, hoping they'd all survive this just so she could ask her where on Earth that machine came from. The robot moved in a hilarious parody of Kate's martial arts, and at one point awkwardly kicked a warship like a football. The more it moved, the more it seemed to imitate Emily, her loose shoulders, her restless legs.

Another alien ship shook Jane out of her thoughts and she dowsed it in flames shot from her hands.

She felt powerful here above the Earth's atmosphere. Jane had flown close to the edge before, had sensed the power of the sun's rays sink into her cells even more aggressively than they did when she was closer to the ground. But here, without the stratosphere to filter light, the solar energy hit her like a direct feed as though plugged right into the outlet.

She was grateful for the extra burst though because Jane needed to utilize every trick, every power, every ability she possessed simply to keep ahead of the fleet.

She ploughed through another ship, let herself glow red-hot and cut through its armor. She exploded out the other side, her flame-powers melting the blackish gunk that came with her, turning it into ash. Jane looked towards the brain-ship situated in the middle of the fleet. Shaped like a whale shark in the front, but more squid-like in the back, it appeared to be a nightmarish spectacle out of a horror movie.

Worse, though, was watching the seed ships, the things that would turn Earth into a dead zone, breaking away from that lead starship and pick up speed, heading for the planet.

"We've got to get those seed ships," Jane said.

"I shall destroy them all! For Aramaias!" Korthos yelled so loudly Jane almost tossed her earpiece aside.

"Hang on, big guy," Jane said. She attempted to assess the size of the ships—difficult with nothing to reference for scale—and unsure of the best course of action. Emily, still nearest the planet, swatted fighters out of the sky before they could break atmosphere. Billy and Seng flew in tandem mid-battlefield, turning space into a dogfight. Korthos, furthest out, made a mess everywhere he ventured, raining destruction down on the fleet in a whirlwind of magic and axe blows.

Doc was still nowhere to be found.

Jane would have to deal with that later.

"New plan," Jane said, aiming at the lead seed ship when it pulled ahead of the pack. "Emily, hit the seed ship to your left."

At another time, the sight of Emily's giant robot arm pointing at something with one metal finger would have been hilarious, but Jane, too worried to be amused, added it to the list of things she'd like to laugh about later.

"That one?" Emily said.

"You got it," Jane said. "How durable is that suit?"

Henry Winter chimed in unexpectedly. Jane hadn't realized he shared the same frequency.

"It'll hold up even if we're forced to ram it," Winter said. "Emily, you'll want to use a bubble of float to launch us."

"Good to hear your voice, Henry," Jane said, relieved that Emily was not alone in the mechanized suit.

"You too," Winter said. The giant robot sped toward its target, arms whacking little wasp-like fighters out of the way as it flew.

"Billy, you and Seng take the one furthest away? You've got the best chance to reach it in time," Jane said.

"On it," Billy said, his tone uncharacteristically focused. Jane watched the two bright white streaks lance across space in the direction of the falling seed ship.

And that leaves me, Jane thought.

Ignoring the smaller ships running interference to her approach, she weaved her way with increasing speed toward the seed ship, her focus entirely on the big craft. A larger warship got in the way, but Jane's momentum allowed her to shoot through the ship like an arrow. The collision split the organic spaceship into pieces.

She tried this same method on the seed ship, but the armor, she discovered, was harder—she did crack the surface, but her whole body became rattled by the impact. The strike shook in her bones and teeth.

New approach, she thought.

Spines and bubbles covered the surface of the vessel. The spines appeared to be some sort of hook or drilling mechanism, allowing the ship to dig into the planet's surface when it hit. Chemicals and spores filled the bubbles. Jane presumed these would change the Earth's atmosphere to be more in line with what the Nemesis fleet required to survive. Jane's fists burst into flames and punched one of the glassy bubbles, sending greenish fluid drifting out into the vacuum of space.

She surveyed the surface of the ship. Hundreds of bubbles, maybe thousands. Too many to destroy by hand, with no guarantee doing so would stop the terraforming device from working. Perhaps the surface bubbles represented just the first of its planet-changing weaponry.

Jane turned her attention down—is it down? she thought, disoriented by the dimensions of space—and saw the rapidly approaching glow of her blue planet. She struck the ship's armor again, both hands on fire, and watched it crumble like charred meat off the grill.

She realized what she had to do and hoped she was strong enough to pull it off.

"Neal, patch me into Kate, private line," Jane said.

"Right away, Designation: Dancer," Neal said.

"Kate?" Jane said, picking up speed to reach the nose of the seed ship.

"Little busy right now." Kate's voice sounded strained. Jane heard her breathing, the sounds of combat rattling the microphone. "What's wrong?"

"I've got a plan to take out one of the seed ships," she said. "The others might need you up here soon."

Kate grunted and punched something on the other end of the line.

"Not sure how much help I can be up there," Kate said. "Why are you telling me this?"

"Just in case," Jane said. "They're going to need your strategic brain to finish this."

"*They*? Not we? What are you going to do, Jane?"

"Hopefully stop this ship from breaking atmosphere," she said. "Be safe, Kate."

All Jane heard was Kate's breathing.

"I'll be there soon," Kate said. "Don't do anything stupid."

"When do I ever do anything stupid?" Jane said, smiling. She reached the nose of the seed ship and positioned herself so that her hands were pushing back against it, her feet aimed at the planet below.

"There's a first time for everything. Luck, Solar."

The sounds of Kate's battles below went silent in Jane's ear. Now or never, she thought, feeling the Earth getting closer and closer. The space around her glowed from the reflection of the sun off the planet's surface.

Jane dug her fingers into the insect-like armor of the seed ship's nose and split the hard but brittle surface. As soon as she got a good grip, she let her hands burn.

The ship's armor crumbled, but as it changed consistency, Jane kept altering her grip, causing the fire—fire she knew shouldn't exist in space, flames that only could happen this close to the sun, where Jane was most powerful—consume the ship's hull. She pushed with more intensity, her whole body igniting, a candlewick in the darkness.

The ship moved forward, and Jane fought right back. She felt every inch of her skin burst into flames, her hair becoming a campfire. Soon all she saw was golden light and the crumbling surface of the ship. Above her, the ship began to glow internally, overheated by Jane's powers, engulfed from the inside out. Jane gritted her teeth, every cell in her body burned hot, emptying out the solar batteries that made up her body. She continued to pour all that heat, all that energy, into setting the seed ship on fire.

The ship broke apart. Blackened ashes glowed red-hot and sputtered, the aftermath of a huge fire. The long vessel splintered and crumbled to inert dust, deteriorating into a dead thing, useless and benign.

Jane drifted in the emptiness of space, feeling empty. Suddenly too weak to move, almost too spent to think, she gazed out at the stars and watched her friends in battle, wondering if she'd have the strength to join them.

CHAPTER 63: THE VALKYRIE

In the months since her transformation, Valerie Snow struggled to understand her place in the world. Was she a human being imprisoned and sharing a body with a storm? Was she a storm trapped in the body of a human? Was she dangerous? Was she a monster?

And so, at first, she hid. She wandered the skies over the ocean, retreating from humanity, avoiding the sight of people, terrified that one move might end a ship full of lives, one lapse in judgment could flood a coastline.

The storm inside her, the other, the living, breathing hurricane that had taken up residence in her body during that horrible experiment performed by the Children of the Elder Star, raged for a long time. Like a feral animal, it slammed against the cages of Valerie's body, feeling cornered and alone.

But as time went on, they came to understand each other. The storm needed freedom. It—she, the storm was a she, Val knew instinctually—wanted to be huge, to pour rain down on vast, open spaces, to stretch its arms in spiraling clouds. And so they did, finding places where the storm would do less harm, unleashing an elemental fury to satiate the needs of the caged sentient hurricane.

And when those rages subsided, Val would be more in control, would bring their shared consciousness more into itself, to contain the storm in the altered body that had once been simply a girl, like any other.

But Valerie Snow still didn't understand her place in the world. Should she be among people? She could not bring herself to speak with her parents, though she visited them, watching from afar. They sensed she lived somehow, though they still had not spoken. Valerie feared what they'd think of her. The Indestructibles would meet with her, to keep her company from time to time, but they were not ordinary people, and Val did not fear being near them—because of their powers, she couldn't harm them, not really, not in the same way she could hurt an ordinary person.

And so she lived outside the world, the girl in the sky, looking down with sad eyes the color of a cloudless day.

She'd learned to control her powers—it used to be that everywhere she went was a stormy day, but she knew now how to pull that energy inward, to the point where she could actually enter a building sometimes. But when she watched the alien warship working its way through the City like a giant slug, she felt her control slipping. The skies, just moments ago so blue—she was always proud of blue skies, because they hinted at her control, they were a sign that she was in charge and not the storm—turned dark gray, thunderclouds rolled in, rumbling and angry.

This wasn't her city, she knew. She grew up in Florida, with sunnier days and stronger storms. But this was her world. And these aliens came to destroy it. The storm inside her raged as well. Elemental, intrinsically part of that world, a function, a moving apparatus of change, the storm could live nowhere else. Only in this world, this place, could the sentient storm exist, and the storm seemed to fully grasp everything Valerie observed. A threat to their world. Monsters here to take their playground away from them. The end of all things.

The skies opened up, heavy rain like a cascading waterfall poured down from above. Winds kicked up, whistled between the buildings and scattered debris on the ground. The clouds nearly black, flashed with blue and purple lightning.

Valerie Snow, Project Valkyrie, discovered her purpose. She found her anger and her moment to be a hero. She flew in closer, locking in on that alien ship. She raised her hand in the air and lightning struck her palm. All around her, windows and street lights exploded and shattered. Valerie, Valkyrie, suddenly transformed as well, her skin became the roiling black and gray of the clouds above, matching them in tone and color, her insides flashing and glowing with lighting.

She pointed at the warship with one finger.

A single, massive bolt of lightning struck the hand she still held above her, and poured back out through the fingertip she aimed at the ship. The electrical bolt exploded into the ship's skin, sparking, splintering it. Smoke and ozone filled the air, and the ship's armor squealed and split like melting plastic.

The spaceship tipped forward, groaning as it banked drunkenly off-course, tearing the façade off an office building and tumbling to the ground. When it landed, digging up pavement with its weight, it crushed a half-dozen cars, but its guns fell silent, the entire ship becoming inert, empty, quiet, dead.

Below her, she saw a man with a camera and a beard that had not grown in properly yet. He seemed familiar somehow. The man fired away with his camera, at the dead starship, at Val herself. She felt a flash of anger at the violation of having her image captured, but then a calmness washed over her.

She stared at the cameraman, who took a few photos of her while she hung in the air, thirty feet off the ground, rain still pouring down in sheets. Her eyes glowed with webs of lightning.

The little earpiece Jane had given her to wear buzzed. The Dancer's voice spoke up.

"Valerie, whatever you just did worked," she said. "We're going to face incoming fighters. Can you do that again?"

"As often as I need to," Valerie said, feeling the power of her sentient storm companion rushing into her limbs, making her heart beat faster.

"Then the sky is yours," Dancer said.

Valerie Snow smiled.

"Yes," she said, glancing up at the black and gray clouds she'd created, the sea of weather. "The sky is mine."

CHAPTER 64:
ONE WAY TRIP ANYWAY

Kate pressed the button on her belt that would summon the hoverbike she'd ridden down from the Tower. Jane's situation sounded desperate; there wasn't time to go back and find the machine where she left it.

Then she saw the lightning strike and started running for the warship a few blocks away.

Kate turned into a wide avenue. "Where am I?" she asked herself—momentarily confused on the streets of her own city. The sudden tropical storm and associated downpour made everything look gray and blurry. Another one of the alien warriors confronted her. She marveled at the variety of them. Were they creatures the Nemesis found and collected as soldiers and slaves? Were they genetically engineered and redesigned like the Children of the Elder Star haltered humans to become hosts?

Its hippopotamus-like face, with four eyes instead of two, stared back at her. The parasite appeared undersized on its wide torso. With arms long like an ape's, the creature prepared to charge, clawed fingers digging into the pavement for traction.

Gotta be a thousand pounds, Kate thought, wondering about the Distribution suit's ability to handle the impact of something that large. I'll get broken if I don't handle this right. I can't let that happen.

The ground rumbled like a low-level earth-quake as the alien charged her. Kate prepared to dodge him when he got close enough, hoping to absorb some of the kinetic energy without getting trampled. Neither option sounded particularly appealing.

One hundred feet away. Seventy-five. Fifty. Twenty-five.

A bolt of green laser light arced out from over Kate's shoulder, striking the alien on the chest—or more specifically, on the parasite itself—and the huge creature tripped over its own massive, tree trunk-like feet, plummeted onto its face, displacing cars as it came to a stop.

Kate whipped around to see who fired the shot, only to find Sam Barren, standing on a car in a soaked hound's tooth suit. Rain dripped off the brim of his fedora. He held a cylindrical gun almost as long as the agent was tall.

"Looks like that stash Prevention sent us hunting for was worth it," Sam said, smiling at Kate. Rainwater ran through his mustache. Sam tried to brush it away.

Kate grunted, then wiped rain from her own eyes.

"That explosion over there," Kate said. "Your guys?"

"Nope," Sam said. He stepped carefully down from the hood of the car and started half-running, half-limping toward the smoking warship.

Kate ran ahead, leaving the old agent behind, knowing he'd catch up. She looked for the hoverbike but couldn't hear its approach yet. She hoped nothing had happened to it. She needed that bike.

Kate arrived at the burning corpse of the warship the same time as Bedlam, who'd been running so fast she slid several feet when she came to a stop.

They both glanced up when they realized what caused this. Valerie drifted slowly down from the sky, the rain catching and falling from her body like a dress.

"Can you do this more than once?" Kate asked.

Valerie nodded.

"Remarkably easy," Val said. "I knew I was powerful, but I had no idea I could pull off something like this."

"Some smaller ships may break through the atmosphere. Do you feel okay about getting up high, trying to take out as many as you can before they're able to get close enough to hit the City?" Kate asked.

"I can do this," Valerie said.

Huffing and wheezing, Sam caught up to them. Several of his agents, wearing suits and bullet-proof vests while carrying a bizarrely inconsistent array of guns like Sam's, each different from the other, joined him and began to secure the area around the ship.

Kate turned to Bedlam.

"I need to get up there," Kate said.

"Into space?" Bedlam said

"Jane thinks I can help," Kate said. "Can you keep things under control down here?"

Bedlam watched the agents patrolling the area. Sam overheard their conversation and shuffled over.

"Unless we get hit with another wave like this one, I think we can lock things down here," Sam said.

"I'll find the stragglers," Bedlam said. "I don't see how I'd be much use in space anyway."

"Nor I," Kate said. "But I'll try to figure that out when I get there. Where's Titus?"

The fur-soaked werewolf chose that moment to come bounding into the scene, covered in alien gore. He smelled like wet dog right now and Kate knew Titus probably felt bad about it.

"Titus!" she yelled. The werewolf cocked his head. "Change back, I need your brain."

He loped over, transforming as he moved. Titus returned to human form by the time he arrived, he shivered in the rain.

"Did we win?"

"We're going into space," Kate said. The soft hum of her hoverbike finally audible, she watched the little aircraft zip toward them.

"Space? We can't—you and me? We can't go into *space*."

"They need us."

"We're not getting there on your flying motorcycle."

"The Tower's a space ship," Kate said. "We're going to stop using it as a tree house and use it as it was originally intended."

Titus examined the carnage around him and gestured at the big carcass of the warship still smoking on the ground.

"We're not needed here?"

"You speak Neal better than anyone," Kate said. "I need you in the air with me."

"Okay," Titus said. He put a hand on Bedlam's shoulder. "You got things down here?"

"The old man and I will hold the fort," Bedlam said, smiling, that old crazy fighter look in her face, the one Titus remembered when they first met returned. "Besides, I absolutely don't want to go into outer space riding in a floating clubhouse."

"Neither do I."

The hoverbike came to rest a few meters away. Kate started for it. She turned back towards Bedlam and Sam.

"Luck," she said.

Sam nodded. Bedlam offered a playful salute.

Titus climbed on the back of the bike and wrapped his arm around Kate's waist, sighing. "I hate these things," he said.

"Don't worry," Kate said. "This is probably a one-way trip anyway."

The duo buzzed into the sky, tearing through sheets of rain, and headed right for the Tower, where it hung in the sky just below the dark clouds of Valerie's storm. Kate felt Titus' grip on her midsection tighten as they tilted vertically to gain height faster. For just a split second, she let herself enjoy the feeling of a warm arm around her waist. But then anger bubbled up inside her—why is it only now, amid disaster, I'm able to feel like this? If we don't die this time, she thought, I need to be better."

They banked into the Tower's landing bay, Kate parked the bike carelessly and hopped off.

"Neal, seal the bay," Titus said.

"Of course, Designation: Whispering," the artificial intelligence said. The doors, heavy, armored things, slid shut behind them.

Kate headed for the control center, leaving puddles of rainwater behind her.

"Neal, what kind of weapons does this ship have?" she said.

There was an awkward, almost sheepish pause from the AI.

"Neal?" Kate said.

"This was a rescue vessel, Designation: Dancer," Neal said. "It was never intended for war. It has some light armaments but nothing that can be effective in full-fledged conflict."

"How's our maneuverability, Neal?" Titus said. "We're about to head into some rough waters. Air. Space. Rough space."

"Poor, Designation: Whispering," Neal said. "But our armor is very durable."

"So we can take some hits," Titus said. "We just can't strike back."

Titus and Kate exchanged a long, concerned glance.

"One way trip, huh?" Titus said.

"We'll figure it out when we get there," Kate said. "Our friends need us."

Titus smiled.

She saw by the light in his eyes, the confident stance, the calmness of his body language—once they got off the hoverbike he'd hated since the first time they rode one—that he seemed happy to be there. He's excited to save the world, Kate thought. Even if it meant a one-way trip.

And at that moment, she felt the same way.

"Take us up, Neal," Titus said as they arrived in the control room. "And call up an inventory of anything we've got lying around we might use as a weapon."

"Done," Neal said.

They watched the monitors as the Earth grew smaller beneath them and the stars above became suddenly so much closer.

CHAPTER 65:
LIGHT SHOW

Billy and Seng worked in tandem, knocking enemy fighters out of the air as they took shot after shot at the seed ship. Billy's own blasts, tearing chunks out of the strange ship's armor, seemed to be far more effective than his teammate's.

He tried not to think about what he saw in the distance, as Jane's target went up in flames like a barn on fire. Or how Jane wasn't answering her communicator.

Where is she, Dude? Billy thought.

Focus on our target, Dude said. *We need to stay focused. There will be time to help our friends later.*

Billy wanted to get angry at the alien, to be furious at his ruthlessness, but he detected the worry in Dude's voice, and the very deliberate way he said "*our* friend," not "your." Jane would never be able to hear Dude's voice—not unless the alien traded host bodies—but the ancient Luminae still considered her a friend. And he worried about her.

The other seed ship, the one Jane destroyed, fell apart in smoldering clumps. She'd done her job, Billy thought. Now pay attention and do yours.

Meanwhile, Seng noticed just how different Straylight's powers were to his own.

"What happened to you," Seng said. "I've never seen a Luminae like you before."

Billy heard strain in the other host's voice. Seng struggled to keep up, lacking Billy's extra speed and power.

"We traveled into the future and accidentally absorbed most of the power of our future selves," Billy said in a hurried tone. He dragged one continuous light blast along the length of the seed ship, leaving a long, blistering scar. "That sounds extra weird when I say it out loud..."

"And you..." Seng started to speak but an incoming attack wing cut him off. Billy and Seng switched dance partners, with Straylight pouncing into the oncoming wing of fighters and scattering them as Seng turned his attention on cutting into the seed ship. "And you didn't burn out?"

Billy laughed despite everything going on around him. He wanted to tell Seng all about the surreal experience, of basically being the surrogate parent for the birth of Dude's mini-me they'd created in the future, but he couldn't keep the thoughts straight in his head.

"Long story," Billy said. "I'll tell you all about it if we don't die out here."

"Fair enough, Earthling," the alien said.

Another wave of fighters headed their way. Billy started toward them, but the flight of ships targeted Seng, his back to them.

And then Billy saw what the fighters had mounted on their hulls.

Null guns, Billy thought, yelling internally.

Go, Dude said.

Billy raced, trying to get between the fighters and Seng, who didn't seem to notice their approach, still too focused on his work searching for the guts of the seed ship to shut it down.

"Seng, look out!" Billy said, pouring on the speed.

They fired familiar, horrific, sickly red-yellow glow of the null guns, unafraid of hitting the seed ship. Lights splashed and bounced off its hull. Seng was trapped within the onslaught of blasts, not quite fast enough to break away. Billy raced in to join him. He watched one fighter take aim and shoot its gun right at Seng. Unthinking, Billy dove in, shielding the alien with his own body.

Well this was stupid, Billy thought, closing his eyes, gritting his teeth, and wondering what the vacuum of outer space would feel like. He'd seen *Total Recall*. He hoped it wouldn't go down like that.

The blast hit him, glanced off his body and ricocheted against the seed ship's hull. His back and shoulder burned. A sharp, bitter ache seeped deep down into his cells. Billy waited for the end.

It didn't happen.

Dude? He thought.

I… am still here, Billy Case, Dude said.

How did that happen?

I can only assume… I can only assume that the doubling of our powers has made our bond strong enough the null guns can't separate us involuntarily.

Does this happen often? Billy thought. He and Seng looked at each other, both equally confused. The expression on the alien's face was so close to normal human shock that Billy almost laughed at him.

I've never heard of one of us becoming immune to null guns, Dude said. *That being said… I don't think we should complain.*

It still hurt pretty bad, Billy said.

It certainly did.

But we can…?

Billy Case, Dude said. *I think you should show these Nemesis ships what a Luminae without fear can do.*

Billy smiled so broadly his cheeks hurt.

You ready, Dude? He thought.

Always, my friend, Dude said.

Billy lit up like a star, engulfing himself in the blue-white light of the Luminae. For the first time, really, he felt unafraid of anything. He wasn't a kid in a costume. He was Straylight, protector of his home world.

And he was about to put on a light show.

Leaving Seng to find cover near the seed ship, Billy flew headlong into the approaching fighters. Not simply scattering them, he disabled more than half on his first attack, blasting some, crashing into others, sending a light-covered fist through the armor of another and throwing it deep into space.

On the offensive, he ran off another set of fighters, emitting arcs of bluish energy from his hands, knocking them out from behind, from below, moving much faster than any of the Nemesis ships could fly. Somehow, Billy's own glee, his acceptance of his own powers, made him even faster, even stronger. The little fighters fled from him rather than attack and abandoned the seed ship.

And then he saw where the fighters were headed.

"Seng, we need to put this seed ship out of commission," Billy said. "They're headed for Earth."

"They want to draw you away," Seng said. "I'll pursue."

"I have an idea," Billy said, turning a wide arc away from the seed ship. "Stand back a bit."

This is going to hurt, Dude said.

A lot? Billy thought.

It not going to tickle.

Well… you only live once, Billy thought. He waited to make sure Seng had flown a safe distance away, and then Billy turned back toward the seed ship, his trajectory aimed at the nose of the vessel, dead center to the spear-like craft's body.

Billy picked up speed, pouring on the power. Dude shifted their protective energy shields up in front like a bumper. At least we're on the same page, Billy thought.

They crashed into the nose of the seed ship, and kept on going.

Later, Billy would only really remember the chaos of it all, broken pieces, parts that looked bone and muscle, as if the ship itself were a living thing. He corkscrewed his way through the center of the terraforming device, spraying blasts of blue-white light in a spinning motion, causing cataclysmic damage to the entire ship, gutting it from within. He had no idea how long it took him to tear through from end to end, but eventually, he burst out of the bio-mechanical engines in the back, feeling their heat against his skin through his shielding. His explosive exit sent him spinning through space, out of control, covered in greasy ship's blood. He couldn't figure out which way was up or down and had no idea if his plan worked.

Then Billy felt a hand on his wrist, catching him, holding him tight.

Seng. The older alien steadied him and kept Billy from floating off into space. He pointed at the seed ship, smoking and crumbling, falling apart from within like wet cardboard. Billy shivered, the expenditure of energy hit him like an ice bath.

"Worked, huh?" Billy said.

"Impressive, my friend," Seng said.

"Yeah," Billy said. "Now let me just puke really quick and we can take on more of those ships before they destroy the planet."

When Billy took stock of what remained of the enemy fleet, his stomach sank. Still more ships than he could count—little fighters, big warships, that one, massive mother ship central to it all... Suddenly, he felt very small. There were just so many of them.

"You've got to be kidding me," he said.

CHAPTER 66:
LUNCH IN THE PARK

While a near-hurricane raged over the City, while panic washed over the streets, while monsters from other planets stormed downtown, a well-dressed woman with eyes made of fire sat down in the park on a tidy gingham blanket and looked up at the sky.

The Lady Natasha Grey wasn't particularly happy to have left her sanctuary by the sea. But, she thought, we must all do our part.

A thousand years ago, a hundred years ago, maybe even as recently as a few decades ago in her long life, if asked, Natasha would have said she'd rather let this world burn. A grumpy little world, bereft of wonder, with scant magic—a gruff place absent of hope or joy. She was born here, yes, but she'd been to other places, storybook lands, heavens and hells. And Earth, she thought, was a drab little hole in the wall. Let it burn.

Funny how things change.

You get attached to a place. You make it your own. You find things to care about. You settle down. Or, instead, you want to keep it safe for other people who care more about it than you do.

No, she thought. Admit it. This is home, and you like it the way it is. Dirty face and all.

The Lady placed a series of objects on the gingham blanket, which remained, like the Lady herself, untouched by the pouring rain. She arranged an amulet, a dagger, a bag of sand, a glass ball, a torch, a bag of tiny bones, in a fussy, deliberate manner, and then started chanting, a sing-songy poem in a language few on Earth would understand.

The ground in front of her opened, and things climbed out. Winged creatures, each and every one, some gray and misshapen, like gargoyles, some lean and scaly like dragons. Little monkeys with wings like bats, angry angels with blackened feathered wings. Demons and monsters and beasts. They all looked to her for a command.

"You summoned us here?" said one, a fork-tongued thing with burnt red skin.

"I did," she said. "Would you like to go home?"

The creatures exchanged confused looks. The red one, acting as some sort of spokesman, nodded.

"We're bound. Not by you. But other masters. Dead wizards. All of us. Bound to objects or the will of dead men," he said.

The Lady Natasha Grey smiled warmly, showing her teeth between bright red lips.

"What if I told you I'd acquired all those old bindings and contracts, and that I could set you free and send you back to the worlds from which you were stolen?" the Lady said.

The red creature quirked a thorny eyebrow.

"What is your price, woman?" he said.

Natasha pointed to the sky, where the first of the alien ships were appearing, headed for the City. Tiny things, now, but en route to the City, more than enough to lay waste to the metropolis.

"Destroy my enemies and you're all free," Natasha said.

"This seems too simple," the demon said. "No black mage would give up our freedom so easily."

Natasha laughed, hard, her belly tightening and eyes glowing brighter.

"Let's just say I'm in a generous mood," she said. "Defend this place from those flying machines, and when the battle is over, I'll break every talisman and untie every spell holding you here. All I ask is your help right now, and that you remember who set you free."

The creature bared his teeth.

"In case you need further favors," he said.

"Come now, you know I'll have no power over you," she said.

"Maybe someday you'll want to return the favor."

The demon laughed, the sound of rocks cascading downhill. He looked at his peers, some nearly human, others not at all. He turned back to Natasha.

"You have a bargain, little wizard," he said.

"Then fly, my pretties," she said, amused at her own phrasing. Maybe this world did have its charms. They knew how to tell wonderful stories here. "Fly, and you'll be free."

CHAPTER 67:
THE BARBARIAN
AND THE MAGICIAN

Doc Silence drifted in space, never quite losing consciousness, but so drained by the massive effort of casting those huge spells he felt drugged and dizzy. He closed his eyes, trying to focus on meditative techniques he'd learned from a vampire in Siberia once upon a time, and pulled himself inward, concentrating on his center. Instead of regaining strength, though, he blacked out.

When he woke, reality had erupted into chaos. He watched in the distance as, with dreamlike imagery, one of the seed ships went up in flames like a match. He knew that had to be Solar. Only Jane could ignite a fire like that in outer space. Swarms of Nemesis fleet fighters, little nasty crafts like flying claws, zipped around in the distance, throw into panic by the loss of one of their ships.

He watched Billy even further away, a beacon of white light destroying another seed ship, so bright he left streaks in Doc's vision as he darted around.

But closer to him, Doc saw what should have been a terrifying sight. Instead, he almost laughed.

Doc had known Korthos of Aramaias, the Truthbringer, the immortal, for half of his adult life. He liked the brute, enjoyed his enthusiasm, and nobody quite knew how to throw back gallons of beer the way he did. But Korthos had always, always, always found a way of biting off more than he should be able to chew and had a special talent for annoying his enemies. So Doc wasn't too surprised when he saw the big man getting tagged by dozens of Nemesis ships, fighters and bigger warships alike, concentrating their fire on him as he raged and hacked at them with that halberd of his.

Korthos gave as well as he took, destroying at least one fighter with each swing, sometimes two at once, but he was completely outnumbered and, while he didn't seem particularly hurt, he was also thoroughly trapped. If it weren't a life and death situation for everyone else, Doc might have compared it to a dog walker who had taken on too many canine companions, all of whom just realized he had a cookie in his pocket.

Doc realized Korthos could handle it. He understood they wouldn't destroy him. An immortal from a time before modern men existed, his story was as old as the planet. Still, he felt bad for his old friend, bound up in laser beams and swinging his poleaxe wildly. So Doc shook off the cobwebs, flexed his fingers, and called up his favorite transmutation spell.

He turned half the ships into tapioca pudding with a sweep of his hand.

Korthos was, seconds later, covered in tapioca pudding.

Somehow, this made the barbarian even angrier. He lashed out at the remaining ships, sundering them with blow after blow, roaring into his earpiece—they'd forced him to wear a small mask that would let him talk into it in space, though hearing the language coming out of Korthos' mouth, Doc kind of regretted it—and, his enemies slain, floated in space, out of breath, eyes raw with anger.

"Nice job, Korthos," Doc said.

"You! Magician! You transformed these ships into a dessert with an alarmingly lumpy consistency! I knew this was your foul magic," Korthos said.

Doc floated over, offering a hand to help the immortal steady himself while he spun in zero-g.

"Your culinary assistance was, in fact, appreciated though, wizard," Korthos said. "Your choice in spells notwithstanding."

Doc got his bearings again, found the brain ship in the sky, tried to count the buzzing smaller ships. There had to be a thousand.

More. So many standing in their way.

"What are we going to do about this?" Doc said. "This is insane."

"We are going to smite them, my friend," Korthos said. "I must return to battle."

"You do that," Doc said.

This was why he'd goaded the barbarian into the fight. Tactically useless from a finesse standpoint, he was tireless and, if aimed in the right direction, a real destructive force. "Don't hurt any of our friends by accident."

"To victory!" Korthos said, flying, in his inexplicable way, toward the center of the fleet. He didn't travel far before he'd once again attracted the attention of too many enemy vessels, but he was keeping them off the backs of the other Indestructibles, so Doc let him continue. That's when he noticed something out of the corner of his eye.

"Is that a giant robot?" he said.

CHAPTER 68:
CANCELING THE APOCALYPSE

Smashing starfighters out of the sky with giant robot hands was fun for a while, Emily thought. Until they started to gang up on her.

The more of them she knocked out of commission the more seemed to swarm her. She swatted at biplanes attacking her like King Kong on the roof of the Empire State Building.

"This is stupid," Emily said. Another ship hit her with some kind of laser beam and the suit rumbled.

"Keep heading for the seed ship," Henry Winter's voice said into her earpiece. "We can do this."

Emily generated a wall of slam to smack a bigger Nemesis ship out of the way, then batted a handful of smaller fighters with the back of her metal hand. The suit grew sluggish, though. Or was it her? She created little pockets of gravity to move the limbs. Was it draining her strength?

"Is this thing slowing down?" she asked.

"It's taking a beating," Winter said. "Things are getting damaged."

"I thought you made this yourself?" Emily said.

"Yeah, and it's a prototype," Winter said.

"This is your test drive? What am I, a gravitational car dealership?" Emily said while punching another enemy out of the way. They had nearly reached the seed ship, which looked like a cross between a missile and a drill. Emily watched enough sci-fi movies in her life to have a terrifying image of what terraforming looked like. She knew that thing couldn't be allowed to reach the planet.

"We're almost there," Emily said. "What do we do?"

"Hit it," Winter said.

"That's so scientific."

"Can you suggest something else?"

Emily used a bubble of float to throw the giant metal suit at the seed ship, slamming into it shoulder first like a football player in a spear-tackle. The shell of the ship cracked underneath the blow, but the suit did too. Pieces grinded and creaked with the strain.

Emily reared back one robotic arm and punched the surface of the ship, trying to get to its innards, hoping to find something to shut it down. But, like a living thing, a fungus or a plant, fibrous and organic, it didn't make sense to her.

"Are there any weapons on this giant action figure? A hidden sword in the arm? Missile launcher in the shoulder?" Emily said.

"Sorry," Winter said. "Didn't have time to put a laser cannon on here."

"What good are you?" Emily said.

"I made you a giant robot," Winter said.

"Okay, you can stay."

Outside, the small Nemesis fighters picked her apart. Wasp-stings disabled armor, scored the robot's hull.

"I can't hit it enough," Emily said. "It's too much machine to break by hand. Do we have fire? Can we kill it with fire? What about nuking it from orbit? It's the only way to be sure."

Winter grew quiet.

It worried Emily that he might have been offended by her Sigourney Weaver reference.

"Emily, throw it," he said.

"Ha. Ha. Ha."

"No. You're stronger than the suit. Your powers are so much more powerful than this robot. It got us here, but destroying this thing is all you," Winter said. "Use one of your bubbles of float and just toss it at the sun."

"Won't that... terraform the sun?" Emily said.

"Pretty sure you can't terraform a ball of gas," Winter said, a slight trace of humor in his voice. "Kill it with fire?"

As if on cue, Emily spied a flash of light in the distance, and watched as the seed ship Jane had been fighting burst into a ball of flames. Always trying to show me up, Emily thought. Or perhaps showing me the right thing to do. Thanks, Jane.

"Here we go," Emily thought. She tried to push off the seed ship to get some distance from it, but something hit them hard from behind and rammed the entire suit against the ship. "What was that?"

"Dammit," Winter said. "They're just throwing themselves at us now. They're flying suicide missions right into the body of the suit."

Another boom echoed in Emily's ears and a second ship battered into them. She tried to turn around to whack the next one out of the air before it could crash into them, but the suit groaned mechanically and could not pull away.

"Are we stuck?" Emily said.

"We are," Winter said, fear rising in his voice. "That last collision must've caused some of our armor to lodge in the surface of the ship."

"Would it help if I got out and pushed?" Emily said in her best Carrie Fisher impression.

"It might," he said.

Emily tried again to dislodge the robot from the seed ship. She shook them, but it was like trying to move an object much too heavy for them to lift. The chest of the suit was lodged in multiple spots, and the right arm of the robot was hooked as well, with some part of the elbow shoved deep into the ragged surface of the ship.

"We got this," Emily said. "We're gonna…"

"Em, you're going to have to get out and push," Winter said.

"I was kidding about that."

"I'm serious," Winter said. "The head of the robot is an escape pod. You're going to eject, and when you're at a safe distance, you'll bubble of float this thing right into the sun. You'll be a big damned hero."

Emily smiled.

"You understood my Firefly jokes this whole time?"

"Locked away for ten years," Winter said. "I had nothing but time. I watched so much TV. I get all your jokes."

Emily looked for the eject button on the console which—covered in lights and dials—seemed more like a Jackson Pollock painting than a computer to her.

"Big red button at the top, the one with the protective cover so you don't hit it by accident," Winter said, reading her mind.

"Thanks," she said. And then realized: "Wait, how are you getting out of here?"

"I'll figure something."

"You can't tell me you didn't build an engineering compartment in this thing without an eject button," Emily said.

"There really isn't an engineering compartment," he said. "The section I'm in wasn't actually meant for passengers, just repairs."

"You're an idiot," Emily said. "I'm not leaving you here."

"Yes you are," Winter said. "I'm going to rig the suit to blow up. Just in case. Nuke it from orbit, only way to be sure, right?"

"Don't start using my jokes against me, Henry," she said sternly.

"The suit I'm wearing has limited oxygen. You'll eject, aim this thing at the sun, and then I'll crawl out and wait for you to find me later. Okay?"

"I don't believe you."

"Have some faith in your scientist."

Another fighter crashed against the robot and the suit shuddered again.

"I'll give you time," Emily said. "I'll eject and then wait sixty seconds or something for you to escape."

"Don't you dare," Winter said. "Those things'll be on you in seconds once you break free. You make your move immediately."

Emily chewed on her lip, almost biting through it when another attacker smashed outside the suit.

"How strong is your armor?" she said.

"I'll be okay. I'm sealed up in this thing. I'll have some time."

"Okay, well," Emily said, before slamming the free fist of the robot into the space around its belly, dredging the surface of the seed ship like fingers through mud, trying to put a little room between the machine and the alien vessel."

"What was that?" Winter said.

"Trying to give you a fighting chance. May the Force be with you, Henry Winter."

"You too, kid. Good luck."

Emily nodded and pounded her fist down on the eject button. Instantly, hydraulics hissed and release valves clicked. Suddenly she was free floating. The head of her giant robot detached and drifted off into space, leaving her behind as the seed ship maintained its trajectory toward Earth.

She stretched one hand out toward the ship, envisioning a bubble of float, the biggest bubble of float she'd ever created, bow to stern, and almost smiled as she watched the ship's forward momentum waver while becoming locked into her gravitational manipulations. She looked toward the sun, the protective glass of the robot's cockpit making it seem less bright, less hot.

She pushed.

The seed ship's course altered immediately, drifting even faster than before toward the waiting sun. Emily couldn't watch the whole trip. The head of the robot started to spin nauseatingly out of control. But she saw the craft's shadow flicker across the sun and the little fighters chasing it, trying to save their master from imminent destruction. Seconds ticked by. Emily waited for some sign. Maybe the suit would break free. Maybe…

In the distance, the suit exploded in eerie silence, a ball of fire with a bigger ball of fire, the sun itself, waiting to consume it. And then it disappeared.

Emily sat in her spinning life raft, suddenly very tired and lonely.

"We did it… I guess," she thought, unsure of the cost.

CHAPTER 69:
DO ANDROIDS DREAM OF
ELECTRIC SHEEP?

Bedlam ran through the downtown area, discovering the occasional alien straggler, hoping to take them out before the Department guys did. Part of her wanted to do so because she knew she was better equipped for the physical challenge of the task; part of her just wanted to keep hitting stuff.

Dark things flew in the cloud cover created by Val. Things with wings. An uneasy feeling stewed in her Bedlam's guts at the sight of them. Her skin crawled, even though she couldn't really make out their actual forms. They destroyed enemy fighters, though, so she shrugged it off and kept running.

She found two more parasite-infected creatures smashing open a shop window, trying to attack civilians hiding inside.

Beldam whistled. The pair, identical insect-like monsters, turned their multi-faceted eyes at her. She searched for where the parasites had taken hold, since knocking the spider-like thing out of commission had been the most effective way of taking out the other aliens. But both of these critters had parasites hanging on their undercarriage, not an easy spot to reach.

That just meant she was forced to improvise. Bedlam scrambled towards one, full speed ahead, metal feet banging against the pavement. At the last second, she dropped, slid under the waiting pincers of the creature's mouth, and grabbed hold of the parasite.

Her feet pressing against the ant-like alien's underside for leverage, she pulled with all her strength.

It shook violently, in pain or frustration, and tried to knock her loose. Bedlam held on tenaciously, even as her back and head banged again the pavement.

The alien reared back giving its companion a chance to bite Bedlam with its sickle-like teeth. She held on to the first, but punched upward, catching the second creature on the jaw with an uppercut. Not her strongest hit, but it knocked the second alien back slightly, allowing Bedlam to continue her attempts to free the first of its parasite.

This is what my life's becoming now, Bedlam thought. I just punched out a giant ant.

She pulled the parasite free of its host with a sickening crack. The giant ant creature flung Bedlam, the disgusting parasitic husk still in her hands. The second alien, after seeing its companion fall, charged at her, seeking revenge or something else, its bug-like eyes incapable of human emotion.

Bedlam threw the dying carcass of the parasite away and readied herself for the next attacker.

She never got a chance, though, as a bright flash of light struck the giant ant from the side. Bedlam blinked, readjusting to the brightness, and saw the alien trapped under some sort of energy net, that kept it pinned to the ground.

"I had that one," Bedlam said.

"Sure you did," a familiar voice said. "But can't blame a guy for wanting to help, can you?"

Agent Black walked out from an alleyway, slinging a futuristic weapon over his shoulder casually. His usually grim countenance lit up with a goofy smile.

"Look at you, playing superhero," he said.

Bedlam ran and threw her arms around him in a bear hug.

"Where have you been?" she asked.

Agent Black gestured to the weapon he carried.

"Would you believe me if I said I've been running errands for the good guys?" he said.

"No," Bedlam said.

The first giant ant stopped moving, dead or unconscious; the second strained against its net cage.

"The good guys never asked before," Black said. "Money's money."

"You always say that," Bedlam said, and approached the still-active alien, trying to figure out a way to get its parasite off. She looked back at Black. "Turning over a new leaf?"

"You seem to be," Black said. "Hanging out with superheroes."

"Well," Bedlam said. "Like you said, they asked."

Black pulled a smaller weapon from his belt, closer to a handgun than a cannon. He crouched down beside the trapped giant insect and fired once. The parasite dropped to the ground, wisps of smoke wafting from the wound where the weapon hit. The alien ant became sluggish and settling down onto its belly.

"You're really working for the good guys," Bedlam said.

"Funny thing," Black said. "It's really a challenge to stay a cold-hearted mercenary when there might not be a world left where you can spend your money."

"Good point," Bedlam said.

"Also when your sidekick decides to go work with the white hats, you begin to feel a bit guilty about being a black hat," he said. "I even recruited some of my boys to be heroes too. They're on the far side of town, blasting aliens with outer-space ray guns. I think we may have helped a few crooks turn over new leaves."

"I'm not your sidekick," Bedlam said, punching Black in the arm.

"Never were," he said, laughing. "What do you say? Want some company putting down the rest of these critters?"

She grinned impishly.

"Are we still allowed to hang out, big guy?" she said. "I'm sitting at the school band kid's table, you're still with the dudes who cut class."

"I think we'll be all right," Black said.

CHAPTER 70:
IF IT HAS A BRAIN, I CAN KILL IT

Shocked at the destruction before them, Kate and Titus surveyed the carnage above the planet in silence from their vantage point on the flying Tower. They saw destroyed enemy ships everywhere, debris from those ships Billy and Jane had obliterated, and miles of rubble and inert biomechanical machinery scattered as far as the eye could see.

In the center of it all, the brain ship continued its slow and ruthless pathway to Earth, now flanked by countless smaller starships. There was a malevolence to it, Titus thought, a ruthlessness, an anger. The Nemesis fleet was a living thing, they knew—but did that mean it could feel rage? Could it be angry at them for destroying its seed ships?

Worse—was it intending to take out that anger on the planet? If it couldn't have the Earth for itself, would it deny the world to anyone else?

The fighters began an attack run, headed planet-side like a swarm of locusts.

"Who's out there?" Titus said into his earpiece. He couldn't see anyone.

"I'm here," Billy said, sounding exhausted. "I think I'm the only one with a functioning radio. Em, you there?"

A long, distressing pause passed before Emily spoke up.

"Yes," she said softly, her tone completely out of character. "Don't worry about me. I'm stuck but okay."

"Stuck?" Billy said.

"Bigger fish, Billy, focus," she said.

"Billy, what do Dude and Seng think the fleet's next move will be?" Kate said. "I'm not seeing any seed ships remaining."

"We got 'em," Billy said. "Three up three down. Dude thinks—"

Seng interrupted him, his voice calm.

"The fleet's pattern right now is aggressive," he said. "They're going to attack the planet. I don't know how to predict what they'll do next though. We've never seen them pushed this close to the brink."

Even as Seng spoke, flights of Nemesis ships were forming in alignment, heading for Earth.

Titus kept looking back at the brain ship. The mother ship. The center of this fleet's universe.

"Billy? Seng? The little fighters, do they think and act independently from the brain ship?" Titus asked.

A few quiet seconds went by before Billy answered.

"Dude says some of the bigger ships can respond independently, but the little ones are controlled by the brain ship," Billy said. "They're less like a queen bee and her hive and more like tools or weapons. They have simple autonomy but can't really act alone cohesively without the lead vessel."

"So if we kill the brain ship," Kate said, "We stop the fleet."

Billy sighed. "I don't think we have the firepower, guys. That ship…"

Seng chimed in. "We've never been able to crack its armor. Even with Straylight's new power levels, even with all of you combined… it's a risk," Seng said. "And all the time we spend fighting the brain ship, your planet will be under attack."

Titus and Kate exchanged a look. Not breaking eye contact, Titus spoke up.

"When you call it the brain ship, is that a euphemism for something? Or does it literally have the brain of the entire fleet in there?" Titus said.

"Dude says it's 'brains,' not brain—there's a consciousness, something controlling the whole fleet," Billy said.

"We know it thinks," Seng said. "And we know it communicates from there. This is the ship that talks to the hosts on the ground, like the ones you defeated earlier, the advanced agents who made ready."

Titus smiled.

Kate shook her head.

"If it has a brain, I can kill it," Titus said. "I just need to get inside."

"That's the stupidest thing I've ever heard," Billy said. "You're going to wolf-out inside its brain and kill it?"

Titus shrugged. "Got a better idea?

"Yeah," Billy said. "Let me do it."

Kate gave Titus a harsh look, then weighed in. "No, you're faster, more maneuverable. You've got to try to keep those fighters from reaching the planet," she said. "Jane too, if we can reach her."

"Sure, we'll simply destroy the twelve hundred enemy ships coming at us right now," Billy. "I've got the six hundred on the left."

Unexpectedly, Doc's voice, ragged and drained, joined the conversation. "It's not a bad plan," he said.

"Great to hear you're not dead, Doc," Titus said.

"Titus, in my study, there's something I want you to take," Doc said, and then he described an amulet he'd left on his desk. "Not much, but if the air isn't breathable, it should help. It carries the same spell I used on myself today."

"What if you can't kill the brain?" Emily said softly.

"I'll do it," Titus said.

"No," she said. "You need a backup plan. Just in case."

Titus rubbed his eyes, looked around the control room, and reflected.

"Neal," Titus said. "The flying machines we've been using. The bikes, the little jet. How combustible are their engines?"

"Don't you dare," Kate said.

"Designation: Whispering. I can give you instructions to make the power source for any number of our vehicles explosive. It would likely not be sufficient to destroy a ship of that size, but it would be enough to cause a blast radius of approximately a hundred meters in each direction."

336

"Do it," Titus said.

Kate and Titus locked eyes again, his expression sheepish, hers furious.

"You said it yourself, Kate," he said, smiling. "It's a one-way trip anyhow."

"I'm coming with you."

"The hell you are," Titus said. "I'm not saying this to be protective. I'm going in there and will let myself go as berserk as I've ever been and I'll gut that ship from the inside. It'll be better if I'm alone." Kate glared.

"C'mon, Kate Miller," he said. "You're just mad that I stole your line about being alone."

Kate shook her head and looked away, her mouth a hard, straight line across her face.

"Billy, get on those fighters," Kate said. "We've got this. Doc?"

"My strength's coming back," he said. "I'll attempt to repeat that spell closer to the atmosphere this time and try to catch more of the fighters."

"Emily," Kate said.

"I'm stuck."

"You find Jane," Kate said. "Stop feeling bad for yourself. You're able to control gravity. There's no such thing as you being stuck. Cut it out."

Titus could almost envision Emily's smile.

"Find Jane," Emily said. "You got it, coach."

Titus and Kate watched their friends scramble on the monitor: Billy and Seng twin streaks of blue-white light headed on an intercept course toward the planet, Doc's magic sparking and glowing in the distance.

"I'm coming with you," Kate said.

"Not like I've ever been able to talk you out of—" Titus started to say, but then stopped as they both saw something they hoped was an optical illusion appear on the monitor.

"Uh, guys?" Emily said. "I'm kinda far away, but is that..."

Emerging from the back of the brain ship, as if from a hidden cargo bay, another seed ship appeared, slowly moving into position to point in the direction of Earth. Identical to the others, its purpose became immediately clear.

"Those bastards had a backup plan," Titus said. "Get Billy. He can take care of that one."

They saw on another screen, however, that the two Luminae hosts were already engaged in a full-on dog-fight closer to the planet's surface. The two men, against untold numbers of enemies, had to hold the line.

"No," Kate said. "This one's mine."

Titus raised a questioning eyebrow.

"I've got it," she said.

"This boat has no weapons, Kate," Titus said.

Kate shot him a vicious smile.

"I'm the master of improvised weapons," she said. "Leave the last seed ship to me."

Titus smiled. All these months together, all these adventures, and barely a second to sit quietly and really get to know each other. We tried, he thought. Even if we don't make it back. We really tried.

"I love you, Kate," Titus said. "I know you're not—"

She moved so quickly he could barely react, crossing the distance between them, pulling him in for a fierce, almost violent kiss, her hands tangled in his hair so he couldn't move. He didn't want to. Not now, and not ever. He wrapped his arms around her, the lean, powerful muscles of her back danced beneath his hands, her heart beat just a little too fast, the way it always had. He knew her heartbeat, with ears that could hear everything. That quick drum of her heart had been his beacon since the first time they spoke.

When she let him go, her face was twisted up with more emotion than he'd ever seen in her, somewhere between sadness and anger and something else. Something unexpected.

"I've always loved you," Kate said softly. "I never said it enough. I should have. I'm sorry I didn't say it more."

"You never had to," Titus said.

He knew her heartbeat. She never had to say anything at all. Maybe that's why they'd worked so well together. He could hear her without ever asking her to say a word.

Titus stepped away, wiping his eyes, sniffing as he spoke to thin air.

"Neal, is that engine ready?"

"Waiting for you in the landing bay, Designation: Whispering."

Titus nodded.

"One way trip," he said.

She just nodded.

"Good luck saving the world, Kate," Titus said.

"Good luck saving the world, Titus. You better not die on me."

Stealing a final look at the monitor before heading for Doc's chambers to pick up that one last trick, Titus wasn't sure of their odds. Not so sure at all.

CHAPTER 71:
LIKE SHOOTING STARS

Jane felt cold.

Never in her life had she been cold. Since her first waking moments, for as long as she had conscious memories, she had been enveloped in warmth, the glow of the sun, the comfort of daylight. Her cells drank in the sun and held onto it, fed her and made her strong.

She was a child of the sun.

In the blackness of space, her body depleted to its core, that solar energy, that glow, disappeared. She felt every ache and pain. Her joints hurt. Her skin felt wrinkled and dry. Her hair, drifting in front of her face without purpose, without fire, looked like anyone else's, dull. Still red and gold, but now simply hair, not the living, dancing flames that the world had become accustomed to when seeing her.

She drifted on nothingness, surrounded by a cloud of ash, the results of giving up her gift, of pouring the sunlight that was her blood into the destruction of the seed ship.

She watched helplessly as her friends struggled in the distance. She saw Billy glow like a comet, a firefly dancing on the vapors of space.

Jane turned her head to see the weird marvel that was Emily manipulate the world's biggest toy. Jane saw the seed ship plummet toward the sun, and the explosion that followed. She wished her earpiece hadn't burned out during the fight. She wanted to know if

Emily was okay. Her vision, usually superhuman, had dulled to an ordinary person's, or worse, as the world faded and blurred.

I've never been so tired, she thought. When she'd been locked up in the Labyrinth, denied access to the sun, she'd been weak, she'd been weary, but not like this, not this empty, crushing exhaustion.

The sun stared back at her, gold and endless. Jane reached out a hand toward the burning globe, appalled at how gray her skin looked, how wrinkled her fingers had become. Am I dying?

She watched the sunlight play between her fingers. I am a child of the sun. I don't know how this happened. I don't know where I came from, not really. But I know your light. Sunlight was my mother's milk. Sunlight is my family's love. Everything I've ever done, I have been able to do because of you.

Don't leave me, Jane thought. She stretched her fingers toward Earth's yellow star. I'm not finished yet. There's still so much more I need to do.

The sun's warmth touched her palm like a soft breath. Her heart beat a little faster. She spread her fingers, and sparkles of light danced around her fingertips, cells reigniting. In the vacuum of space, she turned, closed her eyes, and let sunlight, unfiltered and pure, splash across her face.

Her strength started to return. Color painted her skin. The pain washed away. Her heart raced, and her muscles felt fluid and strong.

Thank you, she thought. Thank you for giving me one more chance. I promise I'll make you proud.

The fleet renewed its attack on Earth, a thousand ships bent on destroying her home world. She watched the Tower—it's a space ship, Jane thought, we've always lived in a space ship, how easy it is to forget the wonder of it—head toward the brain ship, aimed at one last seed ship, one last attempt to ruin their planet. It had to be Kate. Kate always has a plan. I knew I could count on her. She'll never let us down.

Jane's stomach churned at the sheer enormity of the fleet, even without a cadre of seed ships. The hunger of it, the hatred of it. It's too much for us, Jane thought. We're strong, we're brave, but it's too much for us to defeat by ourselves.

And then, as if answering a prayer, she saw them.

Streaking across the sky like shooting stars. A dozen, maybe more, blue-white bolts of light, just like Billy's light. Luminae. They had to be.

And Jane remembered what Billy said. The old man, Horizon, had gone for help. To save our world.

The Luminae joined Billy and Seng, dashing through the Nemesis fleet, a squadron of comets. We're not alone, Jane thought. She clenched her hands into fists and lit herself up, surrounding her body in the flames of the sun.

It's time to end this.

Jane, the solar-powered girl, dove into the fray, to defend her world, the warmth of the sun bright and strong at her back.

CHAPTER 72:
BROTHERS IN ARMS

Billy felt a little overwhelmed. Not worrying about the null guns had been a big relief, but the weapons the alien fighters were throwing at him didn't exactly tickle, and the way they were all pursuing him right now reminded him of photos he'd seen of the Beatles when they first came to America. Crowds chasing the mop tops down the street in black and white photos.

Only instead of being a rock star, Billy was a target, and instead of screaming fans, he was being pursued by hundreds of angry alien space ships through the upper atmosphere of Earth's sky.

A few moments before, Seng had broken off in another direction. Billy hoped the other Luminae host was okay. He didn't possess Billy's protection against the null guns, but then again, Seng also had years more combat experience than Billy. Maybe that translated into being a better dodge ball player Billy thought.

Doc's spells flashed all around him, always just in range of Billy's peripheral vision. Whatever the old magician was doing, it helped, because Billy heard the explosions, but still…

Just when he started to feel his strength flag, the space around him grew warmer, and suddenly a burst of flames behind him, scattered his pursuers. Smiling triumphantly, Jane banked around to catch up with him.

"Glad you're not dead," Billy said. "Why are you smiling?"

"Look up, goofball," Jane said.

Billy twisted so that he was facing back out into space, away from the planet. When he saw them, he started laughing.

"The old man did it!" Billy said. "He actually got help!"

I knew he wouldn't fail, Dude said. *Horizon would never let us down.*

The other Luminae were too far away to make out clearly, but it had to be Suresh and his allies. Who else could it be? They boldly tore through the back end of the fleet, diminishing the Nemesis armada's overwhelming numbers, clearing a path to the Earth.

"We should—"Billy started, but Jane was a step ahead of him.

"You take the left, I'll get the right?" she said.

"You got it."

They split apart, each taking half of Billy's pursuers with them. Billy lifted up, leading them away from the Earth's atmosphere, toward… something, a tangled mass of wreckage near the moon. No, not just wreckage, a ball of combat with Korthos in the middle, that weird loincloth-wearing-Tasmanian-Devil-whirlwind-of-destruction.

"Hey big guy, coming at you!" Billy said.

'Bring forth more of thy enemies, little glowing man!" Korthos yelled into his earpiece, making Billy's ear ring. "I shall smite them all!"

"Get ready to smite like you've never smote before!" Billy yelled. He and the immortal man met in mid-flight. Nemesis ships crashed into each other unable to bank away in time, and the rest began to fall from Korthos' axe and Billy's blasts of light.

One of the other Luminae hosts broke free from their attack pattern and headed straight for Billy. He wasn't surprised when he saw the man approaching him.

Suresh, white hair even crazier and more out of place than the last time Billy saw him, flew up alongside and put a hand on his shoulder.

"Told you I'd be back," Suresh said.

"I don't think you made any promises," Billy said.

"Well, let me tell you something, son. Those guys up there, they've been waiting for this," Suresh said.

"For us?"

"For the chance to help a planet that was fighting back," Suresh said. "They're all survivors of dead worlds. And they've wanted payback for a very long time."

"Y'know, before you came along, I thought I was unique," Billy said.

"Sorry about that," Suresh said, breaking away to take on another wing of Nemesis ships. "We all start out that way."

He saluted Billy and winked, heading back out, a gleeful look on his face.

"Was he always like this?" Billy said.

Horizon always did have odd taste in hosts, Dude said.

"Coming from you, that's a compliment," Billy said.

CHAPTER 73:
PINOCCHIO AND THE WHALE

Titus barely had to fly the little aircraft as it passed into the mouth of the brain ship. He'd headed out of the Tower essentially on a straight course, and shut down the engines to try to mask his approach. Surprisingly, none of the fighters seemed to pay him any mind. Either they were too focused on the bigger picture, or he didn't seem like much of a threat.

His craft passed into the cavernous mouth at the front of the brain ship. Titus kicked the engines back on and landed. Never having practiced flying any of the machines in the Tower, it wasn't a pretty landing, but he figured it didn't much matter. The engine was coming with him. If this worked, he'd have to find another way home.

He opened the hatch and stepped outside, feeling the amulet he'd taken from Doc's office growing cool as it protected him from the environment. Though not armor, it had a spell that would let him breath if the air here turned out to be toxic, which was a start. But he could tell right away it wasn't so different from home. Murkier, yes, with a slight variation of gasses, but Titus would be able to breathe even without Doc's magical help.

He left the amulet on just in case. You never know, he thought.

Titus followed the instructions Neal had provided to open the engine and start pulling out the ship's futuristic fuel core. He'd wanted to ask Neal exactly what the little flyer's power source was comprised of, to really dig down into the mechanics of it, but there just wasn't time. He pulled a dense, glowing blue cylinder out from the chassis and wrapped it up in a backpack, which he slung over his shoulders. Inside that backpack was also an incendiary trigger. A football field in every direction, Titus thought. That should do it.

The brain ship felt like the belly of a whale. It reminded Titus of watching *Pinocchio* as a kid, when Monstro swallows up the puppet at sea. Or maybe a bit like the thing that tried to eat the Millennium Falcon in *The Empire Strikes Back*.

Listen to me, Titus thought. I've turned into Emily.

He wondered briefly if he'd have a chance to tell her about all this. She'd regret missing out on an adventure like setting foot in a living alien space ship.

Titus looked into the darkness, a looming cave lit sporadically with veins of glowing red. Somewhere in there, he'd find the brain itself. The off-switch for this entire fleet.

He willed himself to transform into werewolf, maintaining as much control over it as he possibly could. His amplified senses kicked in. He smelled warm bodies, blood flowing. He heard things moving in the dark.

He set one clawed foot in front of the other and went looking for those bodies. Wherever they were, they had to be protecting what Titus sought.

Titus wound his way through strangely empty corridors, a stray blood cell in a vein. The trail was easy to follow. His internal compass told him that he was heading toward the center of the ship, though he understood he shouldn't fully trust his senses in here. For all Titus knew, he could end up traveling in a circle.

But then he found the first of the parasite-wearing protectors of the ship, waiting for him at the end of a wide hallway. Of course, he thought, staring at the scarred and tusked things. They wanted me somewhere they could gang up on me.

They crouched in the darkness, simple weapons in hand. Titus wished he hadn't left his spear on the Tower. He'd done so thinking that it would be too much to carry, the spear and the engine, but that meant he'd have to take on these warriors with his bare claws.

And they did seem like warriors. Titus wondered what world they'd been conscripted from. All the aliens they'd fought so far had been mind-controlled by those parasites on their chests. Val and Bedlam had been intended for the same fate. If I destroy the brain ship here, will they be set free? Or will they die?

It doesn't matter, Titus thought, baring his teeth and preparing to fight. It's us or them.

I'm so tired of us or them, the werewolf thought.

* * *

An intruder had invaded the ship.

This is what they've kept us here for all this time, the chieftain thought. Warriors for an inevitable battle. Sometimes, when the conscripted soldiers began to degrade, when the control the Nemesis fleet held over them weakened or their bodies started to fail, they'd be assigned on a mission to scout a potential world. Others were sent away because their physiology was well suited for the planet to be invaded, and so they became spies, or first strikers, or suicide missions.

The chieftain envied them. Their valiant deaths. Why the creatures controlling this fleet kept him here, he never knew. Maybe they thought he was stronger than the rest. Maybe he had taken to their control better than others. Or maybe—and this is the assumption the chieftain believed to be true—they just forgot he was here. Another blurry, faceless slave in a ship full of mindless monsters.

But an intruder. They all knew instantly this enemy was on board. The parasites they wore let them know. Fear, anger. Protect the hive, protect the core. Kill it. Kill the thing that threatens the whole.

The chieftain picked up the old weapon he'd brought from his home world, a curved blade, one honed and handed down for generations. For years, he'd wanted to turn the blade on himself, to free him from the endlessness of this existence with the fleet. To die and join his wife and children in the beyond. But the parasite holding tight to his body wouldn't let him. The fleet needed him. Just in case.

The parasite instructed him to find this intruder and kill it. Slowly, reluctantly, the chieftain did as he was ordered. He had no choice. He might have resisted, once upon a time, but the days of fighting back were long gone. He was just a puppet now, an attack dog, a toy.

He walked the familiar reddish pathways of the ship, toward the sound of combat, the smell of blood. The chieftain arrived in time to see the intruder kill his brother, cutting the parasite that had manipulated him for years with one clawed hand while the other lacerated his throat. The chieftain watched his brother die on the floor of this ship and was glad. Finally you are free. Finally you can go home.

The chieftain surveyed this newcomer, tall as he was, almost as big, with silver fur spattered by the black blood of the parasites and the multi-colored bloods of the warriors who wore them. Bodies were scattered all around, some from the chieftain's species, others from more distant stars. All great warriors who had been laid low by these conquerors, who had their dignity and power stripped of them to be used like weapons.

"I'm glad you're a warrior as well," the chieftain said in his own language to the fanged creature whose clawed hands were covered in blood up past his wrists. "This is the death I wanted. The end I've wished for."

The creature seemed to comprehend. Something far in the back of his golden eyes, some rational realization, some connection between the chieftain and the beast.

"This will be a good death," the chieftain said in his own tongue. He raised his blade and charged.

* * *

They must have been collecting these beings forever, Titus thought, putting down another of the parasite-controlled aliens in his way. The deeper he got into the ship the more common it became for them to resemble each other—small groups of the same race or species gathered together, all scarred and strong, clearly saved by the fleet to be guardians against their will. He could easily imagine the werewolves of earth serving this same purpose. If the Nemesis fleet gathered collections of creatures to serve as their warriors, then Titus' own people were a prime choice for the job.

One more alien strode forward from the darkness, carrying a sword that looked older than time. This creature looked older, too, lined face, broken teeth, an empty socket where his left eye should be. His body was a mass of scars.

The creature muttered something in a language that Titus realized would die with him. Stolen from a dead world. Kept here. Forced to fight Titus to the death. The alien looked like a war god on his last legs. He spoke to Titus, locking eyes with him, connecting on some deeper level. Fighter to fighter, warrior to warrior, dead man to dead man.

Titus couldn't comprehend his words, but understood their meaning.

The old alien charged. Titus met him, filled with the werewolf's fury, batting away his sword hand and lashing out with his claws at the parasite on his chest. The alien bashed Titus' mouth with a huge, armored shoulder, stunning the werewolf, making his eyes water. Titus struck back, claws raking across the being's midsection, nearly gutting him.

The alien slashed downward with that old blade, catching Titus in the meat of his ribs, sliding down, cutting into his abdomen. Titus roared, but the monster inside, the beast, beat down the pain, swallowed it, used it. He caught the alien's sword arm, claws dug into his wrist, then snapped it, forcing him to release his blade.

They locked eyes again, like dancers. The alien said something else, in a whisper. A thank you. An apology. For death. For both of them.

Titus couldn't stop the werewolf he shared his body with from piercing the alien's neck with its fangs, blood poured over his face and chest. The alien stopped struggling, and Titus turned his attention to the parasite, tearing it apart more brutally than he'd done any of the others, all the rage and pain and sadness and death washing over him. He threw the dead parasite aside and looked once more at the old warrior, now separated from his captor. Titus realized that the alien had died reaching for one of the others, a creature that looked like him, green-gray skinned, scarred and strong. He dragged the older one's body to the younger and laid them side by side.

They looked like brothers.

The strange blade still protruded from his torso. Titus pulled it free and watched his own blood gush out. He felt weak. His knees wobbled. The wound started to heal, but slowly. Not fast enough for what Titus needed to do.

He limped on, deeper into the ship, carrying the old blade with him, leaving a trail of blood behind.

Down a corridor and up a set of strange, slick steps, he found what he was looking for.

The circular room was lit with a faint green light of bioluminescence; the walls, foggy but translucent, were veined with strands of plantlike bands. When Titus looked inside the almost-clear walls, he understood why.

Beings floated in stasis behind those walls, the round shape of the room allowing them to look at each other. They hung in fluid like a womb, unmoving except to take slow, shallow breaths. Their skin, tree bark in texture, was shiny and black like the Nemesis fleet ships themselves. Their bodies were elfin, thin. They almost looked like part of the fleet, some component to a larger machine.

Titus struck the wall with the blade he'd taken from the dead warrior, the alien metal ringing with each strike but not leaving a mark. He dropped the sword on the ground and started to lash out at the walls with his claws, pounding on it with is feet and shoulder, roaring, screaming. The glasslike substance did start to crack, but not nearly enough. He'd never break through.

The fluid inside the walls began to leak through, grimy and earthy, like swamp water. The creatures behind the glass began to stir. Sleepy yellow eyes opened in their tree-like faces, their mouths, childlike but punctuated by curved pincers like a bug's, moved and twitched.

But they were sluggish. How long have they been behind that glass? Who put them there? Were they born here? Engineered to be this way? Would we ever know?

He tried once more to break the glass with the sword. If he had hours and hours, he might eventually get through, but there were a thousand ships on a mission, receiving commands from this room, and the Nemesis fleet had never, ever left a planet alive.

Titus willed himself to transform back into human shape.

Instantly he felt all the pain from the wound in his side. He looked down. Still raw, not even half-healed, it was bleeding and ragged. He fell to his knees and eased the makeshift bomb on his back down onto the ground. He slid the glowing cylinder from its bag and started attaching the incendiary device to it, exactly as Neal told him to. Titus laughed a little. I could've been an engineer if I'd had an ordinary life.

He checked the settings on the improvised explosive and sat down on the floor, looking at the trigger Neal had helped him build. Just a remote control from one of the machines back in the Tower. Range of maybe twenty or thirty feet. Titus couldn't risk getting too far away.

He sighed and activated his earpiece.

"Who's out there," he said, shocked at how gravelly his own voice was.

"I'm here," Billy said. "Where are you, Titus?"

Titus looked around, wiped blood from his eyes. The aliens behind the glass were stared at him, not in anger, but in curiosity. He wondered what they thought of him. If they realized this was the end.

"I'm on the brain ship," Titus said. "If we have anyone close to it, you better pull back."

"What?" Billy said.

"I can't kill it," Titus said. "I thought I could, but I was wrong. I'm going to have to blow it up."

"The hell you are," Billy said. "I'm coming over there."

"How many fighters would you drag with you if you headed my way, Billy?"

Silence on the other end of the line. Titus heard his friend breathing.

"Who else is out there?" Titus said. "Are we all still alive?"

"Yeah furball, we're all still here," Emily said.

"Do you have the amulet I told you to take," Doc said.

Titus was glad. He'd been wondering if Doc were out there. He wanted to hear the magician's voice one more time.

"I do, boss."

"Don't give up hope then," Doc said. "You're carrying a little bit more luck with you than you think."

Titus smiled, looking around at the tight quarters here in the middle of this hellish ship, at the glowing blue engine full of some sort of fuel that hadn't even been invented yet. He needed more than luck.

"Kate?" Titus said.

Kate didn't answer. Titus smiled. Of course not. He knew she was listening. Talk to her about business. Always business with her.

"Hey Kate, how's the problem with that last seed ship," Titus said. "I don't think destroying the brain ship will stop it from doing what it's intended to do."

"I've got a plan, Titus," Kate said without hesitation.

"You always do."

Neal's voice chimed in.

"Designation: Whispering. Your channel with Designation: Dancer is now direct," Neal said.

"Don't you dare die on me," Kate snapped.

"Trying not to," Titus said.

"You're the one person I've never been able to protect," Kate said. "I hate that."

"Well, that goes both ways Kate Miller," Titus said. "I promise I won't let you down."

Kate sighed. "I mean what I said."

"I know," Titus said. "I've always known. Go save the world, Kate."

"You too," she said.

The line went silent.

Titus activated the incendiary device, then half-walked, half-crawled down the steps that led up to the room where the fleet's controllers still slumbered, using the old alien's sword like a cane to help pull himself along. The stairs wouldn't offer much protection, but maybe that little bit would help.

This is what we were all put here to do, he thought. Defense mechanisms for the world. White blood cells. Immune systems. Here to keep this place spinning for one more day.

He closed his eyes and smiled before pushing the button on the remote and activating the makeshift bomb.

The tunnel filled with horrible noise, then white light. And then nothing.

CHAPTER 74: IMPROVISED WEAPON

Kate watched the Tower's monitors and saw the brain ship crumble from within. The huge vessel crackled and split. Pressure continued to build inside until its shiny carapace exploded, causing it to fall apart like an egg squeezed in a giant invisible fist.

Flames flashed for just a moment before the vacuum of space snuffed them out. Somewhere in the midst of all the destruction, her best friend had stood alone, trying to save a world he'd truly never been comfortable living in.

She gritted her teeth, pushed all other thoughts to the back of her mind, and turned her attention to the seed ship, no longer under control of its brain but still hurtling, with increasing momentum, toward Earth. Still capable of terraforming the planet into something deadly with its organic machinery. A suicide bomb for a dead armada.

How did I get here? Kate thought. I didn't put on this mask to save the world. I did it to stop little crimes, to make things better one life at a time. I'm just a failed dancer in a costume. I don't belong here in a bloody space ship fighting to prevent the apocalypse.

You must be better than this, she reminded herself. Her consistent mantra, her prayer. There's always something you can do.

"Neal," she said. "Are you sure there's no weapons on this ship."

"Nothing beyond personal weapons like the ones in the training room, Designation: Dancer," Neal said. "I apologize."

"How do you build a ship like this without weapons?" Kate said.

"This was a craft designed by hopeful people, Designation: Dancer," Neal said. "From what little I have been able to learn about them, they were healers and wise men. Allowed to travel the stars unharmed."

"Well, they still should have put some damned guns on this ship," she said.

They were rapidly approaching the plummeting seed ship. Do what you always do, Kate thought. When you see a problem, hit it. And, if you see a problem too big for your fist, hit it with something harder.

"Neal, if we ram it with the Tower, will we be able to knock that ship off course enough that it'll miss the Earth?" Kate said.

Neal went silent as he calculated projections, velocities, and angles.

"Designation: Dancer. If we increase our speed by sixty-five point seven percent, we will meet the seed ship before it strikes the Earth and create a sufficient impact to redirect it away from the planet."

"Do it," Kate said.

"Designation: Dancer," Neal said, panic overtaking his voice. "I should warn you there is a seventy-eight percent chance the Tower itself will not survive the impact. This vessel was not designed as a warship. Its hull—"

"—Can you come up with any other options, Neal?" Kate said. "Because I'm not seeing any and I'm not about to let my friends die because I didn't want to break our clubhouse."

Again, silence from Neal.

"Any other options I calculate result in mission failure or destruction of our ship, Designation: Dancer," Neal said.

"Jane told me to find a way to end this," Kate said. "I'm not letting her down. Any of them. Do I need to steer?"

"No. I will pilot the ship for you."

Engines revved up. The whole ship shuddered, moving faster than it had since Kate took up residence. I'm throwing a flying hospital at a living alien missile, she thought.

Kate sat down and watched the seed ship get closer and closer on the monitor. She turned her attention to another screen and watched the ravaged destruction of the brain ship float away. On a third, the chaos of the battle played as the Nemesis fleet's smaller vehicles seemed to have lost all sense of purpose, no longer fighting with the aggressive grace they'd seen in them earlier.

Another screen displayed only stars. A patch of empty sky, not far from the pitched battle in the grand scheme of things. It looked peaceful, a reflection of eternity.

Not a bad way to go, Kate thought.

"Designation: Dancer, I can prepare an escape pod for you," Neal said.

"I don't want to risk it," Kate said. "I need to make sure this works."

"We can jettison the escape pod very close to impact," Neal said, his voice growing concerned. "It is not necessary for you to go down with the ship."

Again, Kate glanced at the monitors and all the carnage floating around. She didn't feel like leaving. A strange sensation, an emptiness in the pit of her belly told her not to leave home.

"Designation: Dancer…"

"Neal, it's okay," Kate said.

"I do not want to die here," Neal said.

Kate bolted upright, shocked by the fear evident in the AI's voice.

"What do you mean?"

"I don't want to end my existence here," Neal said. "I want to leave."

Kate watched as the seed ship grew closer and closer on the main monitor.

"Can you escape?" she said. "When we traveled into the future, there was a, a portable you somehow, can you…?"

"I can download my consciousness into a mobile casing," Neal said. "I prepared for this when we left Earth earlier as a precaution, Designation: Dancer."

"Then go!" Kate said. "What are you waiting around for? Get out of here!"

One more long, soft pause from Neal.

"My programming does not allow me to leave a crewmate behind, Designation: Dancer. If you stay, then so must I."

Kate laughed. Of all the things in the world, it's this ridiculous computer, I'm going to have to rescue this silly living computer…

"Okay," she said, trying to withhold smile, her eyes itchy as she fought back a sense of hope she hadn't wanted to feel. "Where's the casing? I'll get it for you."

She wondered if she was losing her mind when she thought she could hear joy in the AI's voice.

"It is motorized, and on wheels, Designation: Dancer," Neal said. "I can meet you at the escape pod."

Kate released a hard, half-crazy, incredulous belly laugh.

"All this time we thought you were the ship itself," Kate thought. "All this time…"

"This ship has been a better body than I could ever make myself," Neal said. "But I am my own being."

"Get going, you crazy robot," Kate said. She took one last look around the control room. Resting against one chair was Titus' spear, the one he brought back from a training session with the other werewolves months ago. He'd left it behind when he went to the brain ship. Now Kate wondered why. She picked up the weapon and inspected it. She tried to convince herself she was bringing it because Titus would want it later, but the pragmatist in her told her this was only sentiment.

And for just this once, Kate was okay with sentiment.

"On my way," she said. "Meet you there, Neal."

Long strides carried her through the corridors into the bright, sterile halls of the Tower, this place they'd called home, this place where they'd felt secure. Even Kate felt safe here, the one spot she could turn to when she got in over her head, where she'd always be welcome.

She found the escape pods easily enough. Emily was fond of napping in them, since no one ever thought they'd be necessary, a row of cubby holes on the lower level of the Tower.

A blocky robot, not dissimilar from a trash can, dotted with sensors and cameras, waited for her by the pod. It rolled around on what looked like a set of ball bearings, with two segmented arms attached to its sides.

"Neal?" Kate said.

"This chassis has an issue with stairs and ladders, Designation: Dancer," Neal said. "Could you help me?"

Kate wrapped her arms around the little robot, barely half as tall as she was, picked up the surprisingly light machine and jumped inside the nearest escape pod with it. She set him down gently and pounded a button, closing the hatch behind them. Kate took a moment to catch her breath.

"Designation: Dancer, forty-five seconds to impact," Neal said.

"I guess we better go," Kate said.

She took one last look inside through the reinforced glass window on the pod's door. It was a good home, she thought. I'm sorry I had to do this to you. She pressed the release switch.

Kate and Neal plummeted into space, the activation of the pod pushed them away from the Tower itself. They spun in the emptiness, a cork bobbing on the ocean. She watched out the window as the pod's movement turned the view of the impact into a slide show, the Tower racing closer and closer to the seed ship.

The ships collided, hospital crashing into terraforming device.

Like a pair of jousting knights, the two vessels smashed together, shuddering at the impact. Chunks of the seed ship were crushed under the armored hull of the Tower; the Tower itself sundered, a huge rift split open across the undercarriage of the flying hospital. Kate watched the two machines wrestle in space, and then exhaled deeply as the seed ship broke free, its direction altered by forty-five degrees or more, falling away silent and cruel into empty space, trailing broken pieces of its hull behind.

Two internal explosions rocked The Tower, leaving deep, smoking gashes in its hull. The ship's engines sputtered out as it turned and spun and finally, began drifting on its final course.

"Neal, can you see this?" Kate said.

"Yes, Designation: Dancer."

"Will you know where the wreckage lands?"

"I was a part of that ship for decades, Designation: Dancer," Neal said. "And it was a part of me. I will always know where it is."

"I think I understand that feeling," Kate said, watching the remnants of their home tumble silently away.

CHAPTER 75:
ROUTED

Jane, still cut off from the rest of the team without a working earpiece, didn't need one to see the explosion that rocked the Nemesis fleet, its brain ship shattering in a quick, bright instant. She stopped chasing the closest Nemesis fighter to watch the explosion burn out.

"They did it," she said to herself.

The effect was instantaneous. Although the fighters didn't immediately go inert like she'd suspected they would without the brain ship controlling them, there was instant panic as they no longer seemed to have any real directions to follow. Some went blank and just kept flying in a straight line; others kept fighting, but sloppily, and without spirit or purpose. Jane knocked a passing fighter off course and back up into space, and she watched as it just kept going, as if her punch were a subtle suggestion that it might want to choose a different path, just because.

All around her, Billy's fellow Luminae hosts continued to battle, though Jane could see them making the same observation she had. The fighters weren't really a threat anymore. She frowned with concern as a wing or two of fighters took off into deep space together as if fleeing. Were they more sentient than the others? Was this some sort of autopilot instinct? Why were some running and others not?

Jane spotted the last seed ship, still making its way toward Earth. Her fists burst into flames and she prepared to head for it, ready to deplete herself a second time to destroy it if that were necessary. But then, in the distance, she saw the blocky shape of the Tower flying at an almost comical speed toward the seed ship, and watched it as the two crafts smashed together in a soundless, powerful collision.

Billy flew up next to her just as the last seed ship spun off into space, the Tower burning as it fell.

"Kate just flew our house into the seed ship," Billy said.

"I knew she'd figure something out," Jane said. "Where is everyone?"

"Hang on," Billy said, pressing the device in his ear. He shot Jane a worried look, then tossed her the earpiece. "You take this."

"What?" Jane said.

"We've got people missing up there. I gotta go."

Billy erupted in a white light and shot out into space, toward the wreckage of the brain ship. Jane placed the radio in her ear.

"Jane checking in," she said. "Who's out there."

"Still stuck," Emily said. "Jane, I don't know where Henry is."

"Neal and I made it out, Jane," Kate said. "We're fine. Go look for Titus. He was on the brain ship when it blew."

Jane's stomach twisted, the idea of Titus alone out there sent a shock of fear down her spine. Could he survive?

"On my way," Jane said, racing into space. "Doc?"

Doc Silence's comforting voice chimed in. "Already there," he said.

Jane rocketed out into the black, marveling, again, at how vast outer space felt, and wondering, with a growing fear, how they would find their friends in all that emptiness.

CHAPTER 76: HUMAN DEBRIS

All these heroes, constantly looking for a way to die while saving the world, Henry Winter thought. Adrift in space, his suit's life support systems were still operational but nothing else really seemed to be working. Not me. I never wanted to die a hero.

Winter tried to fake his own death ten years before in specific hopes of never dying a hero. He'd pretended to die saving the world so that he could retire early. Winter had every intention of buying an island, marrying a woman people would judge him for being with while they went out in public, and drinking brightly colored beverages on the beach well into his old age. He'd live off patents and inventions he'd created during his lifetime.

He botched that pretty well, got himself captured, and lost ten years of his life.

Winter wanted his beach house and fruity drinks and someone stunning who loved him at least a bit to hang out with. Was that asking too much?

Instead, here he was, lost and alone, and fairly sure nobody would find him. The distress beacon on his suit no longer worked. His radio lost its signal. Rocket boots? Not functioning, and really, not particularly useful for getting home. The suit wasn't designed for reentry through the atmosphere. He'd be human bacon even if he could get back to Earth.

And then he heard the voice in his head. Which was precisely the moment he assumed the oxygen had cut out in his suit and he worried he'd begun to hallucinate.

"Henry Winter," the voice of Prevention, his onetime-jailer and sort-of nemesis spoke in his head. "Fancy meeting you out here."

"Well, this must be the end, then," Winter said, assuming this was the instant his brain would finally shut down. "I'm incredibly disappointed that Prevention was the person you came up with in my twilight moments, brain. Couldn't you have picked someone who actually liked me?"

"I do like you, Henry," Prevention said. "Always did. Sorry about the professional inconvenience of keeping you captive. If I save your life, do you think you'll be able to forgive me?"

Henry laughed, unconcerned that his oxygen was close to zero. I might as well suffocate with laughter on my lips, he thought.

"I'm serious," Prevention said. "Turn your head."

Winter turned to the left. Floating in space maybe thirty meters away was a small spacecraft, reminiscent of a submarine. A United States flag with forty-eight stars on a field of red, with blue and white stripes was printed on its side.

"Yup, I'm so dying right now," Winter said.

"You can if you want to," Prevention said. "But I'm serious about helping."

"Sure, you just happened to be driving along in your alternate reality space submarine."

"First of all, good guess on what this ship is," Prevention said. "Second, I'm a telepath. How do you think I found you out here?"

"That really you, Prevention?" Winter said.

The sound of her laughter filled his brain with just the right combination of warmth and creepiness.

"Call me Laura if you don't mind Henry. And yeah. I heard you were lost. And I figured since I ruined your life, the least I could do is come out and try to save you."

Now Henry really laughed, so hard tears pooled in the corners of his helmet. I don't have to die a hero after all, he thought. I feel like it's Christmas morning.

"Come get me before oxygen deprivation kills too many more

brain cells, and I'll forgive every horrible thing you ever did to me," Henry Winter said. "I don't want to die out here."

"Are you asking permission to come aboard my alternate reality space submarine, Henry?" she said.

"Absolutely."

In his delirium, he couldn't stop himself from asking one last question. "Hey Laura. What's your feeling about fruity drinks?"

Prevention belly laughed, her ship cruised in slowly to pick him up.

"I prefer my hard alcohol neat," she said. "But if you're buying, who am I to say no?"

CHAPTER 77: INDESTRUCTIBLE

D oc Silence moved through the cosmos on unseen waves, spells older than the planet glowing at his back, carrying him through the wreckage of the Nemesis fleet.

He pushed pieces of the brain ship aside with simple hand gestures, telekinetic nudges to make room for him to pass. Broken armor, blackish blood and fuel, pieces of organic machinery so complex it was hard to tell if they were organs or engines filled the vacuum around him.

The dead floated here, as well: enslaved hosts of the Nemesis fleet and its parasites, aliens from hundreds of worlds, powerful and pitiful creatures who had been dragged across light years, to die in a war they should never have been a part of. Doc mourned for them. If they'd learned one thing about the Nemesis fleet, it was that they chose their captives because they were powerful and brave. All these deceased beings floating in space were the finest of their kind, laid low by a force they couldn't stop. They deserved better than this tragedy, every one of them.

Doc searched for one being in particular. The finest of his kind.

He saw a flash of silver and pink behind a slab of armor, a curved wall that once must have been some sort of vein inside the brain ship. Doc flew quickly toward it.

Clinging to that sliver of armor was Titus Whispering.

Reflexively returned to his werewolf form and unconscious, he held on to the debris with claws clenched in silent fury. Black lines of blood and brutality covered his body; blisters and burns marked his skin and patches of his silver fur had been torched away. The amulet Doc had given him still hung around Titus' neck on a metal chain, the gem in its center pulsed softly. A little bit of luck never hurt. Or nothing more than a trinket that provided you air when you couldn't breathe what surrounded you. A wizard's toy, really, but Doc understood all the best tricks began as toys and gimmicks. Not everything had to come from the pages of a book to save a life.

Doc Silence reached out and grabbed Titus' wrist. The werewolf's grip loosened on the slab of wall.

"Come on, my brave friend," he said. "Let's get you home."

Doc stretched out his arms, gestured with both hands and a bluish bubble formed around Titus. Air, clean oxygenated air, and a force field to protect him. Doc's heart skipped a beat. It's said that magic is all transference, that you cannot make something from nothing. But great magicians can create something from nothing, if they sacrifice a little of themselves in return. It cost Doc a piece of himself to provide air in that vacuum of space, but this was the very least he could do for his friend.

Inside the bubble, Titus reverted back to human form, as if his unconscious mind realized that he was now safe, that the beast could rest while the man recovered.

"I've got him," Doc said softly into his earpiece.

"Is he…?" Jane said, even more softly.

"Alive," he said. "I'm bringing him home. You and Billy find the others."

"Doc," Kate's voice said from somewhere in the void.

"Kate, it's going—"

"You don't have to say anything more," Kate said.

He heard something in her tone, an emotion she rarely showed.

"I can always read through what you're saying," she said.

Doc smiled and flew towards Earth.

"And what are you reading now?" he asked.

"That you're not afraid," Kate said. "And it's all I need to know."

CHAPTER 78:
YOU WOULDN'T BELIEVE ME IF I TOLD YOU

Entropy Emily sat inside a giant robot's head in the emptiness of space, convinced she got Henry Winter killed.

This is my fault, she thought. Sure, he built the suit, and sure, he showed it to her—which is tantamount to telling her to use it—but in the end, she was the one flying it, the one who wasn't strong enough to defeat that enemy ship without having to sacrifice the suit.

Henry's dead and it's my fault, Emily thought.

"Where are you?" Jane said over the radio. She'd been quiet through most of the fight, Emily realized. I'm a terrible person for not remembering that until now. But why would I worry about Jane? She's always okay. She's not some old crazy guy I just sent hurtling toward the sun. Jane's made of sunlight. She'll be fine.

"Em?" Jane said again.

"Hush, I'm feeling sorry for myself," Emily said. "I need concentration. I'm not good at feeling like this and it's really weird."

"Billy's out there looking for you. I have his radio. You might have to do something to help him find you."

"I'm in no rush," Emily said, her stomach in knots. Just leave me out here. Y'know, like I did with Henry.

"What's wrong with you?" Jane said.

"Nothing. I got Henry Winter killed. I'm just a horrible, horrible person."

Bedlam, of all people, chirped in next. Clearly their earpieces were partially dependent on the Tower to boost their signal, because her voice sounded even more fuzzy and robotic than usual.

But it was clear she definitely said "Henry's fine."

"Go again, Bedlam?" Jane said.

"Henry… fine… hang on," Bedlam said, her voice breaking up.

A moment passed, and Emily decided that Bedlam was having another conversation completely separate to this one and returned to wallowing. Then Winter spoke.

"Hey, Em," he said, sounding delirious, or possibly drunk.

"You're not dead!" Emily yelled.

"Nope. I hitched a ride with an old friend."

"You're losing it," she said. "Where are you."

"I'm… You wouldn't believe me if I told you, kiddo," Winter said.

Emily pounded her fists on the console.

"I'm so happy you're not dead that I'm not even going to give you a hard time about how belittling calling me kiddo is," Emily said.

"You need a lift?" Henry said.

Emily, about to answer, heard a tap on the glass of her robot's windshield. Billy glowed bright and smiled like a lunatic. He put both hands against the surface and made a face.

"No, I think I'm good, Henry," Emily said. "I'm glad I didn't get you killed."

"Me too," Winter said.

Billy made a telephone with his hands and put it up to his ear, Emily shrugged at him. Billy held up his index finger and, using his light powers, traced a heart in the darkness.

Emily gave him the finger.

"Push me home!" she said.

He mouthed the word: "What?"

"Push me! Take me home, Jeeves!"

Billy pointed at himself. "Me?"

Emily threw her helmet at the window.

He made calming motions with his hands, then darted out of sight. The robot head began to move, and soon, the Earth was dead ahead.

"It really does help when someone gets out and pushes," Emily said. "Princess Leia was right."

CHAPTER 79:
DAY AND NIGHT

Kate curled up in the escape pod, watching stars drift by.

How do we come back from this? Kate thought. How do we return to normal? Do I just begin the normal routine of stopping robberies and patrolling the City? We've seen the future, and what's out in space waiting for us. How do we ever look at the world in the same way again?

The pod spun slowly, and every few minutes Kate would get a good look at Earth. I could fit it in my pocket, she thought. I never wanted to feel this big. I belong down in the alleys and gutters.

Alleys. She wondered about the Hawk, still. Missing for weeks, she thought he might resurface during this last round of attacks, but he hadn't. She felt helpless up here, looking down on the entire planet and didn't like it.

As the pod continued to spin, the sight of Jane hovering outside startled Kate. The solar-powered girl put a hand on the escape pod, stopping its circular movement, then placed her palm on the glass. Kate unfurled her legs and positioned her hand up against Jane's. She felt warmth through the glass.

"Hello in there," Jane said.

Kate nodded back at her. Neal, situated in his new little robot body, spun one of his sensors around to look out the window as well.

"Hello, Designation: Solar," he said.

Jane smiled. "You put Neal in a can," she said.

"Did we lose anyone?" Kate said.

Jane glanced out at the stars. The sun's energy danced across her skin. Kate sometimes found herself mystified at how different they were. Day and night, sun and moon, hope and cynicism, joy and anger. Yet once in a while, if she wasn't paying attention, wasn't forcing herself to think the worst about everything and everybody, Kate would realize she couldn't possibly do this without Jane. Someone had to be optimistic. This type of work drove you mad without hope.

And someone has to be me, Kate thought. Because hope can kill you just as quickly. But there were times, Kate thought, when she could use a little bit more hope.

She gazed past Jane, into the stars, to the cosmos and beyond, into the blackness they knew so much more clearly now than ever before was not nearly as empty as humanity had always believed. Kate wondered what else was in store for them. What other terrors might come their way. We're on the map now, Kate thought. Whatever else is out there, they know we're here. But they've seen us fight, too, haven't they? And we're waiting. Next time, we'll be better.

Jane seemed to sense Kate's mood from outside the pod. She started looking for a place to grab hold of the escape pod, a section where she could get a good grip. She tapped on the glass gently.

"Doc has Titus," Jane said. "He's alive. In bad shape but… Can I bring you home, Kate?"

Kate pressed her head against the glass. Tired, her body ached as if she could feel each individual bruise and cut and scrape from the past few days.

"Let's go home," Kate said.

CHAPTER 80: THE STORY

Jon Broadstreet wandered the streets of the City, taking it all in. He snapped photos with his cheap digital camera and searched for the story.

This is all the story, he thought. Invaders from another planet, a group of super-powered heroes saving the day. Bizarre, bug-like spacecraft zipping over the city while beings covered in light fought them in air-to-air combat.

The aliens on the ground tearing the City apart at the street level, the heroes who stepped up to fight them, Earth's own monsters standing toe to toe with monsters from other worlds. Creatures in the sky, barely visible, winged and horrible things that seemed to disappear as the fight subsided, yet had appeared, incongruously, to be fighting on our side. The girl in the storm, made of clouds and lightning, striking down a huge alien battleship, that came to rest at a location government men were now blocking off to gawkers.

Those government men, using weapons that shouldn't exist. There will be stories about that, too. Was that an example of our tax money at work? Or something more sinister?

The story. There were casualties. Remarkably few, all things considered. Broadstreet knew Jane and her friends would do anything to keep the threat as far away from ordinary people as possible. Buildings were destroyed downtown, though. Streets torn up. People were missing. Some would turn up dead. There would be memorial stories, in the press, on TV. Talking heads will call into question every decision made, by the Indestructibles, by the Department, by the government, by each other.

Always a story. Everyone needs to find their own angle.

Maybe I'm not cut out for this any longer, Broadstreet thought. I'm a terrible newsman. I'm not ruthless enough.

He found himself near a Department staging area, men in dark suits sitting around, tending to the wounded, taking stock of what happened. In the middle of the pack sat Sam Barren, the agent who had been liaison to the Indestructibles as Broadstreet had been their pet reporter. They'd crossed paths a few times. They knew each other. Sam raised a hand at Broadstreet, who waved back. Then, the old agent beckoned him over.

"You I'll talk to," Barren said.

The war appeared to have aged him Broadstreet realized.

"Reporters hounding you?"

"Everyone is," Sam said. "My own men, my own government, you people…"

"I get lumped in with 'you people' now?" Broadstreet said.

"You people," Sam said again, adjusting the battered fedora on his head. "I'll give you three questions because I like you. Go."

"Are they alive?" Broadstreet said without hesitation.

"Who?" Sam said.

"Our mutual friends in the flying headquarters," Broadstreet said. "Did they make it?"

Sam smiled and nodded.

"No casualties," Sam said "Barely. I'll give you more on that later, but I can say they all came home."

"Okay," Broadstreet said. "Speaking of home, where'd the Tower go? It's not above the City anymore."

"That," Sam said, "I really can't tell you. I think they used it in the fight. Where it ended up afterward I don't know."

"So when my readers ask if it's gone…"

Sam turned his eyes up to the sky, his eyes on the verge of watering. Broadstreet was well-versed on the history of the City's heroes. The Tower used to be part of a building, before it became a floating base, but it had been here in the City for a lifetime. If it was gone, it would mark the end of an era, one that Barren had been a part of for decades.

"I don't know what to tell you on that, son," Sam said. "Sorry."

"Last question, then," Broadstreet said.

"Fire away."

"Did we win?"

Sam took his hat off and ran a hand through his thinning hair.

"We're still standing, right?" Sam said. "I'd call that a win."

They shook hands. Broadstreet walked away, leaving Sam to bark orders at his agents. He had a million more questions for the government man, but trying to parse them out overwhelmed him. Who were these aliens? Will they come back? Why were they here? Did we know they were coming?

There will be stories about this for years, Broadstreet thought. Maybe we'll never have all the answers, but we'll ask all the questions.

He cut through the park in the center of the City. People had taken refuge in there of all places. Groups of residents fled the buildings that the aliens seemed to be targeting to hide among the green trees. Broadstreet took pictures, collated quotes from survivors, and chatted with a five-year-old who wanted to be a werewolf when he grew up because of something he witnessed.

Along the way, he crossed paths with an elegant woman shielding her eyes behind huge sunglasses, despite the gray skies and light rain that still fell. He couldn't help but stare at her, and when she saw him, she smiled back.

"Quite the show today, wasn't it?" the woman said. She had an accent. From where, Broadstreet couldn't tell. Perhaps South Africa. Maybe somewhere else.

"Yeah. Were you here the whole time?"

"I was," the woman said. "Doing my part."

"How so?"

She shot him a movie star smile and raised an eyebrow.

"Ugliness will follow, won't it?" the woman said.

"How do you mean?"

"This world. It's full of wonders, and yet it always loves to lay blame. If there was one thing I would change it would be for

375

everyone to realize how lucky we are to be here," she said. "I've been to quite a few versions of hell. It's a shame no one appreciates this place enough."

Broadstreet took a slight step back and studied the woman's face. The corners of her eyes crinkled.

"It was nice to meet you, Jon Broadstreet," the woman said. "Will you quote me in your story?"

Broadstreet shrugged, not sure why she made him uncomfortable.

"Maybe," he said. "Can I get your name, take a quick photo?"

She acquiesced, letting him snap a head and shoulders shot.

"I'm Natasha," she told him. "Natasha Grey."

They shook hands, and Broadstreet watched her walk away. Only after she was out of sight did he realized she knew his name without his ever telling her.

He turned his camera back on and previewed her photo on its small monitor. When he saw the image, he nearly dropped the camera. Behind those huge sunglasses, her eyes burned bright, like balls of flame.

There is always a story, he thought.

CHAPTER 81: WE'RE ALL STILL HERE

Kate sat beside Titus' hospital bed in a secure wing of the Labyrinth, watching him sleep.

Titus hadn't awakened since Doc got him back to Earth. There was little any of them could do for the werewolf. Sam Barren, with his bizarre healing powers, had offered to help despite how much using them hurt him, but on his first attempt, Sam said there was something about Titus' werewolf biology that made his own gifts ineffective. Sam was still a stranger in his own body when it came to the abilities Prevention's people had given him barely a few months before. It didn't surprise Kate that he couldn't explain why they weren't effective.

They tried to locate Titus' tribe to ask for help, but that proved difficult. Finnigan turned down Titus' offer not long ago for a satellite phone, saying that they'd survived all this time without a cell phone and he didn't intend to start now. At the time Kate thought it was charmingly Luddite of him to say so. Now she wanted to throttle the red-headed werewolf for being selfish in his refusal of technology.

Doc mentioned he could send a message to Leto, the leader and shaman of the pack of wolves, one magician to another, but they hadn't heard back. Perhaps they were in trouble, Kate wondered. They wouldn't ignore a call for assistance. The pack was a strange group, but they'd die for each other in an instant. There was no way they'd dismiss an opportunity to help Titus if he needed them.

Titus' wounds were improving, though. Kate could almost watch it happen, as his werewolf healing abilities knitted cuts and lacerations back together and transformed raw burns into pink new skin. The explosion singed the hair on his head, and a silvery gleam of stubble had begun to grow back. Grayer than before, Kate noted. Titus had been turning prematurely gray since they met, it seemed the more he employed his powers, the more the color shift happened. He wasn't getting old, Kate knew. This shift somehow indicated that he was becoming more connected to his abilities.

Still, he hadn't opened his eyes. So she sat beside him, sleeping in the chair next to his bed, only leaving his side for a few minutes at a time. The others stopped by, to bring her food or coffee, and to check on his status. Emily spoke to him for a while, about what happened and what was to come next. Kate felt a flash of annoyance as the blue-haired girl chattered away, but she soon found it comforting as well, the normalcy of it, the endless patter of Emily-speak. If Billy was Emily's best friend, Titus was her big brother. They were all worried.

A knock came at the door. Jane stood in the frame. She wore the uniform of her future self, a bodysuit of white and black and gleaming gold, the girlish costume she'd used before with its cape and skirt cast aside, at least for now. These days, with the Tower gone, all they had to work with was what they'd left back on Earth.

"How is he?" Jane asked.

"No change," Kate said in a rough, quiet voice.

Jane walked in, touched the back of Titus' hand, and examined the room.

"I hate that we had to bring him here," she said.

"The Labyrinth's infirmary is built to treat superhumans," Kate said. "It was the best option. It's my fault the Tower's infirmary was destroyed anyway. I'm the one who should be apologizing."

Jane shook her head. She understood where Kate was coming from. They both had their guilt.

"We're going to meet with the… with Billy's… with the good aliens," Jane said. "I'm not sure what to call them. Humans made up the name Luminae, didn't they? It seems offensive to call them that."

378

Kate shrugged.

"Billy said a while back that Dude's people spoke a language comprised of light," Kate said. "Luminae is probably as good a translation as any."

"I suppose so," Jane said. "We're meeting with them soon. I wanted to ask if you'd like to come, but I assume…"

"I think you can handle this without me," Kate said.

Jane smiled, affection displayed in her eyes. "Just this one time," she said.

"Don't make a habit of it," Kate said.

"I promise not to," Jane said. Suddenly and startlingly, she leaned in to give Kate a hug, wrapping her arms around her shoulders. The solar-powered girl's body radiated the heat of a perfect summer day.

And, not quite sure why or how, Kate returned the hug. Her strong, wiry arms engulfed the other girl. She pressed her chin into Jane's shoulder, biting back a wave of emotion she was not at all comfortable with.

Jane let go and stepped back. "We'll be home soon," she said. "I'll let you know everything that happens."

"I know," Kate said.

She always did. Though Jane was their leader in name, Kate had always been willing to share the burden with her, silent and steady. Sun and moon. Day and night.

"And you let me know if he—"

"I will," Kate said.

Jane nodded again and closed the door behind her.

Kate sat in silence for a few moments, setting her tablet aside, face down on a nearby table. She gazed at Titus, still and quiet in his bed. Then she watched the closed door of the hospital room for a few seconds, slipped her shoes off and crawled into the bed beside Titus. Careful not to touch his burns, Kate rested her head on the pillow beside him. After a few minutes, she started to drift, feeling the battle's exhaustion crashing down on her. Just as her eyes grew heavy, Titus coughed.

"Why does everything hurt?" he said softly, his voice gravely from disuse and smoke.

Kate paused for a moment, unsure if she were dreaming or if he really spoke.

He turned his head slowly to face her, gold eyes bloodshot but open, and offered her a weak smile.

"You made it," he said. "What happened?"

Kate leaned in and kissed him lightly on the lips.

Titus' eyes widened at the uncharacteristic display of affection, her unexpected gentleness.

"Doesn't matter," she said. "We're still here."

CHAPTER 82:
ONCE, ON A FARM

With the Tower now gone, the Labyrinth too public, the options for holding one of the most important and strange meetings in the history of Earth became pretty slim. They needed somewhere private, and out of the way, with room. Lots of room.

Jane said she knew such a place.

Billy laughed when he heard her suggestion. And yet here he stood, in the middle of a field, unfolding tables and setting them up in the mid-day sun. Jane's parents prepared coffee, lemonade, pies and cookies. Of course they did, Billy thought. Everything he knew about Jane—and if he admitted it, most of what he liked about her—came from the fact that she was raised here, by the Hawkins, who would, without batting an eye, host a gathering of aliens to discuss the future of the planet.

And they would put out desserts and other refreshments.

You're nervous, Dude said in Billy's head.

What gave you that impression, Billy thought, pacing back and forth, waiting for the last few arrivals.

What a group, Billy noted, while taking stock of everyone in attendance. Emily helped Mrs. Hawkins carry food from the house and talked her ear off about flying a giant robot. She used bubbles of float to carry items that wouldn't spill if her attention happened to waver. Doc stood to one side with Sam chatting quietly. Valerie Snow, today the color of white clouds on a spring afternoon, hovered near Doc shyly. Billy felt bad for her. The sentient storm was overwhelmed by everything, and he'd overheard her talking with Jane. Val stepped up during the invasion, but he knew what it was like during those days following your first real battle. Terrifying, confusing, guilt-ridden.

Korthos—where did we dig that guy up? Billy thought—sat at one of the folding tables, devouring desserts.

"These round delights are ambrosia!" he said, using a chocolate chip cookie to scoop up a mouthful of apple pie. "I did not know mere mortals were capable of such culinary magicks! Tell me, is this thine superhuman power, Lady Hawkins?"

Doris Hawkins blushed when he spoke to her. A few feet away, big John Hopkins folded his arms across his chest in mock jealousy.

"Flattery will get you everywhere, Mr. Korthos," Doris said.

Bedlam sat at one of the other tables, laughing at the whole event. Billy headed over to join her.

"I feel like I'm in a cartoon," she said.

"Welcome to our lives," he said. "Any word from your boss?"

"Black?" Bedlam said. "He's safe. I tried to explain that he built up a lot of good will for all that he did the past few days, but he'd rather keep a low profile for now."

"He's not a bad guy, is he?" Billy said.

"He can be," Bedlam said. "Or could be. The job required it. But he's also one of the best people I've ever known."

Billy laughed.

"What?" Bedlam asked, and simultaneously, Dude asked the same question in Billy's mind.

Billy answered both of them. "I was just thinking that the world isn't black and white, but... the name... Agent Black? That can't be his real name."

"It is now," Bedlam said. "Just like mine's Bedlam. Sometimes old names fall away. Are you ever going to be Straylight first and Billy second?"

"I dunno," Billy said. "I'm pretty self-absorbed."

Truer words were never spoken, Dude said.

Hey, Billy said. I'm getting better.

382

You are, Dude said. *You've come a long way, Billy Case.*

We've come a long way, Dude, Billy thought. You and me.

Yes, we have, Dude said.

So what's next? Billy asked Dude. I mean, this is why you've existed for all these centuries, right? To fight the Nemesis fleet?

This is what we're here to talk about, Dude said. *Look up.*

Thirteen bright white streaks lanced across the sky, led by one bright ball of fire, Jane, who guided the other Luminae to this place. We didn't lose a man, Billy realized. All these centuries, all these worlds the Luminae had tried to save and failed, and a baker's dozen traveled here to help us and we all made it home. That's a miracle in and of itself, Billy thought.

A wave of emotion flickered through Billy's mind. Not his emotion, he realized. Dude's.

You okay, Dude? Billy thought.

My brothers and sisters, Dude said. *I never thought I'd see so many of us in one place ever again. It's been so long.*

It never occurred to Billy that Dude might be lonely here. Trapped in a host body, unable to live on his own, his partner and friend abandoning him to fight for a world that was not his all alone.

Emily plopped down in the seat next to him, wedging Billy between her and Bedlam.

"Will you look at that," Emily said. "It's like an airshow. What do you think, Billy? You feel any less special now that you know there's a bunch of aliens just like you?"

"You have to ruin my moment, don't you?" Billy said.

Emily punched him on the shoulder.

"What would you do without me, Billy Case?" she said.

"From what I've seen of your friendship, he'd probably either have an incredibly swelled head or a lot more self-confidence," Bedlam said.

"See, I serve a dual purpose. I build you up, I keep you humble," Emily said.

"Story of my life," Billy said, hopping up to his feet. The others joined him, and together they met the delegation of Luminae as Jane landed.

Do you know these guys, Dude? Billy asked.

I do, he said. *Some better than others. But I do.*

The other hosts came in all shapes and sizes, some more human than others. Suresh wore a gleeful look on his face. A blue-skinned creature looked almost like a classic "gray" alien from the movies, aside from its coloring. Something that appeared to be a sentient mass of clay, changed shape as it touched the ground. A reddish centaur-like creature joined them; its body and head were like a rhinoceros instead of man and horse. Two or three resembled some of the aliens they'd seen controlled by Nemesis parasites, clearly stolen from the worlds these Luminae had tried to protect. Seng took the lead, now clearly the most at home with the Earthlings waiting for them.

In the center of the group stood what Billy could only describe as a flying elephant.

Dude, is that...? he asked.

One of the first of our hosts, Dude said. *I thought they were all dead.*

Billy remembered Dude's tale of the first host world of the Luminae and the elephant-like creatures they had joined up with, who sacrificed their lives in an effort to stop the Nemesis fleet. There shouldn't be any left, he thought. Right?

The big creature stepped forward and inspected each member of the gathering.

"I am called Daybreak," the flying elephant said. Hearing it speak at all, let alone in English, caused Billy to nearly freak out. Emily's eyes grew enormous. Bedlam's mouth hung open. Doc smirked a little bit like he was privy to some secret no one else on the team was. And Jane simply offered her hand in welcome.

"I don't, how are... you're..." Billy tried to say. He could hear Dude's amusement in his head, but even Dude seemed confused by this turn of events.

Daybreak looked him over. "You are Straylight," Daybreak said.

"That's me. Billy. Straylight. Case. Me," Billy said.

"I thought all the flying elephants were gone," Emily said.

Billy's stomach filled with acid as he realized what just escaped his friend's lips. He'd said it himself before, but somehow, Emily's tone made it sound so much more flippant.

"Your world is filled with wonders," Daybreak said. "Do you think yours is the only planet with miracles? I am the last of my kind, little one, but I, like you, was no ordinary person when this war started. I am cursed with a longer life than most, longer still than even the Luminae who can extend our lives."

"You've been here since the beginning," Jane said.

"And now at the end," the big creature said. "But we haven't gathered to talk about me."

"Whatever your next move is, we'll help," Doc said. "Anything you need."

Suresh stepped forward and placed a hand on Daybreak's massive shoulder.

"Aside from Straylight and I, all of us are from dead worlds," Suresh said. "They're all Lost Ones. And they aren't the only Luminae out there without an adopted world. There are others wandering the galaxy."

"You need a home base," Emily said. She turned to Doc. "What about Rhode Island?"

Doc laughed and shook his head.

"You already have an idea, don't you, my old friend," Doc said. "You've been busy all those years you were gone."

Billy had forgotten that Suresh and Doc knew each other, that they, along with Dude's partner before Billy, had worked together years before. Suresh looked so much older than Doc and this surprised him. It was easy to forget, with Doc acting as mentor and father figure, that he'd been one of the younger heroes on his team in the old days.

"There's a moon," Suresh said.

"Titan!" Emily yelled.

Everyone turned to look at her.

"What? Everybody knows Titan's the best moon," Emily said.

Suresh roared with laughter, strode over to Emily, and picked her up in a huge hug.

"This one would've fit in so well in the old days," he said, winking at Doc. "And you're right, my little friend. Titan. With your blessing, we'd like to build a base there. Somewhere to call home while we search for our lost friends."

"I knew you weren't just hanging out near Saturn by accident," Billy said.

"Titan does have a hell of a view, kid," Suresh said.

Jane raised her hand politely.

Suresh chuckled at the gesture.

"Go on," he said.

"Is it really over?" Jane said. "The fleet was a living organism. Was it unique? Are there others?"

Suresh and Daybreak exchanged a look.

"We don't know," Daybreak said. "Another reason why we need your help."

"We'll have to keep watch on the worlds the fleet destroyed before," Seng said. "Just in case…"

"If you say anything about eggs or something I'm going to be sick," Emily said.

"Then we shall leave it implied," he said.

"Speaking of 'are there more out there,' one of the seed ships is floating away," Billy said.

"Some of us should go finish that off," Suresh said. "I imagine it will be easy without the brain ship protecting it, but just to be sure I'd like you to help us, Korthos, you big lug."

The barbarian stopped mid mouthful, a mess of Boston cream on his plate. He slammed a fist on the table.

"My axe is yours, Horizon!" Korthos yelled, his mouth still full of food.

Suresh whispered conspiratorially to Doc. "Might help keep the big guy busy," he said.

Doc nodded his gratitude.

Sam, a hand on Jane's shoulder, spoke for the first time. He looked tired. More so than usual.

"We just discovered a bunch of alien tech, some of which we don't even know how to use yet," Sam said. "You're welcome to anything you need."

"Good to see you again, Sam," Suresh said.

The aging Barren nodded. "You as well, you old lunatic," Sam said.

So what about us? Billy asked Dude. If we're not here to guard against the Nemesis fleet, do we… go with them? Must we leave Earth?

Dude remained quiet for a few seconds.

Billy didn't really want to hear what he'd say next.

This is my home, Billy Case, as much as it is yours, Dude said. *My brothers can protect the stars. This is our world to guard.*

"I know what your friend is saying in there, Straylight," Suresh said.

Billy's eyes widened.

"Oh come on now, your partner's always had a soft touch. I knew him before you were born, after all."

"So I don't have to go?" Billy said.

"You are not a Lost One, Straylight," Daybreak said. "You still have a world to care for. It would go against everything we've ever accomplished to take you away."

A wave of relief and regret poured over Billy. Relief to be here, with his friends, but also…

"It'd be nice to see Saturn a second time, though," he said.

Suresh slung an arm around his shoulder, hugging him with comedic aggression. "I knew it," he said.

"Hey!" Emily said. "You're not taking my best friend with you and leaving me here. I want to see Saturn too."

She pointed at Bedlam with one fierce, ramrod straight arm.

"And the cyborg comes too. She's never been off the planet. She's earned it."

Bedlam threw up her arms in surprise.

"Whoa! Whoa! I'm making no demands here! You're the aliens, you do your alien things and I'm totally cool with that!" Bedlam said.

Doc and Jane looked at each other. Both grinned wildly.

"I think we can spare the three of you for a few weeks," Doc said.

Emily grabbed Bedlams wrist and forced her to perform a high-five.

"Yes! Outer space!" Emily said.

"You're not flying us out there in a giant robot," Bedlam said.

"Hey Sam?" Emily said.

The agent shook his head. "Uh-uh, I'm not coming with you," he said.

"Party pooper," Emily said. "But that's not what I'm asking."

Sam threw his arms up in the air in almost the same motion as Bedlam had a moment before.

"I don't know if I should be relieved or offended," he said.

"What I want to know is, did our frenemy Prevention leave that little submarine-looking space ship behind?" Emily said.

A huge smile broke out on Sam's face.

"As a matter of fact, she left it when she dropped off Henry," Sam said. "Who, by the way, says he'd like a sabbatical from the Department. Something about visiting an island and drinking fruity drinks."

Emily whipped around to punch Billy in the arm again.

"That settles it," she said. "We're coming with you to help build your little glowing alien space station thing on Titan."

"Do you hear me arguing?" Billy said. He looked at Bedlam who seemed resigned to be going on their field trip.

"I'm naming the ship," Emily said.

"Okay," Billy said.

"This is the voyage of the Starship Entropy, to boldly go where no Emilies have gone before..." Emily said. "Space, the best frontier."

Gonna be a hell of a trip, isn't it, Dude, Billy thought.

As it should be, Dude said. *As it should be.*

EPILOGUE: INDESTRUCTIBLE LIKE US

Jane felt more powerful under the desert sun than other places. The light that fueled her was purer, more direct here. She flew over the sandy landscape toward a dark patch ahead, a random thatch of clouds locked in place in the distance.

Days before, she'd received a call from Jon Broadstreet. Usually she knew the purpose of his calls, but this time, out of the blue, he caught her off-guard. It had been a quiet yet busy few days, while the Luminae prepared to set out for Titan. Now homeless and out of sorts, the Indestructibles had to figure out what to do with themselves.

"I know you guys haven't been as organized as usual, so I thought you should know about something I heard through the wire," Broadstreet said.

"Tell me we're not being invaded again," Jane said. "We haven't finished cleaning up the last mess."

"I don't think so," Broadstreet said. "But there's rumors of another unexplained UFO crash you may want to investigate. People are saying it's just a hoax, but—"

"—We still have things falling from the sky after the battle," Jane thought. "Thanks, Broadstreet. I owe you one."

"You owe me lots," he said. "I'll put it on my tab."

Jane recruited Valerie to help her scour the desert where the crash was rumored to take place. The two of them could cover a great deal of ground together, while Emily was too slow and Billy too distracted. Jane figured she'd have to call them in if things turned ugly.

She also brought along poor Neal—still in his ridiculously small robot body—in case they needed some sort of analysis of the space debris performed. Flying too fast to have a conversation with him, and feeling absolutely terrible for the AI, she tucked him under her arm like a cask. We need to get him a bigger body, she thought. Maybe there's something kicking around in the warehouse of stuff that Prevention returned to the Department that we could use for an upgrade. The beleaguered artificial intelligence had been downgraded from a massive space ship for a body to little more than a trash can in the past few days. That had to sting.

Valerie found the crash site first, and when she told Jane what she saw the solar-powered girl raced through the desert sky.

"Don't tell anyone yet," Jane said. "I'll be right there."

She contacted Doc privately on her earpiece and asked him to meet her. When she told him what Val had discovered, Jane wasn't surprised that he wasted no time in getting there. Doc appeared out of thin air just as she landed. Val drifted out of the sky to stand beside Jane, leaving wet footprints in her wake.

The burned and battered wreckage of the Tower lay half-buried in the sand.

"Is it your home?" Val said. "I've only been there a few times, I couldn't tell for sure…"

Jane's face split into a huge smile. Broken, cracked and split, still it was the Tower, here on Earth.

Doc smiled and placed a hand on Jane's shoulder.

"I should've checked," he said. "There must be something about this place. This isn't far from where the Tower was found originally. Buried underground."

"So she came home to die?" Jane said.

"Elephant graveyard," Doc said. "But she might not be dead. Neal?"

The AI started scanning the wreckage, sensors spun and whirred softly.

"This may take some time, Designation: Solar," Neal said.

"That's okay," Jane said. She winked at Doc, who nodded back to her, then sat down in the sand. Doc and Valerie joined her, forming a semi-circle around Neal as he worked. "Do what you have to do, Neal. We've got all the time in the world."

* * *

By the time Neal finished his analysis, the sun hung low in the sky, bathing the desert in red and gold. Anyone else would have been baked to a crisp by now, but Jane felt full of life, and Valerie passed the hours creating tiny clouds from nothing, and causing drizzling misty rain to fall onto the sand.

Neal spun a sensor around to look at Jane. She tapped her earpiece.

"Doc, bring them through," she said.

The air beside her shimmered and opened, like a heat mirage. Instantly, a half-circle of purplish light created an arc in the air, and within it she saw her friends waiting in a room somewhere in the City. Jane motioned for them to pass through. Emily charged out first, her replacement Doctor scarf finally complete and wrapped around her head to protect her from the sun. Billy followed, in street clothes, hands in pockets, Bedlam, a couple of steps behind, wore a long skirt and tunic-styled shirt.

"No way," Billy said, spying the wreckage.

"It can't be…" Bedlam said.

"That's our baby," Emily said, grinning like a madwoman.

Titus and Kate entered next, the werewolf used his enchanted spear like a walking stick, his strength not fully returned. He'd pulled a brand new red hooded sweatshirt up over his head to shade against the glare. Bandages covered one hand and were also visible just beneath the collar of his tee shirt, where his burns were still healing.

Kate, uncharacteristically out of uniform, in jeans and a dark cowl-necked top, walked in wearing a pair of unexpectedly stylish boots. Her eyes hid behind a pair of sunglasses, but her lips quirked into a half-smile.

Doc Silence brought up the rear, leaving the portal open with a flick of his wrist.

"This ship should be drifting off into space right now," Kate said.

"Doc has a theory," Jane said. "That it has a landing beacon or something left here. Maybe the last action the ship performed was to send itself home."

"I don't care how it happened," Billy said. "Will she ever fly again?"

Neal spun around so that the "front" end of his temporary robot body faced them.

"I am unsure, Designation: Straylight," Neal said. "Currently eighty-six percent of the ship's functions are offline."

"Only eighty-six percent? We can work with that," Titus said.

"How much of that is irreparable, Neal," Kate asked.

"It will take some time to fully assess, Designation: Dancer," Neal said. "I suspect with the right tools we could restore the Tower to a minimum of fifty percent functionality."

"Half is better than nothing?" Bedlam said, trying to be optimistic.

"Really depends on which half we get running," Titus said. "Big difference if the kitchen works and the communications suite doesn't."

"Can I recommend starting with the lavatory?" Emily said.

"You and your tiny bladder," Billy said.

"Do you want to be flying down to Apollo's Coffee every time you need to pee? I don't," Emily said.

"Still," Titus said. "Even half."

"I don't care if it just ends up an inert shell," Doc said. "This was our home. I'd rather find it here not functioning than let it disappear into space forever."

Jane smiled. Sometimes it was easy to forget how long Doc lived in the Tower. And how much of that time he'd been there alone, wishing his old allies would reappear, or waiting for the next generation to arrive.

"So what are we going to do?" Titus said. "Fix it here?"

"We should bring it somewhere secure," Billy said.

"There's dozens of unused airfields, maybe hundreds in the U.S. alone," Kate said. "One of them must be available."

"Maybe we take it to the one where Emily and I fought the first few Nemesis parasites," Jane said. "Not like there's much going on there now."

Kate nodded. "As good an idea as any," she said. "Question is how do we get it there."

Suddenly the earth rumbled, shaking beneath their feet. Billy and Jane instantly lit up with power, ready to fight. The air turned a little cooler when Valerie reacted as well. Doc's hands shot up in gestures he employed to prepare defensive spells, while Titus' eyes glowed yellow as he began to transform into his monstrous form next to Kate, who stood up on the balls of her feet.

And Emily stretched her arm toward the wreckage of the Tower, lifting the entire thing in a single, massive bubble of float.

"Emily!" Jane yelled.

Entropy Emily turned back to her friends, a wild look of giddy playfulness on her face.

"What?" she said.

Billy laughed, hard enough to start wheezing, and it infected the group, all the tension from the past few months appeared to burn away. Even Titus joined in, kneeling to hold a hand against his ribs. Kate, silently chuckling, locked eyes with Jane and grinned.

"Never mind," Jane said. "You want to carry her home?"

"You got it, boss," Emily said. "Look at that ship. Little dusty, but she's as indestructible as we are, isn't she?"

Jane started to argue, looking at the demolished and cracked hull of their former home. But they'd all made it back. They were all standing. Maybe we are indestructible after all, she thought.

Science experiments and solar-powered girls and werewolves and aliens; wizards and weird gravitational anomalies, and a dancer whose only superpower was that she never, ever gave up. Together, it seemed, nothing could stop them.

"Yeah, Em," Jane said. As indestructible as we are."

Also by Matthew Phillion

Novels in the Indestructibles Series – in print and e-book formats

The Indestructibles (Book 1)
The Indestructibles: Breakout (Book 2)
The Entropy of Everything (the Indestructibles Book 3)
Like a Comet (the Indestructibles Book 4)

Tales from the Indestructiverse

Echo and the Sea

The Indestructibles One-Shots (digital shorts)

The Soloist
Gifted
Blood & Bone
The Monsters We Make
Krampus in the City
Roll for Initiative (an Indestructibles Story) – also available in print

The Dungeon Crawlers Novella Series

The Player's Guide to Dungeon Crawling (The Dungeon Crawlers Book 1)
The Dungeoneer's Bestiary (The Dungeon Crawlers Book 2)
The Ghoul Slayer's Guidebook (The Dungeon Crawlers Book 3)

47670665R00241

Made in the USA
Middletown, DE
11 June 2019